Boris Akunin is the pseudonym of Grigory Chkhartishvili. He has been compared to Gogol, Tolstoy and Arthur Conan Doyle, and his Erast Fandorin books have sold over eighteen million copies in Russia alone. He lives in London.

ALL THE WORLD'S A STAGE

*The Further Adventures
of Erast Fandorin*

BORIS AKUNIN

*Translated from the Russian
by Andrew Bromfield*

WEIDENFELD & NICOLSON

First published in Great Britain in 2017
by Weidenfeld & Nicolson.
This paperback edition published in 2018
by Weidenfeld & Nicolson
an imprint of The Orion Publishing Group Ltd
Carmelite House, 50 Victoria Embankment
London EC4Y 0DZ

An Hachette UK Company

1 3 5 7 9 10 8 6 4 2

Copyright © Boris Akunin 2017
English translation copyright © Andrew Bromfield 2017

A CIP catalogue record for this book is
available from the British Library.

ISBN (Mass Market Paperback) 978 1 4746 0441 3
ISBN (eBook) 978 1 4746 0442 0

Typeset by Input Data Services Ltd, Somerset

Printed and bound in Great Britain by Clays Ltd, Elcograf S.p.A.

MIX
Paper from
responsible sources
FSC® C104740

www.orionbooks.co.uk

CONTENTS

Eight 1s

UNTIL THE BENEFIT PERFORMANCE

A HARMONIOUS MAN

Erast Petrovich Fandorin began regarding himself as a harmonious man from the moment when he mounted the first rung on the ladder of wisdom. This event occurred neither too late nor too soon, but at precisely the right moment – at an age when it is already time to draw conclusions, but it is still possible to change one's plans.

The most substantial conclusion drawn from the years he had already lived resolved itself into a supremely brief maxim that was worth all the philosophical teachings of the world taken together: *growing older is good*. 'Growing older' signified 'maturing', that is, not deteriorating, but improving – becoming stronger, wiser, more complete. If, as a man grew older, he had a feeling of impoverishment instead of enrichment, then his ship had wandered off course.

To continue the maritime metaphor, one might say that Fandorin had cruised past the reefs of the fifties, where men so often suffer shipwreck, under full sail and with his standard fluttering aloft in the breeze. The crew had very nearly mutinied, to be sure, but disaster had been avoided.

The attempted mutiny actually took place on his fiftieth birthday, which, of course, was no accident. There is an indisputable magic in the combination of figures that is not felt only by those who are totally devoid of imagination.

Having celebrated his birthday with a walk along the seabed in a diving suit (at that time Erast Petrovich was a passionate enthusiast of deep-sea diving), in the evening he sat on the veranda, watching the public stroll along the esplanade, sipping on his rum punch and mentally repeating to himself: 'I am fifty, I am fifty' – as if he were trying to get the taste of an unfamiliar drink. Suddenly his gaze fell on a decrepit little old man in a white panama hat, a desiccated, trembling mummy, who was being pushed along in a wheelchair by a mulatto servant. The gaze of this Methuselah was clouded and there was a thread of saliva dangling from his chin.

I hope I shall not live to that age, Fandorin thought – and suddenly realised that he was frightened. And then he felt even more frightened by the fact that the thought of old age had frightened him.

His mood was ruined. He went back to his hotel room – to tell his jade beads and paint the hieroglyph for 'old age' on a sheet of paper. When the sheet had been covered with renderings of the symbol 老 in every possible style, the problem had resolved itself, a concept had been elaborated. The shipboard mutiny had been suppressed. Erast Petrovich had mastered the first stage of wisdom.

Life could not be a descent, only an ascent – right to the very final moment. That was one.

That much-quoted line by Pushkin – 'Days follow days in flight, each day bearing off particles of being' – contained an error of logic. The poet had probably been in a melancholic mood, or it was simply a slip of the pen. The verse should have read: 'Days follow days in flight, each day bringing new particles of being'. If a man lived correctly, the flow of time rendered him richer, not poorer. That was two.

Ageing should be a profitable transaction, a natural exchange of physical and mental strength for spiritual strength, of outward beauty for inner. That was three.

Everything depended on the quality of your wine. If it was cheap, age would sour it. If it was noble, it would only improve. The conclusion from this was: The older a man becomes, the more *his quality* must improve. That was four.

Oh, and there was a fifth point as well. Erast Petrovich had no intention of renouncing his physical and mental strength. And he devised a special programme to ensure that he wouldn't.

In each succeeding year of his life he had to conquer a new frontier. Actually two frontiers: a physical, sporting one and an intellectual one. Then growing old would not be frightening, but interesting.

A long-term plan for the prospective territorial expansion was

4

drawn up quite rapidly – a plan so ambitious that the next fifty years might not suffice.

Of his as yet unfulfilled goals in the intellectual line, Fandorin intended to achieve the following: at long last, learn the German language properly, since war with Germany and Austro-Hungary was obviously inevitable; master Chinese (one year was not enough for this, two would be required – it would have been longer, but he already knew the hieroglyphs); fill a shameful lacuna in his knowledge of the world by familiarising himself thoroughly with the Moslem culture, for which he would have to learn Arabic and make a thorough study of the Koran in the original (set aside three years); read his way through classical and modern literature (Erast Petrovich had always found himself chronically short of time for this) – and so on, and so forth.

His sporting goals, for the immediate future, included the following: learning to fly an aeroplane; devoting a year or so to an intriguing Olympic pastime useful for improving motor coordination – pole-vaulting; taking up mountain-climbing; and, quite definitely, mastering skin-diving, using the new type of rebreather, in which the improved oxygen-supply regulator made it possible to dive to a significant depth for long periods. Agh, there was far too much to list everything!

In the five years that had passed since Fandorin had taken fright at his fright, the methodology of correct ageing had already produced quite decent results. Every year he had ascended one step higher – or rather, two steps – so that now he looked down on his former, fifty-year-old self.

By his fifty-first birthday, as an intellectual accomplishment, Erast Petrovich had learned the Spanish language, the lack of which he had felt so badly while cruising in the Caribbean. The 'step up' for his body had been trick riding. Of course, he had ridden before, but not brilliantly, and this was a useful ability and in addition highly entertaining – far more enjoyable than the automobile races of which he had grown so weary.

By the age of fifty-two Fandorin had learned to speak Italian and significantly improved his level of skill in *kenjutsu* – Japanese swordsmanship. He had been taught this splendid science by the Japanese consul, Baron Shigeyama, a holder of the highest dan. By the end of the assigned period Erast Petrovich was winning two out of every three contests with the baron (and conceding one, but only in order not to offend his *sensei*).

The fifty-third year of Fandorin's life was devoted, on the one hand, to classical and modern philosophy (unfortunately, his education had been limited to the grammar school); and on the other, to motorcycle riding, which, in terms of thrills, was in every way a match for equestrianism.

During the previous year of 1910, Erast Petrovich's mind had been occupied with chemistry, the most rapidly developing of modern sciences, and he had occupied his body with juggling (at first sight a trivial matter, mere foolish nonsense, but it fine-hones the synchronisation of movements and precise motor skills).

In the current season it had seemed logical to him to move on from juggling to tightrope walking – an excellent means for consolidating one's physical and nervous equilibrium.

His intellectual exercises this year were also in part a continuation of the previous year's enthusiasm for chemistry. Fandorin decided to devote this period of twelve months to an old passion – criminalistic science. The appointed term had already expired, but the research continued, since it had taken an unexpected and highly promising direction, a line that apparently no one apart from Erast Petrovich was pursuing seriously.

This development involved new methods for dealing with witnesses and suspects: how could one induce them to be entirely candid? In barbaric times a means that was both cruel and unreliable had been employed – torture. Now, however, it had emerged that the most complete and veracious results could be achieved by using a combination of three methods – psychological, chemical and hypnotic. If a person who possessed the required information, but did not wish to part with it, was first of all assigned to the correct psychological type and appropriately prepared, and his will to resist was weakened with certain specific compounds, and he was then hypnotised, his candour would be absolute and complete.

The experimental results had appeared impressive. However,

serious doubts had arisen concerning their practical value. The problem was not even that Fandorin would never, for anything in the world, have shared his discoveries with the state (it was terrible to think what use could be made of such a weapon by the unscrupulous gentlemen of the Okhrana or the gendarmerie). And in the course of an investigation, Erast Petrovich would scarcely have permitted himself to transform another person, even a bad person, into an object of chemical manipulation. Immanuel Kant, who asserted that human beings must not be treated as a means for the achievement of a goal, would not have approved – and after a year of philosophical studies Fandorin regarded the sage of Königsberg as the supreme moral authority. Therefore Erast Petrovich's research into the criminalistic 'problem of candour' was rather abstractly scientific in nature.

Of course, it remained an open question whether it was ethical to use the new method in investigating especially monstrous atrocities, as well as crimes fraught with serious danger for society and the state.

Fandorin had been pondering intently on precisely this subject for more than three days now – since the moment when news had broken of an attempt on the life of the chairman of the council of ministers, Stolypin. On the evening of 1 September in Kiev a certain young man had fired two shots at the most important figure in the political life of Russia.

Many aspects of this event appeared phantasmagorical. Firstly, the bloody drama had unfolded not just anywhere, but in a theatre, before the eyes of a large audience. Secondly, the show had been an extremely jolly one – an adaptation of Pushkin's *Tale of Tsar Saltan*. Thirdly, the audience had included a real tsar, not of the fairytale kind, whom the killer had left untouched. Fourthly, the theatre had been so well guarded that no one could possibly have infiltrated it, not even Pushkin's hero Gvidon when he transformed himself into a mosquito. Viewers had only been admitted on the basis of individual passes issued by the Department for the Defence of Public Security – the Okhrana. Fifthly, and most fantastically of all, the terrorist had actually been in possession of such a pass, and not a counterfeit, but the genuine article. Sixthly, the killer had not only managed to enter the theatre, but also to carry in a firearm . . .

To judge from the information that had reached Erast Petrovich (and his sources of information were reliable), the arrested man had not yet given any answers that provided a solution to this riddle. Now *this* was a case where the new means of interrogation would have been useful!

While the head of the government was dying (the injury, alas, was fatal), while the incompetent investigators simply wasted their time with fatuous nonsense, an immense empire, already overburdened with multitudinous problems, was trembling and swaying – it could topple over at any moment now, like an overloaded cart after the wagoner has tumbled out of it on a steep bend. Pyotr Stolypin had been altogether too important to the stability of the nation.

Fandorin's feelings about this man, who had governed Russia singlehandedly for five years, were complicated. While respecting Stolypin's courage and resolute spirit, Erast Petrovich regarded many items on the premier's policy agenda as mistaken or even dangerous. However, there could be no doubt whatever that Stolypin's death would strike a terrible blow at the state and threaten to plunge the country into fresh chaos. A very great deal now depended on the speed and efficiency of the investigation.

There could also be no doubt that Fandorin would be invited to take part in this effort as an independent expert. This had happened repeatedly in the past when the investigation of some exceptional case ran into a dead end, and it was impossible to imagine any case more exceptional and important than the assassination attempt in Kiev. Especially since Erast Petrovich had been acquainted in person with the chairman of the council of ministers – on several occasions he had participated, at Stolypin's request, in investigating puzzling or especially delicate cases of national importance.

The times were long over when a quarrel with the authorities had obliged Fandorin to leave his native country and home city for many long years. Erast Petrovich's personal foe had once been the most powerful man in the old capital, but now he (or rather, the little that remained of his most illustrious body) had long been reclining in a grandiose sepulchre, mourned but little by his fellow Muscovites. There was nothing to prevent Fandorin from spending as much time as he wished in Moscow. Nothing, that is, except an addiction to adventures and new impressions.

When he was in town, Erast Petrovich lived in a rented wing of a house on Little Assumption Lane, known in popular parlance as Cricket Lane. A very, very long time ago, about two hundred years in fact, a certain merchant by the name of Cricketinov had built his stone mansion here. The merchant had passed on, the palatial dwelling had changed hands many times over, but the cosy name had been retained in the tenacious grip of Moscow's memory. When resting from his wanderings or investigations, Fandorin lived a steady, quiet life here – like a cricket behind the stove.

The accommodation was comfortable and rather spacious for two: six rooms, a bathroom, plumbing, electricity, a telephone – for 135 roubles a month, including coal for the Dutch stove heating. It was within these walls that the greater part of the intellectual and sporting programme devised by the retired councillor of state was put into effect. Sometimes he enjoyed imagining how, surfeited with travelling and adventures, he would settle down permanently in Cricket Lane, devoting himself completely to the enthralling process of growing old.

Some day. Not just yet. Not soon. Probably after seventy.

Erast Petrovich was very far from surfeited as yet. Beyond the bounds of the cricket world behind the stove, there still remained too many fantastically interesting places, occurrences and phenomena of all kinds. Some were separated from him by thousands of kilometres, some by centuries.

About ten years previously Fandorin had developed a serious fascination with the underwater world. He had even built a submarine according to his own design, which was registered at the distant island of Aruba, and had constantly improved its construction. This had involved immense expenditure, but after he had successfully used his own submarine to raise a precious cargo from the seabed, his hobby had not merely paid for its own costs with plenty to spare, it had freed Erast Petrovich from the need to charge a fee for working as a detective on investigations or as a consultant on criminalistic matters.

Now he could take on only the most interesting cases, or those which, for one reason or another, it was impossible to decline. In any case, the status of an individual acting out of benevolence or kindness was very much more pleasant than the position of a hired functionary, no matter how authoritative.

Fandorin was rarely left in peace for long, because of the reputation that he had acquired in international professional circles over the last twenty years. Since the ill-starred war with Japan, the independent expert's own state had often turned to him for help. There had been times when Erast Petrovich refused – his concepts of good and evil did not always coincide with those of the government. It was only with extreme reluctance, for instance, that he accepted cases involving internal politics, unless it was a matter of some especially heinous villainy.

This business of the attempt on the prime minister's life had a whiff of precisely that kind of villainy about it. There were too many strange, unexplained aspects. According to confidential information received, someone in St Petersburg was of the same opinion. Fandorin's friends in the capital had informed him by telephone that yesterday the minister of justice had set out for Kiev, in order to head up the investigation in person. That meant that he had no confidence in the Department of Police and the Okhrana. If not today, then tomorrow the 'independent expert' Fandorin would also be invited to join the investigation. And if he was not invited, it would mean that the rot in the apparatus of state had spread to the very top . . .

Erast Petrovich already knew what action to take.

Concerning the chemical means of influence, some thought was still required, but the psychological and hypnotic methods could perfectly well be applied to the killer. Fandorin would have to assume that they would prove adequate. The terrorist Bogrov had to reveal the most important thing: whose instrument was he? Exactly who had provided him with the pass and allowed him into the theatre with a revolver?

And it would also be no bad thing to compel the candour of the head of the Kiev Department for the Defence of Public Security, Lieutenant-Colonel Kulyabko, and the deputy director of the Police Department, State Councillor Verigin, who had been responsible for the security measures. There was probably no need to be over-fastidious with these extremely dubious gentlemen, bearing in mind their line of business and general lack of scruples. It was unlikely that they would allow themselves to be hypnotised, but he could sit tête-à-tête for a while with each of them, in an unofficial context, and add a drop or two of his secret formulation to the lieutenant-colonel's favourite cognac and the teetotaller Verigin's tea. And they would tell him about the mysterious pass, and why there was not a single bodyguard present beside the prime minister during the interval, despite the fact that Stolypin had been hunted for years by the Social Revolutionaries and the anarchists, as well as by various solitary crusaders against tyranny . . .

The idea that the organs responsible for the protection of the empire could be implicit in an attempt on the life of the head of the government made Fandorin shudder. This was the fourth day he had spent wandering round his apartment like a man demented, either telling his green beads or tracing out diagrams on paper that only he could understand. He smoked cigars and kept demanding tea, but ate almost nothing.

Masa – his servant and friend, and the only person in the world who was close to him – knew perfectly well that when the master was in this state, it was best to leave him alone. The Japanese remained near by all the time, but he didn't call any attention to himself, he was as quiet as a mouse. He cancelled two assignations and sent the caretaker's wife off to the Chinese shop to get tea. Masa's narrow, oriental eyes glinted fervently – he was anticipating interesting events.

In the previous year the faithful companion had also reached the fifty mark, and he had responded to this milestone date with truly Japanese seriousness, changing his life in an even more radical manner than his master.

Firstly, in accordance with ancient tradition, he had completely shaved his head – as a sign that inwardly he was entering into the condition of a monk and renouncing the vanity of this world as he prepared to withdraw to another. Certainly, Fandorin had not yet noticed that Masa had altered his Céladonesque habits in any way. But then, the rules of Japanese monks do not necessarily prescribe chastity of the flesh.

Secondly, Masa had decided to take a new name, in order to make a complete break with his old self. But here a difficulty arose: it transpired that, according to the laws of the Russian Empire, in order to change one's given name, it was necessary to undergo baptism. However, this was no obstacle to the Japanese. He happily accepted the Orthodox faith, suspended a substantial crucifix round his neck and started crossing himself fervently at the sight of every church dome, and even at the sound of bells chiming – none of which prevented him from continuing to burn incense in front of his domestic Buddhist altar. According to his documents, his name was no longer Masahiro, but Mikhail Erastovich (the patronymic having been taken from his godfather). Fandorin was also obliged to share his surname with this brand-new servant of God – the Japanese had requested this as the very greatest reward that his sovereign lord could bestow on his devoted vassal for long and zealous service.

A passport is one thing, but Erast Petrovich nonetheless reserved the right to call his servant by the name he had always used – Masa. And he ruthlessly nipped in the bud any attempts by his godson to call his master 'faza-san' (father), and especially 'papa'.

So Erast Petrovich and Mikhail Erastovich had been stuck in the house for four days, all the while glancing impatiently at the telephone, anticipating a summons. But the lacquered box had remained stubbornly silent. Fandorin was not often disturbed on trifling matters, since not many people knew his number.

On Monday, 5 September, at three in the afternoon, at last there was a call.

Masa grabbed the receiver – he just happened to be polishing the instrument with a little velvet cloth, as if he were trying to propitiate a capricious deity.

Fandorin walked out into the other room and stood at the

window, preparing himself inwardly for the important clarification of the situation. *Insist on the maximum authority and absolute freedom of action, immediately,* he thought. *Otherwise do not accept. That is one . . .*

Masa glanced in through the door. His expression was intent.

'I don't know whose call you have been expecting for so many days, master, but I think this is the one. The lady's voice is trembling. She says it is a very urgent matter, *of ex-cep-tion-ar im-port-ance.*' Masa pronounced the last three words in Russian.

'A l-lady?' Erast Petrovich queried in surprise.

'She says "Origa".'

Masa considered Russian patronymics an inessential decorative element, remembered them poorly and often omitted them.

Fandorin's bewilderment was resolved. Olga . . . Why, naturally. He should have been expecting this. In a case as tangled and fraught with unpredictable complications as this one, the authorities would not wish to approach a private individual directly in order to ask for help. It was more appropriate to act through the family. Fandorin was acquainted with Olga Borisovna Stolypina, wife of the wounded prime minister and great-granddaughter of the great general Suvorov. A woman of firm will and intelligence, not the kind of individual to be bowed or broken by any blows of fate.

Of course, she was aware that she would be a widow very soon. It was also quite possible that she was telephoning on her own initiative, having sensed something strange in the way the official investigation was being conducted.

Erast Petrovich heaved a deep sigh and took the receiver.

'Fandorin at your s-service.'

OH, HOW VERY AWKWARD!

'Erast Petrovich, for my sake, for the sake of our friendship, in the name of mercy. For the sake of my late husband, do not refuse me!' a woman's voice declared rapidly in resounding tones. A familiar voice, certainly, but distorted by agitation. 'You are a noble and compassionate man, I know that you cannot refuse me!'

'So he has died . . .' Fandorin hung his head, even though the widow could not see it, and spoke with sincere feeling. 'Please accept my p-profoundest condolences. This is not only your personal grief, it is an immense loss for the whole of Russia. You are a strong person. I know your presence of mind will not desert you. And for my part, of course, I will do everything that I possibly can.'

Following a pause, the lady continued in a tone of voice that conveyed a certain perplexity:

'Thank you, but I have come to terms with it one way or another. Time heals all wounds . . .'

'Time?'

Erast Petrovich stared at the telephone in stupefaction.

'Well, yes. After all, it is seven years since Anton Pavlovich died . . . This is Olga Leonardovna Knipper-Chekhov here. I suppose I must have woken you up?'

Oh, how very awkward! Hurling a furious glance at the entirely innocent Masa, Fandorin blushed. It was not surprising that the voice had seemed familiar to him. He had long-standing ties of friendship with the writer's widow – they had both been members of the commission on Chekhov's legacy.

'F-for God's sake f-forgive me!' he exclaimed, stammering more than usual. 'I thought you were . . . It d-doesn't matter . . .'

The consequence of an essentially comic misunderstanding was that from the very beginning of the conversation Fandorin found himself in the position of a man apologising and feeling guilty. If it were not for that, his response to the actress's request would most probably have been a polite refusal, and his entire subsequent life would have turned out quite differently.

But Erast Petrovich was embarrassed, and the word of a noble man is not a sparrow.

'You really will do everything you can for me? I'm taking you at your word, now,' Olga Leonardovna said in a less agitated voice. 'Knowing you as a true knight and a man of honour, I have no doubt that the story I am about to tell you will not leave you unmoved.'

In fact, even without the awkward start to the conversation, it would not have been easy to refuse a request from this woman.

In society Chekhov's widow was regarded with disapproval. It was considered good form to denounce her for preferring to flaunt her brilliance on stage and spend her time in the jolly company of friends from the Art Theatre, instead of nursing the fatally ill writer in his dreary solitude in Yalta. She didn't love him! She didn't love him! She had married the dying man out of cold calculation, in order to acquire Chekhov's fame, while clinging on to her own, in order to secure a name that would be a genuine trump-card in her subsequent theatrical career – such was the generally voiced opinion.

Erast Petrovich was outraged by this injustice. The late Chekhov had been a mature and intelligent man. He knew that he was not simply marrying a woman, but an illustrious actress. Olga Leonardovna had been prepared to give up the stage in order to remain beside him constantly, but it would be a fine husband who agreed to accept such a sacrifice. To love meant to wish happiness for the loved one. Without selflessness, love was not worth a brass farthing. And the wife had been right to let her husband win this battle of magnanimities. The important thing was that she had been with him before he died and eased his passing. She had told Fandorin that on the very last evening he joked a lot and they laughed heartily. What more could one wish for? A good death. No one had any right to condemn this woman.

All these thoughts flashed through Erast Petrovich's mind, not for the first time, as he listened to the actress's rambling, incoherent story. It concerned a certain Eliza, a friend of Olga Leonardovna's and apparently also an actress. Something or other had happened to this Eliza that had 'left the poor thing in a constant state of mortal fear'.

'Pardon me,' Erast Petrovich interposed, when the other party broke off in order to sob. 'I d-didn't quite understand; Altairsky and Lointaine – are they one individual or two?'

'One! Her full name is Eliza Altairsky-Lointaine. She used to go by the stage name of "Lointaine", but then she married and became "Altairsky" as well, after her husband. They soon separated, it's true, but you must agree that it would be stupid for an actress to renounce such a beautiful surname.'

'But even so, I don't quite . . .' Fandorin wrinkled up his forehead. 'This lady is afraid of something, you have described her nervous state most eloquently. But what exactly is frightening her?'

And, most importantly, what is it that you want from me? he added to himself.

'She won't tell me what the problem is! Eliza is a very secretive, she never complains about anything. That's such a rare thing for an artiste! But she came to visit me yesterday, we had a good talk, and something came over her. She burst into tears, fell on my breast and started babbling about her life being a nightmare and saying she couldn't bear it any longer, she was hounded and tormented to death. But when I started badgering her with questions, Eliza suddenly turned terribly pale and bit her lip, and I couldn't drag another word out of her. Eventually she babbled something unintelligible, asked me to forgive her momentary weakness and ran off. I didn't sleep last night and I've had the jitters all day long! Ah, Erast Petrovich, I've known Eliza for a long time. She's not a hysterical girl who imagines things. I'm sure she's in some kind of danger and, what's more, danger of a kind that she can't even tell a friend about. I implore you, in the name of all the bonds between us, find out what the matter is. It's a mere trifle for you, after all, you're a master at solving mysteries. How brilliantly you tracked down that missing manuscript of Anton Pavlovich's!' she said, reminding Fandorin of the story that had marked the beginning of their acquaintance. 'I shall help you gain entry to her circle of acquaintances. Eliza is the heroine now at Noah's Ark.'

'Who? W-where?' Erast Petrovich asked in surprise.

'She's the leading lady in that new-fangled company which is attempting to rival the Art Theatre,' Olga Leonardovna explained in a tone that carried a hint of condescension – either for Fandorin's theatrical ignorance, or for the madmen who had dared to compete with the great Moscow Art Theatre. 'Noah's Ark has arrived on tour from St Petersburg, to astound and conquer the public of Moscow. It's quite impossible to get a ticket, but I have arranged everything. You will be allowed in and given the very finest seat, so that you can get a good look at all of them. And afterwards you can pay a visit backstage. I shall telephone Noah Noaevich (that's their manager, Noah Noaevich Stern). And I shall tell him to render you every possible assistance. He's positively dancing reels round me, hoping to lure me into joining him, so he will do as I ask without any unnecessary questions.'

Erast Petrovich loosed an angry kick at a chair, and it cracked in half. An absolutely worthless, laughable case – the hypochondriacal caprices of some prima donna with a quite incredible name – but it was absolutely impossible to refuse. And this at a moment when he was expecting an invitation to assist with the investigation of a crime of historical, one might even say epochal, significance!

Clucking his tongue, Masa took the mutilated item of furniture and tried to sit on it – the chair sagged crookedly.

'Do you have nothing to say? Surely you will not refuse this little request of mine? I shan't survive it if you too abandon me!' the great writer's widow said with the intonations of Arkadina appealing to Trigorin in *The Seagull*.

'How could I p-possibly dare,' Erast Petrovich said dismally. 'When do I need to be at the theatre?'

'You are an absolute dear! I knew that I could count on you! The performance today is at eight. Now let me explain everything to you . . .'

Never mind, Fandorin consoled himself. *When all is said and done, this outstanding woman deserves to have me spend one evening on her*

17

foolish whim. And if a call about the Stolypin case comes before then, I'll explain to her that it's a matter of national importance.

But no one called before the evening, either from St Petersburg or from Kiev. Erast Petrovich put on a white tie and set off for the performance, struggling in vain to master his annoyance. Masa was ordered to stay beside the telephone and if necessary to come rushing to the theatre on the motorcycle.

ELIZAVETA'S DAY OF REMEMBRANCE

Fandorin himself went by horse cab, knowing that when there were performances taking place simultaneously in the Bolshoi, Maly and Noveishy theatres, there would be nowhere to park an automobile on Theatre Square. The last time, when he went to see Wagner's *Valkyrie*, he had been incautious enough to leave his Isotta Fraschini between two cabs, and a frisky trotter had fractured his chrome-plated radiator – afterwards it had taken two months for a new one to be delivered from Milan.

In the few hours since the actress's telephone call, Erast Petrovich had gathered a little bit of information about the theatre company with which he was about to spend the evening.

He had discovered that this company, which had appeared in St Petersburg the previous season, had created a genuine furore here in the old capital, enchanting the public and dividing the critics into two irreconcilable factions, one of which lauded the genius of the director Stern to the skies, while the other called him an 'artistic charlatan'. They had also written a lot about Eliza Altairsky-Lointaine, but here the range of opinions was somewhat different: from ecstatically adoring among the benevolently disposed reviewers, to condescendingly sympathetic among the malicious – they regretted the waste of talent involved when such an excellent artiste was obliged to squander her gift in the pretentious productions of Mr Stern.

In general, a great deal had been written about Noah's Ark, and written with passion; it was simply that Fandorin never read through the newspapers as far as the pages which discussed the theatrical news. Unfortunately, Erast Petrovich was no lover of the dramatic art and took absolutely no interest in it; if he ever did happen to be in a theatre, it was always, without exception, for an opera or a ballet. He preferred to read good plays with his eyes, so that his impressions would not be spoiled by directorial ambition and poor acting (after all, even in the most absolutely wonderful production there was certain to be one actor or actress who would strike a false note and spoil everything). It seemed to Fandorin that the theatre was an art form doomed to extinction. When the cinematograph came into its own, acquiring both sound and colour – who then would spend a substantial amount of money in order to contemplate cardboard scenery, while pretending that they couldn't hear the prompter's whispering and didn't notice the swaying of the curtain and the excessive maturity of the prima donnas?

For its Moscow tour Noah's Ark had rented the building of the former Noveishy Theatre, which now belonged to a certain 'Theatrical and Cinematographic Company'.

On arriving at the famous square, Erast Petrovich found himself obliged to get out beside the fountain – the congestion created by the carriages and the public made it impossible to drive up to the actual entrance. Moreover, it was strikingly obvious that the crush in front of the Noveishy Theatre was much denser than in front of the Maly Theatre located opposite it, with its perennial production of Ostrovsky's *Storm*, or even in front of the Bolshoi Theatre, where the season was currently opening with *Twilight of the Gods*.

As he had intended, Fandorin first made his way to the playbill, in order to acquaint himself with the membership of the company. It was most likely, since it seemed to be quite customary in the close little world of actors, that the harrowing torments of the leading lady were the result of scheming by one of her colleagues. In order to solve the appalling mystery and be done with this idiotic business as quickly as possible, he had to make a note of the names of individuals relevant to the case.

The title of the show finally ruined the reluctant theatregoer's mood completely. He gazed with a gloomy eye at the foppish poster with its ornamental flourishes, thinking that this evening would prove to be even more distressing than had been expected.

Erast Petrovich very much disliked Karamzin's novella *Poor Liza*, which was regarded as a masterpiece of literary sentimentalism, and for this he had extremely serious, personal grounds of his own, which had nothing at all to do with literature. It was even more painful to read that the production was dedicated 'to St Elizaveta's Remembrance Day'.

It will be precisely thirty-five years ago this month, Fandorin thought. He closed his eyes for a moment and shuddered, driving away the appalling memory.

In an attempt to rouse himself to action, he gave free rein to his irritation.

'What an idiotic fantasy – staging old-fashioned trash in the t-twentieth century!' he muttered. 'And where have they found a plot for an entire "tragedy in three acts", even if there is no interval? And the seat prices have been increased!'

NOAH'S ARK
THEATRE COMPANY

PRESENTS

FOR THE FIRST TIME IN MOSCOW
TODAY, 5 SEPTEMBER, ST ELIZAVETA'S
REMEMBRANCE DAY,

POOR LIZA

A TRAGEDY
IN THREE ACTS,
BASED ON THE NOVELLA BY

NIKOLAI KARAMZIN

DIRECTED BY NOAH STERN

❖ ❖ ❖

CAST:

MME ALTAIRSKY-LOINTAINE — LIZA, A PEASANT'S DAUGHTER
MR EMERALDOV — ERAST, A YOUNG NOBLEMAN
MME REGININA — LIZA'S MOTHER
MR SENSIBLIN — THE SPIRIT OF LIZA'S FATHER
MR SHIFTSKY — YASHA, A YOUNG SHEPHERD
MME APHRODISINA — MARFINKA, A SHEPHERDESS
MME VULPINOVA — A RICH WIDOW
MR MEPHISTOV — A CARD SHARP
MME COMEDINA — FROLKA, THE BOY NEXT DOOR
MR GULLIBIN — SHATSKY, ERAST'S COMRADE-IN-ARMS
MR NONARIKIN — PASSER-BY, MAN AT THE GAMBLING CLUB,
SERVANT, STATUE OF PAN
MR STERN — DEATH

❖ ❖ ❖

THE PERFORMANCE HAS NO INTERVAL
SEAT PRICES INCREASED

'Interested in a seat, sir?' asked a little man with a cap pulled down over his eyes, who had popped up under Fandorin's elbow. 'I've got a ticket for the orchestra stalls. I was dreaming of attending the performance myself, but have been obliged to abandon the idea, owing to family circumstances. I can let you have it. I bought it from a third party, so I'm afraid it's a bit pricey.' He ran a quick glance over the London dinner jacket, the geometrically perfect lapels, the black pearl in the tie. 'Twenty-five roubles, sir . . .'

The sheer gall of it! Twenty-five roubles for a seat, and not even in a box, but simply in the stalls! One of the newspaper stories about the Noah's Ark tour, a highly venomous one, entitled 'Prices Increased', had been devoted to the incredibly high cost of tickets for a performance by the company from out of town. Its manager, Mr Stern, was a remarkably gifted entrepreneur and he had invented a highly effective way of selling tickets. The prices of seats in the boxes, orchestra stalls and dress circle were twice or even three times the usual cost; but tickets for the tiered stalls and the gallery never even reached the box office, they were allocated for purchase by students – through the medium of a cheap lottery. The lottery tickets were distributed among the young men and women for fifty kopecks each and one out of every ten won a ticket for the theatre. Any lucky winner could either attend the production that everyone was writing and talking about, or sell the ticket just before the performance, thereby obtaining a rather handsome return on his fifty kopecks.

This device, which had outraged the author of the newspaper article so profoundly, had seemed ingenious to Fandorin. Firstly, it meant that Stern sold even the very cheapest seats for five roubles each (as much as the price of a good seat in the orchestra stalls in the Bolshoi Theatre). Secondly, the entire student community of Moscow was all agog over Noah's Ark. Thirdly, a lot of young people came to see the show, and it is their enthusiasm that contributes most to ensuring a theatre's success.

Without even condescending to answer the ticket tout, sullen Erast Petrovich made his way over to a door with a plaque that said 'House Manager'. If Fandorin had needed to collect his pass inside, he would have turned round and walked away. Nothing could have induced him to squeeze his way through between so many backs and shoulders. But Olga Leonardovna had told him: 'Five paces to the right of the door there will be a man with a green briefcase, standing on the steps . . .'

And indeed, standing precisely five paces away from the crowd that was storming the door, lounging back against the wall, was a tall man with broad shoulders, wearing a striped American suit that contrasted rather noticeably with his coarse face, which seemed to be moulded out of reddish-brown clay. The man was simply standing there quite impassively, without even glancing at the clamouring votaries of Melpomene, and whistling; he had a flirtatious little green briefcase pressed against his side with his elbow.

Fandorin was not able to approach the striped gentleman immediately – someone was constantly pushing through to the front. In some elusive way these people resembled the rogue who had tried to fleece Erast Petrovich of twenty-five roubles for a ticket; equally shifty and shadowlike, with rapid, muted speech.

The owner of the green briefcase disposed of them quickly, without saying a single word – he just whistled: briefly and mockingly to some, after which the individuals concerned immediately disappeared; menacingly to some, who backed away; and approvingly to others.

The touts' and hucksters' handler, Fandorin decided. Finally wearying of listening to the artistic whistling and observing the incessant flickering of shadowy figures, he set one foot on the first step, holding back by the shoulder yet another shadow that had bobbed up out of nowhere, and said what he had been instructed to say.

'From Madam Knipper.'

The whistler had no chance to respond. Yet another third party pushed in between him and Fandorin. Erast Petrovich did not grab this one by the shoulder, or any other part of his body, out of respect for his uniform: he was an officer, a cornet of hussars and a guardsman to boot.

'Sila Yegorovich, I implore you!' the young man exclaimed, gazing at the striped gentleman with absolutely wild, staring eyes. 'For the orchestra stalls! No farther than the sixth row! Your men have gone totally insane, they're asking twenty roubles a time. All right, then, but on credit. I spent everything I had on a basket of flowers. You know that Vladimir Limbach always pays up. So help me, I swear I'll shoot myself!'

The scalper gave the desperate cornet an indolent glance and whistled indifferently.

'There aren't any tickets. They've run out. I can give you a complimentary pass without a seat, seeing as I'm so well disposed.'

'Ah, but you know an officer can't watch a performance without a seat.'

'Well, take it or leave it . . . Just one moment, sir.'

The last few words were addressed to Erast Petrovich, together with a polite smile, which required a serious effort from that physiognomy of clay.

'There, if you please. A pass for box number four. My respects to Olga Leonardovna. Always glad to be of service.'

Fandorin set off towards the main entrance, to the accompaniment of benign whistling from the tout and an envious glance from the hussar.

'All right, give me the complimentary pass at least!' a voice behind him exclaimed.

A STRANGE WORLD

Box number four turned out to be the finest of them all. If this had been an imperial theatre, and not a private one, it would probably have been called 'the royal box'. The seven armchairs with gilded backs – three in the first row and four in the second – were all entirely at the disposal of a single spectator. All the more impressive, therefore, was the contrast with the rest of the auditorium, which was literally too cramped for an apple to fall to the floor. There were still five minutes left until the beginning of the performance, but the audience were all in their seats already, as if every one of them feared that another claimant to the same place might show up. And not without reason: in two or three places ushers were trying to calm down agitated people who were brandishing tickets. One scene was played out immediately below Fandorin's box. A well-fleshed lady in an ermine boa almost wept as she exclaimed:

'What do you mean, counterfeit? Where did you buy these tickets, Jacquot?'

Red-faced Jacquot babbled that he got them from an extremely presentable gentleman, for fifteen roubles. The attendants, accustomed to such occurrences, were already carrying over two additional chairs.

In the tiered stalls they were sitting even more tightly packed, with some people even standing in the aisles. The area was dominated by the young faces of male students in pea jackets and female students in white blouses.

At precisely eight o'clock, immediately after the third bell, the lights in the auditorium went out and the doors were firmly closed.

The rule of starting a performance on time and not admitting anyone who came late had been introduced by the Art Theatre, but even there it was not observed with such meticulous strictness.

Erast Petrovich heard a creak behind him.

Turning round on the central armchair of the front row, where he was perched like a Padishah, he was rather surprised to see the hussar who had recently promised to shoot himself.

Cornet Limbach – Fandorin thought that was his name – whispered:

'Are you alone? Excellent! Don't object if I take a seat, do you? Why would you need so many places?'

Fandorin shrugged as if to say: By all means, I can spare one. He moved one seat to the right, so that they would not be crowded together. However, the officer preferred to seat himself behind Fandorin's back.

'It's all right, I'll sit here,' the cornet said, taking a pair of field glasses out of their case.

The door of the box creaked again.

'Damn him, what's he doing here? Don't give me away, I'm with you!' the cornet whispered under his breath into Fandorin's ear.

A middle-aged man in tails and a starched shirt walked in, wearing a tie exactly like Erast Petrovich's, only the pearl in it was not black, but grey. *A banker or successful barrister*, Fandorin speculated, casting a brief glance at the pampered beard and the triumphantly gleaming bald cranium.

The man who had walked in bowed urbanely.

'Tsarkov. And you are the incomparable Olga Leonardovna's acquaintance. Always glad to be of service . . .'

From these words it was possible to conclude that Mr Tsarkov was the owner of the miraculous box and he had been asked to provide a seat by the actress. It was not entirely clear what part in all this was played by the whistler with the green briefcase, but Erast Petrovich had no intention of racking his brains over that.

'Is the young man with you?' the amiable owner enquired, squinting sideways at the cornet (who was studying the decorative moulding on the ceiling through his field glasses).

'Yes.'

'Well then, he's welcome . . .'

During the few minutes that remained until the beginning of the show – while the spectators rustled, creaked and blew their noses – Fandorin's new companion told him about Noah's Ark, and with such expert knowledge that Erast Petrovich was obliged to revise his original opinion; *Not a banker, not a barrister, but probably some important theatrical figure or influential reviewer.*

'Opinions differ regarding Stern's talent as a director, but when it comes to business he is quite definitely a genius,' Mr Tsarkov began loquaciously, addressing only Fandorin, as if the two of them were alone together in the box. Cornet Limbach, however, seemed glad that no one was taking any notice of him.

'He began staging his performances a week before the opening of the season and he has exploited his monopoly right up to the hilt, to coin a phrase. The public has come pouring in, firstly because there is nowhere else for it to go, and secondly, because he has fired off in rapid succession three productions that the whole of St Petersburg spent all last season arguing about. First he put on *Hamlet*, then *The Three Sisters*, and now it's *Poor Liza*. And what's more, he announced in advance that each production is being performed just once, without any repetitions. Look at what's happening now, on the third evening.' The theatrical connoisseur gestured round the auditorium, which was crowded to overflowing. 'And this also strikes an astutely cunning blow against his main competitor – the Art Theatre. This very year they were intending to astound the public with new productions of *The Three Sisters* and *Hamlet*. I assure you that after Stern any innovative interpretation will seem stale and insipid. And *Poor Liza* is perfectly outrageous. Neither Stanislavsky nor Yuzhin would have dared to present dramaturgical material of that nature on the modern stage. But I saw the show in St Petersburg. And I assure you, it really is something! Lointaine in the role of Liza is divine!' The bald gentleman kissed his fingertips fruitily and an imposing diamond on one finger sparkled brightly.

He can hardly be a reviewer, Erast Petrovich thought. *Where would a reviewer get a solitaire diamond weighing a dozen carats?*

'But the most interesting part is yet to come. I'm expecting a great deal from the Ark this season. After this volley of three superb absolute sell-outs, they're taking a break from performing for a month. The cunning Stern is giving the Art Theatre, Maly Theatre and Korsh a chance to display their novelties to the public – stepping aside, as it were. After that, in October, he promises to give his own premiere, and, of course, he will lure the whole of Moscow here.'

Although Fandorin had little real understanding of theatrical practices, this seemed strange to him.

'I b-beg your pardon, but surely the building is rented, is it not? How can a theatre exist for an entire month without any takings?'

Tsarkov winked at him cunningly.

'The Ark can afford such a luxury. The Theatrical and Cinematographic Company has granted them fully serviced rental at a rate of one rouble a month. Oh, Stern knows how to find himself a cosy spot! In a month or six weeks they'll prepare a completely new production, starting from scratch. No one knows what the play will be, but people are already giving fifty roubles for a good ticket for the first performance!'

'But what do you mean, no one knows?'

'Precisely that! A deliberately calculated effect. Tomorrow there is a meeting of the company, at which Stern will announce to the actors what play they are putting on. The day after tomorrow all the newspapers will write about it. *Et voilà*: the public will start waiting impatiently for the premiere. No matter what they put on. Oh, trust my intuition, dear sir. Thanks to Noah's Ark, there is a singularly fruitful season in store for Moscow!'

This was said with sincere feeling, and Erast Petrovich glanced at the other man respectfully. Such sincere, selfless love of art could not help but inspire respect.

'But shhhh! It's starting. Now this will really be something – everyone will gasp,' the theatre enthusiast chuckled. 'Stern didn't show them this trick in St Petersburg . . .'

The curtain rose. The entire stage set was concealed behind taut white fabric. It was a screen! A carriage appeared on it, drawn by four horses hurtling along at full gallop.

A combination of the cinematograph and the theatre? Intriguing, thought Erast Petrovich.

The aficionado proved to be right – a rapturous gasp ran through the orchestra stalls and tiered stalls.

'He knows how to capture the audience from the very first moment, the cunning devil,' Tsarkov whispered, leaning forward – and then he smacked himself on the lips, as if to say: Pardon me, I'll keep quiet.

Pastoral music began to play and words appeared on the screen.

'One day, towards the end of the reign of Catherine the Great, a young and brilliant guardsman was returning to his estate from his regiment . . .'

The production proved to be innovative in the extreme, with a host of original ideas; it made playful and at the same time philosophical use of stage scenery and costumes created by a fashionable artist, a member of the World of Art group. The brief parable about a young ingénue, who drowned herself because of her beloved's infidelity, was fleshed out with twists and turns of the plot. Additional characters appeared, some entirely new and others hinted at in passing by Karamzin, the author of the original story. The play dealt with a passionate love that violated all the prohibitions – after all, poor Liza surrenders to her Erast without any concern for rumour or consequences. The play told the story of a woman's self-sacrificing courage and a man's cowardice in the face of public opinion; a story of the weakness of Good and the power of Evil. The latter was personified in a most vivid and lively manner by the rich widow (played by the actress Vulpinova) and the card sharp (played by the actor Mephistov), who is hired by her to ruin the impressionable Erast and force him into marrying for money.

Extensive use was made of the cinema screen in order to recreate historical Moscow and natural phenomena. There was a superlatively conceived scene with the ghost of Liza's father (the actor Sensiblin), who was lit up by a blue beam of light from the projector. Also impressive were the monologue and dance performed by Death as he lured the young woman into the pond (this part was played by Mr Stern himself).

But what the audience found most astounding of all was a trick with a piece of sculpture. Almost the entire second act unfolded beside a statue of Pan, symbolising the pastoral sensuality of the love theme. After a minute or so, of course, the audience stopped paying any attention to the statue, having accepted it as an element of the stage decor. Imagine their delight when, at the end of the act, the classical deity suddenly came to life and started playing his reed-pipe!

It was the first time Erast Petrovich had seen a theatre company in which he was forced to admit that no unevenness could be detected in the quality of the acting. All the actors, even those playing the minor parts, were immaculate, and every entrance by each and every one of them was a genuine firecracker.

However, the numerous merits of the production went almost unnoticed by Fandorin. From the moment when Altairsky-Lointaine first appeared on the stage, for him the play was divided into two parts of unequal value: the scenes in which she played and the scenes in which she was not present.

The moment that delicate voice started singing its simple little song about the wild flowers of the fields, remorseless fingers seemed to squeeze the hitherto indifferent spectator's heart. He recognised that voice! He thought he had forgotten it, but now it appeared that he had remembered it for all these years!

The figure, the walk, the turn of the head – everything was exactly the same!

'Pardon me . . .'

Fandorin turned round and almost tore the field glasses out of the cornet's hand by force.

The face . . . No, the face was different, but that expression of the eyes, that trusting smile, that anticipation of happiness and open acceptance of destiny! How could all of that be reproduced so authentically, so relentlessly? He even squeezed his eyes shut and didn't protest when the hussar took his field glasses back, whispering angrily:

'Give them back, give them back, I want to adore her too!'

To watch poor Liza fall in love with the happy-go-lucky Erast and watch him betray her love for other infatuations, allowing her life to be destroyed, was painful and yet at the same time . . . *revivifying* – yes, that was the strange but absolutely precise word for it. As if Time with its sharp claws had stripped away the horny, calloused skin covering his soul and now it was oozing blood as it recovered its sensitivity and vulnerability.

Fandorin closed his eyes once again; he couldn't bear to watch the scene of Liza's lapse from virtue, which was presented by the director in an extremely bold, almost naturalistic manner. The maiden's naked arm, with the fingers outstretched, was first picked out by a bright beam of light, then it started drooping, sinking downwards like a wilting flower stem.

'Oh, well done, Lointaine!' Tsarkov exclaimed when everyone started applauding. 'Her acting is miraculous! As good as the late Komissarzhevskaya!'

Fandorin cast an angry glance at him. What he had said seemed like blasphemy to Erast Petrovich, who was finding the owner of the box more and more irritating. Several times some person or other came in to whisper with him – although that didn't really matter all that much when Liza, that is, Eliza Lointaine, wasn't on stage. During the musical interludes Fandorin's talkative neighbour leaned across his armchair and began sharing his impressions or telling Erast Petrovich something about the theatre or the performers. For instance, concerning the romantic lead, Emeraldov, Tsarkov said disdainfully that he was 'not a partner up to her level'. This seemed wrong to Erast Petrovich. He was wholeheartedly on the side of this character, he didn't feel jealous when the theatrical Erast embraced Liza and, in defiance of all logic, he hoped that the young nobleman would see reason and return to his beloved.

Fandorin only began listening to the experienced theatre enthusiast's tittle-tattle when Tsarkov said something about the prima donna. Thus, during a long scene that Erast Petrovich found uninteresting – set in a gambling club, with the hero's officer friend trying to persuade him to stop, while the card sharp egged him on to try to recover his losses, Tsarkov communicated something about Altairsky-Lointaine that brought a frown to Fandorin's face

'Ah, yes, Lointaine is definitely a pearl of great price. Thank God that a man has turned up who will not begrudge the funds to provide a worthy setting. I am thinking of Mr Shustrov of the Theatrical and Cinematographic Company.'

'Is he her b-benefactor?' Erast Petrovich asked, suddenly aware of an unpleasant, chilly sensation in his chest and feeling angry with himself because of it. 'Who is he?'

'A very capable young entrepreneur, who inherited a gingerbread and cracknel bakery from his father. He studied in America and manages his business in the tough American style too. He crushed all his competitors and then sold his cracknel kingdom for a very good price. Now he's creating an entertainment empire – a new venture, with great prospects. I don't think he has any romantic interest in Altairsky. Shustrov is an unromantic man. It is really more of an investment, with a view to her potential as an artiste.'

He carried on, saying something else about the Napoleonic plans of the former cracknel manufacturer, but Fandorin, having calmed down now, was no longer listening and he even interrupted the babbler with a rather uncivil gesture when Liza appeared on the stage again.

Although Erast Petrovich's other companion did not importune him with conversation, Fandorin found him just as irksome as Tsarkov. Every time Altairsky-Lointaine made an entrance, he responded with howls of 'Bravo!' and his resounding voice left Fandorin's ears deafened.

'Stop that! You're distracting me,' Fandorin repeatedly told him angrily.

'I beg your pardon,' Cornet Limbach muttered, without tearing himself away from his field glasses, but only a second later he yelled again. 'Divine! Divine!'

The actress had a multitude of ecstatic admirers in the auditorium. In fact it was rather strange that all their howling didn't prevent her from playing her part – it was as if she didn't hear them. Which was not the case with her partner, Mr Emeraldov – when he made his first entrance and women's voices started squealing and shrieking in the hall, he pressed his hand to his heart and bowed.

Under other circumstances the emotional response of the audience would have irritated Fandorin, but today he was almost a different person. He seemed to have a lump in his own throat and did not find the audience's reactions excessive at all.

Despite his own agitation, which was probably provoked less by the actors' performance than by his own memories, Fandorin did note that the reaction of the auditorium was in fact determined by the psychological patterning of the production, in which comic scenes alternated with sentimental ones. By the time the finale came, the audience was sitting there, sobbing in hushed silence, and the curtain fell to thunderous applause and cheers.

A minute before the ending, the striped whistler entered the box and stood respectfully behind its owner. He was pressing his green briefcase against his side with his elbow and holding a little notebook and pencil in his hands.

'Well then,' Tsarkov said to him. 'I'll thank her and Stern in person. Arrange something or other absolutely top class. Emeraldov can make do with you. Give him my card. Well, and some wine, I suppose. Which does he like?'

'Bordeaux, Chateau Latour, twenty-five roubles a bottle,' the striped man said, glancing into the little book. He whistled quietly. 'He certainly has good taste.'

'Half a dozen . . . Hey, you, be quiet!' The final remark was to the hussar, who had started shouting: 'Loi-oin-taine! Loi-oin-taine!' the moment the curtain came down.

Erast Petrovich offended the cornet too.

'Let me have those,' he said, confiscating the boy's field glasses again. He wanted very badly to take a look at what the astounding actress's face was like when she was no longer acting.

'But I have to see her accept my basket!'

The young officer tried to tear the field glasses out of Fandorin's hand, but he might as well have tried to tear the sword out of the hands of the bronze figures of Minin and Pozharsky on Red Square.

'Consider it the price of your seat,' Erast Petrovich hissed, adjusting the little wheel.

No, not the least bit like her, he told himself. *About ten years older. The face isn't oval, but more angular. And the eyes aren't youthful at all, they're weary. Ah, such eyes . . .*

He put down the field glasses, because he suddenly felt unaccountably dizzy. Well, well, what next?

The actors did not come out for their bows by turns, in the way it was usually done in the theatre, but all at once: the male and female leads at the front, with the others in the second row. The one who had played Death, that is, Noah Stern himself, did not appear at all – he remained brilliantly absent, so to speak.

The applause continued unabated as attendants carried flowers out onto the stage from both sides, first the bouquets, and then the baskets – the smaller ones first, followed by the larger ones. About half of the tributes went to Emeraldov and half to Altairsky. Other players received perhaps one or two bouquets, but not everyone got something.

'Now they'll bring mine out. Give me those back! There it is! I spent a month's pay on it!'

The hussar clung on to Fandorin's arm and the field glasses had to be relinquished.

The basket was genuinely sumptuous – an entire cloud of white roses.

'She's going to take mine, mine!' the cornet repeated, seeming not to notice that in his excitement he was tugging on the other man's sleeve.

'Here, if you please. I can see that you are interested.'

Mr Tsarkov politely held out his mother-of-pearl lorgnette on a handle. Erast Petrovich grabbed the trinket, raised it to his eyes and was surprised to discover that the lenses were every bit as effective as those in the officer's field glasses.

Once again the smiling face of Eliza Altairsky-Lointaine appeared close, very close, in front of his eyes. She was glancing downwards and off to one side, and the wings of her delicately chiselled nose were trembling slightly. What could have upset her? Surely not the fact that the final basket presented to Emeraldov (lemon-yellow orchids) was more sumptuous than her white roses? Hardly. This woman could not be infected with such petty vanity!

And then yet another basket, a genuine palace of flowers, was carried out onto the stage. Who was it intended for – the prima donna or the leading man?

For her! This miracle of the florist's art was set down in front of Altairsky to the sound of ecstatic shouting from the entire hall. She curtsied, lowering her face to the buds and embracing the flowers in her slim, white arms.

'Oh, damn it, damn it . . .' Limbach groaned pitifully, seeing that his high card had been trumped.

Erast Petrovich shifted his lenses to Emeraldov for a second. The picturesquely handsome features of Karamzin's Erast were distorted in spiteful malice. Well, well, such passions because of mere flowers!

He looked at Eliza again, expecting to see her triumphant. But the actress's lovely face was a frozen mask of horror: the eyes were gaping wide and the lips were set in a soundless scream. What was wrong? What had frightened her?

Suddenly Fandorin saw that one of the flower buds, still dark and unopened, was swaying to and fro and seemed to be reaching upwards.

Good Lord! It wasn't a bud! Fandorin distinctly made out the diamond form of a snake's head framed in the double circle of his vision. It was a viper, and it was reaching directly towards the petrified leading lady's bosom.

'A snake! There's a snake in the basket!' Limbach howled, and he vaulted over the parapet, down into the gangway.

Everything happened in a few brief instants.

People in the front rows of the orchestra stalls were screaming and waving their arms about. The rest of the audience, not understanding what was happening, launched into a new storm of applause.

The swashbuckling hussar jumped to his feet, snatched his sword out of its scabbard and dashed towards the stage. But the white figure of Pan, made up to resemble marble, came to Altairsky's rescue even sooner. Since he was standing behind the actress's back, the horned god had spotted the fearsome denizen of the flower basket before anyone else. He ran up, fearlessly grabbed the reptile by the neck and snatched it out into the open.

Now the entire audience could see what was happening. The ladies started squealing. Madam Altairsky swayed on her feet and fell over onto her back. Then valiant Pan cried out – the reptile had bitten him on the hand. He swung it hard and smashed it against the floor, then started trampling it with his feet.

The theatre was filled with screams, the clattering of chairs and screeching.

'A doctor! Call a doctor!' voices shouted from the stage.

Someone fanned Eliza with a shawl and someone else led the bitten hero away.

And a tall, very thin man with his head completely shaved appeared right at the back of the stage.

He stood there with his arms folded, contemplating all this babel and smiling.

'Who is that? Back there, behind all the others?' Fandorin asked his omniscient companion.

'One moment,' said the companion, concluding a quiet conversation with his striped minion. 'Find out who was responsible and punish them!'

'It shall be done.'

The whistler walked rapidly out of the box and Mr Tsarkov turned towards Erast Petrovich with a polite smile, as if nothing untoward had occurred.

'Where? Ah, that is Noah Noaevich Stern in person. He has taken off his Mask of Death. Just look how he's glowing! And he has good reason to be delighted. What a stroke of luck! Now the Muscovites will go absolutely mad about the Ark.'

What a strange world, thought Fandorin. *Incredibly strange!*

INITIAL ACQUAINTANCE

The prime minister died at the very time when Erast Petrovich was in the theatre. The next day flags with black ribbons attached to them were hung everywhere and the newspapers appeared with huge headlines of mourning. In the liberal papers they wrote that, although the deceased was a proponent of reactionary views, the last chance for a renewal of the country without turmoil and revolution had died together with him. In the patriotic papers they cursed the Hebraic tribe to which the killer belonged and saw a special meaning in the fact that Stolypin had passed away on the anniversary of the ascension of the Most Orthodox Prince Gleb, thereby augmenting the host of the martyrs of the Russian land. Publications of the melodramatic, gutter-press disposition vehemently quoted Pyotr Arkadievich Stolypin's will, in which he had apparently requested to be buried 'where I am killed'.

This tragic news (they telephoned Erast Petrovich when he got back from the theatre) failed to make any special impression on him. The man who made the call, a high-ranking bureaucrat, also said that the council of the Ministry of Internal Affairs had discussed whether Fandorin should be involved in the investigation, but the commander of the Corps of Gendarmes had categorically objected to this and the minister had made no comment.

It was remarkable that Erast Petrovich did not feel mortified in the least; on the contrary, he actually felt relieved, and if he did not sleep a wink the whole night long, it was not out of resentment, or even out of fearful concern for the fate of the state.

He paced to and fro in his study, looking down at the bright glimmers reflected from the parquet; he lay on the divan with a cigar, looking up at the white ceiling; he sat on the windowsill and gazed hard into the blackness – but all the while he saw the same thing: a slim arm, languid eyes, a snake's head among flower buds.

Fandorin was accustomed to subjecting facts to analysis, but not his own emotions. And even now he did not stray from the path of rational inference, sensing that the slightest sideways step would send him tumbling into a quagmire, and he did not know how to scramble out of it.

Setting out a line of logic created the illusion that nothing special had happened. Just another investigation, the world had not been turned on its head.

Madam Altairsky's fear had been justified. The danger really did exist. That was one, thought Erast Petrovich, bending down one finger – and he caught himself smiling. *She isn't a hysterical girl who imagines things, she isn't a psychopath!*

She obviously had some kind of ferocious enemy with a perverse imagination. Or enemies. That was two. *How could anyone possibly hate her?*

Judging from the theatricality of the attack on her life, the culprit or culprits should be sought first of all within the theatre company or on its immediate periphery. It was unlikely that someone who did not have backstage access could have placed the reptile in the basket. However, that would have to be checked. That was three. *But what if the snake had bitten her? Oh, God!*

He had to go to the theatre, take a close look at everything and, most important of all, try to get Madam Altairsky-Lointaine herself to speak frankly. That was four. *I shall see her again! I shall talk to her!*

The inner dialogue continued in this way right through until the morning, with feverishly agitated emotions constantly hindering the work of thought.

Eventually, after dawn, Fandorin said to himself: *What the blazes is this? I think I must be unwell.* He lay down and with an effort of will forced himself to relax and fall asleep.

Three hours later Fandorin got up well rested, performed his usual physical exercises, took an ice bath and walked on a tightrope stretched across the courtyard for ten minutes. Control over his interior world was re-established. Erast Petrovich ate a hearty breakfast and looked through the Moscow newspapers that had been delivered; a brief glance at the sad headlines – and then rapidly on to the current events pages. Even the publications that lacked a theatre review section had published reports about the play at Noah's Ark and the snake. Some reporters were appalled, some joked about it, but all of them, without exception, wrote about it. The reporters' theories (envy among actors, a spurned admirer, a malicious joke) were of no real interest because they were so obvious. The only useful information that Fandorin gleaned from this reading was the fact that the actor who was bitten (Mr Nonarikin) had been given an injection of antivenom and the state of his health was no longer any cause for concern.

Olga Leonardovna called several times in an agitated state, but Masa had been instructed to tell her that his master was not at home. Erast Petrovich did not feel like wasting time and mental energy on sentimental conversations. Those resources could be put to far better use.

The manager of Noah's Ark met his visitor at the service entrance, shook his hand in both of his own and led him to his office – all in all, he was hospitality itself. During their telephone conversation Fandorin had thought that Stern seemed a little wary, but the theatre director had agreed immediately to meet.

'Madam Chekhov's wish is sacred to me,' Stern said, offering Erast Petrovich a seat in an armchair. His narrow, intent eyes slid over the visitor's impervious face and elegant cream suit and halted on the pointy-toed shoes of crocodile leather. 'She called yesterday and asked for a complimentary ticket for you, but it was too late, there wasn't a single good seat left. Olga Leonardovna said she would arrange things somehow without my help, but she wanted me to set aside some time for you after the performance. She called again this morning to ask if the meeting had taken place . . .'

'I didn't bother you yesterday, in view of the circumstances.'

'Yes, indeed, an absolutely macabre incident. All that screaming backstage! And the audience was so very excited!' The director's thin lips extended into a sweet smile. 'But what is the reason for your visit? Olga Leonardovna didn't explain. "Mr Fandorin will explain that," she said . . . Pardon me, but what line of business is it that you are in?'

Erast Petrovich limited himself to answering the first question.

'Madam Chekhova considers that your leading actress . . .' – he hesitated briefly. He had been about to pronounce the name, but for some reason he didn't – '. . . is in danger. Yesterday's incident d-demonstrates that Olga Leonardovna is right. I promised to get to the bottom of things.'

The theatrical innovator's sharp eyes glinted with curiosity.

'But who are you? Could you really be some kind of psychic? I've heard that fortune-tellers and clairvoyants are all the fashion in Moscow. I find that very, very interesting!'

'Yes, I have made a study of clairvoyance. In Japan,' Erast Petrovich said with a serious expression. It had occurred to him that this story could be very convenient for the forthcoming investigation. And then again, clairvoyance (i.e. 'clear vision') and deduction (that is, clear thinking) did have quite a lot in common.

'Phenomenal!' Stern exclaimed, so enthused that he jumped up out of his chair. 'Perhaps you could demonstrate your art? Well, if only on me, for instance. I ask you please, glance into my future! No, better, into my past, so that I can appreciate your skill.'

What a mercurial gentleman, thought Fandorin. *A veritable bead of mercury.* (The comparison arose in response to the way the theatre director's bald head glinted in a ray of sunlight – the September day had turned out fine.)

The newspaper-reading and telephone calls on which Erast Petrovich had spent half of the present day had thrown very little light on Noah Stern's biography. He had a reputation as a reticent individual who did not like to talk about his past. The only thing known about him was that he had grown up in the Jewish Pale, in extreme poverty, and lived a vagabond life during the days of his youth. He had started as a clown in a circus and then acted in provincial theatres for a long time until eventually he became well known. He had acquired his own theatre company only a year ago, when he won the patronage of the Theatrical and Cinematographic

Company, which had taken a gamble on his talent. Stern told the newspaper correspondents cock-and-bull stories about himself, always different ones – and he quite obviously did it deliberately. Everything added up to just one conclusion: here was a man obsessed by a single, solitary passion – the theatre. He had no family and did not seem to have a home either. Noah Noaevich was not even known to have had any casual affairs with actresses.

'Glance into your p-past?'

The director's high-strung face started quivering in its craving for an immediate miracle.

'Yes, something from out of my childhood.'

Stern was certain that no one knew anything about that period of his life, Erast Petrovich realised.

Well then, if clairvoyance was to be the thing . . .

'Tell me. Is Noah Noaevich your real name?'

'The absolutely genuine article. As stated on my birth certificate.'

'I see . . .' Fandorin drew his black eyebrows in towards the bridge of his nose and rolled his eyes up towards his forehead, across which a greyish lock of hair dangled down (this was exactly the way he imagined that a clairvoyant would have behaved). 'The beginning of your life is a sad one, my d-dear sir. Your father never even saw you. He departed to the next world while you still dwelt in your mother's womb. His death was sudden – an unexpected blow of Fate.'

The chances of being mistaken were not very great. Among Jews there was an old custom of naming children in honour of some relative who had died, but almost never in honour of the living. That was precisely why it was so rare for a son to be given his father's name, except in cases when the father had died. The assumption that the death had been sudden was not so very risky either. Men who had been seriously ill for a long time did not produce such vigorous progeny.

This simple little deduction absolutely bowled the impressionable showman over.

'Phenomenal!' he exclaimed, clutching at his heart. 'I've never told anybody that! Not a single soul! There is no one around me who could know anything about my life! My God, how I adore everything that is inexplicable! Erast Petrovich, you are a unique individual! A miracle worker! From the very first moment I laid eyes on you, I realised that I saw before me an exceptional man. If I were a woman or a disciple of Oscar Wilde, I would absolutely fall in love with you!'

This joke was accompanied by an extremely charming smile. The wide-open brown eyes gazed at Fandorin with an expression of such sincere liking that it was impossible not to respond in kind.

He's overwhelming me, thought Erast Petrovich, *turning on his charm – and with superb skill. This man is an excellent actor and a born manipulator. He was frightened by my little trick and now he wants to know just what sort of creature I am, get my measure and crack open my shell. Well then, bite away, do. Only be careful not to break your teeth.*

'You possess the inner strength of magnanimity,' said Noah Noaevich, continuing with his fawning. 'Oh, I understand about such things. There are not many people with whom I feel a desire to be frank, but you inspire the desire to be defenceless . . . I am terribly glad that Olga Leonardovna has sent you to us. There really is some strange process of fermentation taking place in the company. It would be excellent if you could take a close look at my actors and were able to perceive the villain who hid the snake in the flowers. And at the same time it would be good to find out who poured glue into my galoshes the day before yesterday. An idiotic prank! I had to have a completely new pair of boots resoled and throw the galoshes out!'

Erast Petrovich promised to 'perceive' the destroyer of the galoshes as well, when he was given a chance to meet the company.

'Then we'll see to that straight away!' Stern declared. 'No point in putting it off! We have a meeting scheduled right now. In half an hour. I'm going to announce the new play for production and give out the parts. The actors display their genuine egos most clearly of all when the squabbling over parts begins. You'll see them as if they were naked.'

'What play is it?' Erast Petrovich asked, recalling what his companion in the box had said. 'Or is that still a secret?'

'Oh, come now.' Noah Noaevich laughed. 'What secrets can there be from a clairvoyant? And in any case tomorrow all the newspapers will write about it. I've chosen *The Cherry Orchard* for my new production. Excellent material for routing Stanislavsky with his own weapon and on his own territory! The public can compare my *Cherry Orchard* with their anaemic exercises! I won't deny that the Art Theatre used to be pretty good once, but it has lost its fizz. Any mention of the Maly is simple laughable! And Korsh's theatre is low farce for merchants' wives! I'll show them all what real directing and genuine work with actors look like! Would you like me to tell you, my dear Erast Petrovich, what the ideal theatre should be like? I can see that you would make an intelligent and appreciative listener.'

It would have been impolite to decline the offer, and in any case Fandorin wished to get to grips with the bizarre workings of this world that was so new to him.

'Do t-tell me. I'm interested.'

Noah Noaevich stood over his visitor in the pose of an Old Testament prophet, with his eyes glittering.

'Do you know why my theatre is called "Noah's Ark"? Firstly, because only art will save the world from the flood, and the highest form of art is the theatre. Secondly, because in my theatre company I have a full set of human types. And thirdly because I have two of every kind of beast.'

Noticing the puzzlement on his visitor's face, Stern smiled contentedly.

'Oh, yes. I have a hero and a heroine; a high-minded, no-nonsense father and a *grande dame*, otherwise known as a matron; a male servant-cum-prankster-cum-buffoon and a pert maidservant-cum-prankster-cum-ingénue-cum-coquette; a male villain and a female villain; a simpleton and a principal boy (not a pair – for these two types, singleness is the prescribed arrangement); and then finally, for performing all the other possible roles, there is myself and my assistant director – I play the secondary roles and he plays the tertiary ones. According to my theory of acting, one should not rely on artistes of the so-called versatile type, who are capable of playing absolutely any part. I, for instance, I am an all-round actor. I can play anyone at all to equally good effect – whether it be Lear or Shylock or Falstaff. But one very rarely come across geniuses like that,' Noah Noaevich said regretfully. 'It is not possible to assemble an entire company of them. However, there are any number of actors who are very good in their one and only type. I take a person like that and help him develop his strong but narrow talent to perfection. The type should become inseparable from the individual, that is the very best way. Moreover, artistes are susceptible to that kind of mimicry, and I am very good at guiding them. When I take actors into the company, I even require them to adopt a stage-name that matches the genre of their roles. You know, give a thing a name and that's the way it will be. Only the prima donna and the male lead have kept their former pseudonyms – they both had names that are a draw for the public. My no-nonsense philosopher became Sensiblin, my villain became Mephistov, my coquette became Aphrodisina, and so on. When you take a look now, you'll see immediately that each of them has literally grown into the skin of his or her type. Even offstage they're still working on their characters!'

Erast Petrovich, who had already learned the membership of the company off by heart, asked:

'And what is the type of the god Pan, who demonstrated such bravery yesterday? Nonarikin is not a name that arouses associations with anything in particular, except perhaps the number nine, from the Latin *nonus*.'

'Well he is indeed a number nine in the deck of cards, so to speak, not an ace or any kind of face card. But he's the secondary director, my irreplaceable assistant, one in nine persons and a jack of all trades. And also, by the way, the only one apart from myself who performs under his own natural name. I picked him up in an appalling provincial company, where he was playing heroes quite appallingly under the name of "Lermont", although he is actually more like Lieutenant Solyony in *The Three Sisters*. Now he's in the right place and he's absolutely indispensable; without him I'm all thumbs and no fingers. The basic ploy involved here is that in my theatre absolutely everyone is in the right place. Apart from Emeraldov, I suppose.' The skin on the director's forehead gathered into tragic folds. 'I regret to say that I was beguiled by a striking appearance and a long train of female admirers. A hero should be played by a hero, and our Hippolyte is merely a peacock with bright feathers . . .'

The genius did not grieve for long, however. His face soon recovered its triumphant radiance.

'My theatre is ideal! Do you know what an ideal theatre is?'

Fandorin said no, he didn't know that.

'Well then, I'll explain to you. It's a theatre which has everything that is necessary and nothing superfluous, since a deficit or superfluity of anything is equally injurious to the company. The problem is that there are very few ideal plays in the world. Do you know what an ideal play is?'

'No.'

'It's a play in which all the types are represented vividly. Griboedov's *Woe from Wit* is considered the classic example. However, no one writes like that any more, and you can't exist on a diet of nothing but the classics all the time. The audience gets fed up. It would be good to have something new, something exotic, with a whiff of a different culture. You say you have lived in Japan? You ought to translate something about geishas and samurais. After the war the public became very keen on everything Japanese.' He laughed. 'I'm joking. *The Cherry Orchard* is almost an ideal play. Just the right number of parts that I need. Set a few things right here and there, state some things a bit more distinctly, and there you have an excellent comedy of masks, built entirely on characters, without Chekhov's usual half-tones. We'll see whose orchard has more blossom when the time comes, Konstantin Sergeevich!'

'My name is Erast Petrovich,' Fandorin reminded him, and didn't understand why Stern gave him such a commiserating look.

THE DWELLERS IN THE ARK

At the meeting of the theatre company, which took place in the green room, the director, as agreed, casually introduced Fandorin as a contender for the post of repertoire manager or 'play-picker', that is, head of the literary section. Stern had told him that in the theatre this position was generally regarded as unimportant, and the artistes wouldn't *show off* for such an insignificant figure. And so it turned out. For a moment at the beginning, everyone stared curiously at the elegant gentleman with the picturesque appearance (grey hair streaked slightly with black, parted on a slant, and a well-groomed black moustache), but when they heard who he was, they soon stopped paying any attention to him. This situation suited Erast Petrovich. He seated himself modestly in the farthest corner and started examining them – everyone except Altairsky. Fandorin could feel her presence very keenly (she was sitting opposite him at a slight angle), as if there were a scintillating radiance streaming out of that section of the room, but he did not dare to gaze into it, fearing that the rest of the room would be submerged in twilight, and then he would not be able to work. Erast Petrovich promised himself that he would gaze at her to his heart's content later, after he had studied the others thoroughly.

To begin with, Noah Noaevich delivered an energetic speech, congratulating the company on the colossal success of *Poor Liza* and bemoaning the fact that 'owing to a certain incident' it had not been possible to follow usual practice and review the performance immediately after its conclusion.

'Let me remind you of yesterday's agreement: we are not going to discuss that vile business. An investigation will be carried out, and the guilty party will be unmasked, you have Noah Stern's word . . .' – a brief, suggestive glance in the direction of Fandorin – '. . . But there will be no more of the screaming and oriental ruckus that we had yesterday. Is that clear?'

From out of the zone where the opalescent light was shimmering there came the gentle voice that Erast Petrovich had been yearning to hear again.

'Just one thing, if you will permit me, Noah Noaevich. Yesterday I was in no condition to thank dear Georgy Ivanovich properly for being so brave. He came dashing to help me, at the risk of his own life! I . . . I don't know what would have happened to me . . . If that hideous thing had simply touched me, let alone bitten me . . .' There was a sound of muffled sobbing, which wrung Fandorin's heart. 'Georgy Ivanovich, you are the last true knight of our time! Permit me to kiss you!'

Everyone applauded and for the first time Fandorin allowed himself to glance, but only briefly, at the prima donna. Altairsky was wearing a light-coloured dress, caught in at the waist with a broad, maroon scarf, and a light, wide-brimmed hat with feathers. Her face could not be seen, because she was sitting half-turned away from Fandorin to face a short, pale-faced man with his arm in a sling. The hair at his temples was sleeked down in the style of Lermontov, his high forehead was glistening with sweat and his brown eyes were gazing adoringly at Eliza.

'Thank you . . . That is, I mean to say, don't mention it,' Nonarikin babbled when she took off her hat and touched her lips to his cheek. And then he suddenly blushed bright red.

'Bravo!' a small young lady cried out energetically, jumping to her feet while continuing to applaud. She had an amusing little freckly face with a snub nose, and in his own mind Fandorin immediately dubbed her Halfpint. 'My dear Georges, you are like St George, who defeated the dragon! I want to kiss you too. And shake your poor hand!'

She dashed across to the embarrassed hero, went up on tiptoe and embraced him, but the assistant director received Halfpint's kiss with rather less enthusiasm.

'Don't squeeze so hard, Zoya, it hurts! You've got bony fingers.'

'So this is where my fate was lurking, the threat of death lay in this bone.' The sardonic quotation from Pushkin's poem came from a breathtaking gentleman in a white suit, with a red carnation in the buttonhole. This, of course, was the leading man Emeraldov, who was even more handsome from close up than onstage.

Erast Petrovich glanced cautiously at Eliza, to see what she was like without the hat. But the prima donna was tidying up her hairstyle, and all he could see was her hair raised up and drawn tight in a knot that was either very simple or, on the contrary, incredibly intricate, and lent a certain Egyptian hint to her profile.

'I am obliged to interrupt this touching scene. Enough of all this rapturous admiration and spooning, it's already one minute to four,' said the director, brandishing the watch he had taken out of his pocket. 'Ladies and gentlemen, we have a very important event today. Before we proceed to an analysis of the new play, our benefactor and good angel, Andrei Gordeevich Shustrov, has expressed a desire to meet with us.'

Everyone started and some of the women even shrieked.

Stern was smiling.

'Yes, yes. He wants to get to know everyone. So far only Eliza and I have enjoyed the company of this remarkable patron of the arts, without whom our Ark would never have been launched on its voyage. But we are in Moscow, and Mr Shustrov has set aside the time to greet you all in person. He promised to be here at four, and this man is never late.'

'You villain, couldn't you have warned us? I'd have put on my shot-silk dress and pearls,' a plump lady with a regal appearance, who had undoubtedly once been very beautiful, complained in a rich contralto voice.

'Shustrov is too young for you, dear-heart Vasilisa Prokofievna,' an imposing man with wonderful bluish-grey hair told her. 'I don't suppose he's thirty yet. You won't snare him with pearls and shot silk.'

The lady countered without even turning her head:

'You old buffoon!'

There was a discreet knock at the door.

'What did I tell you: quite remarkable punctuality!' Noah

Noaevich brandished his watch again and dashed to open the door.

Fandorin had been warned about the entrepreneur's forthcoming visit. The director had said it was an excellent way for Erast Petrovich to get to know the members of the company – Stern would be introducing all the actors to their patron.

The owner of the Theatrical and Cinematographic Company did not look much like an industrialist, at least not a Russian one. Young, lean, discreetly dressed and sparing with words. At a first impression it seemed to Fandorin that the most interesting feature of this rather unremarkable individual was a special kind of intensity in the glance of his eyes and a general air of exceptional seriousness. It seemed as if this man never joked or smiled and he never, ever made small talk. Erast Petrovich was usually impressed by people like this, but he took a dislike to Shustrov.

While Stern delivered his welcoming speech – a bombastic oration, with the customary actor's exaggerations ('most esteemed benefactor', 'enlightened patron of the muses', 'custodian of the arts and spiritual values', 'paragon of impeccable taste' and so forth) the capitalist remained silent, calmly surveying the members of the company. He fixed his gaze on Altairsky-Lointaine and from that moment his attention was not distracted by anyone else.

And from that very moment Fandorin began to feel a positive hostility for the 'paragon of impeccable taste'. He squinted at the prima donna – what was her reaction? She was smiling, and tenderly. Her eyes were glued to Shustrov too. And although this was seemingly quite natural – all the members of the company were smiling radiantly as they looked at the young man – Erast Petrovich's mood darkened.

He might at least protest about the compliments, put on a show of modesty, Fandorin thought angrily.

But the truth of the matter was that the actors of Noah's Ark had something to thank Andrei Gordeevich for. Not only had he paid for the move from St Petersburg to Moscow, he had provided a splendidly equipped theatre for their performances here. As Stern's speech made clear, the company had at their disposal a full complement of musicians and attendants, make-up artists and wardrobe mistresses, lighting technicians and labourers, and also all the necessary stage props, with ateliers and workshops, in which experienced costumiers and craftsmen could quickly manufacture any costume or stage set. Probably no other theatre company, including the imperial ones, had ever existed in such pampered conditions.

'The life you have provided us with here is like being in a magical castle!' Noah Noaevich exclaimed. 'It is enough to express a wish and simply clap one's hands – and one's dream comes true. Only in such ideal conditions is it possible to create art without being distracted by degrading and tedious fuss and bother over how to make ends meet. Let us welcome our guardian angel, my friends.'

In response to the applause and ardent exclamations from everyone present, with the sole exception of Fandorin, Mr Shustrov bowed slightly – and that was all.

After that the introductions of the actors began.

First of all Stern led their honoured guest over to the prima donna.

I can do it now, Fandorin thought, and finally allowed himself to focus entirely on the woman responsible for the agitated state in which he had been since the previous day. He knew a lot more about her today than he had known yesterday.

She was almost thirty years of age and came from a theatre family. She had graduated from the ballet department of a theatre college, but had followed a career in drama, thanks to a stage voice of astonishing depth and extremely delicate timbre. She had performed in theatres in both of Russia's capital cities, displaying her brilliance several seasons earlier at the Art Theatre. Malicious gossips asserted that she had left because she did not wish to be on an equal footing with other strong actresses, of whom that theatre had too many. Before becoming the leading actress at Noah's Ark, Altairsky-Lointaine had enjoyed immense success in St Petersburg with performances in the fashionable genre of recitation to musical accompaniment.

That name of hers no longer seemed excessively pretentious to Erast Petrovich. It suited her: as distant as the star Altair ... At the very beginning of her career she had given a vivid performance as Princess Daydream in the play of the same name by Rostand – hence 'Lointaine' (in the French original the heroine is call Princess Lointaine – the Distant Princess, or Princess Faraway). The other part of her pseudonym, which emphasised her inapproachable remoteness, had appeared more recently, following her brief marriage. The newspapers had been rather vague in what they wrote about that. Her husband was an oriental prince, almost a semi-sovereign khan, and some of the articles had referred to Eliza as 'khatun', i.e. a khan's wife.

Well, as he looked at her, Fandorin was willing to believe absolutely anything. A woman like that could easily be a princess *and* a khatun.

Although he had spent a long time preparing himself before he studied her properly at close quarters, it really didn't do very much to soften the blow. Through the field glasses Erast Petrovich had seen her in stage make-up and, moreover, playing the part of a naive village girl. But in life, in her own natural state, Eliza was quite different – not just from her stage image, but simply *different*, unlike other women, unique ... Fandorin would have found it hard to explain exactly how to interpret this thought that made him take a tight grip on the armrests of his chair – because he felt an irresistible urge to stand up and move closer, in order to gaze at her point blank, avidly and continuously.

What is it that's so special about her? he asked himself, trying as usual to rationalise the irrational. *Where does this feeling of unparalleled, magnetic beauty come from?*

He tried to judge impartially.

After all, strictly speaking, she is no great beauty. Her features are rather too small, if anything. The proportions are not classical. A thin-lipped mouth that is too broad. A slight hump in the nose. But instead of weakening the impression of a miracle, all these irregularities merely reinforced it.

It seems to be something to do with the eyes, Erast Petrovich decided. *A certain strange elusiveness that makes you to want to catch her glance, in order to resolve its mystery. It seems to be directed at you, but tangentially somehow, as if she doesn't see you. Or as if she sees something quite different from what is being shown to her.*

Fandorin was certainly not lacking in powers of observation. Even in his present, distinctly abnormal condition, he quickly solved the riddle. Madam Altairsky had a slight squint, that was all there was to the elusiveness. But then another riddle immediately popped up – her smile. Or rather, the half-smile, or incomplete smile that played almost constantly on her lips. *That, apparently, is where the enchantment lies*, thought Erast Petrovich, advancing a different theory. *It is as if this woman is in a constant state of anticipation of happiness – she looks at you as if she were asking: 'Are you the one I'm waiting for? Are you really my happiness?'* And a certain bashfulness could also be read in that marvellous smile. As if Liza were making a gift of herself to the world and was slightly embarrassed by her own generosity.

All in all, it must be admitted that Fandorin failed to resolve the secret of the prima donna's attractiveness completely. He would have carried on examining her for much longer, but Shustrov had already been led on to the person beside her, and Erast Petrovich reluctantly transferred his gaze to Hippolyte Emeraldov.

Now this was a kind of beauty that Fandorin didn't need to rack his brains over. The actor was tall and well set up, with broad shoulders, an ideal parting in his hair, a clear gaze, a blinding smile and an absolutely splendid baritone voice. A sight for sore eyes, a genuine Antinous. The newspapers wrote that he had been followed from St Petersburg to Moscow by almost fifty lovesick female theatregoers, who never missed a single performance that their idol gave and lavished flowers on him extravagantly. Stern had lured him from the Alexandrinsky Theatre for a quite incredible salary of almost a thousand roubles a month.

'You played Hamlet and Vershinin excellently. And you have made a success of Karamzin's Erast too,' the patron of the arts said, shaking Emeraldov by the hand. 'But most important of all, you a have a highly advantageous appearance that can be examined from close up. That's important.'

The millionaire had a peculiar way of speaking. You could tell that he wouldn't squander compliments on anyone. He said what he really thought, without taking too much trouble to make his train of thought clear to the other party.

The leading man replied with a charming smile.

'I could have said: "Look as much as you like, there's no charge for a peek", but with you it's a sin not to ask. So in that connection, I'd like to enquire whether it might not be possible after all to have a benefit performance at the end of the season.'

'Out of the question!' Noah Noaevich snapped. 'The company articles of Noah's Ark state that no one shall have any benefit performances.'

'Not even your favourite?' the handsome devil asked, tossing his head in the direction of Eliza, while still addressing Shustrov.

What an insolent individual, Fandorin thought, and frowned. *Surely someone will put him in his place? And what did he mean by saying that about a favourite?*

'Shut up, Hippolyte. Everyone's sick of you,' the lady who had recently been concerned about her shot-silk dress said in a loud voice.

'And this is Vasilisa Prokofievna Reginina, our *"grande dame",'* the man with the bluish-grey hair put in.

To the sound of muffled giggling, the monumental Vasilisa Prokofievna hurled a withering glance at the joker.

'A voice from the next world,' she hissed. 'Dead men are supposed to hold their tongues.'

The giggling grew louder.

Relationships within the company are strained, Erast Petrovich noted.

'There is no greater calamity for an actress than to cling on for too long to playing the heroine. A woman should know how to move from one age to the next at the right time. I shall be eternally grateful to Noah Noaevich for persuading me to have done with the Desdemonas, Cordelias and Juliets. Good Lord, what a liberation it is not having to act younger than my age, not having a fit of hysterics over every new wrinkle! Now at least I can calmly play the Catherine the Greats and the Kabanyayas until the day I die. I eat cakes, I've put on forty pounds and it doesn't bother me in the slightest!'

This proclamation was made with genuine majesty.

'My queen! Truly a regina!' Stern exclaimed. 'Eat your heart out, dear fellow, for letting your happiness slip away,' he said reproachfully to the grey-haired man. 'This is our *"philosopher"*, Lev Spiridonovich Sensiblin, an extremely wise man, although he can be a bit prickly. He used to be a romantic lead. And not only on the stage, I think, eh, Lev Spiridonovich? Will you finally reveal to us the secret of why you and Vasilisa Prokofievna got divorced? Why does she call you a corpse and a dead man?'

Seeing the sudden animation among the actors, Fandorin guessed that this subject was a popular one in the theatre and felt surprised: surely it was strange to keep a former married couple together in a small company, especially if they had not managed to remain on good terms?

'Vasilisa calls me that because for her I am dead,' the 'philosopher' replied in a meek, sorrowful voice. 'I really did do something absolutely monstrous. Something that is impossible to forgive. Not that I have exactly begged her, by the way . . . But let the details remain our secret.'

'A corpse. A living corpse,' Reginina said, pulling a wry mouth as she spoke the title of the play that everyone in Russia was talking about this season.

Shustrov suddenly livened up.

'That's the idea!' he said. '*A Living Corpse* is an excellent example of how the theatre and the cinematograph support and advertise each other. Count Tolstoy leaves an unpublished play, in some mysterious manner the text finds its way into the hands of my rival Persky, and he has already begun making a film, without waiting for the stage production to appear! No one knows what the play is about, typed copies leak out and are sold on for three hundred roubles! The family of the deceased is taking legal action! I can imagine how the public will go rushing to the cinematograph halls and theatres! An excellent arrangement! We shall talk about that later on.'

His excitement passed off as suddenly as it had arisen. Everyone looked at the entrepreneur in respectful bewilderment.

'My assistant, Nonarikin,' said Noah Noaevich, indicating the man who had been bitten. 'And also an actor without any character type. Monstrously bad, but with a classical repertoire. Our lieutenant is smitten, lovesick, bewitched! He leaves the army and treads the boards under a romantic pseudonym, acting appallingly in appalling productions. And then a new miracle occurs. When he is passing through St Petersburg, he watches my show and finally understands what real theatre is. He comes to me and begs to be taken on in any capacity at all. I have a good understanding of people – it's my profession. I took him on as my assistant and I have never once regretted it. And yesterday Nonarikin showed that he *is* a hero. But of course, you know about that, Andrei Gordeevich.'

'Yes I do.' Shustrov gave the assistant's unbandaged left hand a firm shake. 'Well done. You saved us all some serious losses.'

Erast Petrovich's left eyebrow rose slightly and his mood suddenly improved. If Eliza's health was merely a matter of potential 'losses' for this patron of the arts, then . . . That was quite a different matter.

'I didn't do it to save your losses,' Nonarikin muttered, but the visitor was already being introduced to the next artiste.

'Kostya Shiftsky. As the pseudonym indicates, an actor who plays shifty customers and rogues,' said Stern, introducing a young man with incredibly lively features. 'He has played Goldoni's Truffaldino, de Molina's Lepporello and Molière's Scapin.'

The actor ran one hand through his exuberant, curly hair, bared his teeth in a thick-lipped grin and bowed buffoonishly.

'At Your Excellency's service.'

'A funny face,' Shustrov observed approvingly. 'I have ordered an investigation to be undertaken. The public loves comics almost as much as femmes fatales.'

'We're here to serve. We'll play whoever you tell us to play. You desire a femme fatale? My pleasure!' Shiftsky saluted like a solder and immediately gave a very recognisable imitation of Altairsky: he bleared his eyes, intertwined his hands elegantly and even reproduced the half-smile.

All the actors laughed, even Lointaine herself. Only two individuals were not amused: Shustrov, who nodded with a serious air, and Fandorin, who found this clowning disagreeable.

'And here is our "coquette", little Serafima Aphrodisina. I saw her as Susanna in *The Marriage of Figaro* and immediately invited her to join the company.'

The pretty, plump little blonde bobbed down in a rapid curtsy.

'Is it true what they say, that you're a bachelor?' she asked, and her eyes started twinkling mischievously.

'Yes, but I intend to marry soon,' Shustrov replied equably, without reacting to the flirtatious provocation. 'It's time. My age.'

A gangly woman with a bony face twisted her immense mouth into a wry grin and spoke in a loud stage whisper.

'Sound the retreat, Sima. The fish is too big for the bait.'

'Xanthippe Petrovna Vulpinova – our "villainess",' said the director, extending his open hand in her direction. 'A foxy schemer, so to speak. She used to act comic characters, not very successfully. But I revealed her true calling. I've had an excellent Lady Macbeth from her and she is very fine in *The Three Sisters*; her Natalya had the audience really seething with hatred.'

'The genre of the children's story is very promising too,' Shustrov remarked to that, following some internal logic of his own. However, he did explain. 'You could make a good Snow Queen. A frightening one, the little toddlers will cry.'

'*Merci beaucoup*,' the villainess replied, and starchily ran one hand through her hair, which seemed to have been deliberately combed back so tightly in order to display her disproportionately large ears. 'Oh, do you hear that?'

She pointed to the window

A chorus of female voices was chanting loudly outside.

'Em-er-ald-ov! Em-er-ald-ov!' Erast Petrovich made out.

It must be his admirers, hoping that their idol will glance out of the window.

'What's that they're shouting?' Vulpinova asked, pretending to be listening closely. '"Me-phi-stov", so help me, "Me-phi-stov"!' And she turned to the man beside her in joyful excitement. 'Anton Ivanovich, the Moscow public has recognised your talent! Ah, you played the part of a swindler fantastically well!'

Fandorin was surprised – it was quite impossible to mishear the name.

The person whom the foxy schemer had addressed, a man with dark hair, a large nose and kinked, bushy eyebrows, grinned sardonically.

'If popularity was determined by talent and not appearance,' he said, darting a baleful glance at Emeraldov, 'they would be lying in wait to ambush me at the entrance. But no matter how brilliantly you play Iago or Claudius, they'll never shower you with flowers for it. Pleasures like that are for talentless trash with pretty-pretty faces.'

Listening to the shouts with a smile on his face, the leading man drawled lazily:

'Anton Ivanich, I know you start working your way into the role of a fiendish villain first thing in the morning, but there is no show today, so come back to the world of decent people. Or is that impossible already?'

'I implore you, please don't argue!' Vulpinova exclaimed in exaggerated consternation. 'It's my fault! I misheard, and then Anton took offence . . .'

'You misheard? With your ears?' Emeraldov quipped derisively.

The villainess blushed. *So she does suffer because she is so plain*, Erast Petrovich noted.

'Comrades! Friends!' said a round-faced man in a short, tight jacket, getting up off his chair. 'Come on, really, stop it! We're constantly quarrelling, lashing at each other with barbed remarks, but what for? After all, the theatre is such a fine, great-hearted, beautiful thing. If we don't love each other, if we all keep trying to hog the blanket, we'll rip it to pieces!'

'There we have the judgement of a man who should never direct actors,' Stern responded, putting his hand on the round-faced man's shoulder. 'Sit down, Vasya. And all of you settle down. You see what a madhouse I work in, Andrei Gordeevich? Right, who do we have left? Well this, as you have already guessed, is our villain, Anton Ivanovich Mephistov,' he said, with a rather casual gesture in the direction of the dark-haired man. He jabbed his finger at the man with the round face. 'This is Vasenka, our simpleton, that's why his pseudonym is Gullibin. His particular range includes the roles of devoted brothers-in-arms and likeable birdbrains. In *The Three Sisters* he was Tuzenbach, in *Hamlet* he was Horatio . . . So that's the entire company.'

'What about Zoya?' Altairsky's voice asked reproachfully. It was only a few minutes since Erast Petrovich had heard that voice, but he was already missing it.

'Everyone always forgets about me. Like some insignificant detail.'

The freckle-faced young lady who had kissed the hero Nonarikin and squeezed his injured hand in the intensity of her feelings pronounced these words in a theatrically cheerful voice. She was very short – her legs were dangling in the air because they didn't reach the floor.

'Sorry, Zoya. *Mea culpa!*' said Stern, striking himself on the chest with his fist. 'This is our wonderful Zoya Comedina. Her character is the fool, that is, a female jester. A magnificent talent for the grotesque, parody and general tomfoolery,' he said, really laying himself out, evidently in an effort to make up for his oversight. 'And she's a quite incomparable principal boy as well – she can play boys or girls. And believe it or not, I abducted her from a midgets' circus, where she was playing a monkey most comically.'

Shustrov glanced listlessly at the little woman and started looking at Fandorin.

'The midgets thought I was overgrown, but here they think I'm stunted.' Comedina took hold of the millionaire's sleeve, to make him turn back towards her. 'That's my fate – there's always either too much of me or too little.' She twisted her face into a pitiful grimace. 'But I can do something that no one else can. I'm exceptionally gifted where tears are concerned. I can cry, not only with both eyes, but with just one, whichever I choose. Of course, for my character tears are nothing more than a way of making people laugh.' She suddenly started coughing with surprising hoarseness. 'Pardon me, I smoke too much . . . It helps with playing juveniles.'

'So that's the entire company,' Noah Noaevich repeated, gesturing round at his assembled troops. 'The "dwellers in the ark", so to speak. You can ignore Mr Fandorin. He's a contender for the position of repertoire manager, but hasn't been enlisted into the company as yet. For the present we're still taking stock of each other.'

But for his part, Erast Petrovich had already taken stock. His initial hypotheses had already taken shape and he thought that the circle of suspects had been defined.

He had already clarified everything about the deadly basket of flowers. It had been ordered from the 'Flora' shop, paid for by fifty roubles attached to a note. The note had not survived, but in any case it had not contained anything unusual, merely the instruction to attach to the basket a card that read 'To the divine E. A.-L.'. The basket had been delivered to the theatre by an errand-boy, and there it had stood backstage, in the ushers' room. In principle, anybody could have gained access to the room, even someone from outside.

However, Erast Petrovich was almost certain that the previous day's vile trick had been perpetrated by one of the people presently in the room In any case, he considered it expeditious at this stage not to squander his efforts on any other theories.

The climate in the company was sultry, with an abundance of all sorts of antagonisms, but not everyone fitted the role of the 'snake catcher'.

It was hard, for instance, to imagine the regal Vasilisa Prokofievna engaging in that kind of activity. And despite his sardonic manner, the 'philosopher' would hardly be likely to soil his hands – he was altogether too dignified for that. Fandorin could exclude Gullibin without any qualms. The flirtatious coquette Aphrodisina would never have picked up the reptile with her pink fingers. And Truffaldino-Shiftsky? Pouring glue into the director's galoshes – that kind of hooliganism might, perhaps, be his style, but the dastardly trick with a poisonous snake required an especially malicious nature. There was a feeling of rabid, pathological hatred here. Or of equally incandescent jealousy.

Now Madam Vulpinova, with her crooked mouth and bat's ears, could easily be pictured as a snake charmer. Or Mr Mephistov, with his animus towards 'pretty-pretty' faces . . .

Suddenly Fandorin realised that he had unwittingly been caught on the cunning Noah Noaevich's hook: he had confused real, live people with the character types that they acted. So it was no wonder that the prime suspects had turned out to be the 'villain' and the 'villainess'.

No, he must not allow himself to be guided by first impressions. In general, at this stage it was best to wait a while before drawing conclusions. Not everything was as it seemed in this world. It was all make-believe and pretence.

He had to take a closer look than this. Actors were not like ordinary people. That is, they certainly looked like them, but it was quite possible that they were, in fact, some special sub-species of *Homo sapiens*, with specific behaviours of its own.

The opportunity to continue observing was provided then and there, as Andrei Gordeevich Shustrov began making a speech.

THE DESECRATION OF THE TABLETS

Shustrov's speech matched his appearance very closely. Dry and precise, completely devoid of extravagance, as if the entrepreneur were reading out a memorandum or an official communiqué. This feeling was reinforced by his manner of enunciating his considerations in the form of numbered points. Erast Petrovich himself often had recourse to a similar method for the sake of greater clarity in his reasoning, but on the lips of this patron of the arts the enumeration sounded rather odd.

'Point one,' Andrei Gordeevich began, speaking to the ceiling, as if he could perceive a clear vision of the future up there. 'In the twentieth century public entertainment will cease to be the domain of entrepreneurs, impresarios and other isolated individuals, and will expand into an immense, highly profitable industry. Those industrialists who realise this sooner than others and deploy their efforts more intelligently will occupy the dominant positions.

'Point two. It was precisely with this purpose in mind that one year ago I and my associate M. Simon created the Theatrical and Cinematographic Company, in which I have assumed responsibility for the theatrical side of things, and he has taken on the field of cinematography. At the present stage M. Simon is looking for film-makers and agreeing terms with distribution agents, buying equipment, building a film factory and renting electric theatres. He has studied all of this in Paris at the Gaumont Studio. Meanwhile, I am helping to make your theatre famous throughout the whole of Russia.

'Point three. I decided to back Mr Stern because I see his immense potential, which is perfectly suited to my project. Noah Noaevich's theory of combining art with sensationalism seems to me to be absolutely correct.

'Point four. I shall tell you how my associate and I intend to combine our two spheres of activity at our next meeting. Some things will undoubtedly seem unusual, even alarming, to you. Therefore, I would like first of all to earn your trust. You should realise that my interests and yours coincide completely, and that brings us to the final point, number five.

'And so, point five. I state with all due seriousness that my support for Noah's Ark is no whim or passing caprice. It might possibly have appeared strange to some of you that I have provided the theatre with everything it needs, while making no claim to your proceeds – which I believe to be extremely substantial . . .'

'You are our benefactor!' Noah Noaevich declared. 'Nowhere in Europe do actors receive such salaries as in our, that is, *your*, theatre!'

The others started clamouring too. Shustrov waited patiently for the grateful babbling to subside before continuing his phrase from the precise point at which it had been interrupted.

'. . . extremely substantial and, I fancy, have not yet reached their maximum limit. I promise all of you, ladies and gentlemen, that, having cast in your lot with the Theatrical and Cinematographical Company, you will forget for ever about the financial difficulties with which actors usually have to contend . . .' – more lively hubbub, heartfelt exclamations and even applause – 'and artistes of the first rank will become very seriously wealthy.'

'Lead us into the battle, father and commander!' exclaimed leading man Emeraldov. 'And we will follow you through hell and high water!'

'And to prove the seriousness of my intentions – this, in effect, is point five – I wish to take a step that will secure the financial independence of Noah's Ark for ever. Today I deposited in the bank the sum of three hundred thousand roubles, the interest on which will be credited to you. It is impossible for me or my heirs to take this money back again. If you decide to part ways with me, the capital will still remain the collective property of the theatre. If I die, your independence will be guaranteed in any case. That is all I have to say. Thank you . . .'

They gave their generous benefactor a standing ovation, with whooping, tears and kisses, which Shustrov bore imperturbably, politely thanking each kisser in turn.

'Quiet, quiet!' Stern shouted, straining himself hoarse. 'I have a suggestion! Listen!'

The actors turned towards him.

In a voice breaking with emotion the director announced:

'I suggest that we make an entry in the Tablets! This is a historic day, ladies and gentlemen! Let us record it thus: Today Noah's Ark has acquired true independence.'

'And we shall celebrate every sixth of September as Independence Day!' Altairsky added.

'Hoorah! Bravo!' they all shouted.

But Shustrov asked the question that had occurred to Fandorin.

'What are the "Tablets"?'

'That is what we call our holy book, the prayer book of the theatrical art,' Stern explained. 'Genuine theatre is unthinkable without traditions and ritual. For instance, after a performance we always drink a glass of champagne each and I conduct a critique of each artiste. On the day we made our debut, we decided that we would record all important events, achievements, triumphs and discoveries in a special album entitled "The Tablets". Each of the artistes has the right to record in the Tablets his or her own epiphanies and exalted thoughts concerning our craft. Oh, it contains many items of very great value! Some day our Tablets will be published as a book that will be translated into many languages! Vasya, hand them to me.'

Gullibin went over to a marble plinth with a large, luxurious, velvet-bound tome lying on it. Erast Petrovich had presumed that it was a stage prop from some production, but in reality it was the prayer book of the art of theatre.

'There,' said Stern, starting to leaf through the pages covered in various styles of handwriting. 'For the most part, of course, I'm the one who does the writing. I expound my brief observations on the theory of theatre and record my impressions of the performance that has just been given. But the others write quite a lot of valuable material too. Listen, now. This is Hippolyte Emeraldov: "A perform-ance is like an act of passionate love, in which you are the man and the audience is the woman, who must be roused to ecstasy. If you have failed, she will remain unsatisfied and will run off to a more ardent lover. But if you have succeeded, she will follow you to the ends of the earth." There you have the words of a true hero and lover! That is why his admirers are howling outside the windows.'

The handsome Hippolyte bowed ostentatiously.

'There are witty observations here too,' said Stern, turning an-other page. 'Look, Kostya Shiftsky drew this. And the caption above it reads: "And Noah went in, and his sons, and his wife, and his sons' wives with him, into the ark, because of the waters of the flood. Of clean beasts, and of beasts that are not clean, and of fowls, and of every thing that creepeth upon the earth, there went in two and two unto Noah into the ark, the male and the female." And we are all represented with very fine likenesses. Here I am with my progeny, Eliza and Hippolyte, here are our *grande dame* and Sensiblin as noble beasts, here are the cattle – Kostya himself and Serafima Aphrodisina – here are our villain and villainess creeping upon the face of the earth, here are the fowls – Vasya as an eagle owl and Zoya as a humming-bird – and Nonarikin is shown as the anchor!'

Shustrov examined the caricature with a serious air.

'There is another promising genre in cinematography – the ani-mated drawing,' he said. 'It is little pictures, but they move. We shall have to take that on as well.'

'Hey, someone give me a pen and an inkwell!' Noah Noaevich ordered, and he started solemnly tracing out characters on an empty page. Everyone clustered together, looking over his shoulder. Fandorin walked across too.

Printed out in capital letters at the top of the page were the words: 6 (19) SEPTEMBER 1911, MONDAY.

'Independence Day, made possible by the phenomenal generosity of A. G. Shustrov: to be celebrated every year!' Stern wrote, and everyone shouted out 'Vivat!' three times.

They were about to throw themselves on their benefactor to kiss and hug him again, but he beat a nimble and hasty retreat to the door.

'I have to be at a meeting of the municipal council at five o'clock. An important matter – whether grammar school pupils should be allowed into the evening session at electric theatres. They are almost a third of the potential audience. I bid you farewell.'

After his departure the actors carried on exclaiming rapturously for some time, until Stern told them to take their seats. Everyone immediately fell silent.

Something important was about to take place: the announcement of the new play and – most importantly of all – the allocation of the roles. Faces assumed identical, tense expressions, in which suspicion and hope mingled together. The artistes all looked at their manager. Emeraldov and Altairsky-Lointaine watched him more calmly than the others – they had no need to fear disadvantageous roles. But they seemed to be agitated nonetheless.

Having returned to his observation post, Fandorin also made ready, remembering what Noah Noaevich had said about this being the very moment when players, who were in the habit of dissimulating their feelings, laid bare their genuine egos. The picture might possibly be clarified.

The news that the new production in store for the company was *The Cherry Orchard* failed to arouse any enthusiasm or lighten the atmosphere.

'Couldn't you find anything newer?' Emeraldov asked, and several of the others nodded. 'What's the good of a repertoire manager . . .' – the leading man indicated Fandorin – '. . . if we're choosing Chekhov again? We need something a bit livelier. With more spectacle to it.'

'Where can I find you a new play with good characters for every one of you?' Noah Noaevich asked angrily. 'The *Orchard* resolves itself neatly into twelve parts. The public already knows the plot, that's true. But we'll capture them with the revolutionary impulse of our interpretation. What do you think the play is about?'

Everyone started pondering.

'About the victory of crude materialism over the futility of love?' Altairsky suggested.

Erast Petrovich thought: *She is intelligent, that is wonderful.*

But Stern disagreed.

'No, Eliza. It's a play about the comicality and impotence of cultural refinement and also about the inevitability of death. It's a very frightening play with a hopeless ending, and at the same time very spiteful. But it's called a comedy because fate mocks human beings pitilessly and makes fun of them. As usual with Chekhov, everything is in hints and half-tones. But we shall make everything that has been left unspoken completely clear. It will be an anti-Chekhovian production of Chekhov!' The director grew more and more animated. 'In this drama of Chekhov's there is no conflict, because when he wrote it, the author was seriously ill. He had no strength left to fight against Evil, or against Death. You and I shall recreate the Evil, fully armed. It will be the main motor of the action. With Chekhov's multilevel characters, such an interpretation is perfectly permissible. We shall render the fuzzy psychology of Chekhov's characters clear and distinct, bringing them into focus, as it were, sharpening their edges, dividing them into the traditional character types. That will be the innovative principle of our production!'

'Brilliant!' Mephistov exclaimed. 'Bravo, teacher! And who is the main agent of Evil? Lopakhin, the cherry orchard's destroyer?'

'Well, aren't you setting your sights high!' Emeraldov chuckled. 'Lopakhin he wants!'

'The agent of Evil is the clerk Yepikhodov,' the director replied to his 'villain', and Mephistov's face fell. 'This pitiful little man is the embodiment of the banal, petty evil that every member of our audience encounters in real life far more often than Evil on a demonic scale. But that's not all. Yepikhodov is also a walking Token of Disaster – and with a revolver in his pocket. His nickname is "22 misfortunes". It's a terrifying thing when there are so many misfortunes. Yepikhodov is a harbinger of destruction and death, senseless and pitiless death. It's no accident that the characters keep repeating that ominous refrain: "Yepikhodov's coming! Yepikhodov's coming!" And there he is wandering about somewhere offstage, plucking at the strings of his "mandolin". I shall make it play a funeral march.'

'And which of the women is an agent of Evil?' Vulpinova asked.

'You would never guess. Varya, Ranevskaya's adopted daughter.'

'How is that possible? She's such a sweetheart!' Gullibin exclaimed in amazement.

'You haven't read the play properly, Vasya. Varya is a hypocrite. She is planning to go away on a pilgrimage or enter a convent, but she feeds God's wandering pilgrims on nothing but peas. She is usually played as modest, self-effacing and hard working. But what damned hard work has she ever done? A household manager who has reduced an estate with a luxurious cherry orchard to ruin and destruction. The only bright note in the play is the timid attempt by Petya and Anya to become more intimately involved, but Varya doesn't give this fresh, young shoot a chance to blossom, she is always on guard. Because in the kingdom of Evil and Death there is no place for real, live Love.'

'That's very profound. Very,' Vulpinova said pensively. A rapid sequence of grimaces ran across her face: false piety, saccharine sweetness, envy, spite.

'And who will be the embodiment of Good? Petya Trofimov?' asked Gullibin, apparently trying to prompt the director.

'I thought about that. Garrulous, starry-eyed Good facing up to all-conquering Evil? Too hopeless. Trofimov will be yours, of course, Vasya. Play him in the classic manner, a "lovable simpleton". And the mission of battling against Evil will be taken on by the victorious Lopakhin.' Noah Noaevich gestured in the direction of the company's leading man, who astounded Erast Petrovich by sticking out his tongue at the devastated Mephistov. 'In order to lead Russia out of the beggarly, wretched state that she is in, we have to cut down the cherry orchards that no longer produce a harvest. We have to work on the earth and populate it with energetic, modern people. I advise you, Hippolyte, to play our benefactor, Andrei Gordeevich Shustrov, photographically. But – and this is a very important nuance – Good, by virtue of its magnanimity, is blind. And therefore at the end Lopakhin hires Yepikhodov to work for him. When the audience hears this news, it must shudder in sinister foreboding. Sinister foreboding is the key to the production's interpretation in general. Everything will come to an end soon, and the ending will be wretched and ugly – that is the mood of the play, and also of our epoch.'

'Of course, I'm Ranevskaya?' the *grande dame* Reginina asked in a sweet voice.

'Who else? An ageing but still beautiful woman, who lives for love.'

'What about me?' asked Eliza, unable to restrain herself. 'Surely not Anya? She's still a girl.'

Stern leaned down over her and cooed:

'Come now, you mean you can't play a girl? Anya is Light and Joy. And so are you.'

'Have pity, the reviewers will laugh! They'll say Altairsky has started putting on youthful airs!'

'You will enchant them. I order you to have a dress made, covered in glitter, so that it scatters dots of sunlight everywhere. Every entrance you make will be a celebration!'

Eliza stopped arguing, but she sighed.

'Who do we have left?' asked the director, glancing into a little notebook. 'Mr Sensiblin will play Gaev. An old-style thinker, fine and decent values, but obsolete, everything's clear here.'

'What's clear? Why is it clear?' asked the 'philosopher', flying off the handle. 'Give me a sketch! The development of the character.'

'What development? A global conflagration is about to flare up, and our Gaev will be consumed by it, along with his most venerable cupboard. You're always complicating things, Lev Spiridonovich . . . Right, let's move on.' Stern jabbed his finger at little Comedina. 'We'll age Zoya a bit – and you'll play the conjuror, Charlotta. Shiftsky gets the servant Yasha. Aphrodisina is the maid Dunyasha. I'll take Feers. And you, Nonarikin, will play Simeonov-Pishchik and all sorts of bits and pieces like Passer-By or Station Master . . .'

'Simeonov-Pishchik?' Stern's assistant echoed in a tragic whisper. 'Pardon me, Noah Noaevich, but you promised me a big part! You liked the way I played Solyony in *The Three Sisters*! I was counting on Lopakhin!'

'Most venerable cupboard yourself,' Sensiblin muttered rather loudly, also obviously dissatisfied with his role.

'Ho-ho, Lopakhin!' said Emeraldov, twirling his finger beside his temple as he mocked the director's assistant.

The half-pint 'principal boy' intervened on Nonarikin's behalf.

'And why not! It would be really interesting! What sort of Lopakhin will you make, Hippolyte Arkadievich? You don't look like a peasant's son.'

The handsome devil simply brushed her aside, like a gnat.

'When you gave me Solyony to play, I thought you'd started believing in me,' Nonarikin carried on in a whisper, clutching at the director's sleeve. 'How can I play Pishchik after Solyony?'

'Let go of me, will you!' Stern exclaimed angrily. 'You didn't play Solyony, you simply "represented" him. Because I let you play yourself. A poor man's Lermontov!'

'Don't you dare say that!' The assistant's pale face came out in crimson blotches. 'You know, that's just the last straw. After all, I'm not asking for much, I'm not fishing for the director's job.'

'Ha-ha,' said Noah Noaevich, emphasising the syllables separately. 'That's all we need. So you have ambitions to direct, do you? Some day you'll astound everyone. You'll put on a show that will make everyone gasp.'

He said this in a frankly mocking tone, as if he were trying to provoke his assistant into a fracas.

Fandorin screwed up his face in anticipation of screams or hysterics or some other kind of outrageous behaviour. But Stern demonstrated that he was a superlative psychologist. In response to the direct affront, Nonarikin collapsed, shrivelling up and letting his head droop.

'What am I?' he asked quietly. 'I'm nothing. Let it be as you wish, teacher . . .'

'Right, that's the way now. Colleagues, collect your copies of the text. My remarks, as usual, are in red pencil.'

Dissatisfied silences. Everyone took a copy out of the pile lying on the table, and Erast Petrovich noticed that the folders were different colours. Obviously, each colour signified a particular persona – yet another tradition, perhaps? The leading man unhesitatingly took the red folder. The prima donna took the pink one and handed a light blue one to Reginina, saying: 'Here's yours, Vasilisa Prokofievna.' The 'philosopher' gloomily tugged out the dark-blue folder, Mephistov took the black one, and so on.

Just then an attendant looked in and said that 'Mr Director' was wanted on the phone. Stern had obviously been expecting this call.

'Half an hour's break,' he said. 'Then we get down to work. In the meantime, I ask each of you to glance through your role and refresh your memory of it.'

No sooner had the manager gone out than the taboo on the subject that everyone was excited about ceased to operate. Everyone started talking about what had happened the day before, and nothing could have suited Fandorin better. He sat there, trying not to attract any attention to himself, watching and listening, hoping that the guilty party would give himself or herself away somehow.

To begin with, emotions predominated: sympathy for 'dear Eliza', admiration for Nonarikin's courageous feat. At the men's request, he unwound the bandages on his hand and showed them the bite.

'It's nothing,' the director's assistant said courageously. 'It doesn't even hurt any more.'

But the peaceful phase of the general discussion did not last for long.

The fuse was lit by the female intriguer.

'How deftly you managed to pull your own hand away, Eliza,' Vulpinova remarked with an unpleasant smile. 'I would have just frozen in fright and been bitten. But it was as if you knew there was a snake hidden in the flowers.'

Altairsky swayed back on her feet, as if she had been slapped across the cheek.

'What are you insinuating?' Gullibin protested. 'Surely you're not trying to say that Eliza set the whole thing up herself?'

'The idea never entered my head!' said the schemer, throwing her hands up in the air. 'But now that you bring the subject up ... A yearning for sensational fame drives some people to take even more desperate steps than that.'

'Don't listen to her, Eliza!' said Gullibin, taking the stunned Altairsky by the hand. 'And you, Xanthippe Petrovna, you're doing this deliberately. Because you know that everybody suspects you.'

Vulpinova gave a loud laugh.

'Why of course, who else? But I happen to have noticed a certain curious little detail. As a true knight, during the bows you usually

70

snatch the most beautiful basket and personally hand it to the lady of your heart. But this time you didn't. Why?'

Gullibin couldn't think of any answer to that and merely shook his head indignantly.

Mr Mephistov smacked his lips and declared sombrely:

'I wouldn't be surprised at anything. That is, at anyone.' And he ran his glance over each of them in turn.

Everyone reacted differently when the villain directed his suspicious gaze at them. Some protested, some cursed and swore. Comedina stuck out her tongue. Reginina laughed derisively and went out into the corridor. Sensiblin yawned.

'Oh, to hell with all of you. I think I'll just go out for a smoke and study my part . . .'

However, a genuine fracas failed to materialise. A couple of minutes later everyone had drifted away, leaving the two 'villains' rather disappointed.

'Anton, dear, you could pull a trick like that just to throw the cat among the pigeons,' Vulpinova said to her stage partner, apparently out of sheer inertia. 'Confess, did you do it?'

'Drop that now,' Mephistov responded listlessly. 'Why should we bait each other? I'll go and sit in the theatre and try on Yepikhodov for size. What sort of role is that . . .'

The scheming woman appeared to be still unsatisfied. Since there was no one left in the green room apart from Fandorin, she tried her claws on the newcomer.

'Mysterious stranger,' she began insinuatingly. 'You appeared so suddenly. Just like that basket yesterday, and no one knows who sent it.'

'I beg your pardon, I have no time,' Erast Petrovich replied coolly, and got up.

First he looked into the auditorium. Several of the actors were sitting in there, looking into their various-coloured folders, each of them alone and widely separated from the others. Eliza was not among them. He went into the corridor, where he walked past Shiftsky, who had ensconced himself on the windowsill, past Sensiblin, who was puffing on his pipe, and past gloomy Nonarikin, who was staring at his one and only page of text.

He found Altairsky-Lointaine on the stairs. She was standing at the window with her back to Erast Petrovich and hugging her own shoulders. The text in the pink cover was lying on the banisters.

Enough of this playing the fool, Fandorin told himself. *I like this woman. At any rate, I find her interesting, she intrigues me. So I have to start talking to her.*

He looked at himself in the mirror that happened to be conveniently located close by and felt happy with his appearance. There had never been an occasion when the ladies remained indifferent to the way he looked – especially if he wished to please.

Erast Petrovich walked up to her and cleared his throat delicately. When she looked round, he said gently:

'You shouldn't have got upset. You only gave that wicked-tongued lady more satisfaction.'

'But how could she dare?' Eliza exclaimed piteously. 'To suggest that I . . .'

She shuddered in revulsion.

Keenly aware of how close she was standing – a mere arm's length away – Fandorin continued with a subtle smile.

'Women of the mentality of Madam Vulpinova simply cannot exist without an atmosphere of scandal. You must not allow her to draw you into her games. This psychological personality type is called a "scorpion". Essentially they are unhappy, very lonely people . . .'

The beginning of the conversation had gone well. Firstly, he had managed not to stammer even once. Secondly, Elizaveta was bound to ask about psychological types, and then Fandorin would have a chance to encourage her interest in him.

'Ah, I do believe that is right!' Altairsky-Lointaine said in surprise. 'Xanthippe does seem to be broken inside somehow. She plays mean tricks, but there is something pitiful and supplicating in her eyes. You are an observant individual, Mr . . .' She hesitated.

'Fandorin,' he reminded her,

'Yes, yes, Mr Fandorin. Stern said that you are a connoisseur of modern literature, but you are not simply a repertoire manager, are you? One can sense a certain . . . *specialness* about you.' It took her a moment to find the word, but it caught Erast Petrovich's fancy. And what he liked even more was the enchanting smile that appeared on her face. 'You have such a good understanding of people. You must write theatre reviews, do you not? Who are you?'

After thinking for a moment, he replied:

'I . . . am a traveller. But unfortunately, I don't write reviews.'

The smile faded away, together with the interest that he had read in her magically elusive gaze.

'They say it is fascinating to travel. But I have never understood the pleasure in constantly moving from one place to another.'

The eloquent glance that she cast at the pink folder could mean only one thing: leave me in peace, this conversation is over.

But Erast Petrovich did not want to leave. He had to tell her something to make her realise that their meeting was not accidental, that this was some incomprehensible but incontrovertible scheme of destiny.

'Eliza . . . Pardon me, I don't know your patronymic.'

'I don't acknowledge patronymics.' She picked up the text. 'They exude an odour of stagnation and barbarity. As if you were your procreator's property. But I belong only to myself. You may call me simply Eliza. Or, if you wish, Elizaveta.'

Her tone of voice was indifferent, even rather cold, but Fandorin became even more agitated.

'Precisely, you are Elizaveta, Liza. And I am Erast! D-do you understand?' he exclaimed with an impulsiveness that he had never suspected in himself, and also, stammering quite excessively. 'I saw the finger of fate in that . . . that g-gesture of yours with your arm outstretched . . . And in S-September too . . .'

He hesitated, seeing that she didn't understand a thing. No reciprocal stirring of the soul, no reaction at all apart from slight puzzlement. But there was nothing surprising in that. What meaning did Erast have for her, or September, or a white arm?

He clenched his teeth. The last thing he needed was for Liza, that is, Eliza, to take him for a madman or an overexcited admirer. She was already surrounded by more than enough of both of those, without Fandorin.

'I meant to say that I was astounded by your performance yesterday,' he said in a more composed manner, trying all the time to catch her elusive glance and hold it. 'I have never experienced anything like it before. And of course, the coincidence of the names shook me. I am called Erast, you see. Petrovich . . .'

'Ah, yes indeed. Erast and Liza.' She smiled again, but distractedly, without even a trace of warmth. 'What's all that howling? They're squabbling again . . .'

He looked round in annoyance. Someone really was shouting upstairs. Fandorin recognised the director's voice: 'Blasphemy! Sacrilege! Who did this?' – the voice was coming from the direction of the green room.

'I have to go. Noah Noaevich has come back and he seems to be angry about something.'

Erast Petrovich followed Eliza with his head bowed, cursing himself for flunking the first conversation. Never once since the days of his early youth had he behaved so idiotically with a woman.

'I want to know who did this!'

Noah Noaevich, looking enraged, was standing at the door of the sitting room (sometimes the green room was referred to in that way) holding the 'Tablets' open in his hands.

'Who dared to do this?'

Fandorin glanced into the open book. Immediately below the solemn entry about Independence Day, someone had scribbled in large, crooked letters, using a purple indelible pencil: 'EIGHT 1S UNTIL THE BENEFIT PERFORMANCE. TAKE THOUGHT!'

Everyone came up to look and was left puzzled.

'The theatre is a temple! The actor's ministry is an exalted mission! We cannot survive without reverence and our sacred objects!' Stern exclaimed, almost in tears. 'Whoever did this wished to insult me, all of us and our art! What sort of scribble is this? What does it mean? How many times do I have to repeat that in my theatre there are no benefit performances and there never will be? That's the first point. And the second point is that desecrating our sacred object is the same as defiling a church! Only a vandal could do such a thing!'

Some of them listened to him with sympathy, some shared his indignation, but snickering could also be heard.

'Go away, all of you,' the director said in a weak voice. 'I don't want to see anyone ... It's impossible to work today. Tomorrow, tomorrow ...'

Fandorin took advantage of the fact that everyone was looking at the suffering martyr to keep his own eyes fixed on Eliza. She seemed to him unattainably distant, truly the star Altair, and that thought was painful.

He realised that something would have to be done about this pain, it would not pass off on its own.

THERE ARE NO PROBLEMS THAT
CANNOT BE SOLVED

For the second night in a row Erast Petrovich was unable to get to sleep. And, moreover, his thoughts were by no means occupied with deductive reasoning concerning the snake in the flower basket. The internal condition of the harmonious man had skipped through several consecutive stages at once.

At the first stage a simple truth had been revealed to Fandorin, one that a less intelligent and complex individual would have grasped much sooner. (However, we must make allowances for the fact that Erast Petrovich had considered this page of his life to have been read and closed for ever a long time ago.)

I'm in love, he suddenly told himself, this fifty-five-year-old man who had seen and experienced so many things of every possible kind in the course of his life. He was incredibly surprised and even burst into laughter in the silence of the empty room. *There can be no doubt, unfortunately – so I'm in love, then? In love, like a boy, filled with youthful passion? Ah, what nonsense! How shamefully absurd, how positively vulgar! To burn one's heart out by the age of twenty-two, then live for a third of a century with the feebly glowing ashes, dauntlessly enduring the crushing blows of fate and maintaining one's cold reasoning even in situations of deadly danger; to attain spiritual peace and clarity at an age that is not yet old – and then lapse back into puerility, to find oneself in the laughable position of someone in love!*

And worst of all, with whom? An actress, that is, a creature who is bound to be unnatural, spoilt, false, accustomed to turning heads and breaking hearts!

But that was only half the problem. The second half was even more humiliating. This feeling of amorous infatuation was not mutual, it was unrequited, there was not even the slightest sign of interest from the other party.

In past years so many women – beautiful and intelligent, brilliant and profound, infernal and angelic – had bestowed their adoration and passion on him, but the most he had ever done was allow them to love him, almost never losing his own cool composure. But this one had declared: 'I belong only to myself!' And she had looked at him as if he were a bothersome fly!

In this way Erast Petrovich moved on, without even noticing it, to the next stage – of resentment.

Why, belong to whomever you wish, madam, what business is that of mine? I have fallen in love? How could I ever get such nonsense into my head! He laughed once again (this time not in surprise, but anger). He ordered himself to put this prima donna with the jarring pseudonym out of his mind immediately. Let them work out for themselves in that little theatre of theirs who was playing these vile tricks with vipers on whom. Merely being in that madhouse of theirs was dangerous for the psyche of a rational individual.

Erast Petrovich's will was steely. He had decided, and that was the end of it. He did his evening gymnastics and even ate dinner. Before going to sleep he read some Marcus Aurelius and turned out the light. And in the darkness the apparition descended on him with renewed force. Suddenly her face appeared, with those eyes that looked straight through him, and he heard that gentle, deep voice. And he had neither the strength nor – even worse – the desire to drive away this Distant Princess.

Fandorin tossed and turned until dawn, attempting every now and then to rid himself of the enticing vision. But he was obliged to admit that the dose of venom was too strong and his organism had been poisoned irrevocably.

He got dressed, took his jade beads and set about the problem properly, in real earnest. And so began the third stage – the stage of comprehension.

I am in love, to deny it is absurd. That is one. (He clicked a little green sphere.)

Evidently, without this woman my life will be miserable. That is two. (Another click.)

Which means that I have to do whatever will make her mine – it is that simple. That is three.

Such was the entire chain of logic.

He felt better immediately. For a man of action such as Fandorin, a clearly defined goal stimulates a burst of positive energy.

First of all he had to amend the current constitution, which made absolutely no provision for such a sudden somersault on the harmonious path to old age.

A man walks through that field, the crossing of which is the living of one's life, calmly contemplating the smooth line of the horizon, which appears to be gradually brightening and moving closer. The path he treads is pleasant, his stride is steady. The clouds eddy calmly in the sky above his head – no sun and no rain. And suddenly there is a peal of thunder, a flash of lightning, and a furious lance of electricity transpierces his entire being, darkness swoops down onto the ground, he can see neither the path nor the horizon, he cannot tell which way to walk and – even worse than that – whether he should walk in any direction at all. Man proposes and God disposes.

The electrical vibration swept through Fandorin's body and soul. He felt like a tortoise that has suddenly lost its shell. It was terrifying and shameful, but the sensation was beyond expression in words, as if . . . *as if his entire skin was breathing.* And also as if he had been dozing and had suddenly woken up. To put it in more melodramatic terms: he had risen from the dead. *I seem to have read my own funeral rites too soon,* thought Erast Petrovich, telling his beads faster and faster. *For as long as life goes on, it can throw up any kind of surprise – either happy or catastrophic. And moreover, the most significant among these surprises are combinations of both the former and the latter.*

Fandorin sat in an armchair, watching the window frame slowly filling up with light and focusing his bewildered mind on the changes that were taking place within him.

That was how Masa found him when he glanced cautiously in at the door after seven o'clock in the morning.

'What has happened, master? Since yesterday you haven't been yourself at all. I haven't pestered you about it, but this worries me. I've never seen you like this.'

After a moment's thought, the Japanese corrected himself.

'I haven't seen you like this for a long time. Your face has become so young. Like thirty-three years ago. I think you must have fallen in love!'

Fandorin gaped at his clairvoyant servant in absolute amazement and Masa slapped himself on his gleaming pate.

'Just as I thought! Oh, this is very alarming! Something must be done about it.'

This is my only friend, who knows me better than I know myself, thought Erast Petrovich. *It is pointless trying to conceal anything from him, and in addition, Masa has an excellent understanding of female psychology. Here is a person who can help!*

'Tell me, how does one win the love of an actress?' Fandorin asked, not beating about the bush, but going straight to the point, and speaking in Russian.

'Genuine rove or make-berieve?' his servant enquired in a businesslike tone.

'How's that? What does "make-believe love" mean?'

Masa preferred to speak of these delicate matters in his native language, which he regarded as more refined.

'An actress is the same as a geisha or a courtesan of the highest rank,' he began explaining with an expert air. 'For a woman like that, love can be of two kinds. It is easier to win her acted love – she knows how to act it out superbly. A normal man does not need anything more than that. In the name of such a love a beautiful woman may make certain sacrifices. For instance, crop her hair in proof of her passion. Sometimes even cut off a piece of her little finger. But no more than that. But sometimes, although quite rarely, the heart of such a woman is transfixed by genuine feeling – the kind for which she might consent to a double suicide.'

'Oh, go to hell with your exotic Japanese ideas!' Erast Petrovich exclaimed furiously. 'I'm not asking you about a geisha, but an actress, a normal European actress.'

Masa pondered.

'I have had actresses. Three. No, four – I forgot the mulatto from

New Orleans, who danced on the table . . . I believe you are right, master. They are different from geishas. Winning their love is much easier. Only it is difficult to tell if it is acted or genuine.'

'Never mind that, I'll puzzle it out somehow,' Fandorin said impatiently. 'Easier, you say? Much easier in fact?'

'It would be really easy if you were a director or an author of plays or if you wrote articles about the theatre in the newspapers. Actresses acknowledge only these three types of men as superior beings.'

Remembering the smile that had lit up Eliza's face when she took him for a theatre critic, Fandorin fixed his consultant with an intent gaze.

'Well? Go on, go on!'

Masa continued judiciously.

'You cannot be a director, for that you need to have your own theatre. Writing reviews is not difficult, of course, but much time will pass by before you make a name for yourself. Write a good play, in which the actress will have a beautiful part. That is the simplest way of all. I have engaged in literary composition. It is not a difficult business, and even enjoyable. That is my advice to you, master.'

'Are you making fun of me? I don't know how to write plays!'

'In order to prove one's love to a woman, it is necessary to perform feats of heroism. For such a man as you, overcoming a hundred obstacles or defeating a hundred wrongdoers is no great feat. But to compose a wonderful play for the sake of your beloved – that would be a genuine proof of love.'

Erast Petrovich sent his specialist adviser to the devil and was left alone again.

But the idea that had seemed idiotic at first kept running round Fandorin's head and eventually beguiled him.

The gift given to the woman one loves should be the thing that brings her the greatest joy. Eliza is an actress. The theatre is her life. Her greatest joy is a good role. Ah, if only it really were possible to present Eliza with a play in which she would wish to act! Then she would stop looking at me with polite indifference. Masa has given me a very intelligent piece of advice. It is only a shame that it is quite impracticable . . .

Impracticable?

Erast Petrovich reminded himself of the many times in his life when he had encountered challenges that appeared insuperable at first. However, a solution had always been found. Will, intellect and knowledge were capable of overcoming any obstacle.

He had ample will and intellect. But knowledge was more of a problem. Fandorin's familiarity with the business of playwriting was minimal. The task facing him was comparable to the heroic feats of Hercules. But he could at least try – for the sake of a goal such as this.

One thing was clear. It was unbearable not to see Eliza, but he must not appear before her as merely one more member of the grey crowd. He had already received one fillip to the nose, that was enough. If there was to be another encounter, he must present himself for it fully prepared.

And so the harmonious man moved on to the concluding stage – unswerving determination.

Erast Petrovich set about realising his purpose with comprehensive thoroughness. First he surrounded himself with books: collections of plays, monographs on dramatic art, treatises on stylistics and poetics. Fandorin's skills of rapid reading and concentration, coupled with his feverish excitement, allowed the future dramatist to plough through several thousand pages in four days.

Fandorin spent the fifth day doing absolutely nothing, devoting himself entirely to meditating and creating an inner Void, which would give rise to the animating Impulse that people of the West call Inspiration and people of the East call Samadhi.

Erast Petrovich already knew exactly what kind of play he was going to write – the correct line to take had been prompted by the conversation with Stern about an 'ideal play'. All that remained was to wait for the moment when the words would start flowing of their accord.

As evening was coming on, the inspiration-seeking Fandorin started swaying in a distinct rhythm and his half-closed eyelids opened wide.

He dipped a steel pen into an inkwell and traced out the long title. His hand moved slowly at first, then faster and faster, barely able to keep pace with the torrent of words that came bursting out. Time enveloped the study in a glimmering, undulating cloud. In the dead of night, with the regal full moon shining majestically in the sky, Erast Petrovich suddenly froze, sensing that the flow of magical energy had run dry. He dropped the pen, leaving a blot on the paper, leaned back in his armchair and finally fell asleep for the first time in days. The lamp carried on burning.

Masa entered the room soundlessly and put a warm rug over his master. He started reading what had been written and sceptically shook his large head, as round as the moon.

Seven 1s

UNTIL THE BENEFIT
PERFORMANCE

THE VENGEANCE OF GHENGIS KHAN

She might as well not even go to bed. It was the same thing all over again: a face spattered with cabbage and a red beard surrounding lips that sang without making any sound.

In fact the dream always began very pleasantly, with her apparently driving along a country high road, not in an automobile, but in a carriage: the rhythmic clopping of hooves and jangling of harnesses, the gentle swaying of the springs sending sweet, visceral tremors surging upwards from below. No one there beside her, a mood so buoyant, she felt she could soar up into the air, her soul filled with a premonition of happiness, and she doesn't want anything else at all. Just to keep on swaying like this on the springy seat and waiting for the joy that is already so close . . .

Suddenly there is a tap at the left-hand window. She looks – and sees a livid face with its eyes closed and scraps of cabbage dangling from its luxurious black moustache streaked with white. A hand with a signet ring on one finger adjusts the necktie and it starts wriggling. It isn't a necktie, but a snake!

And then another tap – from the right. She jerks round, and there is the singer with the bright red beard. He looks at her soulfully, opens his mouth wide and even extends his arm in a fluent gesture, but she doesn't hear anything.

Only the tapping on the glass: tap-tap-tap, tap-tap-tap!

At one time the dreams almost stopped. She wasn't even very frightened when she saw that familiar bald spot and that glance blazing with hatred below the fused black eyebrows in the third row of the opera stalls at *Poor Liza*. She had known that he would turn up sooner or later, she was inwardly prepared for it and very pleased with her own self-possession.

But after the performance, when a snake's head with exactly the same frenzied little eyes had suddenly thrust up out of the rosebuds, the nightmare had overwhelmed her again with even greater, more crushing force. If not for dear Nonarikin, so touchingly smitten with her . . . Brrrr, it was best not even to think about it.

For two days afterwards she had not allowed herself to sleep, knowing what it would lead to. On the third day tiredness got the better of her and, of course, the awakening was horrific. With screaming, convulsive sobbing and hiccupping. Since then it had been the same thing every night: the same old dream from St Petersburg, but now the snake had taken up residence in it.

In the dormitory of the ballet school, before she went to sleep little Liza often used to act out for her friends the stories of heroines who were dying. Either from slow-acting poison, like Cleopatra, or from consumption, like the lady with the camellias. Juliet killing herself with a dagger was suitable too, because before she finally stabs herself, she declaims a touching monologue. Liza enjoyed lying there with her eyes closed and listening to the girls sobbing. Later they all went in for dance and some even became well known, but a ballerina's career is short, and Liza wanted to work in the theatre until her old age, like Sarah Bernhardt, and so she chose drama. She dreamed of collapsing lifelessly on the stage, like Edmund Kean, so that a thousand people would see it and sob, even though they thought it was all part of the role, and of drawing her final breath to the sound of applause and shouts of 'Bravo!'

Liza rushed into marriage early. She was playing Princess Reverie (La Princesse Lointaine) to Sasha Lumpin's enamoured Prince Geoffroi. Her first success, the first time she had felt the intoxication of universal adoration. In the season of youth it is so easy to confuse a play with real life! Of course, they separated very soon. Actors should not live together. Sasha faded away somewhere in the provinces, and all that remained of him was his name. But a leading lady cannot be called Liza Lumpina, and so she became Eliza Lointaine.

If her first marriage was simply a failure, the second turned out to be a catastrophe. Once again, she had only herself to blame. She was seduced by the dramatic flair of a sudden shift in the direction of life, by the tinsel and glitter of a superficial effect. And ultimately, by a resounding title. How many actresses had married simply so that they would be called 'Your Excellency' or 'Your Ladyship'? But this had an even more grandiose ring: 'Your Most Exalted Dignity'. That was the title by which the wife of a khan was supposed to be addressed. Iskander Altairsky was a brilliant officer in the Escort Lifeguards, the oldest son of the ruler of one of the khanates of the Caucasus, which had been annexed to the empire during the time of General Alexei Yermolov. He threw his money about and wooed her handsomely, he was good looking, despite his premature baldness, and in addition impetuous and voluble in the Asiatic manner. He declared that he was willing to sacrifice everything for the sake of love – and he kept his word. When his superiors refused him permission to marry, he resigned and abandoned his military career. He ruined his relationship with his father and renounced his rights of inheritance in favour of his younger brother; an actress, especially a divorced one, could not be the wife of the heir to a khanate. But the outcast was allocated a very decent annual allowance. And most important of all, Iskander swore not to make any difficulties over the theatre and consented to a childless marriage. What more could she have wished for? Her stage rivals were positively bursting with envy. Lida Yavorskaya, whose title by marriage was Princess Baryatinskaya, even emigrated from Russia – princesses were ten a penny in St Petersburg, but there was only one khatun.

Her second marriage fell apart even more quickly than the first – immediately after the wedding and the wedding night. And the reason was not that in his exorbitant excitement her husband was incapable of proving himself in the appropriate manner (that was actually quite touching, in fact), but the conditions that he propounded to her the following morning. Altairsky's status as a khatun entailed certain obligations, Iskander told her strictly: 'I promised not to interfere with your passion for the theatre and I will keep my word. But you must avoid plays in which you will have to embrace men or, even worse, kiss them.' Eliza had laughed, thinking that he was joking. When it became clear that her husband was absolutely serious, she spent a long time trying to make him see sense. She explained that it was impossible to play a heroine's roles without embraces and kisses; and furthermore, it was now becoming fashionable to show the act of carnal triumph explicitly on the stage.

'What triumph?' the man of the Caucasus had asked, screwing up his face so expressively that Eliza realised immediately that any explanations would be quite useless.

'The triumph that you failed to achieve!' she had exclaimed, imitating the great Zhemchuzhnikova in the role of Cleopatra. 'And now you never will! Goodbye, Your Most Exalted Dignity, the honeymoon is over! There will not be any honeymoon trip. I am applying for a divorce!'

It was appalling to recall what happened then. This scion of an ancient line, a direct descendant of Genghis Khan, sank to the level of base physical assault and foul barracks language, and then went dashing to the writing desk to take out a revolver and shoot his affronter on the spot. Of course, Eliza ran away while he was fiddling with the key, and after that she refused to meet the crazy Chingizid unless her lawyers were present.

In front of witnesses, Iskander behaved in a civilised manner. He explained politely that he would not agree to any divorce, because in his family this was regarded as a grave sin and his father would take away his allowance. He raised no objections to living separately and even declared his willingness to pay his wife alimony, provided that she observed 'the proprieties' (Eliza rejected the offer disdainfully – thank God, she earned quite enough in the theatre).

The khan displayed his savage nature when they met face to face. He must have had his wife followed, because he appeared in front of her in the most unexpected places, always without any warning. He just popped up like a jack-in-the-box.

'Ah, so that's it!' he would say with a malign glint in those bulging eyes that she had once found handsome. 'So the theatre means more to you than my love? Excellent. On the stage you can behave like a harlot. That is your business. But since you are still formally my wife, I will not permit you to drag my ancient name through the mud! Bear in mind, madam, that you can only have lovers in the glow of the footlights and in full view of an audience. Anyone you let into your bed will die. And you will die after him!'

To be quite honest, she wasn't really very frightened at first. On the contrary, life became a little more exciting. When there was a love scene during a show, Eliza deliberately looked round the auditorium, and if she encountered the withering gaze of her abandoned husband, she played her part with redoubled passion.

Things continued like this until the entrepreneur Furshtatsky became seriously enraptured with her. A distinguished individual with good taste, and the owner of the finest theatre in Kiev, he made her an incredibly generous offer to join his theatre company, showered her with flowers, paid her compliments and tickled her ear with his fragrant moustache. He also made her a proposal of a different kind – of matrimony.

She was prepared to accept both of these proposals. The world of theatre was all abuzz with the news, and once again her rivals were absolutely green with envy.

Then all of a sudden, at a ceremonial banquet held in Furshtatsky's honour by the trustees of the Theatre Society, he died! Eliza herself was not at the banquet, but she was given a very graphic description of the way the entrepreneur turned crimson, started wheezing and slumped over with his face in a plate of thick country soup.

Eliza cried that evening, of course. She felt sorry for poor Furshtatsky and told herself: 'It wasn't meant to be' and so on. But then the telephone rang and a familiar voice with a breathy Caucasian intonation whispered in the receiver: 'I warned you. This death is on your conscience'. Even then she didn't start taking Iskander seriously; he seemed to her like an operetta villain with a bristling moustache and goggling eyes that aren't really frightening. To herself she thought of him mockingly as 'Genghis Khan'.

Oh, how cruelly fate had punished her for her flippancy!

About three months after the entrepreneur's death, which everyone had accepted, without the slightest doubt, as natural, Eliza allowed herself to develop a passion for another man, the heroic tenor at the Mariinsky Theatre. This time no career considerations were involved. The singer was quite simply handsome (oh, that eternal weakness of hers for the good-looking Adonis type!) and he had a breathtaking voice that sent a warm, heady languor flooding through her entire body. At that time Eliza was already working in Noah's Ark, but was still concluding her concert engagements. And then one day she and the tenor (he was called Astralov) were giving a little one-act play-cum-duet called 'Redbeard'. A delightful little piece of nonsense: she declaimed and danced a bit and Astralov sang – and he was so fine and handsome that afterwards they went to Strelna and what was bound to happen sooner or later happened there. And indeed, why not? She was a free, adult, modern woman. He was an attractive man – no great intellect, to be sure, but very talented and gallant. Eliza left in the morning because she had to get to a rehearsal at eleven, and her lover stayed in their hotel room. He was very particular about his appearance and always carried around a toiletry case with a manicure set, all sorts of little brushes, nail scissors and a mirror-bright razor for trimming his beard.

They found him with that razor in his hand. He was sitting in a chair, dead, with his shirt and his beard stained completely red with blood. The police came to the conclusion that after spending the night with a woman, the tenor had slit his own throat while sitting in front of the mirror. Eliza had been wearing a veil and the hotel staff had not seen her face, so it had all passed off without a scandal.

She wept at the funeral (there were quite a number of ladies with tear-stained faces there), tormented by miserable bewilderment: what could she have said or done? This was so unlike the bon vivant Astralov! Suddenly she saw Genghis Khan there in the crowd. He looked at her, grinned and ran one finger rapidly across his throat.

Eliza's eyes were finally opened.

Murder! It was murder! In fact, two murders; there was no doubt that Furshtatsky had been poisoned. For a few days she was completely bewildered and confused, as if she were delirious. What should she do? What should she do?

Go to the police? But, in the first place, there was no proof. They would think it was all the wild ravings of a hysterical young woman. In the second place, Astralov had a family. And in the third place . . . In the third place, she was absolutely terrified.

Genghis Khan had gone insane, his jealousy had become a

paranoidal obsession. Everywhere – in the street, in a shop, in the theatre – she sensed that she was being followed. And this was no persecution mania! In her muff, in her hatbox, even in her powder compact, Eliza discovered little scraps of paper. There was not a word on them, not a single letter, only drawings: a skull, a knife, a noose, a coffin . . . In her suspicious state of mind she dismissed several maids because she thought they had been bribed.

The nights were worst of all. In her distressed and lonely condition (lovers were out of the question!) Eliza had repulsive dreams in which eroticism mingled with appalling images of death.

She thought about him often now. The moment would come when Genghis Khan's insanity reached its climax and then the monster would kill her. It could happen very soon now.

But then why did she not turn to anyone for help?

There were several reasons.

Firstly, as we have already said, there was no proof and nobody would believe her.

Secondly, she was ashamed of her own horrendous stupidity – how could she have married such a monster? *It serves you right, you little idiot!*

Thirdly, she was tormented by remorse for two lives that had been lost. *If you're guilty, then you must pay.*

And in addition – the most terrible reason of all – Eliza had never before felt the fragile beauty of the world so keenly. The psychiatrist she consulted very cautiously about Genghis Khan, without naming any names, told her that the condition of paranoiacs worsened in autumn. *This is the final autumn of my life,* Eliza told herself, as she looked at the poplars starting to turn yellow, and her heart contracted in sweet despair. A moth flying towards a candle flame probably feels much the same thing. It knows it is going to die, but doesn't want to turn aside . . .

The one and only time she had blurted out her fear, in a moment of weakness, had been about ten days ago, to that soul of kindness, Olga Knipper. The dam had burst, so to speak. Eliza didn't explain anything specific, but she wept and babbled incoherently. Afterwards she was sorry she had done it. With her Germanic tenacity, Olga had pestered Eliza with questions. She had telephoned and sent notes, and after that business with the snake she had come rushing round to the hotel, hinted mysteriously about some man who would help Eliza in any situation, gasped and sighed and pried. But it was as if Eliza had turned to stone. She had decided that whatever must be could not be avoided, and there was no point in getting other people involved.

There was only one way to get rid of this good-hearted meddler, and it was a cruel one: to provoke a quarrel with her. And Eliza knew how to do that. She said a lot of offensive, absolutely unforgivable things about Olga's relationship with her deceased husband. Olga cringed and burst into tears and her tone of voice became cold and formal. 'God will punish you for that,' she said – and left.

He will punish me, Eliza thought languidly, *and soon*. On that day she felt so numbed, barely even alive, that she didn't repent in the least. She only felt relief at having been left in peace. Alone with her final autumn, insanity and nightmares.

'Tap-tap-tap! Tap-tap-tap!' The tapping on the glass came again and Eliza rubbed her eyes, driving away the appalling dream. There was no carriage, and no dead men pressing their faces avidly against the glass.

The darkness was lightening. The outlines of objects had already appeared, she could see the hands of the clock on the wall: a few minutes after five. Dawn would break soon and, like a little nocturnal animal, the fear would creep away into its burrow until the evening twilight came again. She knew that now she could go to sleep without being afraid, there were no nightmares in the morning.

But suddenly there it was again, a quiet 'tap-tap-tap'.

She raised herself up on her pillow and realised that her awakening had been false. The dream was continuing.

She was dreaming that she was lying in her hotel room just before dawn, looking out of the window, and there was a dead face with a red, dishevelled beard – huge and blurred. Lord God, have pity!

She pinched herself and rubbed her eyes, which were gluing themselves shut again. Her vision cleared. No, it wasn't a dream!

There was a huge bunch of peonies swaying outside the window. A hand in a white glove appeared out of it and knocked: 'tap-tap-tap'.

Then a face appeared beside it, not a dead one, but very much alive. The lips below the moustache with twirled ends stirred in a soundless whisper, the eyes goggled as they attempted to make out the interior of the room.

Eliza recognised one of her most tenacious admirers – the Life Hussar Volodya Limbach. The St Petersburg cohort of reckless theatre lovers included quite a number of young officers. Any even slightly well-known actress, singer or ballerina always had these noisy, exuberant youths among her retinue. They engineered ovations, threw heaps of flowers, could even hiss at a rival actress, and on the day of a premiere or a benefit performance they unharnessed the horses from the carriage and pulled the sovereign of their hearts through the streets themselves. Their adoration was flattering and useful, but some of the young men did not know where to stop and allowed themselves to cross the line between adoration and harassment.

If Eliza's condition had been different, she might possibly have laughed at Limbach's prank. God only knew how he had managed to clamber onto the cornice of a high first-floor window. But this time she flew into a fury. Damn the young pup! What a fright he had given her!

She leapt up off the bed and ran to the window. Making out an unclad white figure in the half-light, the cornet pressed his face avidly against the glass. Without even bothering to think that the boy might fall and break his neck, Eliza turned the catch and pushed the flaps of the window, which swung wide open.

The bouquet went flying down through the air and Limbach himself was knocked off balance by the blow, but he wasn't sent tumbling into the abyss. In contradiction of the laws of gravity, the young officer hung suspended in mid-air, swaying to and fro and turning gently around his own axis.

The mystery was explained: the impudent young man had lowered himself from the roof on a rope that was wound round his waist.

'Divine one!' Limbach exclaimed in a choking voice, and started speaking in brief phrases. 'Let me in! I wish only! To kiss the hem! Of your nightgown! Reverently!'

Eliza's fury suddenly evaporated, its place taken by the terrible thought that if Genghis Khan found out about this, the foolish boy would be killed!

She cast a glance along Tverskaya Street, which was absolutely deserted at this time in the morning. But how could she be sure that the cursed maniac was not hiding somewhere in a gateway or behind a street lamp?

Without saying a word, Eliza shut the window and closed the curtains. Entering into negotiations, expostulating or scolding would only increase the risk.

But Limbach would not back down. Now she would have no peace from him even at night, in her own room. And the worst thing of all was that the window looked straight out onto the street . . .

During their Moscow tour the company of Noah's Ark was staying in the 'Louvre-Madrid' on the corner of Leontiev Lane. The 'Louvre' was the name of a luxurious hotel with a façade overlooking Tverskaya Street. The director, leading man and leading lady lived here, in deluxe apartments. The more modest part of the complex, the 'Madrid' lodging rooms, had windows that looked out onto Leontiev Lane. This was where the other actors were quartered. Visiting companies often stayed in this twin establishment, which seemed to be specially adapted for the theatrical hierarchy. The wits of the theatre scene had dubbed the long corridor connecting the magnificent hotel and the modest lodging rooms 'the impassable Pyrenees'.

If this happened again, she would have to exchange rooms with someone on the other side of the Pyrenees, Eliza thought, calming down slightly and even starting to smile. After all, it is hard to remain indifferent in the face of such insane amatory follies. He had come dashing down here from St Petersburg, the little devil. Probably without saying a word to his superiors. And now he would spend a long stretch in the guardhouse. But that wasn't the most terrible thing that could happen to him . . .

TERRIFYING

Following the uproar at the performance of *Poor Liza*, the theatre was written and talked about so much that Stern changed his original plans and decided not to halt the performances. The scale of the furore over Noah's Ark was quite unprecedented: speculators were selling on tickets, not for three times their price, but for almost ten times. Additional seats had been set out in the auditorium, at absolutely every point where it was possible. With every entrance she made, Eliza felt two thousand eyes peering avidly at her, as if they were waiting for something outlandish to happen to the prima donna. But she abandoned her former habit and tried not to look out into the hall. She was afraid to see that glance blazing with hatred from under those fused eyebrows . . .

They performed each of the old productions again once: *Poor Liza*, *The Three Sisters* and *Hamlet*. They were received very well, although Noah Noaevich was dissatisfied. During the analytical sessions after the performance, when everyone drank champagne, wrote entries in the 'Tablets' and made flattering or barbed comments to each other, the director complained that 'the emotional intensity' was falling.

'Irreproachable, but vapid,' he exclaimed. 'Like Stanislavsky! We are losing all of our lead. A theatre without uproar, provocation and scandal is only half a theatre. Give me scandal! Give me the pulsing of blood!'

The day before yesterday there had been a scandal in *Hamlet*, and the object of it had once again been Eliza. It was less impressive than on 5 September, but it was hard to say which was more repulsive – to see that snake or to suffer Emeraldov's despicable tomfoolery!

If there was one person Eliza simply could not bear, it was her primary stage partner. A pompous, unintelligent, petty, envious, vainglorious peacock! He simply could not accept the fact that she was indifferent to his chocolate-box charm and that the public appreciated her more. If not for the small group of hysterical young ladies who electrified the rest of the audience with their squealing, everyone would have noticed long ago that the king was naked! He couldn't act properly, only shoot fire out of his eyes. And the brute actually tried to kiss her properly, on the lips. He even tried to thrust his tongue in!

The day before yesterday he had gone way beyond the limit. In the scene where Hamlet tries to woo Ophelia, Emeraldov had played the Prince of Denmark like some licentious ruffian. He had hugged her tight, squeezed her breasts and then, to the horror and delight of the audience, pinched her on the buttock, like an officer's orderly pinching the maid!

Offstage Eliza had slapped him hard across the face, but Emeraldov had only smirked like the cat that got the cream. She was sure that at the critique the impudent scoundrel would get a real roasting, but Stern actually praised this 'innovative discovery' and promised that the next day all the newspapers would write about it. They did write about it, and moreover that yellow-press rag *Kopeck Life* went as far as to hint transparently at a 'special relationship' between Mme Altairsky-Lointaine and the 'irresistible Mr Emeraldov', putting in a comment on 'the African passion that erupted so directly on the stage'.

If things went on like this, in order not to disappoint the public Noah Noaevich would have to come up with new tricks every time – in accordance with his own 'theory of sensationalism'. Would he let crocodiles loose on the stage then? Or make the actresses perform naked? Vulpinova had already suggested that in *The Three Sisters* she should come out on stage in dishabille, supposedly to emphasise how slovenly and shameless Natalya became once she felt at home in the Prozorovs' house. But who would want to feast his eyes on Xanthippe Petrovna's bony ancient relics?

Rehearsals for *The Cherry Orchard* were in full swing – every morning, starting at eleven. But somehow the production wasn't coming together. How much sensationalism could there be in *The Cherry Orchard*, even in a new interpretation? Noah Noaevich himself seemed to realise that he had shot wide of the mark with this play, but he didn't want to admit his mistake. That was a pity. Eliza wanted so much to play something piquant, refined and unusual. She did not like the role of Chekhov's seventeen-year-old ingénue in the least. The character was boring and one-dimensional, there was almost nothing to play. But discipline is discipline.

At a quarter to eleven she got into the automobile. The status of the leading man and the leading lady entitled them to an open car, while the others were given travel allowances for a cab, but today Eliza was travelling alone, thank goodness: Emeraldov had not spent the night at the hotel (that often happened with him).

Holding on to her wide-brimmed hat with the ostrich feathers, Eliza set off along Tverskaya Street. She was recognised – people shouted greetings after her and the driver hooted his horn as a sign of appreciation. Eliza enjoyed these rides, they helped to charge her with creative energy before the rehearsal.

All actors have a special ploy of their own, a cunning little trick that helps them get into the magical condition of Acting. Vulpinova, for instance, always had to quarrel with someone to raise her energy to the required level. Reginina deliberately dawdled and drew things out, so that she would arrive late and the director would shout at her. Plump Aphrodisina smacked herself on the cheeks (Eliza had seen this several times). Everyone knew that Lev Spiridonovich Sensiblin drained his little flask. And Eliza required a brief ride with the wind in her hair, accompanied by cries of greeting – or a walk along the street with a fleeting stride, so that people would recognise her and turn their heads.

With flushed cheeks and all a-jangle inside, she ran up the staircase, threw off her wrap, took off her hat, looked at herself in the mirror (rather pale, but it suited her face) and walked into the hall, punctual to the minute, at precisely eleven. All the others, except for Reginina and Emeraldov, were sitting facing the stage, in the front row. Stern was standing up above them, holding his watch, already prepared to explode. Nonarikin was hovering behind him, empathising with his feelings.

'I don't understand how it is possible to treat one's colleagues, and one's art, come to that, so disrespectfully,' Vulpinova began in a honeyed voice.

Mephistov took up the refrain.

'Would they have been late for the real Noah's Ark too? The man who lays claim to the position of our company's leading actor seems to regard all of us as menials. Including the director. Everyone has to wait, while he condescends to finish his breakfast! And these eternal late arrivals of Reginina's! You work your way into the character, prepare yourself, put yourself in the mood to act, and then instead . . .'

At this point red-faced Vasilisa Prokofievna came running into the hall with her usual cry of: 'I'm not late, am I?' Vulpinova said: 'Ha-ha-ha', Stern grabbed at his temples, Nonarikin shook his head reproachfully. They could have started now, but Emeraldov had still not appeared. It wasn't like him. No matter where he spent the night and with whom, Hippolyte always showed up for rehearsals on time, even when his hangover was so bad that he could barely stagger along.

'Someone go and take a look in the changing room. Our handsome hero's face is probably so puffy he can't powder over the bags under his eyes,' Sensiblin suggested.

'You go yourself. There aren't any servants here,' his former wife snapped contemptuously.

Shiftsky made a joke.

'How's that, no servants? What about me?'

But he didn't get up off his seat. In the end, of course, the ever-dependable Vasya Gullibin went.

What a bore, thought Eliza, suppressing a yawn. *Mephistov's right. This way the mood for acting will evaporate completely.*

She took a little mirror out of her reticule and started practising the facial expressions of her character: innocent joy, touching agitation, tender affection, slight fright. Everything girlish and gentle, in pastel tones.

Stern was scolding Nonarikin for something. Kostya Shiftsky

was making Serafima laugh, Vulpinova was bickering shrilly with Reginina.

'Ladies and gentlemen . . . Noah Noaevich!'

Vasya was standing by the wing of the stage. His voice trembled and broke. Everyone turned round and the noise faded away.

'Did you find Emeraldov?' Stern asked angrily.

'Yes . . .' Gullibin's lips started trembling.

'Well, where is he, then?'

'In his dressing room . . . I think he's . . . dead.'

'Don't talk nonsense!'

Noah Noaevich went dashing backstage, with the others following behind him. The little mirror jolted and bounced in Eliza's hands. At that moment she wasn't really thinking anything, she was simply stunned and followed the others.

They were all frightened, disoriented, bewildered. Although it was clear at first glance that Hippolyte was dead (he was lying on the floor, on his back, with one twisted hand thrust up into the air), someone tried to lift him up and blow into his mouth and someone else shouted 'Doctor! Doctor!'

Eventually Noah Noaevich shouted:

'What are you doing? Can't you see that he's already cold? Everybody get back! Nonarikin, telephone the police. They must have their own doctor . . . What's that they're called? A coroner.'

Eliza cried, of course. She felt terribly sorry for Emeraldov, who had been so impossibly handsome in life, lying there now on the floor with his face contorted; one of his trouser legs was hitched up, but Hippolyte didn't care.

They stood there, huddling in the doorway, waiting for the police. Reginina recited a prayer with solemn feeling. Aphrodisina sobbed, Mephistov and Vulpinova discussed in whispers who the dead man could have spent the night with. Sensiblin sighed: 'This is what all the womanising and drinking got him, the pitiful playboy. But I warned him.' Unable to stand around doing nothing, Nonarikin tried to tidy things up; he righted a chair that had been knocked over and picked up a tin goblet (a stage prop from *Hamlet*). 'Now where do I get a Lopakhin?' Noah Noaevich asked, but it wasn't clear whom he was asking.

Eventually a police officer and a doctor arrived, asked everyone to go out and closed the door. The examination of the body took a long time. With the exception of Noah Noaevich, the men went to the buffet to drink to the memory of the newly departed. The first reporter showed up – God only knew where he had sniffed out the news of the tragedy. And then another one arrived, and another. Photographers appeared too.

Eliza immediately went to her own room (her contract, like Emeraldov's, entitled her to a private dressing room). She sat down in front of the mirror, wondering how to dress for the send-off. The funeral would be in St Petersburg, not here – Hippolyte had a wife, who hated the theatre and everything connected with it. Now her fickle husband would finally return to her and she would consign him to the ground as she saw fit.

Eliza tried out various shades of grief on her face.

Then someone started making a noise in the corridor; she heard footsteps and agitated voices and someone even shrieked. Eliza realised that the police had finished and it was time to go out to the press. She got up and threw on her feather boa from *The Three Sisters* – the line and colour were appropriately funereal. She set her eyebrows at a mournful angle and turned down the corners of her mouth. Her forehead and cheeks were pale, for quite natural reasons. And at the thought of poor Hippolyte her eyes immediately turned moist; in the photographs they would glisten. What terrible misfortune, how ghastly, Eliza told herself, working up her mood.

But this wasn't the really ghastly part yet. That began when Zoya Comedina's little freckled face was thrust in at the door.

'Can you imagine, Eliza? The doctor says that Emeraldov killed himself. And out of unrequited love too! Now who could have expected that, from Emeraldov of all people! The reporters have gone plain crazy!'

And she went dashing on with the astounding news.

But Eliza recalled the entrepreneur Furshtatsky. And something else as well – only now, at this very moment.

When Hamlet-Emeraldov pinched Ophelia and some people in the theatre gasped and others guffawed, Eliza had noticed out of the corner of her eye that someone in a black frock coat jumped abruptly to his feet and walked towards the exit. At the time she was baffled and bewildered and she didn't look more closely, but now that picture appeared in front of her eyes as clearly as if it were a photograph. Eliza's glance possessed a quality that is important for an actress: it registered every detail in her memory.

The man who walked out of the auditorium had square shoulders, a twitchy stride and a gleaming bald patch. It was Genghis Khan, quite definitely – she had no doubt about that now.

Eliza suppressed her scream and grabbed hold of the table to prevent herself from falling. But she fell anyway. Her legs buckled as if they were made of limp rags.

Hippolyte Emeraldov's send-off was managed by Noah Noaevich in person, and he treated this sad event like a theatrical production.

It made an impressive spectacle. The coffin was carried out through the entrance of the theatre with all due honours, to applause and keening from an entire choir of inconsolable female mourners – the leading man's bereft admirers. The square was crowded with people. The procession, extending to well over half a mile in length, travelled halfway across the city to the Nikolaevsky railway station.

Eliza walked immediately behind the hearse with her head lowered and not looking around. She wore a veil, which she occasionally raised to wipe away her tears.

The state of terror and panic that had gripped her since the moment when she guessed the true cause of Hippolyte's death had released her for the present. Eliza sensed people's eyes on her and she was completely in character. The dead man, clad in the costume of Cyrano de Bergerac (that was his most famous role), except for the false nose, was transported in an open coffin, and it was not hard to imagine herself as Roxana seeing her prematurely deceased hero off on his final journey.

Before the train departed, Stern delivered a magnificent speech that set the women in the crowd sobbing, some of them hysterically.

'A great actor has left us, an enigma of a man who carries away with him the secret of his death. Goodbye, friend! Goodbye, most talented of my pupils! Oh, how luminously you lived! Oh, how darkly you have departed! From light through darkness to an even more radiant Light!'

Eliza was also supposed to say some farewell words, as the deceased's partner, but after Stern's airs and graces, she didn't want to appear like a fool, so she flung one hand up to her throat as if trying to force the lump of grief through it. Failing, she wilted and simply dropped a white lily into the coffin without speaking.

That seemed to have gone quite well. What is so good about a veil? You can examine faces through it and no one will notice. So that was what Eliza did. Oh, how they were looking at her! With tears, with admiration, with adoration.

Suddenly her attention was caught by a raised hand in a snow-white glove. It clenched into a fist and the thumb turned downwards in the gesture used to condemn a conquered gladiator to death. Eliza shuddered and shifted her gaze from the glove to the face – and everything was suddenly veiled in mist. It was him, Genghis Khan. Baring his teeth triumphantly in a smile of vengeance.

Eliza fainted for the second time that day. Her nerves had worn very thin.

On the way back from the station to the hotel Noah Noaevich admonished her, shouting above the roar of the engine.

'The scene with the lily was marvellous, I won't argue about that. But fainting was overdoing it. And then, why fall so crudely, so inelegantly? The sound as your head hit the asphalt could be heard ten paces away. When did you become a devotee of the naturalistic school?'

She didn't answer, she hadn't fully recovered yet. Let Stern think whatever he wanted. Her life was over in any case . . .

They didn't go to the theatre to hold a wake. That would have been vulgar philistinism. The director said: 'The best funeral feast with which to honour an actor is the continuation of work on his final show,' and he announced an emergency meeting to redistribute the roles. The company supported the proposal ardently. They had been haggling since the day before over who would play Erast, Vershinin, Hamlet and Lopakhin.

The speech that Noah Noaevich gave to the actors was quite different in kind from the one at the railway station.

'He was a mediocre actor, but he died beautifully. You might say that he sacrificed himself on the altar of his theatre,' he said with deep feeling, and after that he changed to a strictly businesslike tone and didn't look particularly mournful any longer. 'Thanks to Hippolyte everyone is writing about us and talking about us. In view of this, I suggest a bold move. We announce a month of mourning. We won't replace Emeraldov in the existing repertoire. Let's say that we accept the losses as a tribute to the memory of an outstanding artist. We close down the *Sisters*, *Liza* and *Hamlet*.'

'Sublime, teacher!' Nonarikin exclaimed. 'A noble gesture!'

'Nobility has nothing to do with it. The public has already seen our repertoire. Without Emeraldov and his hysterical admirers the shows will lose half their electricity. It would be a mistake to cancel the increased prices, but I can't allow any empty seats in the hall. From here on, my friends, we shall concentrate on rehearsals for *The Cherry Orchard*. I ask everyone to be here on the spot at eleven. And don't be late, Vasilisa Prokofievna, or I shall start fining you, in accordance with the terms of the contract.'

'You always have to bring everything down to money! A trader in the temple, that's who you are!'

'People don't buy tickets for the temple, Vasilisa Prokofievna,' Stern retorted. 'And church lectors don't get paid three hundred roubles a month, regardless of the number of services, that is, performances.'

Reginina turned away haughtily without condescending to reply.

'In order to maintain the impetus and put some money in the till we shall hold several concerts in memory of Emeraldov. At the first one, the auditorium will be filled by his female admirers, who will come especially from St Petersburg. Suicide is fashionable at the moment. If we are lucky, some fool will follow her idol in laying hands on herself. And we shall also honour her memory in a special concert.'

'But that's terrible!' Gullibin whispered. 'How can you be so calculating about such things?'

'Iniquitous cynicism!' the *grande dame* who had been offended by the threat of a fine declared in a loud voice.

But Eliza thought: *Stern isn't a cynic, for him life is unimaginable without theatricality, and theatricality is unimaginable without flamboyancy. Life is a stage set, death is a stage set. He is just like me: he would like to die on the stage to applause and sobbing from the audience.*

'This is all wonderful,' Sensiblin boomed calmly, 'but whom do you intend to introduce into the role of Lopakhin?'

The director had his answer ready.

'I shall try to find someone on the side. Perhaps I'll be able to persuade Lyonya Leonidov to work with us temporarily – out of solidarity with our misfortune. He is familiar with the role and shifting the emphases is child's play for an actor of his stature. And for the rehearsal period I'll put in Nonarikin. You know the text, don't you, Georges?'

His assistant nodded eagerly.

'Well, that's excellent. I'll play Simeon-Pishchik and the passer-by. And we can throw the stationmaster out altogether, Chekhov doesn't give him a single word to say. We'll start this very moment. All of you, please open your folders.'

At that moment the door (they were sitting in the green room) creaked.

'Now who is it?' Noah Noaevich asked irritably; he couldn't bear it when outsiders showed up during a rehearsal or a meeting.

'Ah, it's you, Mr Fandorin!' The expression on the director's thin face changed instantly and it was lit up by a charming smile. 'I'd given up hope already . . .'

Everyone looked round.

Standing there in the doorway, holding a grey English top hat with a low crown, was the candidate for the post of repertoire manager.

THE THEORY OF RUPTURE

'Noah Noaevich, they informed me on the t-telephone that you were here,' he said, stammering slightly. 'I offer you my condolences and beg your pardon for disturbing you on this sad day, but . . .'

'Do you have some news for me?' the director asked with brisk interest. 'Come in, do, come in!'

'Yes . . . I mean no. Not in that sense, but in a d-different one, rather unexpected . . .'

The new arrival was holding a leather folder under his arm. He bowed reticently to the assembled company.

Eliza gave a cold nod and turned away. *How clumsily he portrays embarrassment*, she thought. *He is probably not familiar with the feeling. He didn't look embarrassed yesterday, in a far more awkward situation.*

Yesterday Eliza had been in a state of exalted emotion, sobbing and trembling in a nervous, jittery chill. And late in the evening, overcome by a sudden impulse, she had dashed to the theatre, holding in her hands a huge bouquet of black roses. She wanted to place the flowers on the spot where he had died, this man whom she so much disliked and had involuntarily doomed, as a gesture of repentance.

She had opened the door of the service entrance herself. According to Noah Noaevich's theory, the theatre should not be an actor's second home, but his first, so every member of the company had his or her own key. The nightwatchman was not at his post, but Eliza attached no importance to that. She walked up to the floor on which the dressing rooms were located, then along a long, dark corridor, breathing in the aroma of the roses. She turned a corner – and stopped.

Emeraldov's door was standing wide open. The light was burning inside and she could hear voices.

'Are you c-certain that he stayed here after all the others left?' someone asked. She thought she had heard that stammer before somewhere.

The watchman replied.

'What would I want to lie for? The day before yesterday they played *Hamlet, Prince of Denmark*, a sentimental play. After the performance the gentlemen took a drink and got a bit rowdy. Well, that's always the way. Then they went off home. But Mr Emeraldov stayed here. I glanced in, thinking he hadn't turned the light off again. But he said to me: "You be off now, Antip. I've got an appointment". He was in a merry mood, singing some little song or other. He'd already changed out of his working clothes – you know, them trousers with the baggy knees, the hat with the feather, the sword. And he brought the mugs with him, the ones they drink out of at the feast. Beautiful, they are, with eagles.'

'Yes, yes, you t-told me. And did someone c-come to see him then?'

'I won't tell a lie. I didn't see anyone.'

Eliza stood in the door, outraged.

Well, well, at their first meeting this gentleman, Erast Ivanovich, no, Erast Petrovich, with some rather unusual surname, had made a good impression on her. Handsome, a good age for a man, about forty-five, with the advantageous combination of a fresh face and noble grey hair. The only thing was that his taste in clothes was not quite right – excessively elegant, and what man of insight wore a pearl in his necktie nowadays? But his manner was irreproachable. It was obvious immediately that he was man of society. Perhaps she might even have been interested in him, if only he did something worthwhile. But a repertoire manager – that was boring, that was for someone like Gogol's Bashmachkin. He had called himself a traveller, it was true. Most likely he was a fanatical theatre lover, one of those society drones who dreamed of getting into the world of theatre. Quite a common type. In the Art Theatre there was a former general who played third-level roles without being paid for it.

'I didn't think you were the curious kind, sir,' Eliza said disdainfully when he noticed her.

As soon as the dramatic death of Hippolyte Emeraldov had become known, the building had come under a genuine siege – reporters, inconsolable admirers and lovers of scandal had all but climbed in through the windows. But the 'traveller' had obviously acted more cunningly. He had come at a late hour, after the crowd had dispersed, and slipped the nightwatchman a banknote.

'Yes, madam, there are many curious aspects to this business,' Fandorin (that was his surname) had replied in an equally cool tone, and without even the slightest sign of embarrassment.

'I ask you to leave. Outsiders are not allowed in here. When all is said and done, it's indecent!'

'Very well, I shall go. In any case, I have already seen everything.' He bowed slightly, almost casually, in farewell, and told Antip: 'Madam Lointaine is quite right. Lock the door and don't allow anyone else in. Goodbye, madam.'

'"Goodbye"?' she asked in a hostile tone of voice. 'Have you changed your mind about coming to work as our repertoire manager?'

'Yes, I have. But we shall see each other soon.'

And now they really had seen each other.

'I would like to have a f-few words with you in private,' grey-haired Fandorin said to the director, still acting out his agitation in the same inept manner. A man with eyes of ice could not know what agitation was! 'But I can wait until you have finished . . .'

'No, no, by no means. We will have a talk immediately, and quite definitely in private.'

Stern took the 'traveller' by the arm and led him away.

'Busy yourselves with something. I'll be back soon. Take a close look at the new Lopakhin. You should each work out a sketch of your psychological relationship with this man . . . Please come to my study, Erast . . . mmmm . . . Petrovich.'

However, Stern's 'soon' stretched out into quite a lengthy period.

There was no point in Eliza taking a closer look at the new Lopakhin: firstly, in the course of the play her Anya had hardly any contact at all with the peasant's son; and secondly, in any case Lopakhin would be played in the production by Leonidov or someone else equally great, but most certainly not by Nonarikin, no matter what a lovely man he might be.

The poor soul pestered one of them after the other, but no one wanted to 'establish a psychological relationship' with him.

Eliza sat there, muffled up in her shawl, absent-mindedly listening to the conversations.

Anton Ivanovich Mephistov proposed sardonic conjectures concerning the repertoire manager's 'imposing grey locks' and then asked Sensiblin, as a 'specialist on grey locks', how much bluing was required to maintain such a noble whiteness. The phlegmatic Lev Spiridonovich did not rise to the bait.

'You don't like handsome men, everyone knows that. Drop it, Anton Ivanich, in a man the important thing is not the face, but the calibre,' he said good-naturedly.

'Just listen to him, how judicious and kind-hearted he is,' Reginina whispered about her former husband. 'I don't understand how I could have lived with this man for seven years! Calculating, vindictive, never forgets a thing! Pretends to be a lamb, and then strikes a sly, underhand blow, bites like a snake.'

Eliza nodded. She herself disliked rationalising individuals – both in life and on the stage. She and Vasilisa Prokofievna were allies in their attitude to Sensiblin. Eliza was the only one in the entire company who knew why the *grande dame* hated the 'philosopher' and what she could never forgive him for.

One day, overcome by a sudden impulse to confide in someone, Reginina had told Eliza a story that made her skin creep. How hideously vengeful betrayed husbands could be!

At the time when this story happened, Vasilisa Prokofievna was still playing heroines and she and Lev Spiridonovich worked together in a first-class imperial theatre. Reginina was playing Marguerite in *La Dame aux Camélias* – it was a highly successful adaptation of the novel, and the role of the noble courtesan had been written with heart-rending power. 'The way I died set the entire hall sobbing and blowing their noses,' Reginina recalled, becoming emotional herself and reaching for her handkerchief. 'As you know, Eliza, Sarah Bernhardt is usually considered the finest performer of the role of Marguerite Gautier. But believe it or not, I played her even more powerfully! All the foreigners who saw me simply went out of their minds. The European press wrote about the production. You don't remember, you were still a little girl . . . And what do you think? Word of my Marguerite actually reached Her. Yes, yes, the great Bernhardt herself! And so she came to St Petersburg. Supposedly on tour, but I knew she wanted to take a look at me. The great day came and they told me: she's in the audience! My God, what happened to me! On that day Their Majesties came, but of course, all the people of understanding were looking only at the box where Bernhardt was sitting. Would she approve, I wondered. Ah, how I played! And on a continuously mounting crescendo. They told me afterwards that the great Sarah was sitting there more dead than alive – she was eating her heart out with envy. Finally the culmination of the action was approaching. I have a scene with Armand, I am at death's door. Lev Spiridonovich was playing Armand, he was rather good in that role too. Everyone called us an exquisite couple. But we had had a terrible quarrel, just before the performance. It just happened that in a moment of weakness – I had turned quite dizzy – I yielded to the importunate advances of the second lover, Zvyozdich (he was a very handsome-mannered man) and someone snitched to my husband – well, you know the way it is with us. All right, I'm guilty. Hit me, rip my favourite dress to shreds with a knife, be unfaithful to me with someone else in revenge! But what did Lev do? There I am declaiming my crowning line: "My darling, all I ask is that you cry a little for me". And suddenly . . . Armand had these beautiful, thick false eyebrows. And two jets of water came shooting out from under them! That villain had fastened on a clown's water tubes under his make-up! The audience almost split their sides laughing. The tsar laughed, and the tsarina too. Sarah Bernhardt almost had a fit . . . The worst thing was that I was lying there at my last breath, absolutely shattered, and I couldn't understand a thing! Afterwards, it's true, the reviewers wrote that it was a revolutionary interpretation, that it was a brilliant invention that emphasised the tragi-farcical nature of life and the paltry distance between melodrama and slapstick! But never mind that! He stole the most important moment in my life and trampled it underfoot! And since then that man has been dead to me.'

'That's terrible, terrible,' Eliza whispered. 'Yes, something like that can never be forgiven.'

One actor could not possibly commit a more heinous crime against another. Anything could be expected of a man who was capable of such cruelty.

It was no accident, of course, that the cunning Noah Noaevich had brought the divorced couple together in the same company. According to his 'theory of rupture', the relations within a company should always be seething on the verge of an explosion. Envy, jealousy and even hatred – any strong emotions created a productive field of energy, which, with skilled management from the director and the correct distribution of roles, was transmitted to the acting, lending it an authentic vitality.

'You know, Eliza,' Reginina carried on, whispering, 'I'm not like the others, I don't envy your success in the least. Ah, there was a time when I made the audience faint with passion. Of course, my present line of characters has its own charms too. But let me tell you honestly, as a friend, that the admirers are the thing that is hardest to manage without. When you play the heroines, the persistent suitors who pursue you everywhere like a pack of hounds are annoying. But afterwards, how badly you miss this – pardon my vulgarity – gaggle of young studs! Oh, you have yet to learn that with age feelings – and sensuality, sensuality – do not grow weaker, but stronger. How sweet and fresh that Cherubino of yours in a hussar's uniform is! I mean Volodenka Limbach. Why not give him to me, it won't be any loss to you.'

Although this was spoken in jest, Eliza had frowned. So rumours were already going round? Had someone seen the boy trying to get into her window? What a disaster!

'He's not mine at all. You can take him and keep him, together with the sword, the spurs and all the rest of the trappings! Excuse me, Vasilisa Prokofievna, I'll go and rehearse my part. Or else Stern will come back and start abusing me.'

110

She changed seats and opened her folder, but just then Serafima Aphrodisina sat down beside her and started babbling.

'Kostya Shiftsky's run off. Said he was dashing back to the Madrid. Supposedly he left the folder with his part there. He's lying, probably. He always lies, you can't believe anything he says. But where did you go this morning? I knocked, but you weren't in your room. I wanted to borrow the diamante clip for my hat, it's delightful, and you don't wear it anyway. So where were you?'

Cheerful, bright and thoroughly down to earth, without any inhibitions or duplicity, Serafima had a salutary effect on Eliza's tormented nerves. It's a rare thing in the theatre for two actresses not to become rivals, but there was nothing of that sort between them. With her innate common sense, Aphrodisina explained this very simply. 'You're attractive to one kind of man, and I'm attractive to a different kind,' she said once. 'You're good at playing sad parts, and I'm good at playing jolly ones. There's nothing for us to quarrel over, either on the stage or in real life. They pay you more, of course, but then I'm younger.' Serafima was sweet and spontaneous, a little bit greedy for money, clothes and trinkets, but then at her age that was all understandable and excusable.

Eliza put her arm round Serafima's shoulders.

'I went out for a walk. I woke up early and couldn't sleep.'

'For a walk? Alone? Or with someone else?' Aphrodisina asked breezily. She adored secrets of the heart, affairs and all sorts of provocative subjects.

'Don't tell her anything, Eliza,' said Xanthippe Vulpinova, walking across to them. Here was an individual who simply could not watch calmly while people had a friendly, cheerful conversation. 'Have you noticed that this party here is always trying to pry something out of you and spying on you? The moment you went away just now, she stuck her nose in your notebook.'

'Don't you tell lies!' Aphrodisina exclaimed, jumping to her feet with tears immediately welling up in her cornflower-blue eyes. 'You should be ashamed of yourself! I just took the pencil out of it for a moment. I had to make a note on my part, and my pencil broke!'

'You're the one who's always spying on everyone,' Eliza told the 'villainess' angrily. 'And worst of all, you didn't even hear what we were talking about, you just butted in.'

That was all that Vulpinova needed. She thrust one bony, pointed fist against her side, leaned down over Eliza and proclaimed stridently:

'Attention please! I call all of you to witness! This individual has just called me a spy! Of course, I'm only a little person, I don't play any leading roles, but I do have my rights! I demand a comrades' court, as specified in our statutes! No one has the right to insult the actors with impunity!'

She got her way. Everyone huddled together around the uproar. But Eliza had no need to defend herself, defenders appeared spontaneously. Good-hearted Gullibin tried to make the troublemaker see sense. And a second faithful champion, Georges Nonarikin, shielded the lady against attack.

'In the director's absence, his authority devolves on me!' he declared proudly. 'And I ask you, Madam Vulpinova, not to shout. The statutes include a clause about misconduct and violation of discipline during a rehearsal!'

Xanthippe immediately switched her attention to the new target; it was basically all the same to her who she wrangled with.

'Ah, the Knight of the Mournful Visage! Why are you wandering about with Lopakhin's part, like some nincompoop with a fancy embroidered feed-bag? You'll see your own ears before you ever get to play that part. Because you haven't got an ounce of talent! The general cook and bottle washer!'

Nonarikin turned completely white at this insult, but someone came to his defence in turn. Zoya Comedina jumped up onto a chair – obviously so that she could be seen more clearly – and yelled out with all her might:

'Don't you dare talk to him like that! Don't listen to her, Georges. You're a brilliant actor!'

This despairing appeal defused the tension and there were peals of laughter.

'What a couple, a real sight for sore eyes,' Vulpinova crooned happily. 'You should sit on his shoulder, my dear. And you could go off round the courtyards and the streets singing Beethoven's song "Me and My Marmot".'

The imitation she gave of Comedina sitting on Nonarikin's shoulder and him turning his hurdy-gurdy and singing was so funny that the laughter grew even louder.

For some reason the unfortunate assistant director was not furious with the troublemaker, but with his uninvited intercessor.

'Who asked you to interfere?' he asked her resentfully. 'Everyone has to put their spoke in!'

And he withdrew from the scene.

Eliza sighed. Life was returning to normal. Everything as usual. The 'Theory of Rupture' was still in operation. Only Emeraldov wasn't here . . .

She felt sorry for the little 'principal boy', who was just left there, abandoned on the chair, where she squatted down, looking like a little sparrow with its feathers ruffled up.

'Why are you so blatant about it, men don't like that,' Eliza said gently, moving over to sit by Zoya. 'Do you like Georges?'

'We're made for each other, but he doesn't understand it,' Comedina complained in a quiet voice. 'Actually, I ought to hate you. When you're there, all the men turn towards you, like sunflowers turning towards the sun. Do you think I can't see that he finds my interest irksome, even offensive? I may play comic parts, but I'm not stupid.'

'Why did you interfere?'

'He's so proud, and so unhappy. He has so much passion going to waste inside him. I see that sort of thing very clearly. I don't need much, after all. I'm not you, I'm not pampered.' Zoya bared her teeth in a clownish grin. 'Oh, my demands on life are diminutive, and my demands on love are microscopic. To match my own size.' She pulled a face and slapped herself on the top of her head. 'I'd be satisfied with a smile and a kind word – even just occasionally. I'm not the kind that men love. I'm the kind that they allow to love them, as a special grace and favour. And then not always.'

Eliza felt terribly sorry for her – this plain, skinny girl who was funny even in this moment of frank sincerity. Although (Eliza's professional memory prompted her), hadn't Comedina used the same tone of comic despair in the role of Victor Hugo's Gavroche? Once an actress, always an actress.

They sat beside each other dejectedly without speaking, each thinking her own thoughts.

And then, after being away for half an hour, Noah Noaevich finally returned and the miracles began.

TO HELL WITH *THE CHERRY ORCHARD*!

Eliza hadn't seen Stern in such an elated mood for a long time. Recently he had been acting out an upsurge of enthusiasm rather skilfully, but there is no way to deceive the eye of an actress: she could see perfectly well that Noah Noaevich was dissatisfied, that he was concerned about the success of his new production. And now suddenly this soaring elation. What could the reason be?

'Ladies and gentlemen! My friends!' Stern exclaimed, surveying his colleagues with his eyes all aglow. 'Miracles do not only happen on the stage. Today, as if in recompense for our loss, fate has presented us with a most generous gift. Look at this man ...' He indicated his companion with a sweeping gesture. 'Who is he, in your opinion?'

'The repertoire manager,' someone answered in surprise. 'We've already seen him today.'

'Mr Fandorin, Erast Petrovich,' prompted Shiftsky, who had returned unnoticed at some moment or other. He had always possessed a quite outstanding memory for names.

'No, my comrades! This man is our saviour! He has brought us a quite fantastically promising play!'

Nonarikin gasped.

'But what about *The Cherry Orchard*?'

'To hell with *The Cherry Orchard*! Take the axe to it, your Lopakhin is right! Erast Petrovich's play is new, and no one except me has read it! It is ideal in every respect. In the complement of roles, the theme and the plot!'

'Where did you obtain it, Mr Repertoire Manager?' Reginina asked. 'Who is the author?'

'*He* is the author!' Stern laughed, delighted by the general amazement. 'I explained to Erast Petrovich what kind of play we need, and instead of searching for one he sat down and – hey presto! – wrote it himself. In ten days! Exactly the kind of play that I was dreaming about! Even better! This is phenomenal!'

Of course, there was hubbub. Those who were satisfied with their parts in *The Cherry Orchard* were indignant; the others, on the contrary, expressed their ardent approval.

Eliza said nothing for a while, looking at the handsome, grey-haired man with new interest.

'Enough arguing,' she said eventually. 'When will we be able to acquaint ourselves with the text?'

'This very moment,' Noah Noaevich declared. 'I have run my eyes over it. As you know, I possess the skill of photographic reading; however, this text has to be heard. The play is written in blank verse.'

'Oh, really?' said Gullibin, astounded. 'In the style of Rostand, is it?'

'Yes, but with an oriental flavour. How timely this is! The public is crazy about everything Japanese. Please, Erast Petrovich, take my seat and read.'

'But I have a st-stammer . . .'

'That's not important. Please, ladies and gentlemen!'

Everyone applauded and Fandorin, tugging on his neat black moustache, took a sheaf of paper out of a folder.

'*TWO COMETS IN A STARLESS SKY*,' he read out, and explained: 'This is a title in the tradition of the Japanese theatre. My text is eclectic to some degree, something has been taken from *kabuki*, something from *joruri*, the old puppet theatre form, that is, from . . .'

'Just read it, you can explain everything that's not clear afterwards,' Stern interrupted impatiently, winking at the actors, as if to say: Just you wait, now I'll see you gasp.

'Very well. Of course. I beg your pardon.' The author coughed to clear his throat. 'There is also a subtitle: "A puppet theatre play in three acts with songs, dances, tumbling tricks, sword-fighting scenes and *michiyuki*.'

'What's that?' Sensiblin asked. 'I didn't understand the last word.'

'That is a traditional kind of scene, in which the characters are on a journey,' Fandorin explained. 'For the Japanese the concept of the Path or the Road is very important, and so the *michiyuki* scenes stand out especially.'

'That's all, no more questions!' Stern growled. 'Read!'

Everyone settled down in their seats. No one knows how to listen to a new play like the actors who are going to play in it.

The same tense expression appeared on all their faces – each of them was trying to work out which part he or she would get. As the reading proceeded, one after another the listeners relaxed, having identified their roles. This reaction alone was enough to demonstrate that they liked the play. It's a rare thing to find a play in which every actor has an impressive entrance, but *Two Comets* belonged to precisely this category. The characterisations fitted very neatly, and so there was nothing to quarrel over.

Eliza also identified her own part with no difficulty: the geisha of the first rank Izumi. Very interesting. She could sing and, what was more, dance as well – well, God be praised; Eliza had graduated from ballet school, after all. And she could have such kimonos made, and such hairstyles!

It was simply astounding how she could have been so blind – a woman who apparently wasn't stupid and had seen something of life. How could she have failed to appreciate Mr Fandorin at his true worth? His grey hair and black moustache were so very stylish! And what a pleasant, manly voice he had. While he was reading his stammer disappeared completely. That was actually rather a pity – this slight speech defect really had a certain charm to it.

Ah, what a play it was! Not a play, but a miracle!

Even Xanthippe Petrovna Vulpinova was ecstatic. And no wonder – she didn't often get such an appetising role.

'Bravo, Erast Petrovich!' the villainess called out first of all when the author said: 'Curtain. The end'. 'A new Gogol has appeared amongst us.'

Everyone jumped to their feet and gave a standing ovation. They shouted:

'This is a hit!'

'The season will be ours!'

'Banzai!'

Kostya Shiftsky made everyone laugh by imitating a Japanese accent.

'Nemirovich and Stanislavsky will commit hara-kiri,' and he mimed plump Nemirovoch-Danchenko and skinny Stanislavsky with his pince-nez, slitting open their stomachs.

The only one not to join in the universal jubilation was Nonarikin.

'I didn't understand what parts you and I will get, teacher,' he said with mingled hope and suspicion.

'Well I, naturally, shall be the Storyteller. A unique opportunity to direct the tempo of the action and the actors' playing from right there onstage. A combined producer and director, a brilliant innovation. And you, my dear Georges, will get three roles: the First Assassin, the Second Assassin and the Invisible One.'

The assistant director glanced at the notes he had made during the reading.

'But I beg your pardon! Two of these roles have no words, and the third has words, but no one can see the character!'

'Naturally. He is an Invisible One. But what expressive lines! And then, the Invisible One is the core, the driving motor of the action. And in the roles of the hired killers you can demonstrate your brilliant sword-fighting skills. You told me yourself that at military college you were the top cadet in the fencing class.'

Flattered by these compliments, Nonarikin nodded, but somewhat uncertainly.

'Japanese sword-fighting differs substantially from the Western v-variety,' Fandorin remarked, beginning to stammer again. 'Some d-degree of training will be required.'

'Yes. The problem that concerns me is all the Japanese realia. All those gestures, musical instruments, songs, facial expressions, rhythms of movement, and so on. We shall have to find a live Japanese from somewhere and take him on as a consultant. I cannot allow myself to put on a hotchpotch like the production of *Madam Butterfly* at Milan.' Stern frowned anxiously, but the author of the play reassured him.

'I have thought about that, naturally. Firstly, I myself have a good grasp of Japanese matters. And secondly, I have brought you a Japanese. He is waiting in the foyer.'

Everyone simply gasped, and Eliza thought: this man is a magician, all he needs is a cloak spangled with stars and a magic wand. Just imagine it – he takes a real live Japanese around with him!

'Then call him quickly!' Noah Noaevich exclaimed. 'Truly, you were sent to us by the god of the theatre! No, no, stay here! Gentlemen, call an usher, let him bring our Japanese guest here. And in the meantime, Erast Petrovich, I would like to ask, since you are so prudent, whether you might perhaps have any thoughts concerning who should play the part of this . . . what is his name . . .' He glanced into the play. '. . . this Si-no-bi with the alias of the Inaudible One? As far as I understand it, the *Sinobi* are a clan of professional killers, like the Arab assassins. In your play he juggles, walks a tightrope and dodges a knife blade.'

'Yes, indeed,' said Sensiblin. 'We don't have a hero. If only Emeraldov were alive . . .'

'I find it hard to imagine Hippolyte strolling along a tightrope,' Reginina remarked.

'Yes, that is a problem,' Nonarikin put in. 'An insoluble one, I'm afraid.'

The director disagreed with him.

'Insoluble, my hat. We can find some acrobat from a circus. Circus performers can sometimes be quite artistic.'

'Perhaps we don't necessarily need a professional actor,' the miraculous Erast Petrovich suggested commonsensically. 'The part of the Inaudible One has no words, and his face remains concealed by a mask right to the very end.'

'Tell me,' said Stern, peering hopefully at Fandorin, 'when you were living in Japan, did you engage in all these various oriental tricks? No, no, don't refuse me. With your figure and appearance you could make an excellent partner for Eliza!'

The handsome man hesitated and looked in her direction for the first time.

'Yes, I can do all of that, even walk a tightrope, but . . . I wouldn't dare to go out on stage . . . No, no, please spare me that.'

119

'You ask him, Eliza! Implore him! Go down on your knees!' Noah Noaevich shouted out excitedly. 'Just look at those features. There is so much elegance in them! So much strength! When the Inaudible One takes off his mask at the end and his face is picked out by a beam of light, the audience will go wild!'

Eliza extended her arm towards the author in the gesture of Desdemona begging for mercy and sent him her absolutely most radiant smile – no man had ever been able to stand against that.

But the conversation was interrupted, because an usher glanced in at the door.

'Noah Noaevich, I've brought him. Come in, my good gentleman.'

This remark was addressed to a short, stocky oriental individual in a two-piece check suit. He took several steps forward and bowed to everyone from the waist, without bending his back, at the same time removing his straw boater. His ideally round, shaven head gleamed as if it had been polished.

'Mikhair Erastovit Fandorin,' he proclaimed loudly, introducing himself, and bowed again.

'Is he your son?' Stern asked the author in amazement.

'He's not a relative,' Fandorin replied drily. 'His real name is Masahiro Sibata.'

'Phenomenal,' said Noah Noaevich, drawling his favourite word as he avidly examined the man from the East. 'Tell me, Mikhail Erastovich, do you happen to know how to juggle?'

'Dzugger?' the Japanese asked. 'Ah. I can do a rittur.'

He took a watch out of his breast pocket, a penknife out of his trouser pocket, half of a round cracknel out of a side pocket and started deftly tossing all these things up in the air.

'Magnificent!' A predatory expression with which Eliza was very familiar appeared on the director's face. That was how Noah Noaevich looked when some especially daring creative idea was gestating in his head. 'And have you ever walked on a tightrope?' He clasped his hands prayerfully. 'Even just a little bit! I have read that your nation is exceptionally nimble in physical gymnastics.'

'I can do a rittur,' Fandorin junior replied, and after a moment's thought added cautiously: 'If it is not too high.'

'Phenomenal! Simply phenomenal!' Stern exclaimed, almost with tears in his eyes. 'We won't harass you, Erast Petrovich. I understand that at your age it is strange to go out on to the stage. I have a more grandiose idea. Ladies and gentlemen, we shall have a genuine Japanese acting in our play! That will add authenticity and novelty to the production. Just cast a glance at this face! Do you see that Asiatic modelling, that visceral strength? A statue of the Buddha!' Under the director's outstretched hand, the Japanese thrust out his chest, knitted his brows and narrowed his already narrow eyes. 'We shall keep it a secret until the opening night that the leading male role is being played by a Japanese. But when he removes his mask at the moment of revelation, there will be a furore. There has never been a leading man of this kind on the European stage! And tell me, my friend, could you portray the passion of love?'

'I can do a rittur,' Mikhail-Masahiro replied imperturbably.

He looked round, selected Aphrodisina as his object and fixed her with a glance that was suddenly aflame. The wings of his small nose distended voraciously, the veins stood out on his forehead and his lips trembled slightly, as if he were struggling to hold back a groan.

'*Mamma mia!*' Simochka babbled in a feeble voice, blushing bright red.

'Phenomenal!' Stern boomed 'I've never seen anything like it. But I still haven't asked the most important question; will you agree to act in your foster father's play? We all ask you to do it, everyone here. Ask him!'

'Please do it, please!' the actors roared.

'The success of the play and the new playwright will depend on this,' Stern proclaimed solemnly. 'You wish to help your foster father, don't you?'

'Very much.'

The Japanese looked at Fandorin, who was standing there with a completely stiff face, as if he found everything that was happening extremely unpleasant.

Mikhail Erastovich said something rather long in a strange-sounding language, addressing Fandorin senior.

'*Sore va tasikani soo da kedo . . .*' Fandorin senior replied, as if admitting something reluctantly.

'I agree,' said the Japanese, bowing first to Stern and then to all the others.

The company burst into applause and joyful exclamations.

'I'll order the set design today from Sudeikin or Bakst, whichever one is free,' said Noah Noaevich, switching to a businesslike tone. 'The costumes are not a problem. There is something left over from our production of *The Mikado*, there's something in stock in the storerooms here, and our predecessors staged Jones's *Geisha*. We'll make the rest. And we'll rustle up plenty of props from the Theatrical and Cinematographic Company. We'll restructure the stage. Nonarikin: typewritten texts by roles, in the folders as usual. Absolute secrecy! Until the announcement no one must know what we are putting on. We'll simply inform the press that *The Cherry Orchard* is cancelled. And we'll make sure to announce that we have found a stronger play!'

Eliza noticed that Fandorin shuddered and even squirmed at those words. Perhaps he was no stranger to modesty after all? How sweet!

'Weekends are cancelled!' Stern boomed. 'We are going to rehearse every day!'

UNFORGIVABLE WEAKNESS

He was strange, this Erast Petrovich Fandorin. During the days that followed Eliza became more and more convinced of that. He definitely liked her, there was no doubt about it. But then, she had not often encountered men who looked at her without desire. Except for someone like Mephistov, who seemed genuinely to hate beauty. Or Noah Noaevich, with his obsession for the theatre – he was capable of seeing an actress only as an actress, a means for the realisation of his creative concept.

Men who lusted after a woman behaved in one of two ways. They either flung themselves directly into the attack. Or – if they were of a proud disposition – they pretended to remain indifferent, but nonetheless tried hard to make an impression.

At first Fandorin seemed to be trying to appear indifferent. During the rehearsal, or rather, during the break, he struck up a trivial conversation, with a disinterested air. Something about Queen Gertrude's goblet and the keys to the properties room. Eliza replied politely, smiling inwardly. *How funny he is, thinking he can fool me with this twaddle. He just wants to hear the sound of my voice,* she thought. And she also thought that he was very handsome. And touching. With the way he glanced out from under his thick eyebrows – and blushed. She had always found men who still possessed the ability to blush, even at a mature age, very appealing.

She had already anticipated that he would break off the conversation, as if he was bored with it, and would walk off with a casual air, but would be sure to squint back at her to see what she was thinking. Had she been impressed or not?

But Fandorin behaved differently. He suddenly stopped questioning her about which members of the company had access to the properties room, blushed even more deeply, raised his eyes resolutely and said:

'I won't try to pretend. I'm a poor actor. And I think you cannot be fooled in any case. I am asking you about one thing, and thinking about something completely different. I think I am in love with you. And it is not simply that you are talented, beautiful and all the rest of it. There are special reasons why I have lost my head . . . It doesn't matter what they are . . . I know very well that you are spoilt for admirers and accustomed to ad-doration. It is torment for me to jostle in the crowd of your worshippers. I cannot compete with the freshness of a young hussar, the wealth of Mr Shustrov, the talents of Noah Noaevich, the good looks of the leading men, etc., etc. I had only one chance of attracting your interest – to write a play. For me this was a feat requiring a greater effort than it cost Commodore Robert Peary to conquer the North Pole. If not for the constant g-giddiness that has not left me since the moment we first met, it is most unlikely that I would ever have written a drama, and especially one in verse. Being genuinely in love works miracles. But I wish to warn you . . .'

Here Eliza interrupted him, alarmed by that 'But'.

'How well you speak!' she said agitatedly, taking hold of his hot hand. 'No one ever talks to me so simply and seriously. I can't give you an answer now, I have to puzzle out my own feelings! Swear that you will always be so open with me. And for my part, I promise you the same!'

It seemed to her that her tone and her words had been correct: sincerity in combination with tenderness and a quite clear, but at the same time chaste, invitation to develop their relationship. But he understood her differently and smiled ironically with just his lips.

'Are we going to be "just friends"? Well, that is the kind of answer I expected. I give you my word that I shall never burden you again with my sentimental c-confessions.'

'But I didn't mean it in that way at all!' she exclaimed in alarm, fearing that this dry stick would keep his promise, that would be just like him. 'I have friends without you. Vasya Gullibin, Sima

Aphrodisina, Georges Nonarikin – he's a ridiculous man, but self-lessly devoted and noble. But all that's not the thing . . . I can't be absolutely candid with them. They're actors too, and actors are a special kind of people . . .'

He listened without interrupting. But the way he looked sent an ecstatic tremor through her, like at the most exalted moments when she was onstage. Tears welled up in her eyes, and elation filled her breast.

'I'm tired of playing parts all the time, of always being an actress! Here I am talking to you and I think: a dialogue like Elena Andreeva's with Dr Astrov in the third act of *Uncle Vanya*, only better, much better, because almost nothing breaks through to the outside. That's the way to keep things from now on: fire on the inside, and on the outside – a crust of ice. My God, how afraid I am of turning into Sarah Bernhardt!'

'I b-beg your pardon?' His blue eyes opened wide in surprise.

'My perpetual nightmare. They say that the great Sarah Bernhardt is never natural. That is the principle of her existence. At home she walks about in a Pierrot costume. She lies down to sleep in a coffin, not a bed, in order to imbue herself with the tragic spirit of exist-ence. She is entirely feigned passion, entirely affectation. That is the terrible danger lying in wait for every actress – to lose oneself, to turn into a shadow, into a mask!'

And she burst into tears, putting her hands over her face. She wept bitterly and in earnest – until her nose turned red and her eyes puffed up – but she still kept glancing through her fingers to see how he was looking at her.

Oh, and how he was looking! She wouldn't barter a look like that for an ovation from a full house!

Of course, the relationship could not remain at this stage for long. Friendship with a handsome man is something out of a romantic ballad. Such things don't happen in real life.

On the third day, following the regular rehearsal, Eliza went to his house, to a small annexe hidden away in an old, quiet side street. The pretext for the visit was a respectable one: Erast had suggested that she choose a kimono for her role, as well as some fans and some other Japanese trinkets, of which he had a huge number at home. She didn't have anything of *that sort* in mind at all, word of honour. She was simply curious to take a look at how this mysterious man lived. A house can tell a great deal about its inhabitant.

And the house did, indeed, tell her a great deal about Erast Petrovich – almost too much, in fact, she couldn't make sense of all of it at once. There was ideal order everywhere here. You could even say there was lifeless order, as is often the way with inveterate, pedantic bachelors. There were no traces at all of permanent female inhabitation, but here and there Eliza's keen glance spotted little bits and pieces that looked like keepsakes from previous passions: a miniature of a young blonde in the depths of a bookcase; an elegant comb of the kind that was fashionable about twenty years ago; a little white glove, seemingly forgotten under a mirror. Well, so he had not lived like a monk all his life, that was only natural.

There were no awkward silences. Firstly, in the company of this man, it was not uncomfortable in the least to say nothing. Erast Petrovich had a quite fantastic mastery of the difficult art of the pause; he simply looked at her and she no longer felt bored. And secondly, there were so many interesting things in the house, she wanted to ask him about everything, and he gladly started telling her, after which the conversation moved on of its own accord, in any direction.

Eliza felt absolutely safe – even with just the two of them alone in an empty house, a gentleman like Erast Petrovich would not stoop to doing anything improper. There was only one thing she had failed to take into account: intelligent conversations with an intelligent man always had an arousing effect on her.

How did it all happen?

It began with an absolutely innocent thing. She started examining some prints and asked about an outlandish creature: a fox in a kimono, with a tall hairstyle.

'That's a *kitsuné*, a Japanese werewolf,' Fandorin explained. 'A supremely guileful creature.' She said that the *kitsuné* looked terribly like Xanthippe Vulpinova, and indulged herself by passing several pejorative comments about that rather unpleasant individual.

'You speak of M-Madam Vulpinova with bitterness,' he said, shaking his head. 'Is she your enemy?'

'But surely you can see? That malicious, petty creature simply hates me!'

And then he delivered one of those little speeches, of which she had heard so many in the last three days and to which, although she thought of them ironically to herself as 'sermons', she had already become accustomed. She had even come to like them. They were, perhaps, even the most charming thing about talking to the 'traveller'.

'Never make that mistake,' Fandorin said with a very serious air. 'Don't denigrate your enemies, don't call them offensive names, don't describe them as paltry and contemptible. By doing that, you demean yourself. Who are you in that case, if you have such a despicable enemy? If you respect yourself, you will not be the enemy of those who are not worthy of respect. If a stray dog barks at you, you won't go down on all fours and b-bark back at it. Furthermore, if an enemy knows that you regard him with respect, he will respond in kind. This does not s-signify reconciliation, but it helps in avoiding mean tricks in the course of the struggle, and it also makes it possible to conclude the war with a peace, instead of killing.'

He was remarkably handsome when he talked this charming nonsense.

'You are a man of genuine culture,' Eliza said with a smile. 'At first I took you for an aristocrat, but you are a classic member of the intelligentsia.'

Fandorin immediately launched into a diatribe against the intelligentsia – he was unusually talkative today. It was probably her nearness that affected him in that way. Although there was another possible explanation (it occurred to Eliza later). As an intelligent man and connoisseur of psychology, Erast Petrovich might have noticed how powerfully his 'sermons' affected his listener and deployed this weapon to the full. Ah, she still hadn't learned to understand him!

The oration in the course of which Eliza finally melted completely was this:

'I do not regard that as a compliment!' Fandorin exclaimed heatedly. 'The "classic member of the intelligentsia" is a b-being who is harmful, even ruinous, for Russia! The estate of the intelligentsia might seem likeable enough, but it possesses a fatal flaw, which was noted so accurately and mocked by Chekhov. A member of that estate is capable of bearing hardships with dignity, he is capable of maintaining his nobility in defeat. But he is absolutely incapable of winning in a battle with a boor or a blackguard, who are so numerous and so powerful here. Until such time as the estate of the intelligentsia learns to f-fight for its ideals, there will never be anything decent and worthwhile in Russia! But when I say "fight", I do not mean a fight according to the rules of the boor and the blackguard. Or else you will become exactly the same as they are. It has to be a fight according to your own rules, the rules of an honourable individual! It is customary to think that Evil is stronger than Good, because it places no limitations on its means – it ambushes slyly, strikes furtively and below the belt, it attacks with odds of ten against one. So it would seem that if you fight Evil according to the rules, it is impossible to win. But assertions like that result from stupidity and, b-begging your pardon, impotence. The intelligentsia is a thinking estate, and that is where its power lies. If it loses, that is because it has made poor use of its main weapon, the intellect. One need only apply the intellect for it to become clear that the noble man has an arsenal more powerful and armour far more impregnable than those of even the most adroit conspirators from the Okhrana or revolutionary leaders who send altruistic young boys to their deaths. You will ask what they consist of, this arsenal and the armour of the noble m-man, who does not stoop to base means of struggle . . .'

Eliza had no intention of asking about anything of the sort. Erast Petrovich's excitement as he spoke and his tone of voice affected her more powerfully than any aphrodisiac. She finally gave up trying to resist the weakness flooding through her body, closed her eyes and laid her hand on his knee with a gentle sigh. Eliza never did find out what the arsenal and armour of the honourable individual consisted of. Fandorin stopped speaking in mid-phrase and, naturally, drew her towards himself.

After that, in the way that things happened with her in such cases, she remembered snatches and separate images – mostly touches and smells, rather than visual impressions. The world of love was magical. In that world she became a completely different being, she did unimaginable things and was not even slightly embarrassed. Time altered its pace. Reason blanked out benignly, ineffably beautiful music played and she felt like a classical goddess, soaring on a cloud.

But then there was a flash of lightning and a peal of thunder. Quite literally – a storm had blown up outside. Eliza raised her head, glanced towards the window and saw that it was completely black. Darkness had already fallen, and she hadn't even noticed. But when the darkness was illuminated by a flash of sheet lightning, Eliza's reason returned instantly, bringing with it its constant companion, the fear that she had completely forgotten about.

What have I done? Oh, egotist! Criminal! I'll destroy him, if I haven't already.

Pushing her beloved's head, which glimmered silver in the faint light, off her shoulder, she jumped up, rummaged about on the floor and started getting dressed.

'What's wrong? What's happened?' he asked in astonishment.

Eliza shouted frantically, with tears in her eyes:

'This must never, do you hear me, never happen again!'

He gaped at her open-mouthed. But Eliza ran out of the house, straight into the lashing downpour.

Oh, horror! Horror! Her very worst fears were confirmed: there under the awning of the gates was a dark, thickset figure. Someone had been lurking opposite the open window and spying . . .

'Oh God, save him, save him!' Eliza pleaded, running along the wet pavement with her heels clattering. Running with no idea of where she was going.

A HEART ON A CHAIN

Afterwards, of course, she calmed down a bit. Probably a chance passer-by had simply been sheltering from the storm under the arch of the gates. Genghis Khan was a terrifying man, but not a ubiquitous devil.

But what if it really had been him? Should she not warn Erast about the danger?

She hesitated for a while before deciding not to. If she told Fandorin everything, as a man of honour, he would start watching over his beloved, and would refuse to leave her alone. And then Iskander would be certain to find out about their relationship. Eliza would never survive yet another loss, especially one *like this*.

She allowed herself one indulgence: she dreamed a bit about how everything could have worked out for them, if it weren't for her bad karma (she had gleaned that croaking Japanese word from the play). Ah, what a couple they would have made! A famous actress and a dramatist who, though no longer young, was insanely talented. Like Olga Knipper and Chekhov, only they wouldn't have parted, but lived together happily for a long, long time – until they were old. Eliza didn't go on to dream about old age, though. Oh, bother that!

That was another reason why she couldn't put Erast's life at risk: her responsibility to literature and the theatre. A man who had never taken up the pen before and then suddenly created a masterpiece – yes, yes, a masterpiece! – could become a new Shakespeare! Let Mephistov pull a wry face and whisper that this little play was convenient for Stern's theory, but there was nothing else interesting about it. He was simply furious that he had been handed a skimpy little role, the most disagreeable of all. A play that was dictated by love could not help but be great! And there was no greater homage for a woman than to be an artist's inspiration, his muse. Who would remember a girl called Laura, that little girl Beatrice or the frivolous Anna Kern if not for the great works dedicated to them? Thanks to Eliza Lointaine, a glorious new name would shine in the firmament of dramatic art. So how could she allow it to be extinguished because of her?

She took a grip on herself and chained up her poor heart. The next day, when Fandorin came rushing to see her in order to discover what was wrong, Eliza was reserved and even cold with him. She pretended not to understand why he addressed her in such a familiar manner. She made it clear that what had happened the day before had been cancelled out. It quite simply *had not happened* – and that was all there was to it.

She only had to hold out for the first two minutes. Eliza knew that as a proud man he would not start trying to clarify their relationship, let alone pursuing her. And she was right. After two minutes Fandorin turned deadly pale, lowered his eyes and chewed on his lips as he struggled with himself. When he looked up again, the expression of his eyes was completely different – as if someone had closed the curtains tightly.

'Well then, goodbye,' he said. 'I shall not trouble you again.' And he left.

God only knew how she managed not to burst into tears. She was only saved by an actor's habit of controlling the external expression of her feelings.

After that he stopped coming to the rehearsals. In fact, there was no particular need for him to come. All the questions about the Land of the Rising Sun could be answered by the Japanese, who took his work with exemplary seriousness: he arrived before everyone else and left after everyone else, and proved to be exceptionally diligent. Noah Noaevich could not have been more delighted with him.

All in all, getting rid of Fandorin had proved even easier that Eliza thought. She even felt rather annoyed about it. Arriving at the theatre at eleven, she kept waiting to see whether he would show up, and summoning up the inner strength to be firm. But Erast didn't come and the effort of summoning was wasted. Eliza was suffering. She consoled herself with the thought that it was all for the best and the pain would be blunted in time.

Working on her part helped her a lot. There were so many interesting things about it! It turned out that Japanese women, and especially geishas, walked differently from European women and bowed differently, and they spoke and sang and danced in special ways. Eliza imagined herself as a living embodiment of the most elegant of the arts, a devoted acolyte of 'yugen', the Japanese ideal of unmanifest beauty. It was not easy to grasp this concept: what was the point of Beauty if it concealed itself from sight and shrouded itself in veils?

Noah Noaevich spouted new ideas every day like a fountain. He suddenly started restyling the already complete design of the play: 'Since the play is written for a puppet theatre, let's play it in puppet style!' he declared. 'The actors not involved in a scene put on black robes and turn into puppeteers. They seem to lead a character about, tugging on his strings.' And he demonstrated a jerky style of movements. 'The point is that the characters are puppets in the hands of karma, of implacable Fate. But at a certain moment, Eliza, your puppet suddenly snaps its strings and starts moving like a living person. That will be spectacular!'

During the breaks, emerging from the enchanted onstage condition in which one feels neither fear nor pain, Eliza seemed to clench up tight as the appalling burden of reality descended on her with all its dead, dusty weight. The phantom of Genghis Khan hovered in the dark depths of the wings, murdered love scraped at her heart with a cat's sharp claws, and if she went out into the corridor, there was a dead maple leaf sticking to the windowpane – autumn, probably the last autumn of her life . . .

The only breath of air during these unavoidable intervals in work were her conversations with Fandorin junior. Naturally, Eliza didn't dare to demonstrate her interest in Erast Petrovich too clearly, she had to restrain herself, but even so, every now and then, between the discussions of Japanese bits and pieces, she managed to direct the conversation to more important matters.

132

'But you have been married?' Eliza asked one day when Mikhail Erastovich happened for some reason to mention that he was a bachelor.

'No,' the Japanese replied with a joyful smile. He smiled joyfully almost all the time, even when there was no apparent reason for it.

'And your . . . stepfather?' she went on casually. As a matter of fact, she still hadn't discovered in what circumstances Erast had acquired such an unusual stepson. Perhaps as a result of marriage with a Japanese woman? She decided to investigate that subject later.

Mikhail Erastovich thought for a bit, thought again and replied:

'Not to my recorrection.'

'Have you known him for a long time?'

'More than cirty years,' the Japanese said radiantly. Eliza had already grown accustomed to his imperfectly pronounced but entirely understandable and almost correct Russian.

She cheered up a bit at that: so Erast (he was about forty-five, wasn't he?) had never been married. For some reason she felt glad about that.

'Why hasn't he ever married?' she asked, pursuing the theme.

The round face of the Japanese took on a serious expression. He rubbed the stubble on the top of his head (Stern had ordered him not to shave his head for the show, it was unromantic).

'He was unabur to find a woman worthy of him. That is what he tord me many times.'

'Well, well, what high self-opinion!' A caustic note crept into Eliza's voice. 'And did he try very hard?'

'He tried very hard,' Mikhail Erastovich confirmed. 'Many women wished to marry him. He tried and he tried – he used to ask me: What do you cink, Masa? No, I said, she is not worthy. He agreed. He orways ristens to what I say.'

Eliza sighed and took note of that.

'So he tried a lot of women?'

'Very many! There were genuine princesses, there were revorutionaries. Some women were rike andjers, others were worse than the devir.'

'Beautiful?' she asked, forgetting about caution. The conversation had turned out too enthralling altogether.

Masa (that name suited him better, she thought, than 'Mikhail Erastovich') grimaced in a strange manner.

'My master has sutrange taste,' he said, and then, seeming suddenly to recall something, he corrected himself. 'Very beautifur.'

And he even demonstrated exactly how beautiful they were: with a huge bust, full sides, immensely wide hips and tiny little eyes.

Fandorin really does have strange passions, Eliza concluded. *He likes big women, I'm not to his taste at all.*

At that point she started pondering and became sad, and the conversation ended. Eliza didn't even ask why Masa called Fandorin 'master'.

On closer acquaintance, however, it emerged that not all information acquired from the Japanese should be taken on trust. Her stage partner proved to be no novice when it came to telling a few fibs, or at least fantasising a little.

When, following some complicated manoeuvring, Eliza once again succeeded in directing the conversation to the subject of Erast and asked what he actually did, Masa replied briefly.

'He rescues.'

'Whom does he rescue?' she asked, astounded.

'Whoever he has to, he rescues them. Sometimes he rescues his homerand.'

'Who?'

'His homerand. Mother Russia. He has saved it about ten times arready. And he has saved the whore worrd three or four times,' Masa declared, dumbfounding her and continuing to glow with his usual smile.

Well now, Eliza said to herself. *It could well be that the information about the princesses and revolutionaries is from the same category.*

September came to an end. The city turned yellow and was pervaded with a smell of tears, sadness and nature's dying. How well this matched the condition of her own soul! At night Eliza hardly slept at all. She just lay there with her hands set behind her head. The pale orange rectangle on the ceiling, a projection of the window illuminated by a street lamp, looked like a cinema screen, and on it she saw Genghis Khan and Erast Petrovich, the geisha Izumi and the

Japanese assassins, pale images of the past and the blackness of the future.

During the second night of the month of October the regular 'screening' concluded in a sudden shock.

As usual, she was running through the events of the day and the course of today's rehearsal. She counted the number of days since she had seen Fandorin (an entire fifteen!) and sighed. Then she smiled, recalling the latest scandal in the theatre company. Someone had played the hooligan again and written an idiotic entry in the 'Tablets': 'SEVEN 1S UNTIL THE BENEFIT PERFORMANCE'. No one knew when it had appeared – they hadn't looked into the log for a long time, since there were no performances. But then some 'phenomenal aphorism' had occurred to Stern and he opened the book – and there were the scribbles in indelible pencil on the page for 2 October. The director threw a hysterical fit. His target was the venerable Vasilisa Prokofievna, who had only just recalled what magnificent benefit performances she used to have in the old days: with silver trays, and grandiloquent addresses, and box-office takings of thousands. Only Noah Noaevich could possibly have imagined Reginina secretly slavering over the indelible pencil and vandalising the sacred book with those crooked letters. How amusingly he had pounced on her! And how thunderously she had expressed her outrage! 'Don't you dare to insult me with your suspicions! I'll never set foot in this den of iniquity again!'

Suddenly two immense black legs appeared, aimlessly swinging to and fro, on the 'ceiling screen' that Eliza was watching. She squealed and jerked upright on the bed. It was a moment before she thought of looking in the direction of the window. And when she did look, her fear turned to fury.

The legs were not chimerical, but perfectly genuine, in cavalry boots and jodhpurs. They were descending slowly, with a sword scabbard beating against them; then came a hitched-up hussar's jacket and finally Cornet Limbach *in toto*, lowering himself down on a rope. He hadn't shown up for two weeks after the previous incident – no doubt he had been sitting in the guardhouse. But now here he was back again, out of the blue.

This time the brat had prepared more thoroughly for his invasion.

Standing on the windowsill, he took out a screwdriver or some other tool (Eliza couldn't see it very well) and started fiddling with the window frame. The closed catch grated quietly and started turning.

This was just the last straw!

Jumping up off the bed, Eliza repeated the same trick as the last time: she pushed opened the window flaps. But this time the result was different. While he was twisting his screwdriver or whatever it was that he had, Limbach must have loosened his grip on the rope, or perhaps he had let go of it completely. In any case, he cried out pitifully at the sudden blow, turned a somersault in mid-air and went flying downwards.

Transfixed with horror, Eliza leaned out over the windowsill, expecting to see a motionless body on the pavement (after all, it was a high first floor, a good fifteen feet), but the cornet proved as agile as a cat and landed on all fours. Spotting the empress of his heart leaning out of the window, he pressed his hands imploringly to his breast.

'To fall to my death at your feet is happiness!' he shouted out in a ringing voice.

Eliza laughed despite herself and closed the window.

However, things could not go on like this. She would have to swap rooms with someone after all. But with whom?

It could be with Comedina. The 'leading boy' was always given the worst accommodation. And if Limbach climbed in the window again, Zoya, tiny little thing that she was, would still be able to see him off. If she wanted to, of course, Eliza thought slyly. And if she didn't want to, then two birds would be killed with one stone: Zoya would have her amusement, and the little officer would leave Eliza alone.

She spluttered with laughter as she imagined the brash cornet's amazement when he discovered the substitution. And there was probably no need to warn Zoya. It would turn out more interesting that way – a little scene from the *commedia dell'arte*. It was only one short step from the appalling to the comic in life.

Only was there a mirror in Zoya's little kennel? She could ask to have the one here moved.

Eliza couldn't live in a room without any mirrors. If she didn't look at herself at least once every two or three minutes, she got the feeling that she didn't really exist. This psychosis, rather common among actresses, goes by the name of 'reflectiomania'.

ACROSS THE PYRENEES

Eliza herself observed the events that transpired in the 'Louvre-Madrid' the following night only in part, and so she had to reconstitute the overall picture from the accounts of eyewitnesses.

It should be mentioned that late that evening the electricity went off in the hotel and the lodging rooms. It was too late to call the electricians and the dramatic events took place either in complete darkness or by the uncertain light of kerosene and candles.

The best place to start is with Zoya Comedina's account.

'I always fall asleep like a cat. As soon as my head touches the pillow, I'm gone. And this was an imperial bed, you could say. A bed of swan's down! Pillows of angels' feathers! And before that I lounged in a hot bath to my heart's content. Anyway, there I am, sleeping sweetly and dreaming that that I'm a frog, sitting in a swamp and it's warm and damp there, but I'm lonely. I swallow unappetising mosquitoes and croak. What are you laughing at, Eliza? It's true, honestly! Suddenly – thwack! – an arrow thrusts itself into the ground. And then I realise that I'm not just any amphibian, I'm a frog-princess, and now a handsome prince will appear to get his arrow back. If I grab hold of that arrow and hold on tight, it will bring me good fortune.

'The prince immediately appears and puts me on the palm of his hand. "Oh," he says, "how green you are and how pretty! And what wonderful little warts you have! Let me give you a kiss!" And he really does kiss me, hotly and passionately.

'Then I suddenly wake up and what do you think? The prince isn't a prince, but some fop or other with a little moustache and he's panting into my face and slavering my lips with kisses. Oh, did I yell! He tried to put his hand over my mouth – and I sank my teeth into his finger.

'I sat up and I was going to yell again, only when I looked, I saw I knew him. That cornet of hussars. The one who showers you with flowers. The window was wide open and there were tracks on the windowsill.

'So he looks at me and waves his finger about, with his face all twisted.

'"Who are you?" he hisses. "Where did you come from?"

'With my short hair, he took me for a boy.

'I say to him: "No, where did *you* come from?"

'He puts his fist up against my nose. "Where is she?" he whispers. "Where's my Eliza? Tell me, you little devil!" And then he goes and twists my ear, the rotten beast.

'I got frightened. "She's moved to the Madrid, to room number ten," I said. I don't know why I said that. I just blurted out the first thing that came into my head. Word of honour! What are you laughing at? Don't you believe me? Well, you should. Why didn't I kick up a rumpus when he left? Well, I was really frightened, I couldn't even catch my breath. Honest to God.'

No witnesses were found to the bold cornet's traversal of the dark Pyrenean corridors from the Louvre to Madrid, so the next episode of the drama was played out directly in room number ten.

'I don't know how the miscreant managed to open the door without waking me up. I'm a very light sleeper, I wake up at the slightest stirring of the air . . . Don't lie, Lev Spiridonovich, I have never snored. And anyway, how would you know how I sleep now? Thank God, it's a very long time since you kept me company. I want him to go out. I won't tell the story with him here!

'. . . And through my light doze I hear someone whispering: "Queen, Empress, ruler of heaven and earth! I am ablaze with passion at the aroma of your perfume". I should mention that at night

I always perfume myself with "Fleur de Lys". And then someone starts kissing me on the neck and the cheek, and presses his lips against mine. Naturally, I decided that I was dreaming. And what point is there in being shy in a dream? And then, since there are no men around, I ask you, which of us wouldn't like to have a dream like that? Well, naturally, I fling my arms open to embrace this miraculous reverie . . . Stop giggling, or I won't tell you!

'Now it all happened in pitch darkness, note, so I couldn't even recognise that despicable boy . . .

'But when he turned brazen and tried to take the kind of liberties that I don't permit myself even in dreams, I finally realised that this wasn't a dream, but an absolutely genuine assault on my honour. I pushed the blackguard off, and he fell onto the floor. I started shouting. And that disgusting Limbach, realising that his intentions had been foiled, ran off into the corridor.'

Whereas Zoya's story inspired absolute trust (apart from her directing the villain to room number ten by accident), Reginina's story required a few corrections. Otherwise it was hard to explain why she took so long to shout out to the rest of Madrid and why Limbach had suddenly become 'despicable' and 'disgusting' to her, although previously she had been well disposed towards him.

It was far more probable that Limbach, drowning in Vasilisa Prokofievna's monumental corpulence, realised he had come to the wrong place, started floundering about and had broken free, thereby provoking the *grande dame*'s indignant howling.

However that might be, the next point on the night raider's route was known for certain. At the sound of screaming, Sensiblin looked out of room number eight with a lamp in his hand and saw an agitated figure with a sword dangling on its belt running hell for leather along the corridor.

Turning a corner, Limbach ran into Xanthippe Petrovna. She had also stuck her nose out of her room, clad only in her nightshirt and curlers.

This is her story.

*

'I was served a bad turn by my perpetual kind-heartedness. When I heard shouting, I got out of bed and looked out into the corridor, in case someone needed help.

'A young man came dashing towards me. I didn't recognise him immediately as your admirer, Limbach. But he told me he who he was and clasped his hands together imploringly on his chest.

'"Hide me, madam! They're chasing me! If I end up with the police, I'll get at least a month in the guardhouse!"

'You know, I'm always on the side of anyone who's being pursued by the police. So I let him in and bolted the door shut, like a stupid fool!

'And what do you think? That ingrate started molesting me! I tried to make him see reason, I lit the lamp, so he could see that I'm old enough to be his mother. But he was like a madman! He tried to tear off my shirt and chased me round the room, and when I started screaming and calling for help, he bared his sword! I don't know how I'm still alive. In my place anyone else would take the brute to court, and instead of the guardhouse, he'd end up serving hard labour – for attempted rape and murder!'

Of course, there was even less truth in this than in what Vasilisa Prokofievna had said. There was no doubt that Limbach had spent several minutes in Vulpinova's room. It is also possible that he entered the room of his own accord, hoping to sit out the commotion. But as for molestation – that seemed rather doubtful. Most likely Vulpinova herself had tried to solicit his attention, but committed the blunder of lighting the lamp, and the poor cornet was horror-struck at the appearance of his rescuer. It was also entirely possible that he lacked the tact to conceal his revulsion, and Xanthippe Petrovna would most certainly have been insulted by that. Offended and infuriated, she was capable of reducing anyone to fear and trembling. It was easy to imagine that Volodya, already badly frightened, had been obliged to snatch out his sabre – just as D'Artagnan bared his sword when he fled from Her insulted Ladyship.

He had definitely darted out into the corridor with his blade bared. A bevy of agitated actors had already congregated there: Anton Ivanovich Mephistov, Kostya Shiftsky, Sima Aphrodisina and

Nonarikin. At the sight of an armed villain, everyone except the bold Georges hid in their rooms.

By that time these incredible reversals of fortune had rendered Volodya half berserk.

He dashed at the deputy director, brandishing his sabre.

'Where is she? Where is Eliza? Where have you hidden her?'

Georges – a bold heart, but not the brightest of intellects – backed away towards the door of room number three, blocking it off.

'Only over my dead body!'

But it was all one to Limbach at this stage – so be it, over a dead body. He knocked Nonarikin to the floor with a blow of his sword hilt to the forehead and found himself facing the room that had previously been occupied by Zoya.

Subsequent events required no reconstruction, because Eliza had observed them herself and been directly involved.

Exhausted by her chronic lack of sleep, the previous evening she had drunk a tincture of laudanum and slept through the entire ruckus. She was only woken by the loud toing and froing right outside her room. Eliza lit a candle, opened the door – and found herself face to face with Limbach, anguished and crimson-faced from all his running about.

He flung himself at her with tears in his eyes.

'I've found you! My God, all the torments I've suffered!'

Still drowsy and not thinking clearly, she moved out of the way and the cornet evidently took this as an invitation.

'This whole place is full of erotomaniacs!' he complained (these words explain Eliza's subsequent assumptions concerning Reginina and Vulpinova). 'But I love you! Only you!'

The explanation in the doorway of her room was interrupted when Vasya Gullibin came running out from round the corner. He was a heavy sleeper and the last inhabitant of 'Madrid' to wake up.

'Limbach, what are you doing here?' he shouted. 'Leave Eliza alone! Why is Georges on the floor? Did you strike him? I'm going to call Noah Noaevich!'

Then the cornet nimbly darted inside, locking the door behind him. Eliza and he were left alone together. One couldn't exactly say that she was frightened by this. In her time she had seen all sorts of hotheads. Some of them, especially officers and students, had committed worse antics than this. And in any case, Volodya behaved rather meekly. He went down on his knees, dropped his sword on the floor, grasped the hem of her negligee and pressed it reverently to his breast.

'Let me be killed for your sake . . . Let them even throw me out of the regiment . . . My aged parents will never survive it, but even so, there is no life for me without you,' he declaimed rather inarticulately but with true feeling. 'If you spurn me, I shall slit my stomach open, as the Japanese did during the war!'

At the same time his fingers seemingly inadvertently crumpled up the fine silk fabric, so that it gathered into folds, rising higher and higher. The hussar broke off his tearful lament in order to lean down and kiss Eliza on her bare knee – and there he stayed, his kisses creeping higher and higher.

A chilly shudder suddenly ran through her. Not from the shamelessness of his touches, but from a terrible thought that had occurred to her.

What if fate has sent him to me? He is desperate, he is in love. If I tell him about my nightmare, he will simply challenge Genghis Khan to a duel and kill him. And I shall be free!

But immediately she felt ashamed. To risk the boy's life for egotistical considerations of her own was a shameful idea.

'Stop,' she said in a weak voice, putting her hands on his shoulders (Limbach's head was already completely hidden under the negligee). 'Get up. I need to talk to you . . .'

She herself did not know how it would all have ended: whether she would have had the courage or, on the contrary, the cowardice to embroil the boy in a deadly intrigue.

Things never reached the stage of an explanation.

The door was torn off its hinges by a mighty blow. The hotel doorman, Gullibin and Nonarikin – with a crimson lump on his forehead and his eyes blazing – jostled in the doorway. They were moved aside by Noah Noaevich, who ran an outraged gaze over the indecent scene. Eliza smacked Limbach in the teeth with her knee.

'Get out from under there!'

The cornet got up, tucked his cold weapon under his arm, ducked under the outstretched arms of the doorman and darted out into the corridor, howling: 'I love you! I love you!'

'Leave us,' Stern ordered.

His eyes hurled lightning bolts.

'Eliza, I was mistaken in you. I regarded you as a woman of the highest order, but you take the liberty . . .' And so on and so forth.

She didn't listen, but just looked down at the toes of her slippers.

Terrible? Yes. Shameful? Yes. But it is more forgivable to risk the life of a stupid little officer than the life of a great dramatist. Even if the duel were to end with Limbach being killed, Genghis Khan would still disappear from my life. He would go to prison, or flee to his khanate, or to Europe – it doesn't matter where. I would be free. We would be free! This happiness can be paid for with a crime . . . Or can it?

Five 1s

UNTIL THE BENEFIT
PERFORMANCE

FISHING WITH LIVE BAIT

Some wise man, Erast Petrovich thought it was La Rochefoucauld, had said that very few people know how to be old. Fandorin had assumed that he belonged to that happy minority – and he had turned out to be mistaken.

Where has the rational, dignified equilibrium disappeared to? Where are you, calm and liberty, detachment and harmony?

Fandorin's own heart had played him a trick that he had never expected. Life had been turned upside down, and all the immutable values had been reduced to dust. He felt twice as young as before and three times as stupid. The latter assertion was perhaps not entirely true. His intellect seemed to have deviated from its established course and lost its singleness of purpose, but it had retained its perpetual acuity, relentlessly noting all the stages and twists and turns of his illness.

At the same time, Fandorin was not certain that what was happening to him should be considered an illness. Perhaps, on the contrary, he had recovered his health.

It was a philosophical question, and he was helped in finding the answer to it by the very best of philosophers – Kant. The philosopher had been sickly from the day he was born, he was constantly unwell and this distressed him very badly, until one fine day the sage was struck by the excellent idea of regarding his sickly condition as good health. Being unwell was normal, there was nothing here to be sad about, *das ist Leben*. And if it suddenly happened that nothing was hurting in the morning – that was a gift of fate. And life was immediately filled with the light of joy.

Fandorin acted in similar fashion. He stopped obstinately setting his reason and his heart at odds. If this was love, so be it, let it be considered a normal state of soul.

He immediately felt slightly better. At least an end had been put to his inner discord. Erast Petrovich had enough reasons for torment without self-flagellation.

Falling in love with an actress was a truly heavy cross to bear – a thought to which Fandorin's mind returned a hundred times a day.

With her he could never be sure of anything. Apart from the fact that in the next moment she would be different from the way she was in the previous one. Now cold, now passionate, now false, now sincere, now sweetly clinging, now spurning! The first phase of their relationship, which had lasted only a few days, had made him think that Eliza, despite her actress's affectation, was nonetheless a normal, real, live woman. But how could he explain what had happened at Cricket Lane? Had it really happened, that explosion of devastating passion, or had he imagined it? Did it really happen that a woman flung herself into a man's arms and then ran away – and ran in terror, even revulsion? What had he done wrong? Oh, Erast Petrovich would have paid dearly to receive an answer to the question that was tormenting him. Pride did not permit him to ask. Present himself in the pitiful role of a petitioner, a *quibbler* over feelings? Never!

In fact, everything was clear enough anyway. The question was rhetorical.

Eliza was firstly an actress, and secondly a woman. A professional enchantress, who needed powerful effects, emotional rupture, morbid passions. The sudden shift in her behaviour was dual in nature; firstly, she had taken fright at a serious relationship and didn't wish to lose her freedom, and secondly, of course, she wanted to get him more securely fastened on the hook. Such paradoxical motivation was typical for women of the theatrical caste.

He was a wise old bird and he had seen all sorts of things, including the eternal female game of cat-and-mouse. And he had seen it performed with greater skill. In the art of binding a man to herself, a European actress was no match for an experienced Japanese courtesan with a command of *jyojutsu*, the 'skill of passion'.

But although he understood this uncomplicated game perfectly well, he succumbed to it nonetheless and suffered, and his suffering was genuine. Self-reproach and logic were no help.

And then Erast Petrovich started trying to convince himself that he was very lucky. There was a stupid saying: 'If you want to fall in love, then love a queen'. But a queen was some kind of nonsense, she wasn't even a woman at all, but a walking set of ceremonial conventions. If you wanted to fall in love, then love a great actress.

She embodied the eternally elusive beauty of *yugen*. She was not one woman, but ten, even twenty: Juliet and the Distant Princess, Ophelia and the Maid of Orleans and Marguerite Gauthier. To conquer the heart of a great actress was very difficult, almost impossible, but if you succeeded, it was like conquering the love of all the heroines at once. And if you failed to conquer, nonetheless you loved the very best women in the world all at once. You would have to devote your entire life to the struggle for requited feelings. For even if you did win the victory, it would never be final. There would be no relaxation and peace – but who had ever said that that was a bad thing? Genuine life *was* this eternal trepidation, and not at all the walls that he had built round himself when he decided to grow old correctly.

Following the break-up, after having denied himself any possibility of seeing Eliza, he frequently recalled one conversation with her. Ah, how well they had spoken together during that brief, happy period! He remembered that he had asked her what it meant to be an actress. And she had answered.

'I'll tell you what it is to be an actress. It is to experience perpetual hunger – hopeless, insatiable hunger! A hunger so immense that no one can assuage it, no matter how greatly they love me. The love of one man will never be enough for me. I need the love of the whole world – all the young men, and all the old men, and all the children, and all the horses and cats and dogs and, most difficult of all, the love of all the women too, or at least most of them. I look at a waiter in a restaurant and I smile at him in a way that will make him love me. I stroke a dog and I tell it: love me. I walk into a hall full of people and I think: "Here I am, love me!" I am the unhappiest and the happiest person in the world. The unhappiest, because it is impossible to be loved by everyone. The happiest, because I live in constant anticipation, like someone in love before a tryst. This sweet ache, this torment is my happiness . . .'

At that moment she had been straining her ability to be sincere to its very limit.

Or had it been a monologue from some play?

But feelings were one thing, and work was another. The vicissitudes of love must not interfere with the investigation. That is, they quite definitely did interfere, periodically stirring up his line of deduction and obfuscating its clarity, but they did not distract Fandorin from his investigative activities. The viper in the basket of flowers was more like some piece of villainy out of an operetta, but a premeditated murder was no joke. Concern for the woman he loved and, when it came down to it, his civic duty, required that he expose the treacherous criminal. The Moscow Police were free to come to any conclusions at all (Erast Petrovich's opinion of their professional abilities was not very high), but he personally had no doubt at all that Emeraldov had been poisoned.

That had become clear on the very first evening, in the course of his nocturnal visit to the theatre. Not that Fandorin had suspected from the very first that something was amiss with the suicide of the leading man – not in the least. But since another event that was both ominous and hard to explain had occurred in Eliza's immediate vicinity, he had to get to the bottom of it.

What had become clear?

The actor had remained behind in the theatre because he had an appointment to meet someone or other. That was one.

He was in a wonderful mood, which is strange for someone intending to commit suicide. That was two.

Thirdly. The goblet from which, according to the police report, Emeraldov had voluntarily drunk poison had, naturally, been taken away by the investigator. However, the polished surface of the table bore marks from *two* goblets. So the actor had received his unknown visitor after all, and they had drunk wine.

Fourthly. Judging from the marks, one of the goblets was intact, but the other had a slight leak. The first had left behind rings of water, the second had left rings of wine. Obviously, before the stage-prop goblets were used, they had been rinsed under the tap and not wiped dry. And then a little wine had seeped out of the second one.

Erast Petrovich had taken away dried-out particles of the red liquid for analysis. There had not been any poison in the wine. So the presumptive murderer had drunk out of the goblet that had disappeared. That was five.

The next day the picture had become even clearer. The following morning, once again employing the useful method known as 'greasing the palm', Fandorin had gained entrance to the properties room with the help of an usher. Or rather, the usher had simply shown him where the room was located and Erast Petrovich had opened the door himself, with the help of an elementary picklock.

And what had he found? The second tin goblet was standing on the shelf perfectly calmly, beside the crowns, jugs, dishes and other properties from *Hamlet*. Fandorin immediately recognised the item he was looking for from its description: it was the only one there like it, with an eagle and a snake on its hinged lid. Judging from the dust, some little time ago two goblets had stood here. On the evening of the murder, Emeraldov had taken them directly from the stage, and then someone (presumably the murderer) had returned only one to its place. Examination through a powerful magnifying glass had revealed the microscopic crack through which the wine had seeped out. And in addition, it was clear that the goblet had been well washed, and as a result, unfortunately, no fingerprints were left.

Nonetheless, half the job had been done. The list of suspects had been drawn up. All that remained was to infiltrate that circle, in order to identify the murderer.

Another day went by and everything had arranged itself in ideal fashion. There would be no more need to act by stealth or bribe attendants. The play about the two comets had been accepted for production and Fandorin had become an acknowledged member of the company. A genuinely fortunate coincidence of civic duty and personal interest.

During the rehearsal, after asking various different people a few apparently casual questions, he had discovered the most important thing: who in the company had unlimited access to the properties room at any time of the day or night. The list of suspects had immediately shrunk to a minimum. The stores of stage properties, accessories and costumes were managed by the director's assistant, Nonarikin. He took his responsibilities very seriously, never gave the keys to anyone and always accompanied everyone who needed to take anything out of storage. It was easiest of all for him to have returned the goblet to its place.

But there was one man in the company who would not have needed Nonarikin's sanction – the manager of the theatre. In order to discover whether Stern had taken the key from his assistant, Fandorin would have had to ask questions, and that was not a good idea, so he decided to keep them both under suspicion.

The third subject had been added almost accidentally. In the Japanese play the 'rogue' Shiftsky had been given the part of Kinjo, a pickpocket, or rather, putting it more correctly, a 'pick-sleeve', since Japanese clothes were not equipped with any pockets and valuable items were usually kept in the sleeves. Kostya had played a pickpocket in a play based on *Oliver Twist*, and at the time he had studied that difficult craft assiduously in order to appear convincing on stage. And now, recalling the old days, the young man had yielded to the imp of mischief and decided to demonstrate his skill. During the break he rubbed up against one, two, three people and later chuckled as he returned Reginina's purse, Nonarikin's handkerchief and Mephistov's bottle of some kind of medicine. Vasilisa Prokofievna good-naturedly called the artful dodger a 'scallywag', Nonarikin simply blinked, but Anton Ivanovich created an uproar, shouting that a decent man would never go rummaging through other people's pockets even as a joke.

After this comical incident Fandorin added Shiftsky to his mental list too. Shiftsky had taken Nonarikin's handkerchief, so he could have taken the key.

A day later a rather simple operation in the old detective genre of 'fishing with live bait' had been conceived and put into action.

During the afternoon Erast Petrovich had paid a stealthy visit to the properties room, once again resorting to the picklock. He placed his Bure chronometer beside the goblet. Turning round on hearing a rustling sound, he saw a large rat sitting on the shelf to his left and observing him with contemptuous equanimity.

'We'll m-meet again soon,' Fandorin told the rat, and walked out.

Later, when at five o'clock everybody was drinking tea from the samovar (yet another tradition), the conversation turned to Emeraldov again and the actors started guessing what misfortune had made him decide to depart this life.

As if he were thinking out loud, but nonetheless speaking loudly, Erast Petrovich had drawled:

'Suicide? I rather think not . . .'

Everyone had turned towards him.

'But what was it, if not suicide?' Gullibin asked in amazement.

'I'll answer that question for you soon,' Fandorin had said confidently. 'I have a few conjectures. Actually, not even conjectures, but facts. Don't ask me about anything yet. I shall know for certain tomorrow.'

Eliza (this was still the very beginning of their relationship) rebuked him.

'Stop talking in riddles! What have you found out?'

'Is it from the realm of clairvoyance?' Stern asked entirely seriously, without even the slightest irony. (His cheek twitched in a nervous tick. Or had Fandorin imagined that?)

Mephistov stood with his back to Fandorin and didn't look round. That was strange – had his interest really not been piqued by such a tantalising subject?

Two cups of tea were standing in front of Erast Petrovich. He picked them up in his hands, looked at one, then at the other, and pensively repeated Claudius's line as Gertrude drinks poison in front of him:

'"It is the poisoned. cup. It is too late . . ." Yes, that is exactly what happened, two goblets, and in one of them d-death . . .'

He deliberately pronounced these words in a barely audible voice, almost a whisper. In order to make them out, the murderer would have to move close or crane his neck. An excellent method, invented by the Prince of Denmark in the 'mousetrap' scene. Once the suspects have been ascertained, it is not hard to follow their reactions.

Stern hadn't heard anything – he had started talking to Sensiblin about something else. Mephistov still hadn't turned round. But the director's assistant had leaned bodily towards Fandorin and his strange smile had suddenly seemed more like a grimace.

That's the entire investigation, Erast Petrovich thought, with a slight twinge of regret. *We've had to deal with trickier charades than that.*

He could, of course, have taken the criminal to task there and then, there was enough circumstantial evidence. A possible motive could also be postulated. But to anyone unacquainted with the theatrical milieu, the theory would seem fantastic. The justice system would hardly believe in it either, especially since the evidence was circumstantial through and through.

So the criminal would have to be caught dead to rights, so that he couldn't squirm out of it.

Well then, let us proceed to the third act.

Erast Petrovich reached into his waistcoat pocket.

'Oh, what's this! Where's my c-chronometer. Ladies and gentlemen, has anyone seen it? A gold "Pavel Bure"? And it has a special fob, a magnifying glass.'

Naturally, no one had seen the watch, but most of the actors, wishing to help the dramatist, immediately started looking for it. They glanced under chairs and asked Erast Petrovich to remember whether he could have left the chronometer in the buffet or, begging his pardon, in the water closet.

'Ah yes, in the propert . . .' – then he suddenly checked himself and started coughing.

An extremely primitive little interlude, played out for a fool. But in all honesty, it must be said that Erast Petrovich was not inclined to overestimate the intellectual abilities of his opponent.

'Never mind, don't c-concern yourselves, ladies and gentlemen, I've remembered where I left it,' he announced. 'I'll collect it later. It's safe enough where it is.'

Nonarikin behaved so much like the caricature villain in some provincial production, it was almost grotesque. He came out in red blotches, chewed on his lips and kept throwing furious glances at Erast Petrovich.

Fandorin did not have to wait long.

The rehearsal came to an end and the actors started going their separate ways.

Erast Petrovich deliberately dawdled. He sat down, crossed his legs and lit up a cigar. Eventually he was left on his own. But even then he didn't hurry. Let the criminal's nerves suffer a bit, let him languish in suspense.

The building was absolutely quiet now. Probably it was time.

THE JUDGEMENT OF FATE

He went out onto the stairs and walked down to the service floor. The dead-end corridor, onto which the doors of storerooms and workshops opened, was dark.

Fandorin stopped in front of the properties room and jerked on the door handle. It was locked – from the inside, he presumed.

He opened the door with the picklock. Inside it the darkness was pitch black. Erast Petrovich could have switched on the electric light, but he wanted to make the criminal's task easier for him. The strip of pale light seeping in from the corridor was entirely adequate for him to walk over to the shelf and pick up the watch that he had left there.

As he walked through the darkness, expecting an attack at any moment, Fandorin felt a slight prick of shame at the extreme pleasure of his excitement: his pulse was beating out a drum tattoo, his skin was covered with goosebumps. This was the real reason why he hadn't backed this home-grown Borgia up against the wall, why he hadn't tangled him up in the chain of evidence. Erast Petrovich wanted to shake himself up, refresh himself, set the blood coursing through his veins. Love, danger, the anticipation of victory – this was genuine life, and old age could wait.

He wasn't taking much of a risk. Not unless the criminal decided to shoot, but that was not very likely. Firstly, the watchman would hear and call the police. Secondly, judging from the impression that Fandorin had formed of the director's assistant, this 'poor man's Lermontov', as Stern had called him so accurately and pitilessly, Nonarikin would choose some more theatrical method.

Nonetheless, Erast Petrovich's hearing was stretched to the limit, prepared to catch the quiet click of a firing hammer being raised. It wasn't so very easy to hit a fast-moving black cat in a dark room (Fandorin was wearing a black suit today).

He had already determined the killer's location from a very faint rustling that he heard coming from the right-hand corner. No one but Fandorin, who in his time had made a special study of listening to silence, would have attached any importance to that sound, but Erast Petrovich immediately recognised it as the rustle of fabric against fabric. The man waiting in ambush had raised his hand. What was in it? A cold weapon? Something blunt and heavy? Or was it a revolver after all, and the hammer had been raised in advance?

Just to be on the safe side, Fandorin took a rapid step to one side, out of the greyish strip of light and into the darkness. He started whistling Alyabiev's romance 'Nightingale, My Nightingale' in a special way, shifting his lips to one side and pursing them up. If the criminal was taking aim, he would have the illusion that his target was standing one step farther to the left.

Come on now, Monsieur Nonarikin. Be bold! Your victim suspects nothing. Attack!

However, there was a surprise in store for Erast Petrovich. A switch clicked and the properties room was flooded with light that was very bright by contrast with the darkness. There now, so that was why the assistant director had raised his hand.

It was him, naturally – with his forelock tousled and his eyes glinting feverishly. Fandorin's powers of deduction had not let him down. But even so, there was yet another surprise, apart from the light. Nonarikin was holding in his hand not a knife, not an axe, not some vulgar kind of hammer, but two rapiers with cup-shaped hilts. They had previously been lying one shelf below the goblet – stage props from the same show.

'Very impressive,' said Erast Petrovich, clapping his hands silently. 'It's a pity that there's no audience.'

There was one spectator, however: Fandorin's acquaintance, the rat, was sitting in its former position with its little eyes glittering in fury. No doubt from the rat's point of view they were both ignorant louts who had impudently invaded its private domain.

The assistant director blocked off the way out of the room. For some reason he was holding out the rapiers with the handles forward.

'Why d-did you switch on the light? It would have been easier in the dark.'

'It's against my principles to attack from behind. I'm offering you up to the judgement of Fate, you false playwright. Choose your weapon and defend yourself!'

Nonarikin was strange. Calm, one could even say solemn. Exposed murderers didn't behave like that. And what was this fairground burlesque with stage weapons? What was the point of it?

Even so, Fandorin took a rapier, the one that was closer to hand, without examining them. He glanced briefly at the point. You couldn't stick that through a man, but you might just scratch him with it. Or raise a lump on his head if you took a good swing.

Erast Petrovich had not yet assumed a defensive posture (that is, he had not even decided yet whether to participate in this charade) when his opponent launched into the attack with a cry of '*Gardez-vous!*', making a rapid lunge. If Fandorin had not possessed outstandingly fast reactions, the rapier would have pricked him straight in the chest, but Erast Petrovich swayed to one side. Even so the rapier tip tore through his sleeve and scratched his skin.

'*Touché!*' Nonarikin exclaimed, shaking the drop of blood off the blade. 'You're a dead man!'

An excellent frock coat had been completely ruined, and the shirt together with it. Erast Petrovich ordered his clothes from London and he was dreadfully angry.

It should be said that he fenced rather well. Once in his youth he had almost lost his life in a sabre duel and after that incident he had taken care to fill this dangerous gap in his education. Fandorin moved onto the attack, cascading blows on his opponent. *So you want some fun? Then take that!*

Incidentally, from the psychological point of view, one sure way to crush your opponent's will is to defeat him in some kind of competition.

Nonarikin was under serious pressure, but he defended himself skilfully. Only once did Erast Petrovich succeed in striking the assistant director a serious blow to the forehead with the length of the blade, and once he caught him on the neck with a slashing blow. Backing away under the onslaught, the assistant director gaped in ever greater amazement at Fandorin, who was pale with fury. Nonarikin evidently hadn't expected this kind of sprightliness from the playwright.

Right, that's enough playing the fool, Erast Petrovich told himself. *Finiamo la commedia.*

With a double thrust he hooked up his opponent's weapon, performed a twist – and the rapier went flying into the farthest corner. Forcing Nonarikin back against the wall with his blade, Fandorin said scathingly:

'Enough theatre. I suggest a return to the confines of real life. And real death.'

His defeated enemy stood there quite still, squinting downwards at the rapier point pressed against his chest. Beads of sweat glinted on his pale forehead, where the lump was flooding with crimson.

'Only don't stab me,' he gasped hoarsely. 'Kill me some other way.'

'Why would I kill you?'' Fandorin asked in surprise. 'And in any case, that is rather hard to do with a blunt piece of metal. No, my good fellow, you will serve hard labour. For cold-blooded, villainous murder.'

'What are you talking about? I don't understand.'

Erast Petrovich frowned.

'My dear sir, don't try to deny the obvious facts. From a theatrical point of view it will turn out very b-boring. If you did not poison Emeraldov, then why on earth would you arrange an ambush for me?'

The assistant director raised his round brown eyes and started batting his eyelids.

'Are you accusing me of murdering Hippolyte? *Me*?'

For an actor of third-level parts he portrayed astonishment rather well. Erast Petrovich even laughed.

'Who else?'

'But surely you did it, didn't you?'

Fandorin had not often encountered such barefaced insolence. He even felt slightly disconcerted.

'What?'

'But you gave yourself away! Today, during the tea break!' Nonarikin cautiously touched the rapier blade, moving it away from his chest. 'I'd been tormented by doubt since the day before yesterday. A man like Hippolyte couldn't kill himself! It simply doesn't make any sense. He loved himself too much. Then suddenly you started talking about goblets. And it hit me! There was someone there with Hippolyte! Someone drank wine with him. And slipped poison in his drink! I went to the properties room to take a look at the other goblet. And then I saw the Bure watch. It was as if a veil fell from my eyes! It all fitted together! The mysterious Mr Fandorin, who turned up here for no obvious reason, then disappeared and then appeared again – the day after Hippolyte was killed! That slip about the goblets! The lost watch! I guessed that you would come back for it. You know, I'm no great master at solving mysteries, but I believe in the justice of Fate and God's judgement. So I decided that if you came, I would challenge you to a duel. And if Fandorin was the criminal, Fate would punish him. I went to my dressing room, came back here and started waiting for you, and you came. But you're still alive, and now I don't know what to think . . .'

He shrugged in bewilderment.

'Raving nonsense!' Fandorin sniggered. 'Why on earth would I want to kill Emeraldov?'

'Out of jealousy.' Nonarikin gave him a look of weary reproach. 'Emeraldov was pestering her far too openly. And you're in love with her, that's obvious. You've lost your head over her too. Like so many others . . .'

Feeling himself blushing, Fandorin didn't even bother to ask who Nonarikin meant by that and raised his voice.

'We're not talking about me, but you! What was that nonsense you were spouting about the judgement of God? You can't kill anyone with these twigs!'

The assistant director cast a wary look at the blade.

'Yes, it's a stage-prop rapier. But with a precisely directed blow you can pierce the skin with it – I did that with my first thrust.'

'What of it? No one has ever died from a little scratch.'

'It depends what kind of scratch. I told you that I went to get something from my dressing room. I have a medicine chest there, with remedies for every possible occasion. All sorts of things happen in the company, you know. Mr Mephistov has epileptic fits, Vasilisa Prokofievna has the vapours, and there are injuries too. And I'm responsible for everything and everyone. I have to be a jack-of-all-trades. They taught us that in the officers' school: a good commander must know how to do everything.'

'What are you t-telling me this for? What business is your medicine chest of mine?' Fandorin interrupted him irritably, annoyed that the secrets of his heart had been so obvious to an outsider.

'Along with everything else in there I have a little bottle of concentrated venom of the central Asian cobra. I brought it from Turkestan. An indispensable remedy for nervous ailments. Our ladies often suffer very serious hysterics. If Madam Vulpinova gets really carried away, she can go into convulsions. But I just have to put a couple of drops on cotton wool, rub her temples – and it's gone, like magic.' Nonarikin demonstrated how he rubbed the venom into the skin. 'So I got this idea. I smeared the tip of one of the rapiers. The way Laertes did in *Hamlet*. I thought: if Fandorin poisoned Hippolyte, let him die of poison too, it will be God's judgement. The rapiers are absolutely the same to look at, I didn't even know myself which of them was poisoned. So our duel wasn't theatrical at all, it was absolutely, genuinely, to the death. If the venom gets into the blood, the terminal spasms set in after two minutes, and then the breathing is paralysed.'

Erast Petrovich shook his head – this was raving lunacy after all.

'But what if you'd been scratched by the poisoned rapier?'

The assistant director shrugged and replied:

'I told you, I believe in Fate. Those are more than just empty words to me.'

'But I don't believe you!' Fandorin raised the tip of the rapier right up to his eyes. It really did seem to have a damp gleam.

'Careful, don't prick yourself! And if you don't believe me – let me have it.'

Erast Petrovich willingly handed him the weapon, but also lowered his hand into his left pocket, where his revolver lay. This assistant director was a strange individual. It wasn't clear what to expect from him. Was he pretending to be half-witted? Would he attack again now? That would be the simplest finale. Fandorin deliberately turned his back, since he could follow Nonarikin's movements from the shadow on the floor.

The former lieutenant's silhouette swayed, then folded over double at lightning speed, with his outreached arm ending in the thin line of the rapier. Erast Petrovich was prepared for an attack, he jumped to the left and turned round. However, the shadow had misled him. It turned out that Nonarikin had made a thrust in the opposite direction.

With a cry of: 'I lay a ducat that it is dead!' he jabbed the rapier at a rat sitting peacefully on the floor, but didn't run it through, merely pricked it slightly and flung it against the wall. The little beast squealed and darted away, knocking over cardboard goblets and papier-mâché vases.

'You've l-lost your ducat. Now what?' Erast Petrovich asked spitefully. He felt embarrassed about his desperate leap. At least he hadn't pulled out his revolver.

But Nonarikin didn't seem even to have noticed that Fandorin had shied away from him. The assistant director wiped the tip of the blade very cautiously with a handkerchief and started moving out the shelves.

'Feast your eyes on that.'

The rat was lying there belly up, with all four legs twitching.

'On this little animal the venom acted almost instantaneously. I told you, I wanted to punish a murderer. But Fate has acquitted you. You have been purged in my eyes.'

Only at this point did Erast Petrovich really believe that he had escaped an absurd, cruel death by a miracle. If not for his eternal good luck, which had prompted him to choose the poisoned weapon without even pausing for thought, he would be lying on the floor now, like that rat, with his open mouth straining convulsively. It would have been an idiotic death . . .

'M-merci beaucoup. Only you have not yet been purged in my eyes. Afterwards the poisoner brought the second goblet back to the properties room. You are the only one with free access to the properties room. And you also had a motive: Emeraldov had been given the part that you were counting on.'

'If we killed each other over parts, the theatres would have turned into graveyards a long time ago. You have an excessively romantic idea of actors.' Nonarikin actually smiled. 'As for the properties room, I certainly do have the key. But your example shows that it is possible to gain entry without it. And another thing. Do you know when exactly Hippolyte met his killer?'

'I do. The nightwatchman saw him shortly after nine. And according to the post-mortem results, death occurred no later than midnight. I enquired from the police.'

'So the crime was committed some time between shortly after nine and twelve o'clock. Then I have an alibi.'

'What is it?'

Nonarikin hesitated before he replied.

'I would never have said, but I feel guilty for almost having killed you. I repeat, I was certain that you were the poisoner, but now it turns out that you are searching for the poisoner. Fate has acquitted you.'

'Stop talking about Fate!' Erast Petrovich exploded, angry because he realised that he had missed the mark with his theory. 'It gives me the impression that I'm talking to a lunatic!'

'You shouldn't talk like that.' Nonarikin flung out his arms and looked up at the ceiling, or, to use a more solemn expression, raised his eyes to the heavens. 'The man who believes in a Higher Power knows that nothing happens by accident. Especially when it is a matter of life and death. And the man who does not believe in a Higher Power is in no way different from an animal.'

'You said something about an alibi,' Fandorin interrupted him.

The assistant sighed and spoke in an ordinary voice, without any declamatory intonation.

'Naturally, this is strictly between the two of us. Give me your word of honour. It concerns the reputation of a lady.'

'I won't give you any k-kind of word. You were with a woman that evening? With whom?'

'Very well. I rely on your common decency. If you ever tell *her* about it (you understand who I mean), it will be a base and dishonourable act.' Nonarikin hung his head and sighed. 'That evening I left the theatre with Zoya Nikolaevna. We were together until the morning . . .'

'With Comedina?' Erast Petrovich asked after a second's pause: he hadn't understood immediately who Nonarikin meant. No one had ever called the little 'leading boy' by her first name and patronymic in his presence. However, if he was surprised by this confession, it was only for a moment.

'Yes.' The assistant director rubbed his bruised forehead unromantically. 'As Terentius said: "I am human and nothing human is alien to me". You are a man, you will understand me. After all, there are physiological needs. Only don't ask me if I love Zoya Nikolaevna.'

'I won't,' Fandorin promised. 'But I shall definitely have a word with Madam Comedina. And you and I will continue this conversation . . .'

A MILLION TORMENTS

Despite the rather late hour, he drove directly from the theatre to the hotel in his automobile, so that Nonarikin could not get there ahead of him and conspire with Comedina. The precaution was strictly superfluous: Erast Petrovich had no doubt that the alibi would be confirmed, but in a serious case like this every detail had to be checked.

After Fandorin had managed, not without some difficulty, to locate the little actress's room in the Madrid, he apologised to her for this unexpected visit and apologised even more profusely for the bluntness of the question he was about to ask. He had to talk to this young lady without any beating around the bush. And that was what he did.

'It concerns the circumstances of Mr Emeraldov's death,' he said. 'Let us therefore temporarily set aside questions of d-decorum. Tell me, where were you on the evening and the night of 13 September?'

Comedina's freckled features extended into a foolish smile.

'Oho! So you think I look like a woman who could spend the night with someone? That's actually rather flattering.'

'Don't waste time on playing games. I'm in a hurry. Just tell me if you were with Mr Nonarikin. Yes or no? I am not interested in your morals, madam. I simply want to know the t-truth.'

The smile didn't disappear, but every trace of contrived merriment evaporated, leaving the green eyes gazing at this uninvited visitor without any expression at all. It was impossible to guess what the owner of those eyes was thinking. *It's a good thing that Madam Comedina plays children on the theatrical stage, and not in the cinematograph*, Erast Petrovich said to himself. *With an expression like that you couldn't possibly act the part of a child in a close shot.*

'You said today that Emeraldov didn't kill himself,' Comedina said slowly. 'So you have your suspicions . . . And you suspect Georges, am I right?'

Fandorin was familiar with this type of personality. Other people were inclined not to take these individuals seriously, simply because of the way they looked and behaved. And more often than not other people were mistaken about them. Small individuals, regardless of their gender, usually possessed a strong character and were far from stupid.

'I don't know who you really are. And I don't wish to know,' Zoya went on. 'But you can exclude Georges from your calculations. He spent the night on that bed over there.' Without looking round, she jabbed her finger in the direction of the narrow iron bedstead and grinned even more unpleasantly. 'First we abandoned ourselves to sinful passion. Then he slept and I lay beside him, watching. It's a narrow bed but, as you can observe, I don't take up very much space. Are you interested in the details?'

'No.' He lowered his eyes, unable to withstand her glittering gaze. 'I beg your p-pardon, but it was necessary . . .'

After that he examined the rapier taken from the properties room in his home laboratory. Mr Nonarikin proved to be a very thorough individual. A genuine jack-of-all-trades. The point had been smeared with the venom of *naja oxiana*, mixed with animal fat, obviously added so that the toxin would not dry out. An injection of this filthy muck would undoubtedly have resulted in a very rapid and agonising death.

In the morning, before the rehearsal, Fandorin completed his essential check with a visit to the criminal police department, where he was very well known. He asked a question and received an answer. Emeraldov had been killed with a completely different poison – classic cyanide.

On his way to the theatre Erast Petrovich yielded to gloomy thoughts about how he had frittered away his detective skills and how remarkably stupid being in love had made him. Not only had he constructed a mistaken theory, he had also revealed himself to that whimsical eccentric, Georges Nonarikin. He would have to clarify the situation with Nonarikin today, and insist that the assistant director keep his mouth shut – otherwise he could frighten off the real poisoner.

However, he didn't manage to talk to Nonarikin on that day, because Eliza suddenly agreed to go to Cricket Lane with him to choose a kimono, and first the miracle happened, and then the enchantment was shattered, leaving Erast Petrovich alone in a deserted, absolute dead house.

Nonarikin showed up himself in the afternoon of the following day. Fandorin had not left the house since Eliza had fled. He had just remained sitting there in his dressing gown, immersed in a strange lethargy and smoking one cigar after another. Every now and then he suddenly became agitated and started walking round the room, talking to someone invisible, then he sat down, sinking back into immobility. The hair of this habitual stickler for neatness dangled down in loose white locks, his chin was covered with black stubble and below his blue eyes matching blue circles had appeared.

The assistant director presented a stark contrast with the seedy-looking dramatist. When Fandorin finally shuffled feebly to the door in his slippers and opened it (the bell must have been ringing for five or ten minutes), he saw that Monsieur Nonarikin had decked himself out in a new morning coat, buttoned on a gleaming white shirt collar and knotted on a silk necktie, and he was clutching a pair of white gloves in his hand. His officer's moustache jutted out to the sides in bellicose fashion, like two cobras poised to attack.

'I asked Noah Noaevich for your address,' Nonarikin said austerely. 'Since you didn't condescend to spare me any time yesterday and did not even put in an appearance today, I have come to you myself. There are two matters concerning which we need to clear the air.'

He has probably just seen Eliza, was the only thought that occurred to Fandorin when he saw the assistant director.

'Is the rehearsal already over, then?' he asked.

'No. But Mr Stern has let everyone go apart from the two leads. Madam Lointaine and your stepson are rehearsing the love scene. I could have stayed, but I preferred to leave. He is far too eager altogether, this Japanese of yours. It was painful for me to watch it.'

This was a painful topic for Erast Petrovich too and his face contorted in a wry grimace.

'What does that matter to you?'

'I love Madam Lointaine,' Nonarikin declared calmly, as if merely affirming a well-known fact. 'Like many others. Including yourself. I would like to clear the air on this subject.'

'Well, then, c-come in . . .'

They sat down in the drawing room. Georges held his back straight and kept hold of the gloves. *Is he going to challenge me to a duel again?* Fandorin chuckled languidly to himself.

'I'm listening. Please c-continue.'

'Tell me, are your intentions concerning Madam Lointaine honourable?'

'They could not p-possibly be more so.'

Never to see her again and to try to forget her, he added to himself.

'Then as one honourable man to another, I propose an agreement not to resort to any base, deceitful tricks in the contest for her hand. Let her be united in marriage with the one who is more worthy, who will be hallowed by the light of heaven!' Following his penchant for lofty expression, the assistant director raised his eyes to the chandelier, from which little Japanese bells dangled, swaying in the draught. Ting-a-ling, ting-a-ling, they tinkled gently.

'L-let her. I don't mind.'

'Excellent! Give me your hand! But bear in mind that if you break our agreement, I shall kill you.'

Fandorin shrugged. He had listened to similar threats from more dangerous opponents.

'All right. That's the first matter dealt with. We won't come b-back to it again. What is the second matter?'

'Hippolyte's murder. The police aren't doing anything. You and I must find the murderer.' Georges leaned forward and tugged belligerently on his moustache. 'In cases of this kind, I am even less adroit than you.' (Erast Petrovich raised his eyebrows at that.) 'But even so I can still come in useful. It will be easier if there are two of us. I am willing to be your deputy, the position of an assistant is one to which I am accustomed.'

'Thank you, but I already have an assistant,' Fandorin would have replied a few days earlier. But now he answered in a dull voice:

'Very well. I shall bear that in mind.'

The sufferings occasioned by the rift with the woman he loved were aggravated by another that was equally onerous: the breach in his relationship with Masa, the only person with whom he was close. For thirty-three years they had been inseparable, they had come through a thousand trials together and were accustomed to relying on each other in everything. But in recent days Erast Petrovich had been feeling increasingly irritated with his old comrade.

It had begun on the fifteenth of the month, the day when the play was read. Fandorin had taken Masa with him to the theatre in order to make the strongest possible impression on Stern. When dealing with theatre people, act theatrically. Here is a play drawn from Japanese life for you, and here as an appendix to it is an absolutely genuine Japanese, who can act as your consultant on any questions you might have.

Erast Petrovich had foreseen that the question would arise of where to find someone to play the male lead – someone who could juggle, walk a tightrope and perform various acrobatic tumbles – and he had been quite certain that no such actor existed anywhere in the world, so Stern would be obliged to invite the dramatist himself to play the part. In fact Fandorin had written this role for himself. It had no words, so that his damned stammer would not cause any problems; there was no need for him to show his face (except just once, at the very end); and most importantly of all – there was a love scene with the heroine. Imagining how he would embrace Eliza had lent the author's inspiration a powerful additional impulse . . .

But what had happened? The Japanese had been given the part! The director had found Masa's round face, with its narrow eyes, more interesting than Erast Petrovich's features. And Masa, the swine, had had the insolence to accept the offer. And when he saw that his master was displeased, he had explained in Japanese that this way it would be much more convenient to observe the theatre company from the inside. That was entirely logical and Fandorin had muttered sourly: *'Sore va tashikani soo da kedo . . .'** He couldn't possibly argue about the role in front of witnesses. In his own mind he cursed himself: firstly, for not acquainting Masa with his plans; and secondly, for dragging the Japanese along with him.

Afterwards he had told his servant everything that he thought. He had emphasised in particular the fact that Masa would not be able to play a *sinobi* because, unlike Fandorin, he had not been trained in the clan. Masa objected that Russians would never notice subtle points like that, they couldn't even tell the difference between *udon* noodles and *soba*. He was right, of course. In any case, the director had already made his decision. Erast Petrovich's hopes of achieving intimacy with Eliza, at least in the role of her stage lover, had been wrecked.

True, intimate relations had been established anyway, and not onstage, but in real life. Only the conclusion had been a catastrophe, which would probably not have happened if they were acting in the same play. Erast Petrovich already knew enough about the psychology of actors to realise that a leading artiste would never allow herself to break off a relationship with her stage partner – it would have ruined the production.

However, even before the catastrophe there had been more than enough occasions of suffering. When Fandorin was still attending rehearsals, he was constantly tormented by his painful envy of Masa, who had the right to touch Eliza, and in the most intimate fashion too. That damned director, who was obsessed with sensuality, wanted to make the love scene look 'convincing'. For instance, he introduced an unprecedentedly bold element: driven by his rampaging emotions, Masa's hero did not simply embrace the geisha, but slipped his hand inside her kimono. Noah Noaevich assured everyone that a natural touch like that would absolutely stun the audience. Meanwhile, it was Erast Petrovich who was stunned. There was not a trace of naturalism in his play, which dealt with spiritual love.

Masa's behaviour was simply repulsive. He kissed Eliza fervently on the neck, reached eagerly into the top of the actress's kimono

---

* That's right, I suppose.

and toyed so freely with her bust that Fandorin got up and walked out. He was especially infuriated by the generous praise that the Japanese showered on Eliza. 'Her lips are very soft, but her breasts on the contrary are firm and springy! My master has made a good choice,' he said after the rehearsals, gleaming with sweat and smacking his lips – and all this with an air of the keenest possible friendship and sympathy!

The hypocrite! Oh, Fandorin knew all about his servant's habits. And that avaricious glint in his eyes, and that voluptuous smacking of his lips. It was the riddle of all riddles how Masa managed to win women's hearts (and bodies), but in that area he could give his master a clear hundred points' start.

On the other hand, it was unjust to condemn the Japanese for being unable to resist Eliza's magic. She was that kind of woman. Everyone lost their head over her.

True love and true friendship are incompatible, Erast Petrovich ruminated bitterly. *It's either one or the other. This is a rule which admits no exceptions . . .*

THE COURSE OF THE ILLNESS

What had happened to Fandorin is what happens to every strong-willed, cerebral man who is accustomed to keeping his feelings on a tight rein when his prancer suddenly zooms off, flinging its abhorrent rider out of the saddle. This had already happened to Erast Petrovich twice before, on both occasions because of love that had been broken off tragically. Of course, this time the finale appeared farcical, rather than tragic, but that only made the helpless condition that had overwhelmed the former rationalist all the more humiliating.

His will had evaporated, not a trace remained of his mental harmony, his reason had declared a strike. Fandorin sank into a shameful apathy that dragged on for many days.

He didn't leave the house, but just sat there for hours, staring at an open book without even seeing the letters. And when a period of agitation set in, he started exercising furiously, to the point of physical exhaustion. Only when he had drained his strength completely could he get to sleep. Then he woke up at some unpredictable time of day – and everything started all over again.

I am unwell, he told himself. *Some day this will end. The other times were far, far worse, and it passed off after all.* Ah, but then, he protested, he had been young. A long life made the heart grow weary and weakened its capacity for recovery.

Perhaps the illness would have passed off more quickly if not for Masa.

Every day he returned from the rehearsal at the theatre exhilarated and greatly pleased with himself, and started reporting on his success: what he had said to Eliza and what she had said to him. Instead of telling him to shut up, Erast Petrovich couldn't help listening, and that was bad for him.

The Japanese was not surprised by his master's pitiful condition. In Japanese it was called *koi-wazurai*, 'love disease', and was considered perfectly respectable for a samurai. Masa advised him not to fight against the melancholy, to write poetry and 'water his sleeves with tears' as often as he could, in the way that the great hero Yoshitsune did when parted from the beautiful Shizuka.

On that fateful night when Eliza had made Fandorin the happiest and then the unhappiest man in the world (in his sick condition Erast Petrovich thought in precisely such ludicrously stilted expressions), Masa had seen everything. The Japanese had slipped out discreetly through the rear entrance and loitered in the courtyard for several hours. When the heavy rain set in, Masa had hidden under the archway of the gates. He had only come back into the house when Fandorin was left alone. And he had immediately begun pressing him with questions.

'What did you do to her, master? Thank you for not closing the curtains, it was interesting. But at the end it turned really dark and I could not see anything any more. She ran off wildly and aimlessly, sobbing loudly and even slightly unsteady on her feet. You must have permitted yourself something quite exceptional. Tell me, in the name of our friendship – I am dying of curiosity!'

'I don't know what I did,' Fandorin replied in bewilderment. 'I don't understand what happened.'

His expression was wretched, and his servant stopped pestering him. He patted the tormented man on the head and made him a promise,

'Never mind. I will set everything right. She is a special woman. She is like an American mustang. Do you remember the American mustangs, master? They have to be tamed gradually. Trust me, all right?'

Fandorin nodded listlessly – and condemned himself to the torment of listening to Masa's stories every day.

If the Japanese could be believed, he went to the theatre exclusively in order to 'tame' Eliza. Supposedly he did nothing else there but describe his master's virtues to Eliza as advantageously as possible. And supposedly she was gradually mellowing. She had begun asking after Fandorin without displaying any resentment or animosity. Her heart was thawing day by day.

Fandorin listened morosely, without believing a single word. He found the sight of Masa abhorrent. Envy and jealousy choked him. The Japanese spoke to her and as part of his role he hugged her tight, kissed her and touched her body (damn it!). Was it possible to imagine a man who would not submit to the necromantic charms of this woman in those circumstances?

September came to an end and October began. There was no difference between one day and another. Fandorin waited for the next report about Eliza in the way that a totally degraded opium addict waits for the next dose of his drug. And when he got it, he didn't feel any relief, he merely despised himself and hated the supplier of this poison.

The first sign of a recovery appeared when it occurred to Erast Petrovich to take a look at himself in the mirror. In normal life he paid a considerable amount of attention to his appearance, but now it was more than two weeks since he had combed his hair.

He looked – and was horrified (also an encouraging symptom). His limply dangling hair was almost completely white, while his beard, on the contrary, was completely black, without even a single thread of grey. Not a face, but a drawing by Aubrey Beardsley. A noble man does not descend to the crudeness of the brute even in the most onerous of circumstances, said the sage. *And there is nothing onerous about your circumstances*, Fandorin told his reflection reproachfully. *Merely a temporary paralysis of the will*. And he immediately realised the first step that must be taken in order to restore his self-control.

Leave the house, in order not to see Masa and not listen to what he said about Eliza.

Erast Petrovich tidied himself up, dressed with the most meticulous possible care and went out for a stroll.

It turned out that while he was lurking in his lair, sucking on his paw, autumn had made itself undisputed master of the city. It had recoloured the trees on the boulevard, washed down the road with rain, lightened the sky to a piercing azure and set ornamental flocks of birds flying southwards across it. For the first time in all these days Fandorin attempted to analyse what had happened.

There are two causes, he told himself, scattering the dry leaves about with his cane. *Age – that is one. I decided to inter my feelings too soon. Like Gogol's Pannochka, they have jumped out of the coffin and frightened me half to death. The strange coincidence – that is two. Erast and Liza, the anniversary year, St Elizaveta's day, the white arm in the beam of light from the projector. And three is the theatre. Like the exhalations of a swamp, this world clouds the mind and distorts the outlines of all objects. I have been poisoned by this pungent air, it is contraindicated for me.*

It was comforting to think and set out a line of logic. Erast Petrovich was feeling better with every minute that passed. And not far from Strastnoy Monastery (he had not even noticed that his stride had carried him all the way round the Boulevard Ring to this spot), a chance encounter occurred that finally set the sick man on the road to recovery.

He was distracted from his thoughts by a crude howl.

'You boor! You swine! Watch where you're going!'

The usual story; a cab driver had driven through a puddle close to the pavement and splashed a passer-by from head to foot. The splattered gentleman (Fandorin could only see a narrow back in a pepper-and-salt jacket and a grey bowler hat) broke into a torrent of abuse, jumped up on the running board and started lashing the gargantuan man around the shoulders with his stick.

The driver looked round and must have determined in an instant that the individual before him was a person of no great significance (as everyone knows, cabbies are true psychologists in such matters), and being twice as broad across as his assailant, he snatched the stick out of the other man's hand and snapped it in two, then grabbed him by the lapel and drew back a massive fist.

Half a century without the slavery of serfdom has blurred the boundaries between the social orders somewhat after all, Erast Petrovich thought distractedly. *In 1911 a member of the lowest class no longer allows a gentleman in a hat to inflict punishment on him with impunity.*

The gentleman in the hat started jerking about, trying to break free. When he turned his profile towards Fandorin, he turned out to be an acquaintance – Anton Ivanovich Mephistov, the actor who played the roles of villains and mischief-makers. Erast Petrovich decided it was his duty to intervene.

'Hey, badge 38-12!' he shouted, running across the street. 'Keep your hands to yourself! It's your own fault!'

The 'psychologist' required only one glance to see that this was a man who should not be wrangled with. The cabby released Mephistov and expressed the praiseworthy intention of fighting for his rights in a civilised manner.

'I'll take him to the magistrates' court. Oho, fighting with a stick! That's not in any rules!'

'Q-quite right,' Erast Petrovich said approvingly. 'They'll fine him for fighting and fine you for his ruined clothes and broken cane. You'll be even.'

The cabby glanced at Anton Ivanovich's trousers, figured something out, croaked and lashed at his horse.

'Hello, Mr Mephistov,' said Fandorin, greeting the pale-faced 'villain'.

Mephistov brandished his fist at the receding carriage and exclaimed:

'The brute! The proletarian! If not for you, I'd have smashed his face to pulp . . . But anyway, thank you for intervening. Hello.'

He wiped off his clothes with a handkerchief, his bony features shuddering in fury.

'Mark my words, if Russia is destroyed by anything, it will be exclusively by loutishness! A lout sits on another lout and drives a lout along! Nothing but louts from top to bottom.'

However, he calmed down quite quickly – he was, after all, an actor, a creature with feelings that are tempestuous, but shallow.

'I haven't seen you for a long time, Fandorin.' He looked Erast Petrovich up and down more closely and his sunken eyes glinted with curiosity. 'My, but you certainly look the worse for wear. You've started looking like a human being. You used to be like a picture from a ladies' magazine. Are you unwell, then? Your Japanese didn't mention anything.'

'I was a little unwell. I have almost recovered now.'

Fandorin found this encounter distasteful. He touched his fingers to his top hat, intending to take his leave, but the actor grabbed hold of his sleeve.

'Have you heard our news? A scandal! Pornography!' His lizard-like face glowed with happiness. 'Our great touch-me-not beauty, our Egyptian princess, has utterly disgraced herself. I mean Eliza Altairsky, if you haven't realised yet.'

But Fandorin had understood him perfectly well. He had also realised that this chance encounter had not come about entirely by accident. He was about to learn something important, and it might possibly accelerate his recovery. However, crude talk about *her* could not be permitted.

'Why do you speak so spitefully about Madam Altairsky-Lointaine?' he asked in a hostile tone.

'Because I cannot bear beauties and all sorts of prettiness,' Mephistov explained with great eagerness. 'A certain ugly writer once spoke some stupid words that are repeated endlessly by all sorts of blockheads: "Beauty will save the world". Gibberish, sir! It will not save it, but destroy it! This truth is expounded remarkably well in your little play. Genuine beauty does not assault the eye, it is concealed and accessible only to the chosen few. It is invisible to the blockhead and the lout! The first reaction to a powerful, innovative work of art is the fear and revulsion of the crowd. If I had my way, I would mark every pretty-pretty face with a fiery brand, to prevent it glowing with its chocolate-box prettiness! I would replace all the sumptuous palaces with structures of steel and concrete! I would shake all the mouldy old rubbish out of the museums and . . .'

'I have no doubt that is precisely what you would do, if you had your way,' Fandorin interrupted him. 'But what, after all, has happened to Madam Altairsky-Lointaine?'

Anton Ivanovich started shaking with silent laughter.

'She was caught with an admirer in a most titillating pose! In her hotel room! With Limbach, the cornet of hussars, the young Adonis. She wearing almost nothing, and her lover was down on his knees, with his head stuck right up under her nightshirt and kissing away for all he was worth. I told you – a pornographic postcard!'

'I don't believe it,' Erast Petrovich said in a strangled voice.

'I wouldn't have believed it either. But the hussar didn't sneak in to see her quietly, on the sly – he demolished half the hotel in his amorous fury. And the indecent scene was witnessed by people who wouldn't make it up: Stern, Vaska Gullibin and Nonarikin.'

Fandorin's face must have contorted in pain. In any case Mephistov said:

'It seems strange now that I used to think of you as a saccharine-sweet pretty face. You have a rather interesting appearance, the face of a Roman patrician from the period of the empire's decline. Only the moustache is superfluous. If I were you, I'd shave it off.' Anton Ivanovich indicated his own upper lip as an example. 'I just decided to stroll to the hotel after the rehearsal, to clear the fumes. Won't you keep me company? We could drop into the buffet for a drink.'

'Thank you. I'm busy,' Erast Petrovich replied through his teeth.

'And when will you come to see us in the theatre? We've made great progress, it would be interesting for you. Really, do come to a rehearsal.'

'Most definitely.'

The damned 'troublemaker' finally left him in peace. Fandorin looked at the pieces of Mephistov's cane lying on the pavement, then snapped his own entirely innocent stick of the strongest ironwood in half and snapped the pieces in half again.

He also recalled the idiotic compliment about his appearance. It was Dostoyevsky's Fyodor Karamazov who had 'the face of a Roman patrician from the period of the empire's decline'! *And as it happens, the repulsive old erotomaniac was about the same age as me*, he thought. And in that very instant his blighted will shuddered and came to life, flooding his entire being with the strength he had been waiting for.

'With red-hot iron,' Fandorin declared out loud, and stuck the fragments of the broken stick in his pocket, in order to avoid littering the pavement.

And then he added:

'Enough of this p-puerility.'

It was fate: a depraved actress, a sprightly cornet and a vicious-tongued 'villain' who turned up along his way at just the right moment had mercifully combined forces to return the sick man's reason and calmness of mind.

It was over.

The world felt free, cool and spacious.

At breakfast the next day Fandorin read the newspapers that had accumulated and for the first time he listened to Masa's chatter without feeling irritated. The Japanese clearly wanted to tell him about the disgusting incident with the cornet: he began delicately with comments regarding the special moral character of courtesans, geishas and actresses, but Erast Petrovich redirected the conversation to the astounding events in China, where a revolution was beginning and the throne of the Manchurian Qing dynasty had been shaken.

Masa tried to turn the conversation back to the theatre.

'I shall call in there today. Later on,' said Fandorin, and the Japanese fell silent, evidently trying to understand the change that had come over his master.

'You don't love her any more, master,' he concluded after a moment's thought, with his perennial perspicuity.

Erast Petrovich could not resist passing a spiteful comment.

'No, I don't. You can feel absolutely free.'

Masa didn't reply to that. He sighed and started pondering.

Fandorin drove up to Theatre Square at two o'clock, counting on arriving exactly in time for the lunch break in the rehearsal. He was calm and collected.

Madam Lointaine is free to arrange her private life as she sees fit, that is her business. However, the investigation that has been interrupted by my psychological indisposition must be continued. The killer must be found.

Fandorin had barely emerged from his Isotta Fraschini before a nimble little man came scurrying up to him.

'Sir,' he whispered, 'I have a ticket for the premiere of the new Noah's Ark production. A superb play of oriental life. An original title – *Two Comets in a Starless Sky*. With quite incredible tumbling tricks and astoundingly frank scenes. The tickets have not reached the box office yet, but I have some. Fifteen roubles in the circle and thirty-five in the orchestra stalls. It will be more expensive later.'

So the title and the subject of the play were no longer a secret, and what was more, the day of the premiere had been set. Well, these matters did not concern Erast Petrovich now. To hell with the play.

As he walked to the entrance, hucksters pestered him again twice. They were doing a brisk trade. And some distance away, in the same spot as last time, the grand marshal of the touts was loitering with his perennial green briefcase under his arm. He kept glancing up at the autumn sky, stamping his shoe with its thick rubber sole on the ground and whistling absent-mindedly, but at the same time he seemed able to survey everything around him. Erast Petrovich caught the gaze of those little eyes boring into him with either curiosity or suspicion. God only knew why he had provoked such a lively reaction from this murky individual with a face of clay. Perhaps he had remembered about the pass for the box? What about it? But then, that was of no importance.

During the time since Fandorin had last been here, certain changes had taken place. A large photograph of the deceased Emeraldov was hanging to the left of the entrance – with a lighted icon lamp and a heap of flowers piled up directly on the pavement. There were two smaller photographs beside it, apparently of hysterical women who had taken their own lives in their inconsolable grief for their idol. An announcement in a flirtatious little mourning frame informed people that there would be an 'Evening of Tears' in the small auditorium 'for a small circle of invited individuals'. Naturally, the prices had been raised.

Erast Petrovich felt a slight stabbing sensation in his heart when he saw the photograph on the other side of the entrance – the leading lady in a kimono, with a *takashimada* hairstyle. The curt caption read: 'Mme ALTAIRSKY-LOINTAINE IN HER NEW ROLE AS A JAPANESE GEISHA'. There were flowers lying in front of the famous actress's portrait too, although not as many.

I did feel a twinge nonetheless, Fandorin noted, and hesitated. Perhaps he should put off his visit until tomorrow? Apparently the wound had not yet healed over sufficiently.

A horse cab pulled up behind him and a ringing voice shouted out:

'Wait!'

There was a jangle of spurs and a clatter of heels and a hand in a yellow glove set a basket of violets in front of the actress's portrait.

At this point Erast Petrovich felt a more powerful stabbing sensation in his chest. He recognised the cornet whom he had once admitted to the box. Limbach recognised him too.

'I put some here every day!' The fresh, youthful face lit up in an ecstatic smile. 'I consider it my duty. Have you brought flowers too? Don't you recognise me? We were at *Poor Liza* together.'

Erast Petrovich turned away without speaking and walked off to one side, indignant at the furious pounding of his heart.

Sick, I'm still sick . . .

He had to wait a little and take himself in hand. Fortunately he was standing right in front of the announcement of the new production.

Just a theatre-lover, studying a poster. Nothing special.

TWO COMETS IN A STARLESS SKY
A play of Japanese life

The letters attempted to look like hieroglyphs. The artist had drawn some stupid little figures in a style that was more Chinese than Japanese. And for some incomprehensible reason the whole composition was crowned by a branch of *sakura*, although it was a blossoming apple tree that was mentioned in the play. But that didn't matter. The most important thing was that the condition he set had not been broken: where the author's name should have been, there were only the initials 'E.F.'

I need to forget about this shameful episode as soon as possible, thought Fandorin. And in his own mind he prayed to the Russian and the Japanese gods and the muse Melpomene for the play to be a resounding failure, so that it would be excluded from the repertoire and expunged for ever from the annals of theatrical art.

Without even wishing to, every now and then Erast Petrovich squinted sideways at his fortunate rival. He felt furious and the humiliation of it tormented him, but the urge was too strong.

The boy still didn't go away – the man with the briefcase moved closer to him and they started talking about something. The conversation gradually grew more animated. In fact, the leader of the ticket touts behaved calmly and didn't raise his voice, and it was the cornet who did most of the shouting. Fragments of phrases reached Fandorin's ears.

'This is monstrous! You can't dare to do that! I'm an officer of His Majesty's guard!'

And then there was a phrase that sounded very strange, coming from 'an officer of His Majesty's guard'.

'You and your Tsar can both go to hell!'

The man with the briefcase whistled again, not mockingly this time, but menacingly, and said something else in a quiet, insistent voice.

'I'll pay everything back! Soon!' Limbach exclaimed. 'On the word of a gentleman!'

'You've given the word of a gentleman before!' the other man finally exploded. 'Either cough up the money, or . . .'

The tout-in-chief grabbed the cornet crudely by the shoulder, and his hand was clearly not a light one – the youth's knees even buckled slightly.

What a pity that she cannot see her lover grovelling to his creditor, Fandorin thought in a malicious impulse that was unworthy of a noble man. *In my time an officer of the hussars didn't behave like a stray puppy dog. He would have challenged him to pistols at five paces, and that would have been the end of it.*

However, Limbach found a different way out of the scandalous situation. He shoved his assailant in the chest, took a run up, jumped into the horse cab and yelled:

'Drive! Drive!'

The shove sent the creditor's hat flying off his head and the brief-case fell out from under his arm. The lock came open and papers slid out onto the pavement, including a yellow cardboard folder that seemed familiar to Fandorin.

He took several steps forward to take a better look at it. He was right: Stern had handed out the parts to his actors in similar folders. Erast Petrovich's keen glance made out the words printed in large capitals: 'TWO COMETS . . .'

Rapidly stuffing the papers back into his briefcase, the whistling enthusiast scowled at Fandorin.

'What are you doing always hanging around here, trying to sniff everything out, Nat Pinkerton?'

Now this was interesting.

'So you kn-know me?' Erast Petrovich asked, standing over the ruffian, who was squatting down on his haunches.

'That's the job – knowing everything.' The other man stood up and turned out to be half a head taller than Fandorin. 'What interests keep you hanging about here, Monsieur Sleuth? Professional matters, or perhaps affairs of the heart?'

These impudent words were accustomed by winking and derisive whistling.

Fandorin was in a foul mood today, and his nerves were not in good order. So he behaved in a manner that was less than absolutely worthy. Normally he considered it impossible to touch a gentleman of this type with his hands unless there was some urgent necessity to do so, but this time he broke his own prohibition. He took hold of a button on the man's jacket between two fingers, tugged gently – and the button was left in his hand. He did the same with the other three buttons. Then he stuck them in the ruffian's breast pocket.

'Well, since you know who I am, don't be impertinent with me. I don't like it. And sew on your buttons, you're improperly dressed.'

Good grief, a retired state councillor, a respectable man of fifty-five, and I behave like some pugnacious whippersnapper!

He had to give the scalper-in-chief credit. He obviously really had found out something about Fandorin, because he didn't look for trouble. But there wasn't even a hint of fear in his spiteful little eyes either. This time the whistle was mockingly respectful.

'Jupiter is angry. So it's an affair of the heart. Well, I wish you luck. No more, no more. I'm going to sew on my buttons.'

He tipped his hat and backed away.

This little outburst finally convinced Fandorin that his state of mind had not yet normalised.

Tomorrow, he told himself. *I shall be in better form tomorrow.*

He got into his automobile and drove away.

THE PREMIERE

The painful operation was carried out the next day, and on the whole it was a success. Only in the very first moment, when *she* glanced round, looked at the new arrival in the room and threw her hand up to her throat, as if she couldn't catch her breath, Fandorin's breath also faltered, but he controlled himself. Everyone dashed to shake his hand and greet him noisily, complaining about his pallor and rebuking 'Mikhail Erastovich' for not telling them that his 'step-father' was unwell.

Erast Petrovich said hello to everyone, including even Eliza – politely and distantly. She didn't look up. The aroma of her hair presented a clear and distinct danger. Catching the dizzying scent of Parma violets, the convalescent moved away quickly.

That's it, he told himself in relief, *it will be easier now.*

But it didn't get any easier. Every encounter, every accidental (and especially non-accidental) clash of glances, and in particular every exchange of even a couple of entirely insignificant words, paralysed his breathing and triggered a twinge in his chest. Fortunately Fandorin attended rehearsals infrequently. Only if the director asked him to come or the investigation required it.

After the embarrassment with Nonarikin and the enforced break of two weeks, he had to start over again almost from scratch and draw up his list of suspects anew.

He had no answer to the most important question: why had someone wanted to poison that fatuous popinjay Emeraldov? And was there any connection between the murder and the snake in the basket?

He had come up with about ten theories – effectively the number of members in the theatre company – but they were all unconvincing and contrived. On the other hand, in this strange world, many things seemed contrived: the actors' behaviour, their manner of speaking, their relationships, the motivations for their actions. In addition to the 'internal' theories (those that were limited to the bounds of the Ark) there was one 'external' theory, which was rather more realistic, but a serious effort was required to elaborate it, and Erast Petrovich was not really in a fit state for serious effort. Although he regarded himself as recovered, he was still subject to fits of apathy and his brain was not working as well as usual.

Conducting the investigation in this condition, all on his own, without an assistant, was like rowing with one oar, setting the boat endlessly describing the same circle over and over again. Fandorin was used to discussing the progress of his deductions with Masa, it helped him to systematise and clarify the direction of his thinking. The Japanese often made useful comments, and in this grotesque case his common sense and close knowledge of the possible suspects would certainly have come in very useful.

But one of the proofs that Erast Petrovich was not yet fully recovered was the fact that he still found it hard to tolerate his old friend's company. Why, oh why, had he spoken those words: 'You can feel absolutely free'? The damned oriental Casanova had eagerly taken advantage of his permission and now hardly ever left Eliza's side. It was more than Erast Petrovich could bear to see them rehearsing the passionate love scene. If he happened to be in the auditorium at the time, he immediately got up and left.

Thank God, the Japanese knew nothing about the investigation, or it would have been impossible to get rid of him. At the very beginning, when it was only a matter of the operetta viper in the basket of flowers, Fandorin had not seen any need to involve his assistant in such a frivolous case. And at the initial stage the matter of Emeraldov's death had not seemed too complicated to him either. And, as we know, before the fiasco of the 'Fishing with Live Bait' operation, relations between master and servant were already ruptured – Masa had arrogantly usurped the role that Fandorin wrote for himself.

The days stretched out in this way. The theatre company was in a feverish state ahead of the premiere. Masa came back from rehearsals late in the evening – and invariably discovered that his master had already retired to the bedroom. And Fandorin, hating himself for the feebleness of his thinking, kept going round and round the same circle. He wrote out names and hypothetical motives on a sheet of paper.

'Mephistov: pathological hatred of beautiful people?

'Vulpinova: resentment: pathological psychology?

'Aphrodisina: was she having a secret affair with the murdered man?

'Reginina: extremely hostile relations with Emeraldov.

'Stern: a pathological passion for sensationalism.

'Gullibin: by no means as simple as he seems.'

And so on in the same vein.

Then he angrily crossed it all out: puerile babble! The word 'pathological' appeared in the list more frequently than was permissible in criminalistic theory. But then, beyond the slightest doubt, this environment was itself pathological. Stern loved to repeat Shakespeare's phrase: 'All the world's a stage, and all the men and women merely players'. The actors really were convinced that the whole of life was one big stage, and the stage was the whole of life. Here appearance became immutable reality, the mask was inseparable from the face and dissimulation was the natural norm of behaviour. These people regarded as insignificant those things that constituted the meaning of greatest significance for an ordinary person; and vice versa, they were willing to lay down their lives for things to which everybody else attached no importance . . .

A few days before the premiere Noah Noaevich called Fandorin in for an urgent consultation. He wanted to know whether the author would object to the main accent of the ending being shifted slightly – from the text to a visual effect. Since in the final scene the heroine was sitting in front of an open jewellery casket, 'the prop had to be put to work', for in the theatre there should not be any guns that did not fire. And so Nonarikin had come up with an interesting idea. He spent a long time fiddling about with wires and hanging suspended from the ceiling in a cradle, tinkering with the casket before eventually presenting the fruits of his engineering concept to the director. Stern was ecstatic – the invention was exactly to his taste.

After the phrase with which the author concluded his play, a miracle would occur: two comets consisting of little light bulbs would suddenly blaze up above the hall. Throwing her head back and raising her right hand, to which the attention of the audience would be riveted, with her left hand the heroine would imperceptibly press a little button – and everyone would gasp.

Georges demonstrated his invention. The work had been carried out impeccably, and in the front of the casket, where the audience could not see it, the master craftsman had mounted an electrical panel that showed the time: hours, minutes and even seconds.

'I was taught that on an electrical combat-engineering course,' he said proudly. 'Beautiful, isn't it?'

'But what is the clock in the casket for?' Eliza asked.

'Not what is it for, but who is it for. It's for you, my dear,' Noah Noaevich told her. 'So that you won't drag out the pause. That's a little fault that you do have. Watch the seconds, don't get carried away. An excellent idea. Georges! It would be good to have a blinking clock, a big one, to hang above the stage on the inside. For the actors. We have too many ladies and gentlemen who like to hog the limelight.'

His assistant was nonplussed.

'Oh no, that's not what I did it for . . . I thought that afterwards, when the play's taken out of the repertoire, Eliza could keep the casket – as a souvenir. A clock is a useful thing . . . There's a little wheel here at the side, you can turn it if the clock's running too slow or too fast. There are lots of wires inside it now, but later on I'll disconnect them all, and the casket can be used for various cosmetics and such . . . And it runs off an ordinary electrical adaptor.'

Eliza smiled tenderly at Nonarikin, who was blushing.

'Thank you, Georges. That's very sweet of you.' She looked at Fandorin. 'You won't object if the performance ends with a light show, will you? Mr Nonarikin has made such an effort.'

'Whatever you wish. It's all the s-same to me.'

Erast Petrovich turned his eyes away. Why was she looking at him imploringly? Surely not because of this little trinket? It must be the usual actress's affectation – if you have to make a request, then do it with a tear in your eye. And all she wanted to do was encourage the zeal of yet another admirer. After all, she had to be loved by everyone around her – including even 'all the horses, cats and dogs'.

As far as the finale was concerned, that really was all the same to him. He would have been glad not to come to the premiere – and not at all because of author's nerves. Erast Petrovich was still hoping that the show would be a resounding flop. If the audience felt even a hundredth part of the revulsion that this sloppy romantic melodrama now inspired in the dramatist, then the result was not in any doubt.

Alas, alas.

The premiere of *Two Comets*, which took place exactly a month after the company was first acquainted with the play, was a resounding triumph.

The audience ecstatically drank in the exoticism of the *karyukai* or 'world of flowers and willow trees', the Japanese name for the chimerical kingdom of tea houses where unbelievably elegant geishas indulge their demanding clients with ephemeral, recherché, incorporeal pleasures. The stage sets were miraculously good, the actors performed splendidly, transforming themselves into puppets and then back into living people. The mysterious chiming of a gong and the honeyed recitation by the Storyteller alternately lulled and galvanised the audience. Eliza was dazzling – there was no other word for it. Under cover of darkness, from his position as one of a thousand spectators, Fandorin could watch her unhindered and he relished the forbidden fruit to the full. A strange feeling! She had nothing to do with him, but at the same time she spoke in his words and obeyed his will – after all, he was the author of this play!

Altairsky-Lointaine was given a magnificent reception and after every scene in which she appeared there were cries of 'Bravo, Eliza!' However, the completely unknown actor playing the part of the fateful killer enjoyed even greater success. In the programme it simply said 'The Inaudible One: Mr Swardilin' – that was how Masa had translated his Japanese name, Shibata, which consisted of the hieroglyphs for 'meadow' and 'field'. His somersaulting and pirouetting (performed in a very mediocre fashion in Erast Petrovich's biased view) sent a theatrical public not pampered by acrobatic tumbling into raptures. And when, as the plot required, the ninja pulled off his mask and turned out to be a genuine Japanese, the auditorium erupted into shouts of acclaim. No one had been expecting that. Caught in the beam of the spotlight, Masa glowed and shimmered like a golden Buddha.

The audience was also astounded by Nonarikin's electrotechnical invention. When the lights went out and the two comets blazed into life high above their heads, a sigh ran through the auditorium. The stalls were a solid expanse of white faces raised to the ceiling, which was quite an effect in itself.

'Brilliant! Stern has outdone himself!' said the influential reviewers in the director's box, where Fandorin was sitting. 'Where did he get this miraculous Oriental? And who is this "E.F." who wrote the play? He must be Japanese. Or American. Our playwrights don't know how to do this sort of thing. Stern is deliberately concealing the name, so the other theatres won't poach the author. And what about that love scene? Bordering on the scandalous, but so powerful!'

Erast Petrovich had not seen the love scene. He lowered his eyes and waited until the audience stopped gasping and gulping. The repulsive sounds could be heard quite clearly in the shocked silence that filled the hall.

The curtain calls went on for absolutely ages. Some people in the hall tried calling out 'Author! Author!' – but rather uncertainly: no one knew for certain whether the author was even in the theatre. It had been agreed with Stern that Erast Petrovich would not be invited up onto the stage. The audience clamoured briefly and stopped. They had quite enough people to celebrate and shower with flowers without the dramatist.

Erast Petrovich looked through his opera glasses at Eliza's face, glowing with happiness. Ah, if only just once in his life she would look at him with that expression, nothing else would matter . . . Masa bowed ceremoniously from the waist and immediately started blowing kisses to the audience like a regular leading man.

But that was not the end of Fandorin's trials. He still had to survive the backstage banquet – it was absolutely impossible not to go.

A RUINED BANQUET

Erast Petrovich spent a long time smoking in the foyer after the public had gone home and the bustle in the cloakroom had faded away. Eventually he heaved a sigh and went up to the actors' floor.

First Erast Petrovich walked along the dark corridor onto which the doors of the actors' dressing rooms opened. He suddenly felt an irresistible urge to glance into the room where Eliza prepared for her entrances, transforming herself from a real, live woman into a role: sitting in front of a mirror and exchanging one existence for another, like a *kitsuné*. Perhaps the appearance of the space that she used for these metamorphoses would somehow help him to understand her mystery?

He looked round to make sure there was no one near by and tugged on the brass door handle, but the door didn't yield, it was locked. That was strange. As far as Fandorin was aware, the actors of the 'Ark' were not in the habit of locking their dressing rooms. Erast Petrovich found this small fact symbolic. Eliza would not allow him into her secret world, she wouldn't let him get even a brief glimpse of it.

He walked on, shaking his head. Not only were most of the dressing rooms not locked, their doors were actually standing ajar. The very last door was firmly closed, but when he turned the handle tentatively, it swung open immediately.

The scene revealed to Fandorin's surprised gaze was in the spirit of the indecent Japanese *shunga* prints that are so popular with foreigners. Right there on the floor, between the make-up tables with their mirrors, Masa, wearing a close-fitting ninja jacket, but without the lower half of his costume, was intently turning up the kimono of Serafima Aphrodisina, who played the part of a trainee geisha in the show.

'Oh!' the 'coquette' exclaimed, jumping to her feet and adjusting her clothing. Erast Petrovich did not get the impression that she was seriously embarrassed. 'Congratulations on the premiere!'

Gathering up the hem of her kimono, she darted out through the door.

The Japanese watched her go regretfully.

'Do you need me, master?'

'So you're having an affair with Aphrodisina and not . . .?' Fandorin didn't finish his question.

Masa got up and said philosophically:

'Nothing turns women's heads like a Great Success. This beautiful girl showed no interest in me before, but after a thousand people applauded and shouted and cheered, Sima-san started making such wide eyes at me, it would have been stupid and impolite to leave the matter without any continuation. Many women in the hall were looking at me in exactly the same way,' he concluded, examining himself in the mirror with satisfaction. 'Some of them said: "How handsome he is! A genuine Buddha!"'

'Put your trousers on, Buddha.'

Leaving the newborn star to admire his irresistibly handsome features and adjust his clothing, Fandorin walked on. He really had come to dislike Masa. The worst thing was that this puffed-up nobody was right: now he would become even more attractive to Eliza – after all, actresses were so susceptible to the tinsel glitter of success! He ought to tell her about Masa's monkey business with Aphrodisina – but unfortunately, for a noble man, that was quite inconceivable . . .

Erast Petrovich was so consumed by his misery, it didn't occur to him that he was also enveloped in the glittering cloud of a Great Success. This fact was only made clear to him when he entered the buffet quietly, trying not to attract any attention. No such luck!

'Here he is, our dear author! At last! Erast Petrovich!' Everyone came dashing towards him, vying with each other to congratulate him on the brilliant premiere, the superb triumph and his new-found fame.

Stern raised a glass of champagne.

'Here's to a new name on the theatrical Mount Olympus, ladies and gentlemen!'

Madam Reginina in her purple kimono, her eyes extended with mascara (all the actors were still in their stage costumes and make-up), declared with feeling:

'I have always been an advocate of an author's theatre, not a director's or actors' theatre! You are my hero, Erast Petrovich! Ah, if only you had written a play about a woman who is no longer young, but whose heart is still vibrant and filled with powerful passions!'

She was elbowed aside by her former husband, with his gleaming false bald patch and waxed samurai pigtail.

'It is only now that I have really understood the concept of your work. It is majestic! You and I have a lot in common. Some day I shall tell you the story of my life . . .'

But the company's female 'intriguer' was already pushing herself forward, her lips extended to reveal a small-toothed smile.

'The most interesting plays in the world are the ones in which the central character is on the side of evil. You have shown that brilliantly.'

On the other hand, Vasya Gullibin, who had still not removed the swords from his belt, thanked Fandorin for 'giving villainy its comeuppance' – which, in his opinion, was the most important idea of Fandorin's play and of existence in general.

And then Erast Petrovich stopped seeing and hearing them, because Eliza came up to him, took his neck in her hot hand, stunning him with an aroma of violets, kissed him and whispered every so quietly:

'My best one, my very best! Forgive me, my darling, there was nothing else I could do . . .'

She slipped away, yielding her place to others and leaving Fandorin tormented by uncertainty: had she really said 'my darling' and not just 'my dear'? He wasn't sure that he had heard her correctly. So much depended on that! But he couldn't just ask her, could he?

Calm down, it means absolutely nothing, he told himself. *Madam*

Lointaine is an actress, and she is also under the spell of a Great Success. For her I am no longer just a man, but a Highly Promising Dramatist. That kiss is not worth a thing and I cannot be lured into the same trap for a second time, no thank you very much. And he deliberately added an extra dash of bitterness by asking: *But why is your chosen favourite nowhere to be seen, my lady?*

He actually had not seen Limbach at the premiere today and had drawn the only possible conclusion: there was no need for the cornet to besiege the fortress, if it had already been taken. He must be waiting in a hotel room with flowers and champagne. *Well, good luck to him. To coin a phrase – may your bed be feather-soft!*

After the actors, the dramatist was congratulated by the very small number of guests – the banquet was for the 'inner circle' only. The influential reviewers whom Erast Petrovich had seen in the box came over and paid him condescending compliments. Then his elbows were taken by two extremely amiable gentlemen, one with a pince-nez and the other with a perfumed beard. They were interested in whether he had any more compositions in hand or 'on the drawing board'. Stern immediately came flying across and wagged his finger at them jokingly.

'Vladimir Ivanovich, Konstantin Sergeevich, no pilfering our authors now. Or I'll poison both of you, as Salieri poisoned Mozart!'

The last person to approach him, when all the others had gone back to the table, was the patron of the muses, Shustrov. He didn't pay any compliments, but took the bull by the horns immediately.

'Could you write a scenario on a theme from Japanese life?'

'I b-beg your pardon? I don't know that word.'

'A scenario is the word for a cinematographic play. It's a new idea in the field of film-making. A detailed exposition of the action, with dramatic instructions and scenes described in detail.'

Fandorin was surprised.

'But what for? As far as I'm aware, the film-maker simply tells the actors playing the roles how to stand and which way to move. After all, there isn't any dialogue, and the plot can change, d-depending on money, the weather and how busy the actors are.'

'That's how it used to be. But all that will change soon. Let's have a talk about it later.'

The director tapped his fork against a glass and called the millionaire.

'Andrei Gordeevich, you wished to make a speech! This is the right moment, everyone is here!'

The heartbreaker Swardilin had just shown up, with the bristles of his freshly grown hair gleaming. The scoundrel sat down beside Eliza, who said something affectionate to him. But then, where else was the person playing the male lead supposed to sit?

Erast Petrovich was also seated in a place of honour, at the opposite end of the table, beside the director.

Mr Shustrov began the speech in his usual manner.

'Ladies and gentlemen, this is a good show, people will write about it and talk about it. I have been convinced yet again that I calculated correctly when I put my money on Noah Noaevich and your entire company. I was especially delighted by Madam Altairsky-Lointaine, who has a great future ahead of her . . . If we can see eye to eye . . .' he added after a pause, gazing intently at Eliza. 'Permit me, madam, to make you a small symbolic gift, the meaning of which I shall explain in a little while.'

He took a small velvet case out of his pocket and extracted from it a very delicately made rose of reddish gold.

'How charming!' Eliza exclaimed. 'What craftsman could possibly have produced such intricate work?'

'That craftsman's name is nature,' the entrepreneur replied. 'You are holding in your hands a living flower bud, sprayed with a layer of gold dust – the very latest technology. Thanks to the film of gold the beauty of the living flower has been rendered eternal. It will never wilt.'

Everyone applauded, but the capitalist raised his hand.

'The time has come to explain the main idea behind the establishment of our Theatrical and Cinematographic Company. I decided to invest money in your theatre group because Noah Noaevich was the first person working in the theatre to realise that truly colossal success is impossible without sensationalism. But that is only the first stage. Now that the newspapers of both of Russia's capital cities are writing about Noah's Ark, my plan is to elevate your fame to an even higher level – first of all, right across the whole of Russia, and then right around the world. This cannot possibly be achieved by means of theatrical touring, but there is another means: the cinematograph.'

'You wish to make a film of our production?' Stern asked. 'But what about the sound, the words?'

'No, my partner and I wish to create a new type of cinematograph, which will become a fully fledged art form. The scenarios will be written by authors with a literary reputation. We won't ask just anyone to act in the films, but first-class actors. We will not be satisfied, as others are, with cardboard or canvas scenery. But the most important thing is that we shall make millions of people love the faces of our stars. Oh, this concept has an immense future! The art of an outstanding theatrical actor is like a living flower – it is spellbinding, but the enchantment comes to an end when the curtain closes. I wish to render your art imperishable by coating it in gold. What do you think about that?'

No one said anything, and many of the actors turned to look at Stern. He got up. It was clear that he did not wish to upset his benefactor.

'Mmmm . . . Highly respected Andrei Gordeevich, I understand your desire to earn greater profit, that is only natural for an entrepreneur. And I myself, God knows, never let slip an opportunity to milk the golden calf.' A ripple of laughter ran round the room and Noah Noaevich inclined his head comically, as if to say: Guilty, I admit it. 'But surely you find the results of our Moscow tour satisfactory? I don't think any theatre has ever had takings like this – no offence intended to my colleagues in the Art Theatre. Today's premiere brought in more than ten thousand roubles! Naturally, it would only be just for us to start sharing, in mutually advantageous proportions, with the company that has given us shelter.'

'Ten thousand roubles?' Shustrov repeated. 'That's a joke. A successful film will be watched by at least a million people and on average each of them will pay fifty kopecks at the box office. Minus the production costs and the theatre-owners' commission, plus foreign sales and the trade in photocards – and the net profit will be at least two hundred thousand.'

'How much?' Mephistov gasped.

'And we intend to produce at least a dozen pictures like that in a year. So count it up for yourselves,' Andrei Gordeevich continued. 'And at the same time bear in mind, ladies and gentlemen, that one of our stars will receive up to three hundred roubles for a day of filming, a second-level actor like Mr Sensiblin or Madam Reginina will receive a hundred, and a third-level actor will get fifty. And that's not counting the nationwide adoration that will be guaranteed by our own press, working together with Noah Noaevich's brilliant gift for creating sensations.'

Eliza suddenly stood up, her face blazing with inspiration and the pearl droplets in her tall hairstyle glittering.

'When money is the cornerstone of everything, it is the end of genuine art! You have given me this rose and, of course, it is beautiful. But you are mistaken when you say that it is alive! It died as soon as you condemned it to this golden captivity! It was transformed into the mummified corpse of a flower! It is the same with your cinematograph. The theatre is life! And like all life, it is instantaneous and unrepeatable. There will never be another moment exactly the same, it cannot be halted, and that is why it is beautiful. You Fausts, who dream of halting a beautiful moment, fail to grasp that beauty cannot be recorded, it will die immediately. That is what the play we acted today is about! You must understand, Andrei Gordeevich, that eternity and immortality are the enemies of art, I am afraid of them! A play may be good or bad, but it is alive. A film is a fly in amber. Exactly as if it were alive, only it is dead. I shall never, do you hear, *never* act in front of that box of yours with its big glass eye!'

God, how lovely she was at that moment! Erast Petrovich pressed his hand against his left side, feeling a stabbing pain in his heart. He looked away and told himself: *Yes, she is magnificent, she is magical and miraculous, but she is not yours, she doesn't belong to you. Don't give way to weakness, don't lose your dignity.*

It should be said that not many of those present liked Shustrov's mathematically dry address. If they had applauded the entrepreneur, it was merely out of politeness, while Eliza's impassioned speech was greeted with loud exclamations of approval and clapping.

The *grande dame* Reginina asked in a loud voice:

'Well, sir, so you assess my value at only a third of Madam Altairsky's?'

'Not your value,' the entrepreneur began explaining, 'but the contribution of your roles. You see, during filming I intend to make extensive use of a new approach known as "blow-up", that is, showing an actor's face across the entire screen. For this technique flawlessly attractive and young faces are preferable . . .'

'But the cinematographic business has no interest in old fogeys like you and me, Vasilisochka,' the company's 'philosopher' put in. 'We shall be cast aside, like worn-out shoes. But everything is in God's hands, I'm an old stager, I've been around the block on my own account, and I'll certainly get by without the protection of the cinematograph. Am I right, my foxy little sister?' he asked Vulpinova, who was sitting next to him.

But she was looking at the millionaire, not Sensiblin, and smiling at him in an extremely pleasant manner.

'Tell me, my dear Andrei Gordeevich, is it your intention to make films in the Gothic style? I read in a newspaper that the American public has fallen in love with films about vampiresses, sorceresses and witches.'

It really was quite incredible, the way Mr Shustrov had of saying appalling things to people in the politest possible tone of voice.

'We are thinking about it, madam. But research has indicated that even a negative heroine, whether it be a sorceress or a vampiress, must possess an attractive appearance. Otherwise the public will not buy the tickets. I think that with your distinctive face it would be best to avoid close-ups.'

Xanthippe Petrovna's 'distinctive face' immediately shed its smile and contorted in a malign grimace, which suited it far better.

The discussion of the cinematograph soon stumbled to a halt, although Shustrov tried to go back to the subject. When everyone got up from the table and started wandering about at will, he came over to Erast Petrovich and started explaining that cinematic scenario writing was a career with a wonderful future; it promised great fame and an immense income. The capitalist offered to arrange a meeting with his partner, Monsieur Simon, who would be able to explain all this better and was a highly engaging individual altogether. But Fandorin failed to show any interest in the profession with a wonderful future or the engaging partner, and he fled from his tedious conversation partner just as soon as he could.

Then Shustrov set to work on Eliza. He took her aside and started saying something to her with a very serious air. She listened, twirling the golden rose in her hands and smiling benignly. When the impudent fellow permitted himself the liberty of taking her by the elbow, she did not pull away from him. And Fandorin did not like it at all when the young man led her out of the room. As he walked past them with a cigar, Erast Petrovich heard Shustrov say:

'Eliza, I need to talk to you alone about an important matter.'

'Well then, see me to my dressing room,' she replied, running a rapid glance over Fandorin's face. 'I need to remove my make-up.'

And out they went.

I can't take any more, Erast Petrovich told himself. *What this woman does is no concern of mine, but there is no point in my watching her flirt with men. It smacks too much of masochism.* He calculated when he could leave without it looking like an insult, and decided that it would be in about ten minutes.

Exactly ten minutes later he approached Stern and said goodbye in a whisper, trying not to attract anyone's attention to his departure.

Noah Noaevich was looking either disconcerted or preoccupied. He had probably been alarmed by his patron's speech.

'A brilliant debut, brilliant, congratulations,' he murmured, shaking Erast Petrovich by the hand. 'Let's think about the next play.'

'D-definitely.'

Fandorin set off towards the way out with a sense of relief, manoeuvring between the actors and the guests, most of whom were holding cups of tea or glasses of cognac.

The doors opened towards Erast Petrovich of their own volition and he barely managed to catch Eliza as she literally fell against him bodily. Her face was frozen in a mask of horror and her pupils were so distended that her eyes seemed black.

'Aaaaah . . .' she moaned, not seeming to recognise Fandorin. 'Aaaaah . . .'

Shustrov came running along the corridor, dabbing at his forehead with a handkerchief.

'What have you done to her, damn you to hell?' Erast Petrovich shouted at him.

'Back there . . .' mumbled the entrepreneur, who was always so calm, pointing with a trembling finger. 'There, in the dressing room . . . Eliza took the key off the board and opened the door . . . And there . . . We have to call the police! The telephone . . . Where's the telephone?'

The dead man was lying in the dressing room right next to the door, in a fetal pose – curled up, with his hands pressed against his stomach. Trying not to step in the vast pool of blood, Fandorin cautiously removed a folding knife with a very sharp, slightly curving blade from the clenched fingers.

'A clasp knife,' Masa said behind him.

'I can see that for myself. Move back and don't let anyone through. There's a lot of evidence here,' Erast Petrovich told him drily.

There were splashes of blood everywhere in the room, the inside of the door was covered with bloody hand prints and the red tracks of boots with pointed soles could be seen on the floor. The dead man was wearing cavalry boots exactly like that.

'Let me in!' Stern shouted angrily. 'This is my theatre! I have to know what's happened.'

'I advise you not to g-go in. The police won't like it.'

Noah Noaevich glanced into the dressing room, turned pale and stopped insisting.

'The poor boy. Was he stabbed to death?'

'I don't know yet. I believe the cornet died from loss of blood. The broad knife wound on the stomach didn't kill him instantly. He floundered round the room and grabbed at the door handle, then his strength deserted him.'

'But . . . why couldn't he get out into the corridor?'

Fandorin didn't answer. He remembered how he had walked along the corridor before the banquet and been surprised that the door was locked. Apparently Limbach must have been lying there, only a step away, obviously already dead or unconscious.

'A sea of blood,' Stern told the others, looking back. 'The hussar was stabbed or he stabbed himself. Either way, we'll be in all the newspapers again tomorrow. The reporters will sniff out in an instant that the youngster was one of Eliza's admirers. How is she, by the way?'

'Simochka and Zoya Comedina and Gullibin are with her,' Vasilisa Prokofievna replied. 'She's barely conscious, the poor soul. I can imagine what it's like, to open the door of your own dressing room and see something like that . . . I don't know how she'll survive it.'

These words were uttered with a special significance, which Fandorin understood perfectly well.

'At least now it's clear why the cornet wasn't on the rampage at the premiere,' Sensiblin remarked cold-bloodedly. 'I wonder how on earth he got in here. And when.'

Stepping on the toes of his shoes between the splashes of blood, Fandorin took hold of a card protruding from the pocket of the formal red hussar's jacket and pulled it out. It was a pass to the artistes' floor, without which no outsider would have been allowed in here on the day of a premiere.

'In view of the fact that none of the actors saw Limbach, he must have found his way into the corridor after the performance had already begun. Mr Stern, who hands out passes like this one?'

Noah Noaevich took the card and shrugged.

'Any of the actors. Sometimes myself or Georges. Visitors normally use their passes during the interval or after the performance. But we performed without an interval, and everybody went to the buffet immediately after the show. No one came in here.'

'Painfur,' said Masa.

'What do you mean?'

'When the sutomach is cut right across, it's painfur. He is not a samurai, he yerred. Very roud.'

'Of course he yelled. But there was music playing in the hall, and there wasn't a soul here. No one heard.'

'Rook, master.' Masa's finger was pointing at the door.

In among the drying streaks of blood, two crudely daubed letters could be made out: 'Li'. The second letter was smeared, as if the writer had run out of strength.

'Right, listen to me,' said Erast Petrovich, switching to Japanese.

'Keep a close eye on everyone here. That's all I need you to do. I'll handle this case myself, and Subbotin will assist me. The police have to be involved in any case.'

'What are you saying?' Noah Noaevich asked with a frown. 'And why didn't you let Georges call the police?'

'I just told Masa that it's time to do that now. First I had to make sure that no one would enter the dressing room and ruin the evidence. With your permission, I'll make the telephone call. I have a police detective acquaintance, a very good specialist. Ladies and gentlemen, I ask you all to go back to the b-buffet! And you, Mr Stern, post two ushers at this door.'

SPECIALISTS AT WORK

'No doubt about it – it's suicide,' said Moscow criminal police investigator Sergei Nikiforovich Subbotin, pressing the yoke of his spectacles into the bridge of his nose in his habitual manner and smiling as if in apology. 'This time, Erast Petrovich, your hypothesis has not been confirmed.'

Fandorin couldn't believe his ears.

'Are you joking? A man ripped open his own stomach and then, all on his own, locked the door from the outside and hung the key on the board?'

Subbotin giggled in acknowledgement of the joke. He blotted his sparse white hair with a handkerchief – it was getting close to dawn and he had already put in several hours of intense work.

'I'll follow your method, Erast Petrovich, and run through the points. You told me that Cornet Limbach had no reason to commit suicide, since he had won a victory in love. According to your information the artiste Altairsky had bestowed her ... er ... favours on him, is that correct?'

'Yes,' Fandorin confirmed in an icy tone. 'The cornet had no reason to do away with himself, especially in such an appalling manner.'

'I'm afraid you are mistaken,' Sergei Nikiforovich said with an even more guilty air, embarrassed at having to correct his former mentor. A very long time ago, twenty years in fact, the young police officer had begun his career under the stewardship of State Counsellor Fandorin. 'While you accompanied the body to the autopsy room in order to establish the precise time of death I did a bit of investigating here. The artiste concerned and the hussar were not involved in an intimate relationship. The rumours are without any substance. You know what a stickler I am, I established the fact for certain.'

'They were n-not involved?'

Erast Petrovich's voice shook.

'Absolutely not. And what's more, I spoke to a friend of Limbach's on the telephone, and the witness claimed that just recently the cornet had been driven distracted by the torments of love and he had declared repeatedly that he would kill himself. That, as you say, is one.'

'And what will be two?'

Subbotin took out his notebook.

'Witnesses Gullibin and Nonarikin testified that on the night when Limbach found his way into Madam Altairsky's hotel room, they heard him on the other side of the door, threatening to rip open his stomach in the Japanese manner if she rejected him. That is two for you.' He turned over the page. 'In some way as yet undetermined, Limbach got hold of a pass and sneaked into the dressing room of the queen of his heart. I believe he wanted to punish his tormentor when she returned in triumph after the performance, smothered in flowers. Having lost all hope that his feelings might be requited, Limbach desired to kill himself in the terrible Japanese manner. Like a samurai committing hiri-kiri for a geisha.'

'Hara-kiri.'

'Isn't that what I said? He carves himself open with the knife, suffering appalling agony, he's bleeding to death and he tries to write her name – "Liza" – on the door, but his strength runs out.'

Getting carried away, the investigator started demonstrating how it had all happened: here was the cornet clutching at his stomach, writhing in agony, dipping his finger into his wound, starting to write on the door and falling. Well, Sergei Nikiforovich didn't actually fall, it's true – the floor of the dressing room had just been washed and it hadn't dried out yet.

'By the way, the incomplete name is three.' Subbotin pointed to the door which, on his instructions, had been left untouched. 'What did the coroner tell you? When did death occur?'

'At approximately half p-past ten, plus or minus a quarter of an hour. That is, during the third act. The death agony lasted no more than ten minutes.'

'There, you see. He waited until the performance was almost over. Otherwise there was a risk that someone else, and not Madam Lointaine, might glance into the dressing room, and then the entire effect would have been ruined.'

Fandorin sighed.

'What's wrong with you, Subbotin? All your deductions and the reconstruction aren't worth a bent farthing. Have you forgotten that the door was locked? That someone must have locked it with a key?'

'Limbach himself locked it. Obviously he was afraid that if he couldn't bear the pain, he would go running out in his semi-conscious state. I found the key – or rather, a duplicate – in the pocket of the suicide's breeches. Here it is – and that is four.'

A key glinted on the investigator's open hand. Fandorin took out his magnifying glass. Yes indeed, it really was a duplicate, and one made recently – the marks of a file could still be seen on the bit. There was not the slightest trace of triumph or – God forbid! – gloating in the investigator's voice, only calm pride in a job honestly done.

'I checked, Erast Petrovich. The keys of the actors' dressing rooms hang on a board, unattended. The rooms are not usually locked anyway, so the keys are almost never used. Limbach could have had a copy made during some previous visit.'

And Fandorin sighed again. Subbotin was rather a good detective, thorough. Not quite the sharpest pencil in the box, but a police officer didn't have to be. He could have gone far. Unfortunately, after Erast Petrovich was obliged to resign, things had not worked out well for the young man. In post-Fandorin times quite different qualities were required for a policeman to make a successful career: delivering elegant reports and currying favour with superiors. Sergei Nikiforovich had not learned to do either of these from the state counsellor. Fandorin had always laid more emphasis on teaching him how to gather evidence and question witnesses. And here was the result of an incorrect education; the man was already past forty, and still only a titular counsellor, and he was always given the least advantageous, dead-end cases, which gave him no chance to distinguish himself. If not for Erast Petrovich's direct request, there was no way that Subbotin would ever have been entrusted with a plum job like a bloody drama in a fashionable theatre. After all, the newspapers would all write about it, and he would become an instant celebrity. Provided, of course, that he didn't make a mess of things.

'And now you l-listen to me. Your theory of a "Japanese-style suicide" won't hold water. I assure you that no one b-but a samurai from a previous age, who has prepared for such a death since he was a child, is capable of performing hara-kiri on himself. Except perhaps for a violent madman in a fit of acute insanity. But Limbach was not insane. That is one. Secondly: did you notice the angle of the cut? No? Well, that is why I went t-to the autopsy room with the body, to study the wound properly. The blow was delivered by a man who was standing face to face with Limbach. At the moment of the attack the cornet was sitting d-down, in other words he was not expecting the attack at all. As you recall, a substantial pool of blood collected beside the overturned chair. That is where the blow was struck. That is three. Now pay attention to the knife. What kind is it?'

Sergei Nikiforovich picked up the weapon and turned it over in his hands.

'An ordinary clasp knife.'

'Precisely. The Moscow b-bandits' favourite tool, which is replacing the sheath knife in their arsenal. Using a weapon like this, a slicing blow can be delivered with no backswing, on the sly. You open it behind your back or quietly slip it out of a sleeve, so that your victim doesn't see it. The strike is made holding it in a closed fist with the handle towards the thumb. Let me have it, I'll show you how it's done.'

He made a swift movement, pulling his hand out from behind his back. Subbotin doubled over at the sudden surprise of it.

'It leaves a characteristic wound, shallow at the end where penetration occurs and gradually deepening towards the point of withdrawal. That is, the opposite picture as compared with the blow of hara-kiri, in which the blade is first thrust in deeply and then jerked out at an angle. I repeat: only a samurai with incredible tolerance of pain, who has trained his hand for a long time, is capable of inflicting a wound as long as Limbach's on himself. A Japanese suicide usually had only enough strength to thrust the dagger in, after which his second immediately severed the p-poor man's head.' Fandorin looked reproachfully at his former pupil. 'Tell me, Sergei Nikiforovich, where would a cornet get a bandit's knife?'

'I don't know. He bought it for some reason. Possibly for this very purpose, judging from the sharpness of the blade,' replied Subbotin, shaken, but still not convinced. 'Let me remind you of the writing on the door.' He pointed to the bloody letters 'Li'. 'If those are not the first letters of the name of the woman who was the reason why the young man decided to end his life, then what are they?'

'I have an inkling, but first let us ask the witnesses a few questions. Now is precisely the right time.'

Eliza was waiting in the green room with the director and his assistant. The actress had been asked to stay by the investigator; Stern and Nonarikin had been asked to stay by Fandorin.

Subbotin sent a police constable for them. But he came back with only the actress and the assistant director.

'Noah Noaevich flew into a fury and left,' Nonarikin explained. 'It really is awkward, gentlemen. A man like that being made to wait to be summoned, like some petty thief. I can answer any questions concerning procedures, schedules, the general organisation of the dressing rooms and all the rest of it. That's my area of responsibility.'

'How are you feeling?' Fandorin asked the actress.

She was very pale and her eyes were puffy. Her geisha's hairstyle had slumped to one side and traces of mascara could be seen on the sleeves of her kimono – Eliza must have wiped away her tears with them. Her face, however, had been washed clean and there was no make-up left on it.

'Thank you, I'm feeling better,' she replied in a quiet voice. 'Simochka was with me almost all the time. She helped me to tidy myself up – I looked like a witch, covered in black streaks . . . Sima left half an hour ago, Mr Masa volunteered to see her home.'

'I s-see.'

He's jealous because I'm working with Subbotin, Erast Petrovich guessed. *Well, to hell with him. He can console himself with his Aphrodisina, we'll manage without him.*

'Two questions, madam,' he said, adopting a businesslike tone of voice. 'The first is: Was the door handle like that before?'

Erast Petrovich pointed to the inner surface of the door. The brass handle was slightly bent.

But apparently Eliza could see only the traces of blood. She screwed up her eyes and answered in a weak voice.

'I . . . don't know . . . I don't remember . . .'

'I remember,' Nonarikin announced. 'The handle was in perfectly good order. But what's that written there?'

'That will b-be my second question. Madam Lointaine, did the deceased ever call you "Liza"?' Erast Petrovich tried to make the question sound completely neutral.

'No. No one ever calls me that. Not for a long time.'

'Perhaps in . . . intimate moments?' The questioner's tone of voice became even drier. 'Please be frank. It is very important.'

Her cheeks turned pink and her eyes glittered angrily.

'No. And now goodbye. I don't feel well.'

She turned and walked out. Nonarikin dashed after her.

'You can't go anywhere in the kimono!'

'It doesn't matter.'

'I'll see you to the hotel!'

'The car will take me.'

She left.

What did that 'no' of hers mean, Fandorin wondered in torment. *That even in intimate moments Limbach never called her 'Liza', or that there weren't any intimate moments? But if there weren't, then why such turbulent manifestations of grief? This is more than simply shock at the sight of death, there is powerful, genuine feeling here . . .*

'And so,' he summed up dispassionately. 'As you see, the cornet never called Madam Altairsky-Lointaine "Liza", and it would be strange if he decided to use a new name for her at the moment of his departure from this life.'

'Then what does this incomplete word signify? Did he really decide to sign off with his own name: "Limbach, with best regards"?'

'B-bravo. I've never observed any tendency towards irony and sarcasm in you before.' Fandorin smiled.

'With the life I have, I'd be finished without irony. But really, Erast Petrovich, what did happen here, in your opinion?'

'I think it was like this. The murderer – someone well known to Limbach, who didn't arouse his suspicion – sliced open the cornet's stomach with a sudden blow and then walked or ran out into the corridor and locked the door, or simply leaned his body against it. The officer, fatally wounded, bleeding to death, but not yet unconscious, shouted, but apart from the criminal no one heard him. Then Limbach tried to get out of the dressing room, he grabbed the door handle and even bent it, but it was no good. Then the dying man tried to write his killer's name, or some other word that would expose him, on the door, but his strength ran out. When the groaning and thrashing about stopped, the criminal entered the dressing room and slipped the duplicate key into the dead man's pocket. He used the other k-key, taken from the board, to lock the door again from the outside. To make the police think that the suicide had locked himself in. Do you remember the testimony of Madam Lointaine and Mr Shustrov? When they reached the door and found it locked, the actress was rather surprised, but she found the key in its usual place – on the board. The fact that the criminal failed to notice the letters written in blood when he entered the room after Limbach died is hardly surprising – they don't stand out among the other blotches and streaks. I didn't notice them immediately myself.'

'How convincingly you describe it all,' simple-hearted Nonarikin exclaimed. 'Like a real detective!'

The investigator cast a sideways glance at Erast Petrovich and grinned, but he didn't pass any ironic comments.

'You've convinced me,' he admitted. 'I expect you already have some theories?'

'Several. Here is the f-first for you. Limbach had a strange, convoluted relationship with a certain individual who, as far as I can understand, runs the theatre ticket touts. An entirely criminal type. Very tall and unpleasant, with a face the colour of brick. Dresses in American suits and whistles all the time . . .'

'His nickname is actually "Mr Whistle",' Sergei Nikiforovich said with a nod. 'A well-known figure. The right hand of Mr Tsarkov, the so-called "Tsar", who rules over an entire empire of ticket touts, a very influential man. On friendly terms with everyone in the municipal authorities and has his own box in every theatre.'

'I know who you mean. And my next question would have been about Mr Tsarkov. I had the pleasure of sharing a box with him. Mr Whistle showed up there too. So that's the "Tsar" the hussar was t-talking about . . .' The theory was becoming more and more convincing. 'You see, a few days ago, I happened to witness a contretemps between Mr Whistle and Limbach. The tout demanded repayment from the cornet for some debt or other, but the young man said: "You can go to hell, you and your Tsar". I was surprised by that . . . I don't know exactly what the conflict was about, but if a criminal character like Whistle happened to have a clasp knife in his pocket, I wouldn't be surprised in the least. And a man like that wouldn't stop at m-murder, you can read that in his eyes. That's theory number one for you. Let's leave it for the time being and move on to theory number t-two . . .'

But they never even started on theory number two.

'I know that Whistle!' put in Nonarikin, who had been listening avidly. 'And I know Tsarkov. Who doesn't know them? Mr Tsarkov is a very polite and personable individual, the actors always receive bouquets and gifts from him after a successful show. As a sign of gratitude, so to speak. He usually thanks the director and the leading artistes in person, and he sends Mr Whistle to the others. But you're mistaken, Erast Petrovich, Whistle isn't a criminal at all, quite the contrary. Isn't that right, Mr Policeman?'

'Well, it's like this,' said Subbotin, happy to go back to the first theory – he found it interesting. 'He used to be the inspector of the Myasnitsky district. And his departure wasn't entirely voluntary. Something to do with bribes, but there were no judicial consequences. You know our people don't like to hang the dirty linen outside in public view.'

'I know. But g-go on.'

'Gentlemen,' Nonarikin butted in, shifting anxiously from one foot to the other. 'If you don't need me any more . . . What if the automobile didn't wait for Madam Altairsky? She can't walk home through the city at night alone – in a costume like that, and in such a distressed state! I'll check and, if necessary, I can catch up with her. She can't have got far in those Japanese sandals of hers.'

And he ran off, without waiting for permission. Erast Petrovich watched the assistant director go with an envious gaze.

'. . . And Mr Whistle's real name,' the investigator continued, 'is Sila Yegorovich Lipkov . . .'

He stopped short with his mouth hanging open. His light eyelashes started fluttering.

'There, you see,' Fandorin said in a slow, soft voice, instantly forgetting all about Eliza and her faithful paladin. '"Liza" has nothing to do with the case. So it's Lipkov, then? Ye-es, let's wait a while before moving on to theory number two.'

He took a chair, set it in front of himself and straddled it, facing the back.

'You sit down as well. The real discussion is only just beginning. We have the scent now.'

Subbotin sat down too – beside him, in exactly the same manner. The investigators were like two mounted knights at a crossroads.

'Where do you want to start?'

'From th-the head. That is, from Tsarkov. And to add to the fun, I'll throw a little more k-kerosene onto the flames for you. Do you remember that at the beginning of the season someone slipped a snake into Madam Lointaine's flowers?'

'I read something in the newspapers. What does that have to do with this?'

'This is what.' Erast Petrovich smiled sweetly. 'I recall – and, as you know, I have a good memory – a certain phrase that Tsarkov spoke to his adjutant general. What he said was more or less: "Find out who did it and punish them". That is one. Before that he ordered Whistle to take half a dozen bottles of expensive Bordeaux to the leading man as a gift. That is two. And the third thing is that Emeraldov did not poison himself as the newspapers reported. He was poisoned, and with wine. A pity I didn't think of analysing it to see exactly what kind. In any c-case, that is three. And the fourth thing is that, bearing in mind the character of the deceased leading

211

man and his rivalry with Madam Lointaine, it is entirely possible that Emeraldov played that vile trick himself.'

'A second murder in the same theatre!' Subbotin jumped to his feet and sat back down again. 'Whistle could have poisoned the artiste Emeraldov! But isn't that too harsh a punishment for such a petty piece of nastiness?'

'Not so very petty. A viper's bite, together with the shock, could quite easily have dispatched the l-lady to the next world. And furthermore, as I recall, Tsarkov held a very low opinion of the Ark's leading lover. He could have flown into a violent fury if he discovered that Emeraldov was responsible for the vile trick with the snake. But tell me more about Tsarkov, so that I can understand how dangerous his rage is. Everything you know.'

'Oh, I know a lot about him. I collected a bit of material last year and I was thinking of trying to nail him, but there was no way.' Sergei Nikiforovich gestured dismissively. 'Too big a fish for me. With protectors in places that are too high. I can tell you straight out that August Ivanovich Tsarkov's fury and his threats should be taken with the maximum possible seriousness. He's quite a staid, restrained individual, who rarely gives free rein to his feelings. But once he gets his dander up . . .' The investigator ran the edge of his hand across his throat in an eloquent gesture. 'Speculation in theatre tickets is his favourite activity, but by no means his most important one. The Tsar can guarantee a production's success. And he can make it fail. Stirring up scandal about a theatre, rumours, hecklers, reviews – he can control all of these. He can make an unknown newcomer a celebrity, but he can also destroy an actor's career. The boxes that he owns are always at the disposal of the city's bigwigs, and so they regard August Ivanovich as a delightful and courteous individual, whom riff-raff like Titular Counsellor Subbotin must not dare to bother with his petty little quibbles.'

The policeman smiled bitterly.

'Can the black market trade in tickets really bring in such large profits?' Fandorin asked in surprise.

'Make the calculation for yourself. In order to counter speculation, a municipal council regulation restricts the number of tickets that box offices can issue to any one individual to a maximum of six.

But that's no obstacle for the Tsar. He has about twenty so called "buyers" working for him, and they are always first in line at the box office window – it goes without saying that all the ticket sellers have been bribed. If we take a super-fashionable show like yesterday's premiere, the Tsar's net income from reselling tickets will be at least one and half thousand. And then there's the Art Theatre, which you can't simply walk into just like that. There's the Bolshoi. There are shows in the Maly and Korsh theatres for which tickets are also hard to come by. There are high-demand concerts and functions of various kinds. The Tsar got his start in theatrical profiteering and he maintains a keen interest in this area, a profitable one in every possible sense, but his main income is derived from elsewhere. According to my information, he now has all the expensive brothels in Moscow under his control. The Tsar also provides services of an even more delicate nature to certain interested parties: he provides perfectly decent young ladies, not official whores with yellow tickets, to respectable men who wish to avoid publicity. And he provides a similar service to bored ladies – for good money he finds handsome young men to act as their male escorts. As you might expect, everything in Tsarkov's enterprise in interconnected: dancers, both male and female, from the corps de ballet or the operetta, and sometime even rather well-known actors and actresses, are often not averse to acquiring an influential patron or a generous mistress.'

'So T-Tsarkov has an entire organisation. How is it set up?'

'In ideal fashion. It runs like clockwork, with both full-time and part-time employees. At the lowest level, the "buyers" work for a daily rate. Whistle's assistants hire petty bureaucrats and students who have taken to drink from among the derelicts on Khitrovka Square. They queue at the box offices overnight and buy up all the best places for the fashionable shows. The "buyers" are dressed up for the job – they're issued with shirtfronts, hats and jackets. Special "foremen" keep an eye out to make sure a Khitrovkan doesn't just run off with the money and get drunk. There are specially trained "pushers" who create a crush at the box office, forcing their own people through and shoving everyone else out of the way. There are the "touts", who hang about outside every theatre and peddle the tickets. They're watched over by "pinschers", who are responsible for arranging things with policemen on the beat and putting an end to any activity by amateur touts. Oh yes, I forgot about the "informants". They're the secret agents, so to speak. The Tsar has someone from the management or the acting company in his pay in every theatre. They report on what's going to be in the repertoire, changes in productions, internal events, the leading men's drinking bouts and the leading ladies' migraines – you name it. Thanks to his "informants" the Tsar never makes a mistake. He has never once bought all the tickets for a show that ended up being cancelled, or for a premiere that turned out to be a flop.'

'Well, that's all fairly clear. Now tell me about Mr Whistle, please. What exactly is he in charge of in this hierarchy?'

'A little bit of everything, but mostly the "pinschers". They're a kind of "flying squad". Whistle has recruited dashing young blades who can give anyone a sound thrashing, or even finish them off if need be. The Tsar didn't win control of the brothels without offending a few people, he had to take that juicy morsel away from some very serious characters.'

'I used to know those serious characters,' Erast Petrovich said with a nod. 'Levonchik from Grachovsky Park, Acrobat from Sukharev Square. I haven't heard anything about them for a long time now.'

'Well, this is why you haven't. Last spring Levonchik went back home to Baku. In a wheelchair. Just imagine, he accidentally fell out of a window and broke his back. And Acrobat announced that he was retiring from the business. That was just after his house burned down and his two closest deputies disappeared.'

'Last spring? I was in the Caribbean. I m-missed that.' Fandorin shook his head. 'Well, nice going, Mr Whistle. And no trouble with the police?'

'Zero. My reports don't count for anything. Official instructions were not to do anything about it. And in a confidential conversation I was told: "We shall be grateful to August Ivanovich for doing our job for us and clearing the city of gangster elements". And there's another thing too, Erast Petrovich. Lipkov is very popular with the municipal police, especially the district inspectors. He's their hero and idol, you could say. Once a year, on his birthday, he organises a special function, by invitation only, at the Bouffe Theatre – it's actually called "The Police Inspector's Ball". They reminisce about that occasion the whole year round in all the police districts. I should think so too: a superb concert with satirical rhymers, a cancan and clowns, swanky food and drink and the company of vivacious young ladies. Mr Whistle gets an opportunity to show off to his former colleagues – there, just look how rich and powerful I've become! And at the same time he keeps up useful contacts. Police raids on the racketeers are a waste of time. Whistle's little friends in the force always warn him in advance. When I was getting close to the Tsar, I thought about raiding his so-called "Office" to obtain evidence and proof of criminal activity. But I had to abandon the idea. My own assistants would have been the first to inform Whistle about the operation, and the Office would have moved to a new address in the twinkling of an eye. It moves constantly from place to place anyway.'

'What f-for? If the Tsar isn't afraid of the police?'

'But he is afraid of the hoodlums, they've got it in for him. And in any case, August Ivanovich is obsessively cautious. A week or two is the longest he stays anywhere. He seems like a conspicuous sort of gentleman, his automobiles and carriages can be seen at all the theatres, but just you try finding out where he's living at the moment – no one knows.'

Erast Petrovich got up and swayed back slightly on his heels, pondering.

'Mmmm, and what kind of clues were you expecting to find in his Office?'

'The Tsar follows the American accounting system and keeps scrupulous records. He ordered two large filing cabinets on wheels from Chicago to help him do it. They contain all his records, his accounts . . . you name it. August Ivanovich respects order, and he's not afraid of a search. And there's the fact that there are armed guards protecting all the documents and their owner. The Tsar always resides where his Office is. And Mr Whistle lodges with him. They're as inseparable as Satan and his tail.'

The investigator pressed his spectacles into the bridge of his nose, giving Fandorin an incredulous look.

'Surely you're not going to . . . Don't even think about it. It's far too risky. Especially on your own. You can't rely on the police. My men will only be a hindrance, I've explained that. I could help in a private capacity, of course, but . . .'

'No, no, I don't wish to compromise you in the eyes of your superiors. Especially since they have specifically warned you not to bother Mr Tsarkov. But perhaps you might at least know where the infamous Office is located just at the moment?'

Sergei Nikiforovich shrugged and spread his hands.

'Unfortunately . . .'

'Never mind. That's no g-great problem.'

BACK TO THE GOOD OLD DAYS

Fandorin thought that he would determine the current location of Mr Tsarkov's 'Office' in elementary fashion: by following Mr Whistle. But it all proved to be a bit more complicated than that.

It was a job he was familiar with and it had its pleasant side. Erast Petrovich justifiably regarded himself as a master when it came to trailing someone. In recent years however, he had only rarely had to play the part of the 'tail' himself, which made him all the more keen to shake off the cobwebs.

An automobile was also a very convenient thing – he could take several changes of dress with him, and his make-up materials, and all the tools that he needed, and even tea in a Thermos flask. In the nineteenth century he would have had to conduct the pursuit in less comfortable conditions.

Erast Fandorin didn't find his mark at Theatre Square, so he moved to Kamergersky Lane, where he spotted the commander of the touts at the entrance to the Art Theatre. As usual, Lipkov was standing there whistling, as if he had nothing much to do, and people occasionally came up to him – no doubt 'touts' or 'pin-schers', or possibly 'informants'. The conversation was always brief. Sometimes Whistle opened his green briefcase and took something out of it or, on the contrary, put something into it. Basically, he was labouring by the sweat of his brow, without leaving his post.

Fandorin stopped his car about fifty paces away, beside a ladies' dress shop, where several carriages and automobiles were already parked. He conducted his observation with the assistance of an excellent German innovation: a pair of photo-binoculars, with which he could take instant photos. Just to be on the safe side, Erast Petrovich photographed everyone Mr Whistle talked to – not really for any practical purpose, but simply to check the apparatus.

At half past two the mark moved from his spot – on foot, which indicated that he was not going far. At first Fandorin was going to follow him in the automobile, since Kamergersky Lane was lively, with plenty of pedestrians around, but he realised in time that Whistle had escorts: two substantially built young men were walking fifteen or twenty strides behind him, one on each side of the street. Erast Petrovich had captured both of their images with his camera a little earlier. They were obviously 'pinschers', performing the function of bodyguards for their boss.

The Isotta Fraschini had to be left behind. Fandorin was dressed in an inconspicuous short jacket (on one side it was grey, but when turned inside out, it was brown). In a shoulder bag of the kind that commercial travellers carried, he had a spare costume – another double-sided jacket. His false beard, secured with an adhesive of his own concoction, could be removed in a single movement; and spectacles with a tortoiseshell frame rendered his face almost unrecognisable.

The mark proceeded along Kuznetsky Most Street, turned right and took up a position by the final column of the Bolshoi Theatre. Here everything was repeated all over again. Whistle clicked the lock of his briefcase and exchanged a few words with fidgety little men.

Probably it was safe now to go back for the automobile, Fandorin reasoned. It was already clear that the mark would move on from the Bolshoi to Noah's Ark – that was obviously his usual route.

Ten minutes later the Isotta Fraschini was standing between the two theatres, at a point from which it was convenient to conduct observation in both directions.

Mr Whistle moved on to the box offices of Noah's Ark at precisely four o'clock. The touts here were different from the ones at the Art Theatre and the Bolshoi, but the 'pinschers' were the same. They kept an eye on their commander from the left and the right, but didn't come close to him.

There was another man with his hat pulled forward over his eyes and a light coat of shantung silk, loitering close to the stage door.

Fandorin noticed the man, because he was acting strangely. Every time the door opened, he hid behind a pillar that was completely covered with posters. Erast Petrovich was obliged to get out of his car to examine this intriguing individual from closer quarters. He had a dark complexion, with a large Caucasian nose and eyebrows that grew together across its bridge. To judge from his bearing, he was a military man. Erast Petrovich photographed him – not with the binoculars, of course. For inconspicuous photography at short distances, he had a Stirn detective camera: a little flat box, attached under his clothing, with a powerful high-aperture lens that was disguised as a button. The inconvenient aspect of this miraculous invention was that it was single-loading, and Fandorin was soon convinced that he had wasted the camera shot for nothing. The Caucasian individual didn't demonstrate the slightest interest in Mr Whistle and didn't communicate with him in any way. Shortly after six o'clock, when the rehearsal was over, the actors started coming out of the door. When Eliza appeared, accompanied by Gullibin and Aphrodisina, the suspicious character hid.

Fandorin pressed the binoculars to his eyes avidly. The woman who had robbed him of his harmony of soul was looking pale and sad today, but inexpressibly lovely nonetheless. She waved her hand to let her automobile go and set off with the other two towards Hunters' Row. They had clearly decided to stroll back to their hotel.

The man in the shantung silk coat followed the actors, and Erast Petrovich realised that he was nothing more than yet another admirer. He had been waiting for the beautiful woman to appear, and now that she had, he would creep along after her in a rapturous transport of delight.

No, I'm not going to dance along with the other extras, Erast Petrovich thought angrily, and forced himself to move the binoculars from Eliza's elegant silhouette to Lipkov's repulsive features of clay

'It's time you were going home, my friend. No point in working yourself to a frazzle,' Erast Petrovich whispered.

As if he had heard, Mr Whistle waved his hand and an enclosed black Ford automobile that had been standing by the fountain drove across to the theatre. The 'pinschers' dashed over to the car. One swung the door open, while the other looked around. Then all three men got in.

Fandorin started his engine, preparing to follow the Ford. He suppressed a yawn. *The job will soon be over. Now we'll find out where the Tsar has his den.*

But it was not to be.

When the Ford pulled away from the pavement another automobile, an open Packard, blocked the roadway. Three young men of the same build as Lipkov's bodyguards were sitting in it. Of course, Fandorin could have followed the covering car – it must be about to travel the same route – but it wasn't worth taking the risk. He would have to abandon his motorised surveillance. Moscow was not New York or Paris, there were not many cars in the street, and every one stood out. The bodyguards in the Packard would be certain to spot a tenacious Isotta, that was precisely the kind of reason for which the second car acted as escort.

So the day had been wasted. Apart, that is, from the fact that Fandorin had been convinced of the difficulty of attaining the goal that he had set himself. And the fact that he had looked at Eliza for a few seconds.

For Erast Petrovich unforeseen obstacles had never been anything more than a reason to mobilise the additional resources of his intellect. And that was exactly what happened this time, although no exceptional effort was required. The task was not a complicated one, after all, and a new solution was quickly found.

The next day he went to the theatre with Masa. According to the rules established by Stern, rehearsals of the current production had to take place every day. Noah Noaevich's credo stated that the premiere was only the beginning of the real work and every new performance of a play had to be more perfect than the one before it.

Master and servant ate their breakfast in a graveyard silence and remained silent all the way to the theatre. Masa actually gazed demonstratively out of the window. The Japanese was still offended because Erast Petrovich had not informed him about how the investigation was going. And that was very good, thought Fandorin, who did not yet feel any desire to make peace.

At the beginning of the rehearsal Erast Petrovich waited until the individual he was interested in was free and then did what he had come here for.

Fandorin was interested in the actor Konstantin Shiftsky, who played the part of a petty thief.

'Are you an "informant"?' Erast Petrovich asked without any preliminaries, after first leading the actor out into the corridor.

'How do you mean?'

'Do you work for the Tsar? Don't t-try to deny it. Ten days before the premiere I saw the folder containing your role in Mr Whistle's briefcase. The colour for your roles is yellow, isn't it?'

The prankster's mobile features face started twitching and his eyes blinked rapidly. Kostya didn't answer.

'If you start getting stubborn, I'll tell Stern about your earnings on the side,' Fandorin threatened.

'Don't,' Kostya said quickly, and looked round to make sure that there was no one near by. 'I'm not doing anything bad, after all . . . Well, I answer a few questions about how things are going, what's happening . . . I tell him about changes in the repertoire. When the new play appeared, the Tsar was interested, of course. He liked it a lot, by the way, and predicted it would be a great success.'

'*Merci beaucoup*. So, are you constantly in contact with the Tsar?'

'No, I deal more with Whistle. Only occasionally with the Tsar. The last time we talked about you. He was very curious . . .'

'Was he really?'

'Yes. He asked my opinion about whether he could give you a valuable gift on the occasion of the premiere. I advised him against it. I said: Mr Fandorin is a reserved kind of man, not very sociable. He might not like it . . .'

'Why, you're a psy-psychologist.'

'The Tsar wasn't surprised. I think he knows more about you than I do . . .'

Erast Petrovich remembered his confrontation with Whistle. Everything was clear now. The Tsar had taken an interest in the new playwright, made enquiries about him and learned all sorts of interesting things. Well now, that was most opportune.

'Where did you meet the Tsar? In his Office?'

'Yes. They took me somewhere out past Ostankino.'

'Do you remember the place?'

'I remember it. But Whistle said they were moving out of there the next day. And that was almost two weeks ago . . .'

'Do you know where the Tsar is staying now?'

'How could I?'

Fandorin thought for a moment and said:

'Then I tell you what. You go and give Whistle a n-note to deliver to the Tsar. He's loitering in front of the theatre right now. Write: "Fandorin was asking questions about you. We need to meet." They'll take you straight to the Office.'

Shiftsky immediately wrote down everything as dictated, although he pursed his thick lips sceptically.

'But why would they do that? What's the big deal if a dramatist is asking a few questions? You don't know what kind of man the Tsar is. Oho, he's a big kind of man.'

'Whistle will take you straight to the Tsar,' Erast Petrovich repeated. 'They'll be nervous. And you'll tell them that when I talked to you I mentioned my suspicions. Say that Fandorin thinks Emeraldov was killed by the Tsar's people.'

'What do you mean, killed? He committed suicide,' said Kostya, starting to get flustered. 'If I were you, I wouldn't rub these people up the wrong way. They might take offence.'

'When I come round to your hotel this evening, you can tell me if they've taken offence or not. But the most important thing you have to do is remember exactly where they take you.'

Fandorin watched through the window of the foyer as his prediction came true.

Shiftsky walked out and went over to Mr Whistle. He said something, with his head pulled into his shoulders ingratiatingly, and handed Whistle the folded sheet of paper. Whistle unfolded it and frowned. Then he waved his hand – and after that, everything happened exactly as it had the previous day. Two 'pinschers' ran over, the Ford drove up, the second car blocked off the street and the actor was taken away to have a talk with the autocrat of the Moscow scalpers.

222

Before evening arrived Erast Petrovich took action on another front and had a meeting with Mr Shustrov, after first telephoning the Theatrical and Cinematographic Company. The entrepreneur said that he would receive the dramatist immediately.

'Well, have you changed your mind?' Andrei Gordeevich asked as he shook his visitor's hand. 'Are you going to write scenarios for me?'

The style of his office was strangely non-Russian. Fine-boned furniture, constructed out of sticks and metal poles; huge windows stretching from the floor to the ceiling, with a view of the River Moscow and the factory chimneys towering up beyond it; strange pictures on the walls – nothing but cubes, squares and zigzag lines. Erast Petrovich did not understand modern art, but he attributed that to his advanced age. Every new era had its own eyes and ears – people wanted to see and hear something different. At one time even the snug, cosy Impressionists had seemed like hooligans, and now this respectable capitalist had an appalling purple woman with three legs hanging above his desk, and that was just fine.

'The game you are getting involved in is a serious one,' Fandorin said gravely, letting his eyes linger on posters for the latest films from Europe (*Dante's Inferno*, *Ancient Roman Orgy*, *Sherlock Holmes versus Professor Moriarty*). 'And I am a serious man. I have to know the rules and understand them.'

'Naturally,' the young millionaire said with a nod. 'What is it that concerns you? I'll answer any questions you have. I am extremely interested in collaborating with someone like you. Why do you hide from the reporters? Why have you only put your initials on the posters, and not your full name? That's not right, it's a mistake. I'd like to make you a star.'

This was a gentleman who had to be spoken to bluntly, so Fandorin asked his question without beating about the bush.

'How do you get along with Tsarkov? As far as I can understand, if one is not on good terms with this wheeler-dealer, it is rather d-difficult, if not impossible, to establish a theatrical and cinematographic industry in Moscow.'

Shustrov was not embarrassed by this direct question.

'I get along excellently with the Tsar.'

'Oh, indeed? But you are a protagonist of civilised entrepreneurial activity, and he is a gentleman who likes to fish in murky waters, a semi-bandit.'

'First and foremost, I am a realist. I have to take into account the specific features of Russian business. In this country the success of any large-scale initiative requires support from above and from below. From the clouds up above . . .' – Andrei Gordeevich pointed to the towers of the Kremlin, visible through the window at the end of the room – '. . . and from underground . . .' – he jabbed his finger down towards the floor. 'The powers that be permit you to do business. And nothing more than that. But if you want that business to make progress, you have to turn to the unofficial power. In our state, which is so clumsy and inconvenient for business, the unofficial power helps to lubricate the rusty gearwheels and trim the rough edges.'

'You are t-talking about figures such as Tsarkov?'

'Of course. Cooperation with this underground magnate is absolutely essential in my field of work. Working without his help would be like trying to get things done with one arm missing. And if he were hostile, our enterprise would be entirely impossible.'

'What does his help consist of?'

'Many things. For instance, are you aware that pickpockets don't ply their trade at Noah's Ark productions? One newspaper article attributed this phenomenon to the beneficial influence of high art on callous criminal hearts. But in fact the pickpockets have been frightened off by Tsarkov's people. That was done as a favour to me. He also stirs up the ballyhoo around touring performances – if he regards them as promising. It's useful for him as concerns speculation in the tickets and for me in that it increases the value of the theatre that I have backed. But the Tsar will be at his most useful to us when we develop the cinematographic side of our activity. Then his underground enterprise will expand to cover the whole of Russia. We shall have to control the distributors, maintain order in the electric theatres, curtail the production of illegal copies. The police will not be able to do this work and will not wish to. And so the Tsar and I have great plans for each other.'

Shustrov explained enthusiastically and at length how the empire of performance and spectacle that he was in the process of creating would function. Everyone in it would do the job that he had the talent for. Brilliant writers like Mr Fandorin thinking up plots and storylines. Brilliant directors like Mr Stern making films and staging inventive theatrical productions, with the former sharing a thematic connection with the latter: that is, if the current emphasis is on orientalism, a play on Japanese life is followed by two or three films on the same subject matter. This develops demand, while at the same time providing a saving on scenery and costumes. The company's own newspapers and magazines inflate the cult of its own actors and actresses. Its own electric theatres mean that takings do not have to be shared with anyone. The entire system is safe and secure from top to bottom in all its branching ramifications. Good relations with the authorities provide protection against any difficulties with the law, and good relations with the Tsar guarantee protection against criminals and sticky-fingered employees.

As Erast Petrovich listened, he wondered why, here in Russia, in all ages, the most important requirement for the success of any venture was 'good relations'. It must be because the Russians regarded laws as irritating, arbitrary obstructions invented by a certain hostile power in its own interests. And that hostile power was called 'the state'. There was never anything rational or benevolent in the actions of the state. It was an immense, sprawling, vicious monster. The only salvation was that it was also half-blind and rather stupid, and every one of its greedy gullets could be fed. Without that, it would be absolutely impossible to live in Russia. Establish good relations with the gaping, toothy maw closest to you and do whatever you like. Only don't forget to fling chunks of meat into it on time. That was the way things had been under the Rurikoviches, that was how things were under the Romanovs, and that was how things would remain until relations between the general population and the state changed fundamentally.

Having promised to give the millionaire's proposal serious thought, Erast Petrovich walked out of the Theatrical and Cinematographic Company pondering the situation seriously. The opponent he had challenged had proved to be more serious than originally thought.

The technological spirit of the twentieth century was already making inroads into the dense thickets of the criminal world of Moscow. This Tsar had American bookkeeping, a sound business structure, automobiles, and professionally organised protection. It was probably not really wise to go up against an organisation like that on his own. Like it or not, he would have to make peace with Masa . . .

A TRUE FRIEND

The Japanese did not come home to spend the night, but Erast Petrovich did not attach any importance to that. *Out chasing after skirts again*, he thought. *Well, that's all right, the plan for a little visit to Sokolniki can be discussed tomorrow.*

That evening Shiftsky had reported on his visit to the Tsar. The actor was frightened and intrigued, because the news of Fandorin's suspicions had seriously alarmed the lord of the speculators.

'But who are you? I mean, really?' Kostya asked Erast Petrovich fearfully. 'They ordered me to report every word you say immediately . . . Why are they so frightened of you?'

'I have no idea,' Fandorin replied, fixing the actor with an unblinking gaze. 'But I advise you very seriously not to inform Mr Whistle about every word I s-say.'

Shiftsky gulped.

'I g-get it . . .' And then he panicked. 'Oh, I didn't mean to make fun of you! It just happened!'

'I believe you. So, a two-storey detached house in Sokolniki, at the end of Deer Grove Street? I tell you what, sit down and draw the area as accurately as you can. I'm curious about the surroundings . . .'

At home on Cricket Lane, with the help of a detailed police map of the Meshchansky district, which included Deer Grove Street, along with all the rest of Sokolniki, Erast Petrovich identified Mr Tsarkov's present address. The building to which Shiftsky had been taken was once a country house outside the city, but now it stood on the grounds of the park. On the map it was actually marked as 'Deer Grove'. Under cover of night Fandorin paid a visit to the north-eastern sector of Sokolniki in order to take a look at the objective and, if the opportunity arose, carry out his plan there and then.

He was obliged to abandon the idea of a full-frontal cavalry charge. At first glance the house appeared to be located conveniently. Dense bushes ran almost right up to it from three sides. However, this apparent ease of access was deceptive. The Office was well protected. There was one 'pinscher' on guard all the time on the porch, keeping his eyes fixed on the alley leading to the isolated house. When Fandorin trained his binoculars on the windows, he counted another four of them on watch inside. All the curtains were tightly closed, but even so there were little gaps left at the top, just below the cornice. In order to get some idea of how the ground floor was arranged, Erast Petrovich had to climb trees on three sides of the house. It was an undignified kind of activity, but refreshing – it made Fandorin feel a bit younger. And at the same time he gained a fairly accurate impression of the layout of the Office.

The upper floor contained the Tsar's chambers and Mr Whistle's room. Down below there were two large spaces. One of these, to judge from the furnishings, was the dining room. The other – where guards loitered constantly – was the working office. Fandorin even managed to examine two large, lacquered cabinets of unusual design which glinted in the orange light of the kerosene lamps. Without a doubt, they were the personal archive of His Speculative Majesty.

It was no Plevna fortress, of course, but it couldn't be taken by storm, especially by one man acting alone. But two men – himself and Masa – now that was a different matter.

After his successful reconnaissance, feeling restored for the first time in an entire month, he went back home and slept for four hours, and then it was time to go to the theatre. Erast Petrovich had to catch Masa before the rehearsal began, so at half past ten he was already sitting in the auditorium, concealed behind a newspaper – an excellent way to avoid the idle chatter of which actors were so fond. He had observed long ago that reading a newspaper, especially if one assumed an air of concentration, inspired respect in others and warded off any superfluous contact. But Fandorin did not even have to act out any pretence. Today's *Morning of Russia* carried an extremely interesting interview with the minister of trade and industry, Timashev, about the excellent fiscal situation in the empire: liquidity reserves of more than 300 million roubles had been accumulated from budget surpluses, the Russian currency's exchange rate was strenghtening day by day and the government's energetic policy was quite certain to set Russia on the road to a bright future. Erast Petrovich's own prognoses concerning the future of Russia were not optimistic, but how glorious it would be to be mistaken!

From time to time he glanced at the doors. The theatre company was gradually gathering. Everyone was in their normal clothes – the established rules called for rehearsals to be conducted with scenery, but without make-up or costumes. The brilliant Noah Noaevich believed that this laid bare an actor's technique, rendering the errors and miscalculations more obvious

Aphrodisina came in. Erast Petrovich did not lower his eyes back to the newspaper, expecting that Masa would appear after her, but he was mistaken – the 'coquette' had arrived alone.

He had to read another article, about the historical events in China. A revolt by a single battalion in the provincial city of Wuchang, which had begun a week earlier, had led to Chinese everywhere cutting off their pigtails, refusing to submit to the authority of the emperor and demanding a republic. It was incredible to think what an immense behemoth had been set in motion by such a little spark – 400 million people! And the Europeans were apparently not even aware that mighty, somnolent Asia had awoken. It could not be stopped now. As its oscillations slowly gathered amplitude, spreading wider and wider, it would submerge the entire planet under its waves. The world was ceasing to be white and – as the Japanese put it – 'round-eyed'; now it would turn yellow and its eyes would inevitably grow narrower. How interesting all this was!

He looked up from *Morning of Russia*, trying to picture to himself newly awoken, black-haired Asia in alliance with enlightened, golden-haired Europe. And he froze. There was Eliza walking into the hall, arm-in-arm with Masa. They were smiling at each other and whispering about something.

The newspaper rustled as it slid down off Fandorin's knees.

'Good morning, gentlemen,' said the vilest, loveliest woman in the world. Spotting Erast Petrovich, she glanced at him with obvious embarrassment, even timidity. She hadn't been expecting to meet him.

But Masa looked at his master with a most independent air and thrust his chin out proudly. The Japanese also had newspapers under his arm. He had only recently developed a passion for reading the press – since the journalists had started writing about the director Stern's 'oriental discovery'. Now Masa bought all the Moscow publications early in the morning.

'Nothing today. They only write that the day after tomorrow is the second pu-er-o-form-ance,' he enunciated painstakingly, placing the newspapers on the director's little desk. 'And that the pubric is waiting impatientry for the next triumph of Madam Rointaine and the inimitabur Swardirin. Look, here.' He pointed out a tiny article circled in thick red pencil.

Some of the actors came over to see whether there was anything written about them as well. To judge from the expressions on their faces, no one was mentioned apart from the two leading artistes.

Fandorin gritted his teeth, feeling completely crushed by this new, double, betrayal. He no longer remembered that he had intended to patch things up with his friend. The only thing he wanted to do was to leave. But he could only do that without attracting attention to himself after the rehearsal began, and for some reason it simply didn't begin.

Nonarikin walked out onstage.

'Noah Noaevich telephoned. He apologised and said he was with Mr Shustrov and has been delayed.'

The actors, who had been about to take seats in the front row, got up again and scattered throughout the hall.

The 'villainess' Vulpinova walked over to the desk; beside which the two leading artistes were seated like a pair of turtle doves. She picked up *The Capital Rumour* and spoke to Masa in a sweet voice.

'Dear Swardilin, please read us something interesting.'

'Yes, yes, I love to listen to you too!' Mephistov put in, smiling with his entire immense mouth.

The Japanese did not have to be asked twice.

'What sharr I read?'

'Anything you like, it doesn't matter,' said Vulpinova, winking at Mephistov. 'You have such a resonant voice! Such enchanting delivery!'

At any other time Fandorin would not have permitted these spiteful characters to mock his comrade, but just at this moment, he experienced a repulsive gloating. Let this puffed-up turkey, this brand-new 'star', make a laughing stock of himself in front of Eliza and all the others! This wasn't as easy as tumbling around the stage without a single line to speak!

Masa was very fond of the sound of his own voice, so he did not find the request surprising. He gladly opened the double page of newsprint, cleared his throat and with the intonation of a genuine orator started reading out everything, with no exceptions. There were advertisements in handsome frames at the top of the page – he didn't even omit those.

He began with an advertisement for 'Sobriety' pastilles, which promised a cure for drinking bouts, and read the text expressively all the way to the end.

'. . . A huge number of habituar drunkards have sent touching expressions of gratitude, enthusiasticarry praising the miracurous effects of the pastirres.'

'We've tried these "Sobriety" pastilles,' Sensiblin boomed in his deep voice. 'They're no good. Just give you heartburn.'

Masa read out with equal feeling an invitation by 'the firus-crass artist V. N. Reonardov' to enrol as one of his pupils in a course of painting and drawing.

'What is "firus-crass"?' he asked.

'"Crass" means "very good", "very beautiful",' Mephistov explained without batting an eyelid. 'For instance, you could be called a "really crass actor".'

Erast Petrovich frowned, seeing the grins on some of the actors' faces as they listened to Masa. The jealous man was unable to take any pleasure in them.

However, not everyone was mocking the Japanese as he distorted his words. Aphrodisina, for example, was smiling wistfully. In the eyes of a woman of her character, infidelity probably only increased the value of a lover. The *grande dame* Reginina was also listening with a touching smile.

'Ah, read something about animals,' she requested. 'I'm very fond of the "Zoological Gardens News" section on the last page.'

Masa turned over the sheet of newsprint.

'"Pyton Attacks Doctor Sidorov".'

And he did not simply read but in effect he reproduced the entire appalling scene of the python's attack on the head of the terrarium. The doctor had been bitten on the arm and the reptile had only unclenched its teeth when it was doused with water.

'How terrible!' Vasilisa Prokofievna exclaimed, clutching at her ample bosom. 'I immediately recalled the nightmarish snake in the basket! I can't imagine how you survived that, dear Eliza. Really, I would have died on the spot!'

Madam Lointaine turned pale and squeezed her eyes shut. Masa (the scoundrel, the scoundrel!) got up, stroked her shoulder soothingly and carried on reading – about a newborn lion cub that had been rejected by its mother. The little mite had been saved by a stray mongrel bitch who agreed to feed it with her milk.

Reginina liked this article far more.

'I can just imagine it, how charming – the tiny little lion cub! And that wonderful, magnanimous mongrel! Really, I could just go and take a look at that!'

Encouraged by his success, Masa said:

'Farther on here there's a very interesting rittur articur. "Bears' Rives in Danger".' And he read out an article about the mysterious illness of two brown bears and how the mystery had been solved by the veterinarian Mr Tobolkin. It had been suspected that the animals were suffering from plague but, as Masa joyfully informed his listeners: '"In the doctor's opinion, the irrness was the resurt of the intensive masturbation in which the bears indurged from morning untir evening. This fate is rare among bears, but it often affects monkeys and camers." That's absorutery true! In the jungur I myserf have often seen rittur monkeys . . .'

232

Masa stopped short, with an expression of incomprehension on his round face: why had Vasilisa Prokofievna turned away indignantly and the two 'villains' burst into hysterical laughter?

Fandorin suddenly felt sorry for the poor fellow. The difference in codes of education, in conceptions absorbed in childhood concerning what was decent and what was not, were an almost insuperable barrier. The callow youth from Yokohama had lived far away from Japan for almost thirty years, but he still could not completely accustom himself to the mores of the 'redheads': either he blurted out something that was scandalous from the viewpoint of a *grande dame*, or blushed bright red in shame at something which to the Western eye was entirely innocent – for instance, a seated woman has dropped her umbrella and pulled it closer with the toe of her little shoe (monstrous vulgarity!).

From sympathy it was only a single step to understanding. Erast Petrovich looked at Masa's red face – and suddenly seemed to see the light. The Japanese had quite deliberately made up to Eliza, and the fact that he had arrived with her following his overnight absence was no coincidence either! This was not the action of a traitor; on the contrary, it was the action of a true and faithful friend. Knowing his master as well as he did and seeing the pitiful state that he was in, Masa had tried to cure him of his fatal obsession, using a method that was cruel but effective. He had not tried to persuade Erast Petrovich by wasting empty words on him – they would not have had any effect in any case. Instead of that he had graphically demonstrated the true worth of the woman who – exclusively through a perfidious concatenation of circumstances – had forced a breach in a heart encased for so long in horny defences. It was all the same to this artiste whom she conquered – just as long as the trophy was presentable. She had turned the boy-cornet's head, but not allowed him into her bed – he was not a high enough flyer. A successful playwright or a fashionable Japanese actor, now that was a different matter. There was nothing surprising here, nothing to wax indignant about. Fandorin had intuitively sensed that from the very beginning, had he not, when he was figuring out the most reliable path to Madam Lointaine's heart (no, only to her body)? Indeed it was Masa, that connoisseur of women's hearts, who had prompted him to take that path.

Of course, Erast Petrovich was no longer angry with his comrade. He was actually grateful to him.

But even so, to watch the way Eliza smiled affectionately at the Japanese and the way he took her by the elbow and whispered something in her ear was beyond all enduring.

Without an assistant Erast Petrovich could not carry out the operation he had planned. But he felt that he could not take Masa with him; he did not wish to. The very idea seemed intolerable to him, and Fandorin immediately found logical grounds for his feeling. A surgical incision, although it was made for a virtuous purpose, always stung and bled. Time was required for the scar to heal over.

'Ladies and gentlemen!' the assistant director appealed loudly to the assembled company. 'Do not let yourselves be distracted! You know that Noah Noaevich demands absolute concentration before a rehearsal! Let us begin the first scene. And when Noah Noaevich arrives, we'll go through it again.'

'Now look what he wants,' Sensiblin growled. 'A rehearsal of a rehearsal – that's something new.'

The others took no notice of Nonarikin's appeals either. In his anguish, the assistant director pressed his hands against his breast – the edge of a false cuff protruded from the sleeve of his skimpy little jacket.

'None of you genuinely love art!' he exclaimed. 'You only pretend to believe in Noah Noaevich's theory! Ladies and gentlemen, that isn't right! You have to devote yourself wholeheartedly to your calling! Remember: "All the world's a stage!" Let us try to begin! I shall read the Storyteller's part myself!'

No one apart from Fandorin was listening to him. But Erast Petrovich was struck by an unexpected idea.

Why not take Georges Nonarikin with him on the job?

He had his eccentricities, of course, but he was very brave – one only had to recall the poisoned rapier. That was one.

A former officer. That was two.

And also – a point of particular importance – not indiscreet. He wouldn't let anything slip to anyone about Fandorin's investigation into Emeraldov's death. And, what was more, not once since that incident had he made any attempts to talk about it, although Erast

Petrovich had caught his curious, enquiring glance. Truly exceptional restraint for an actor!

Yes, really. The plan of the operation could be adjusted to reduce
the role of the assistant to a minimum.

Basically, Masa's talents – his fighting skills, initiative and
lightning-fast reactions – would not be required here. A sense of
duty and firm resolution would be enough. And Georges certainly
had no lack of those qualities. It was no accident that Stern had
chosen him as his assistant . . .

The conversation with the assistant director confirmed the correct-
ness of the spontaneous decision.

Erast Petrovich led the distressed Nonarikin into the side apron
of the stage.

'You once offered t-to help me. The hour has come. Are you
ready? But I must tell you that the job entails a certain risk.' He
corrected himself: 'I would even say, a significant risk.'

Nonarikin didn't think about it for even a moment.

'I am entirely at your disposal.'

'Are you not even going to ask what it is that I want from you?'

'There is no need.' Georges looked at Fandorin unflinchingly
with his big, round eyes. 'Firstly, you are a man who has seen the
world. I saw how respectfully the police officer listened to you.'

'And secondly?' Fandorin asked curiously.

'Secondly, you could not suggest anything unworthy to me. You
are a man of noble spirit. That is clear from your play and from your
manner. I especially appreciate the fact that since our conversation
on that occasion your conduct with regard to a certain individual
has been beyond reproach. And neither have you told anyone about
my own unfortunate weakness (I mean Mademoiselle Comedina).
In short, whatever idea you may have come up with, I am prepared
to follow you. And all the more so if the business that lies ahead is
dangerous.' The assistant director jerked up his chin in a dignified
manner. 'If I refused, I should lose all respect for myself.'

Of course, he was slightly comical with that high-flown manner
of speaking that he had, but moving at the same time. Erast
Petrovich, who was accustomed to playing close attention to his own

attire, could not help noticing that Nonarikin was dressed poorly; a jacket that was neat, but had seen better days; a shirtfront instead of a shirt; shoes that were well polished, but had patched heels. Noah Noaevich did not reward the efforts of his assistant very generously – in fact, he paid him as a 'third-level' actor, in accordance with the significance of the roles that he played.

And all because, Fandorin mused, *the model of humanity created by Stern lacks one important set of parts. It is somewhat exotic, but without it the palette of dramatic roles is incomplete and life is insipid. Moreover, this type is encountered more often in literature than in everyday life. Georges would suit the role of a 'noble eccentric' quite excellently – Cervantes' Don Quixote, Griboedov's Chatsky, Dostoevsky's Prince Mishkin.*

Certainly, Nonarikin's awkwardness could result in unexpected problems. Erast Petrovich promised himself to reduce his assistant's role to the absolutely simplest possible. Never mind, it was better to go on serious business with a man who might be slightly inept, but was noble, than with some self-seeking police careerist, who at the crucial moment would decide that his own interests were more important. Someone who possessed a highly developed sense of his own dignity could let you down through an inadvertent blunder, but never out of base villainy or cowardice.

How much easier it would be to live in this world, if only everybody regarded himself with respect, Fandorin thought after his conversation with the assistant director.

There was a class of human individuals that Erast Petrovich had always regarded with disgust. There were people who said quite calmly, without the slightest embarrassment: 'I know that I'm shit'. They even saw a certain virtue in this, a distinctive kind of honesty. Of course, the immediate continuation of this remorseless confession was this: 'And everyone around me is shit too, only they hide behind beautiful words'. In every noble action a person like this immediately searched for a base motive and he was furious if he could not guess it immediately. But in the end, of course, he figured something out and heaved a sigh of relief. 'Oh, come on!' he exclaimed. 'You can't fool me. We're all cut from the same cloth.' The philanthropist was generous, because he felt flattered by the awareness of his own superiority. The humanist was kind only in words, but in actual fact he was false through and through and only wanted to show off. Anyone who went to serve hard labour for his beliefs was a stupid ass, pure and simple. The martyr offered himself up for slaughter because individuals of that kind derived perverted sexual pleasure from feeling victimised. And so on. People who were willing to consider themselves shit could not live without rationalisations – that would have shattered their entire picture of existence.

THE DEER GROVE OPERATION

On the way there he asked his partner to demonstrate the result of his training once again. It was evening time, almost night, the Isotta Fraschini was hurtling along between the ill-famed vacant lots and flophouses of the Sokolniki streets and the undulating trill that Nonarikin emitted after applying his fingers, folded into a ring, to his teeth rang out ominously. If there was anyone wandering belatedly through the darkness somewhere near by, the poor devil's heart must surely have sunk into his boots.

After the rehearsal Erast Petrovich had secluded himself with Georges in the empty make-up room and informed him of the results of the investigation.

According to the conclusions drawn by Fandorin, the sequence of events was as follows:

Emeraldov's male jealousy and envy of his stage partner's success drive him to commit the vile trick with the viper. The Tsar instructs his lieutenant to find out who is responsible for the trick. Mr Whistle reports to his boss that the actor is the guilty party. Aware that the success of the extremely profitable tour by Noah's Ark depends first and foremost on Eliza, and fearing that Emeraldov will play another mean trick on her, the Tsar orders the threat to be removed. In his opinion (and he has been proved right), a leading man like Emeraldov will be no great loss for the company in any case. When Whistle shows up at Hippolyte's dressing room with the wine, the actor doesn't suspect anything bad. They have probably drunk together before. The former policeman slips poison into the Chateau

Latour. If not for the crack in the second goblet, the staged suicide would have passed off entirely successfully.

Not everything about the second murder was so clear. Obviously, Limbach owed the Office a lot of money and he did not want to repay it, and, what's more, he did everything he could to avoid any discussion of the matter – Fandorin had witnessed one such scene in front of the entrance to the theatre. During the premiere of *Two Comets*, Whistle somehow found out that Limbach had sneaked into Eliza's dressing room and was waiting for her there – probably in order to congratulate her face to face. This time there was no way the cornet could avoid the discussion. Apparently the conversation had ended in an argument and Whistle had been obliged to make use of his clasp knife. The murder was most likely not premeditated – otherwise the criminal would have finished off his victim. Instead of that, he panicked, ran out into the corridor and waited until the wounded man went quiet. The duplicate key had probably been made by the cornet, especially so that he could sneak into the dressing room – it was possible to surmise that Whistle had discovered this in the course of their turbulent discussion. While Whistle was holding the door to prevent the wounded man from getting out into the corridor, a plan had occurred to him. If he locked the door with the key from the board and the second key was discovered on the dead man, everybody would be certain that Limbach had locked himself in and slashed his own stomach. All that was required was to put the knife in the dead man's hand, and this had been done. However, as in the case of the leaking goblet, Mr Whistle had again failed to pay close enough attention. He hadn't noticed that the dying man had traced out in blood on the door the initial letters of the name 'Lipkov', which had eventually led the police (as Fandorin modestly put it) onto the trail.

Nonarikin had listened with rapt attention.

'When this is all over, you should write a play about it,' he declared. 'It would be a sensation – a criminal drama hot on the heels of the villainous crime! Noah Noaevich would like the idea. And that profit-hungry Shustrov would like it even more. It would be my dream to play Whistle! Will you write that part for me?'

'First play yourself,' said Erast Petrovich, cooling Nonarikin's ardour and inwardly regretting that he had become involved with the actor. 'Tonight. Only watch out: in this theatre of ours a flop can result in death. Of the real kind.'

Not in the least bit frightened, Georges exclaimed:

'Then let's rehearse. What do I have to do?'

'Whistle artistically. Consider it practice for playing the part of Mr Whistle. Every self-respecting Moscow gang has its own way of communicating. It's like in the animal world – a sound signal serves a double function: to allow your own kind to recognise you and to frighten away strangers. I have assembled an entire music collection of bandits' whistles. The Sukharev Square gang, led by a certain Acrobat, which was driven away from its rich feeding trough some time ago by our f-friends, uses a trill like this.' Erast Petrovich folded his fingers together in a special way and gave a resounding, rollicking, hooligan whistle that rang through the empty theatre. 'Right, then, you try to repeat that.'

'What for?' Nonarikin asked after thinking for a moment.

'Let's agree,' Fandorin said with a polite smile, 'that if I tell you to do something, you don't think about it and ask me "what for", but simply do it. Otherwise our p-plan could turn out badly.'

'Like in the army? Orders are not to be discussed, but carried out? Yes, sir.'

Fandorin's assistant asked his commanding officer to show him one more time and then, to Erast Petrovich's amazement, at the first attempt he produced a rather convincing imitation of the Sukharev Square villains' battle call. 'Bravo, Georges. You have a talent.'

'I'm an actor, after all. Imitating is my profession.'

By nightfall, after practising zealously, Georges had achieved genuine mastery, which he demonstrated with every possible diligence.

'N-no more! You've deafened me.' Erast Petrovich took one hand off the steering wheel and gestured to stop the enthusiastic whistler. 'You do that excellently. The Tsar and his guards will be absolutely convinced that the Sukharev Square gang has attacked them. Tell me once again what you have to do.'

'Yes, sir.' Nonarikin flung up his hand in military style to the rakishly angled peaked cap that had been issued to him especially for the operation. The smart blades from Sukharev Square flaunted headgear like that – unlike the Khitrovka bandits, who preferred soft, eight-sided caps, or the Grachovka hoodlums, who considered it chic to go around bareheaded.

'I wait in the bushes to the south-west of the house . . .'

'Where I position you,' Fandorin specified.

'Where you position me. I look at my watch. Precisely every three hundred seconds I start to whistle. When men come running out of the house, I fire two shots.' Fandorin's assistant took his officer's Nagant revolver out of his belt. 'Into the air.'

'Not simply into the air, but vertically upwards, hiding behind a tree trunk. Otherwise the pinschers will identify your location from the flashes and start firing straight at you.'

'Yes, sir.'

'And then?'

'Then I start moving in the direction of the Yauza river, firing every now and then.'

'Into the air as before. It is not our intention to kill anyone. You simply have to lure the guards away.'

'Yes, sir. In tactics that is called "drawing the main forces of the enemy against oneself".'

'Yes, that's it.' Erast Petrovich cast a dubious sideways glance at his passenger. 'For God's sake, don't let them cut down the distance between you. Don't go playing the hero. Your job is to get them to follow you to the river, and there you'll stop firing and simply run off. That's all. That will be the end of your mission.'

Nonarikin protested with a dignified air.

'Mr Fandorin, I am an officer of the Russian army. In tactical matters I can perform a false retreat, but I do not consider it possible to run away, especially from some riff-raff or other. Believe me, I am capable of more than that.'

What am I doing? Erast Petrovich asked himself. *I'm putting a dilettante's life in danger. And all because I took offence at Masa, like a stupid idiot. Perhaps I should call off the operation before it's too late?*

'On the other hand, discipline is discipline. The order will be carried out,' Nonarikin sighed. 'But promise me this: if you need any help, you'll whistle to me in the Sukharev Square style, and I'll come rushing to assist you.'

'Excellent. Agreed. If I don't whistle, it means I don't need your help,' Fandorin said in relief. 'But there is nothing to be worried about. There will not be any complications. Trust my experience.'

'You're in command, you know best,' the retired lieutenant replied briefly, and Erast Petrovich felt almost completely reassured.

Now, according to the science of psychology, in order to dispel any excessive nervousness, he ought to strike up a conversation on some distracting subject. There were still ten minutes left until they reached Sokolniki Park. A fine rain had started falling. That was most opportune for the operation.

'I find it strange that a man of your character left military service in order to walk the boards,' Fandorin said in a light tone of voice, as if they were on their way to some kind of society event. 'The uniform probably suited you and a military career is an excellent match for your character. After all, you're an idealist, a romantic. And the life of a theatre director, such as you wish to be, ultimately consists of highly p-prosaic matters: is a play good, will it bring in money at the box office, will the public come to see your actors . . . The status of a theatre is not determined by the quality of the art, but by the price of a ticket. Noah Noaevich and the famous Stanislavsky are regarded as geniuses because on their posters it says: "Seat prices increased".'

This attempt to distract his companion with an alternative topic was successful.

'Oh, how mistaken you are! I'm an absolute theatre addict. For me, not only is all the world a stage, for me the theatre is the centre of creation, its ideal model, stripped of banal and unnecessary impurities! Of course here, just as in the ordinary world, everything has its price. But the point is precisely that the price has been *increased*. Its value is higher than that of pitiful reality. When I'm on the stage, everything else ceases to exist! Nothing has any significance – neither the audience in the hall, nor the city outside the walls of the theatre, nor the country, nor the entire globe of the earth! It is like genuine love, when all you want in the whole, wide world is one woman. You are prepared to love the whole of the human race in her, and without her the human race is worth nothing to you, it has no meaning.'

'You exaggerate s-somewhat, but I understand what you have in mind,' Erast Petrovich remarked morosely.

Georges muttered discontentedly.

'I never exaggerate. I am a very precise individual.'

'Well then, carry out everything precisely as we agreed. We've arrived. We go on from here on foot.'

There was quite a distance to walk. A long alley led from Sokolniki Avenue to Deer Grove House. Naturally, it was impossible to drive along it in the automobile – in the silence of the night the rumbling of the motor would have alarmed the guards. They moved along without speaking, each of them thinking his own thoughts. *Or perhaps our thoughts are about the same thing*, Fandorin suddenly thought. *That is, about one and the same person . . .*

Because of the low clouds and the lingering drizzle, they couldn't see the road. Erast Petrovich was wary of switching on a torch. In pitch darkness even a feeble gleam can be seen from a long distance. They walked side by side, but not in step. Suddenly Nonarikin exclaimed loudly and disappeared – quite literally.

'What's happened to you?'

'Here I am . . .'

A head wearing a cap appeared straight up out of the ground.

'There's a ditch here. Give me your hand . . .'

For some reason a narrow ditch really had been dug across the road. On the vehicular section it had been covered over with planks, but on the margin, along which the two accomplices were walking, there was no covering. Erast Petrovich had been lucky – he had stepped over it without noticing, but Georges' foot had hit the precise centre of the hole.

'Never mind, I'm not hurt. . .' Fandorin's assistant clambered out. 'Thank you.'

This little incident did not appear to have disturbed Nonarikin's equilibrium. Erast Petrovich mentally acknowledged the strength of the former sapper's nerves. Dusting off his clothes, Nonarikin said pensively:

'Not long ago I would have regarded this fall as a bad omen, a sign of the ill-disposition of Fate. I told you that I am in the habit of trusting providence blindly. But I have reconsidered my views. There is nothing fatalistic in the fact that you strode over the ditch and I fell. It is simply that you are luckier than I am. You know, I think now that there is no Fate. Fate is blind. Only the artist is sighted! Everything is decided and determined by one's own will.'

'I am more or less of the same opinion; however, if you have put your c-clothing in order, let us move on. And for God's sake, watch your step!'

When the house appeared in the distance, in the middle of a small clearing, with its curtained-off windows glowing dully, Erast Petrovich moved off the margin of the road into the bushes. He wanted to get this simple job that was dragging on for so long over and done with.

'Stay here,' he whispered to Nonarikin, leaving him behind an old birch tree on the edge of the clearing. 'Here, take my watch. It has phosphorescent hands. Precisely five minutes.'

'Your word is my command.'

Georges waved his Nagant cheerfully.

Fandorin took off his leather jacket and cap and was left clad in a black gymnastic leotard. He bent down and ran out into the clearing, then flattened himself out completely and started creeping along, counting off the seconds. At two hundred he was already in position, fifteen strides from the porch where the bored sentry was languishing.

The plan for luring out the 'pinschers' was primitive in the extreme, but Fandorin was always guided by a rule that said: do not complicate anything that does not need to be complicated. The opponents he was up against were not spies or saboteurs, or even a gang of killers. These thugs were not used to waging war; the way they would behave in a critical situation was easy to predict. Obviously, the Tsar was not seriously afraid of a frontal assault – otherwise he would not have moved into such an isolated spot. He and Whistle regarded the mobility of the Office and their distance from the city neighbourhoods as the guarantee of their safety. So a

visit from the Sukharev Square gang, whom they regarded as defeated, would come as all the more of a surprise to them . . .

Just as long as the absolute theatre fanatic didn't mess things
up . . .

He didn't. When Erast Petrovich's count reached three hundred
a rakish whistle rang out from the bushes. Georges managed superbly, reproducing the Sukharev Square whistle in three distinct
registers, as if there were several of the whistling bandits there. That
was exactly how the Acrobat's men would have behaved if they had
found out where the Office was and made a drunken decision in the
middle of the night to get even with their old foes. They would have
rushed to the park in a cab, driving with reckless derring-do, but
as they got closer to the Office, their wild belligerence would have
evaporated. They would have had just enough courage to whistle
out of the bushes, but no one would have crept out into open space
to face the pinschers' bullets.

The sentry flew down off the steps, grabbing a revolver out of his
pocket. Apparently Mr Whistle hired serious troopers, not the timid
kind. Two shots rang out in the thickets – Nonarikin was playing his
part irreproachably. The pinscher also fired a shot at random. Thank
God, not in the direction of the spot where the assistant director
was hiding.

The other four guards were already running out of the house,
holding their guns at the ready.

'Where are they? Where?' the watchmen shouted.

Mr Whistle came darting out – in his braces, with no jacket.

A window frame banged on the upper floor. It was the Tsar glancing out. He was wearing a dressing gown and a nightcap.

'It's bunkum, August Ivanich!' Whistle exclaimed, throwing his
head back. 'The Sukharev louts have gone crazy. We'll soon teach
them a lesson. Piebald, you stay here. Everyone else, forward! Give
them a good thrashing!'

The four pinschers went dashing forward, firing haphazardly and
shouting. There was the indistinct retort of a shot in the bushes too
– already some distance away.

'They're sloping off. Over that way!'

Boots tramped and branches cracked, and the pack was lost to sight. The shooting and the howling started moving farther away.

So far everything was going ideally.

'I told you, Lipkov,' the Tsar shouted angrily from up above. 'We should have eliminated that gorilla Acrobat from the Sukharev mob! Come up here! We'll have a talk.'

'Eliminate him – it's never too late, August Ivanich. We'll do it.'

But the Tsar was no longer in the window.

Whistle scratched his cheek perplexedly and called curtly to the sentry who was nicknamed Piebald.

'You keep your eyes peeled.' And he disappeared into the house.

Meanwhile, Fandorin had picked up a conveniently sized cobble. Erast Petrovich had been a master at the art of throwing stones since his time in Japan.

A dull, sappy thud – and Mr Piebald tumbled down off the steps without a shout or a groan. The profession that he had chosen for himself was fraught with various kinds of risks. The risk, for instance, of incurring a moderately serious concussion.

Fandorin entered the house, moving soundlessly. He ran through the dining room and found himself in the study.

No, this isn't a genuine adventure, he thought disappointedly. *This is some kind of Detective Putilin's Diary.*

He had brought an entire set of picklocks with him, for every kind of lock. But the much vaunted American cabinets opened with the very first of them, the most elementary.

All right now, let's see what kind of secrets of the court of Madrid we have here . . .

The first cabinet was divided into sections containing all the legal and illegal amusements of the first capital city of Russia (Erast Petrovich immediately dubbed this depository 'The Garden of Delights'). There were six drawers. Each had a beautiful little label with a typed title and a small graphic symbol – a truly delightful sight. There was 'Theatre' with a mask, 'Cinematograph' with a little beam of light, 'Circus' with a strongman's dumbbells, 'Restaurants and Inns' with a little bottle, 'Sport' with a boxing glove and 'Love' with a symbol that made Fandorin wince – he was not fond of obscenity. It turned out that Sergei Nikiforovich Subbotin did not have the full picture of the extent of the Tsar's domain. Or perhaps the underground empire's borders had expanded since last year, when the titular counsellor collected his information. It was a well-known fact that highly profitable corporations with multiple profiles expanded rapidly.

Erast Petrovich took out one folder at random from the sport section. All right, then, the Samson Wrestling Club. A surname on the cover, with 'nominal owner' in brackets; a second surname with the word 'owner' and the note: 'see Personnel'. Inside there were dates, figures, sums of money and a list of fighters with payouts. The Tsar obviously made money from fixed fights as well as on the tickets. No ciphers or codes – sure testimony that the person who drew up the archive felt safe and was not even slightly concerned about unexpected visits from the police.

As he went about his task quickly and confidently, Fandorin listened carefully for a creak on the stairs. He could still hear shots, as before, but from a significant distance away, and the shouting could not be heard at all. Good for Nonarikin; apparently he had already led the pinschers all the way to the Yauza. The second cabinet should have been named, in the manner of a library, 'The Personal Catalogue'. Here the labels on the drawers said: 'Actors', 'Debtors', 'Friends', 'Informants', 'Clients', 'Girls', 'Boys', 'Our People', 'Sportsmen' and so on – at least twenty of them altogether. No playful little pictures, everything very businesslike. Inside there were more folders, with names on them. Erast Petrovich ran rapidly through the 'Friends' section and shook his head: almost the entire municipal council of Moscow, the councillors of the city parliament, an immense number of police officers. There was no time now to work out which of them were paid wages by the Tsar and which of them simply benefited from his favours. The job had to be carried out first.

Fandorin opened the drawer with the label 'Debtors' and found what he was looking for under the letter 'L': 'LIMBACH, Vladimir Karlovich, born 1889, St Ptsbg, cornet of the Life Guards regiment'. The sums were noted on lined paper, from fifty to two hundred roubles. Some had been crossed out and marked 'paid'. One entry said: 'bouquet for 25 roubles'. The last two entries were these:

'4.10. In liaison with Altairsky-Lointaine (?). Make him an offer.

'5.10. He refused. Take measures.'

Well then, that seemed to be all. Probably the Tsar was alarmed when he heard that Limbach had become Eliza's lover. The business of Emeraldov's punishment demonstrated that the underground magnate was counting on great things from this actress. Obviously, like the millionaire Shustrov, he saw immense potential in her. (Erast Petrovich found that thought comforting: he hadn't lost his head over some ordinary, run-of-the-mill coquette, after all, but over a great artiste, a truly outstanding woman.) While Eliza's unpredictable and dangerous stage partner had simply been done away with, they had at least first tried to 'make an offer' to the tiresome cornet: let's say, that he leave the actress alone in return for his debts being written off. Or, on the contrary: that Limbach take on the role of an informant, reporting to the Tsar on the leading lady's behaviour and mood. Outside the theatre Fandorin had been a chance eyewitness to this attempt to clarify relations (or one of them). Limbach had refused ('I am an officer of His Majesty's guards!'). His next conversation with Mr Whistle had ended in a quarrel and a blow from a knife.

Just in case, Erast Petrovich glanced into the 'Actors' section, but he didn't find Emeraldov there. That was only natural: why keep the folder if the man was already in the graveyard?

Unable to resist, he took out Eliza's folder. He learned a few new things about her. For instance, her date of birth (1 January 1882); in the 'preferences' section it said: 'perfume with the fragrance of Parma violets, the colour purple, don't send her money, likes ivory'. Fandorin recalled that she often had fanciful grips made of something white in her hair. So the aroma of violets, which he had taken to be her natural scent, was explained by perfume? Erast Petrovich frowned at the 'Lovers' section. There were two names. The first was his own, crossed out. The second was Limbach's, with a question mark.

All this, however, was mere nonsense, of no significance at all. The important thing was that his theory had been confirmed, so he could now proceed to the stage of clarifying matters face to face.

If the pinschers should return while the conversation was in full flow, that was no disaster. Those ruffians did not represent any danger for a professional. Nonetheless, Erast Petrovich laid his flat, compact Browning on the desk and covered it with a sheet of paper. He sat down in an armchair, crossed his legs and lit up a cigar. Then he called loudly:

'Hey, you up there! Enough of that whispering! Come down here if you please!'

The vague muttering coming from the upper floor stopped.

'Look lively, gentlemen! It is I, Fandorin!'

The sound of an overturned chair. Feet tramping on the stairs. Whistle burst into the study, clutching a Mauser in his hand. When he saw the visitor peaceably smoking a cigar, he froze. Mr Tsarkov stuck his head out from behind his henchman's shoulder – he was still in his dressing gown, but without the nightcap, and his hair was sticking up in clumps round his bald patch.

'Have a seat, August Ivanovich,' Fandorin told him calmly, taking no notice of the Mauser. His relaxed pose was deceptive. The instant Mr Whistle's finger started moving, the chair would have been empty and the bullet would merely have drilled a hole in its upholstery. Since the time when he had mastered the difficult art of instantaneous relocation, Erast Petrovich had taken good care to maintain his form.

Casting a significant glance at his assistant, the autocrat of all Moscow moved forward cautiously and stood facing his uninvited visitor. Whistle kept the seated man in his sights.

Excellent. The other man must have the illusion that he was in control of the situation and could break off the conversation at any moment – in a fashion fatal for Erast Petrovich.

'I was expecting a visit from you. But under less extravagant circumstances.' Tsarkov nodded at the window, from where they could hear the sound of shots, although less frequently now. 'I am aware that you suspect me of something. Actually, I even know what it is. You could have made civilised arrangements to meet, and I would have disabused you.'

'I wanted to take a look into your archive first,' Fandorin exclaimed.

Only now did the Tsar notice the rifled cabinets. His pudgy face contorted in fury.

'Whoever you might be, even if you're Nick Carter or Sherlock Holmes a thousand times over, this is impudence that you will have to answer for!'

'I'm willing. But f-first you answer me. I accuse you – or, to be technically precise, your principal assistant – of two murders.'

Lipkov whistled ironically.

'Well, two might as well be three,' he said menacingly. 'Why be petty about things?'

'Wait.' The Tsar raised his hand to stop Whistle butting in. 'Why on earth would I kill Emeraldov and that . . . what was the name now . . .' He clicked his fingers, as if he couldn't remember. 'Well, that hussar . . . Damn it, I don't even remember what he was called!'

'Vladimir Limbach, and you know that perfectly well. There's a dossier on him in your archive, with s-some extremely intriguing entries.' Fandorin pointed to the folder. 'So let's start with Limbach.' Tsarkov took the folder, glanced into it and tugged on his imperial.

'I have all sorts of people in my filing cabinet . . . Am I supposed to remember all the small fry? Ah, yes. Cornet Limbach. "Make him an offer". I remember.'

'B-bravo. What did it concern? Was the boy not to pester Madam Lointaine with his attentions? And did the boy prove obstreperous?'

His fury mounting, the Tsar flung the folder back onto the desk.

'You have broken into my lodgings in the middle of the night. Organised a cheap farce with all this whistling and shooting! You have rifled through my documents, and after that you dare to demand explanations from me? I only have to click my fingers to have you blasted to kingdom come.'

'I don't understand why you haven't done that yet,' Mr Whistle remarked.

'They told me that you were a genius of intellectual deduction,' the Tsar hissed through his teeth, ignoring Whistle. 'But you are simply a presumptuous, puffed-up idiot. The very idea of it – breaking into my Office! And with trivial nonsense like this! Let me tell you, great luminary of the sleuths, that . . .'

'Drop that pistol! I'll shoot!' a voice roared out from behind Lipkov's back. Georges Nonarikin appeared in the doorway of the dining groom. His Nagant was aimed at Mr Whistle.

'Erast Petrovich, I got here in time!'

'Damn! Who asked you to inter . . .'

Before Fandorin could finish, Lipkov swung round rapidly and flung up the hand holding the Mauser. The assistant director fired first, but the former policeman had foreseen that and he swayed nimbly to one side. The Mauser gave a dry squawk, much quieter than the Nagant, and there was a metallic clang as the bullet struck the door hinge. Splinters were sent flying, and one of them thrust itself into Nonarikin's cheek.

Erast Petrovich was left with no choice. He grabbed his Browning from under the sheet of paper and, before Whistle could squeeze the trigger again, he fired, taking no chances, straight to the back of his head.

Killed outright, Lipkov slumped against a cabinet and slid down onto the floor. The pistol fell out of his limp fingers.

But Mr Tsarkov displayed unexpected speed and agility. He gathered up the hem of his dressing gown, set off at a run and sprang straight towards the window with a despairing cry. The curtains swayed, the windowpanes jangled, and Moscow's Lord of Delights disappeared into the nocturnal darkness. Instead of setting off in pursuit, Fandorin dashed over to Georges.

'Are you wounded?'

'Fate protects the artist,' said Nonarikin, jerking the splinter out of his bleeding cheek. 'That's to continue with the question of *fatum* . . .'

Fandorin's relief was immediately replaced by rage.

'What did you come back for? You've ruined everything!'

'My pursuers scattered along the bank of the river, and I thought I ought to come back and make sure that you were all right. I didn't intend to interfere . . . The door was wide open, there was shouting . . . I simply glanced in. I saw he was aiming at you, about to fire at any moment. But what am I apologising for?' Nonarikin exploded. 'I saved your life, and you . . .'

What point was there in arguing? Erast Petrovich merely gritted his teeth. It was his own fault, after all. He knew who he was taking with him!

He ran out onto the porch, but the Tsar's tracks were long cold, of course. Pursuing him through the dark park would be hopeless.

Fandorin went back into the study and telephoned Subbotin at home – thank God, under the present rules every detective police officer was allocated a home telephone. After Erast Petrovich gave him a brief account of what had happened, Sergei Nikiforovich promised to send police officers from the nearest police district, the Fourth Meschansky, and to come himself.

'Now leave,' Erast Petrovich told his assistant. 'Only, for God's sake, in a different direction – towards the main avenue. The pinschers will probably get here before the police do.'

'I wouldn't even think of it.' Nonarikin bound up his cheek with an absolutely immense handkerchief and became even more like the Knight of the Sad Visage. 'How could I leave you here alone? Never!'

Ah, Masa, how badly I miss you, thought Erast Petrovich.

Strangely enough, the police arrived first. Or perhaps there was nothing strange about it: one could surmise that the pinschers had met the Tsar on their way back to the house and he had led them off out of harm's way. It was hard to imagine August Ivanovich in the role of a general commanding a frontal assault against an armed position.

In order not to waste any time while waiting for an attack or reinforcements – it didn't make any difference which – Fandorin told his wretched assistant to keep an eye on the approaches to the house, while he set about studying the archive in greater detail. By the time Subbotin arrived (he drove up in a horse cab about half an hour after the local police) the plan of subsequent action had more or less been defined.

'There are two questions,' Erast Petrovich said to the civil servant in their tête-à-tête conversation, after first informing him of how things stood. 'The first is: where do we look for the Tsar? The second is: what do we do with this?' He nodded at the American cabinets.

'Do you want to destroy me? I won't take the folders. There's half of Moscow in there, including almost all my bosses. It doesn't surprise me. The world and the people living in it are imperfect, I've know that for a long time. Sooner or later the Lord God repays everyone according to his deeds.' The titular councillor nodded towards Mr Whistle, already laid out on a stretcher, but not yet loaded into the police carriage. 'I tell you what, Erast Petrovich. You'd better take that dynamite yourself. It will be safer with you. In the search report I'll say that the cabinets were empty. And as for Mr Tsarkov, we won't see him in this city again. He's no fool and he realises perfectly well that he could get away with any kind of caper, but not losing those files. Consider that the Tsar has abandoned the throne and gone into voluntary abdication.'

'But I haven't abandoned the Tsar,' Fandorin said menacingly, stung by the failure of the operation. 'He has two murders to answer for. I'll dig August Ivanovich out wherever he hides.'

'But where are you going to look for him? The world's a big place.'

Erast Petrovich pointed to a pile of folders.

'Our friend's concern has three branch offices: in St Petersburg, Warsaw and Odessa. The Tsar has his own people there, and his own business interests. The names and addresses are all clearly stated. I'm certain he'll slink off to one of those three c-cities. I have to calculate exactly which way the criminal will go – north, west or south.'

'Calculate? But how?'

'D-don't worry. That's what deduction is for. I'll work that out and deliver him all neatly parcelled up,' Fandorin promised, smiling pensively in anticipation of engrossing work in which he could bury his woes.

THE RETURN

Fandorin returned to Moscow on the first day of November. Empty-handed, but almost cured.

Erast Petrovich had only kept half his promise. He had correctly calculated the city to which Tsarkov had fled: Warsaw. August Ivanovich's enterprise was established on a broader basis there than in St Petersburg or Odessa. And in addition, in case of any unpleasantness, the border was close at hand. The Tsar had availed himself of this emergency exit as soon as he got wind of the fact that a certain grey-haired gentleman, who was very well informed about all of the Moscow fugitive's Warsaw contacts, had arrived in the governorate-general.

The pursuit had continued right across Germany and ended in the port of Hamburg. Fandorin had got there only twenty minutes too late – just in time to glimpse the stern of the ship on which the Tsar was making his escape to America. In the heat of the moment Erast Petrovich almost bought a ticket for the next sailing. Nothing could have been simpler than to have the emigrant held at New York – it would suffice to send the Pinkerton Agency a telegram telling them to meet the visitor at the quayside and not let him out of their sight until Fandorin arrived.

But the vehement thrill that had fuelled Erast Petrovich's efforts through all the days of the pursuit was beginning to wane. The game was not worth the candle. The extradition proceedings would drag on for months and the outcome was uncertain. And after all, the Tsar had not murdered anyone himself; the actual killer and only witness was dead, and proving that the suspect was involved in crimes committed on the other side of the world would be practically impossible. But even if Tsarkov was handed over, Fandorin could be quite certain that no one in Moscow would bring him to trial. The last thing the municipal authorities wanted was scandalous legal proceedings with all the inevitable exposures. If Fandorin were to deliver the Tsar to Moscow, no one would be delighted.

Erast Petrovich travelled back, refreshed by the pursuit, and two days spent in a railway carriage compartment allowed him to put his thoughts and feelings in order. He considered that now he was ready to return to a life in which reason and dignity predominated.

It was a profound error to believe that an intelligent man was intelligent about everything. He was intelligent in matters that required intellect, but in matters involving the heart, he could be very, very stupid indeed. Erast Petrovich admitted his stupidity, sprinkled his head with ashes and firmly resolved to reform.

What exactly were 'intelligence' and 'stupidity', in essence? The same as 'maturity' and 'infantility'. In this absurd business he had acted like a child all the time. But he had to behave like an adult. Restore normal relations with Masa. Stop feeling offended with Eliza, who was not to blame for anything. She was what she was – an exceptional woman, a great actress, and if she didn't love him, there was nothing to be done about it. As they said, the heart knows no law. Did it know how to love at all, the heart of an actress? Be that as it may, Eliza deserved to be treated with calm, equable respect. Without any sneaking, puerile glances, without any idiotic resentments, without any jealousy to which he was not entitled.

From the Alexander Station he went straight to the theatre, where a rehearsal was due to be taking place. Fandorin knew from the newspapers that during his absence the *Comets* had been played twice, and triumphantly. Madam Altairsky-Lointaine had been praised greatly, and no less admiration had been expressed for her partner, who was referred to as 'the genuine Japanese, Mr Swardilin'. The reviewers noted with particular satisfaction that tickets for the production had become more accessible, since the valiant Moscow police had finally succeeded in breaking up a network of theatre ticket touts. The calculating Stern had postponed the next performance of the 'oriental play' for two weeks – obviously to give the frenzied interest no chance to abate.

Erast Petrovich ascended the stairs leading to the auditorium in a perfectly calm state of mind. However, there was a surprise waiting for him in the foyer: Eliza was striding about there. At the sight of that neat figure, with the broad belt round its waist, his heart stood still, but only for a moment – a good sign.

'Hello,' he said in a low voice. 'Why aren't you at the rehearsal?'

Her cheeks turned pink.

'You . . .? You've been away for so long!'

'I travelled to Europe, on business.'

He could be pleased with himself: his voice was steady and its tone cordial, his smile was affable, there was no stammer. Eliza looked more agitated than he was.

'Yes, Masa said that you left a note and went away . . . And you wrote to Nonarikin too. Why to him precisely? That's strange . . .' She said one thing, but seemed to be thinking of another. She looked as if there was something she wanted to say, but couldn't bring herself to do it.

Erast Petrovich heard shouting from the auditorium. He recognised the director's voice.

'What is Noah Noaevich ranting about?' Fandorin asked with a gentle smile. 'Surely you didn't commit some offence and he put you out of the room?'

He pretended not to notice her embarrassment. He didn't want to succumb to an actor's wiles. With her female instinct, Eliza had probably sensed that he had changed, untangled himself from the web, and now she wanted to draw him back into her insubstantial, deceptive world. Such was the nature of an artiste – she could not accept the loss of an admirer.

But Eliza took up his jocular tone.

'No, I came out myself. We have another scandalous incident going on in there. Someone has written something about a benefit performance in the Tablets again.'

It was a moment before Fandorin realised what she meant. Then he recalled that when he met the theatre company for the first time, in September, an inexplicable entry had appeared in the sacred journal – a certain number of 1s remaining until a benefit performance – and Stern had been outraged by the 'sacrilege' of it.

'A j-joke repeated? That's stupid.'

I'm stammering again, he thought. *Never mind. It is a sign of reduced tension.*

'This is the third time.' Her eyes, as always, looked at him and past him at the same time. 'About a month ago someone wrote about 1s again. The first time there were eight 1s, the second time there were seven, and today, for some reason, there are five. The joker has probably lost count . . .'

'Three times?' Fandorin frowned. 'That's rather too m-many for a joke, even a stupid one. I'll ask Noah Noaevich to show me the Tablets.'

'And you know,' Eliza said suddenly. 'I've had a proposal.'

'What kind of proposal?' he asked, although he had guessed immediately what she meant.

Ah, his heart, his heart! Supposedly he and it had agreed about everything, but still it betrayed him and started fluttering.

'Of the hand and the heart.'

He forced himself to smile.

'And who is this bold fellow?'

I should not have spoken ironically, it sounded bitter!

'Andrei Gordeevich Shustrov.'

'Aha. Well now, a serious man. And young.'

Why did I say 'young'? As if I were complaining that I am no longer young myself!

So that was what she had wanted to talk about. She was going to ask his advice, was that it? Well, no, thank you very much.

'An excellent match. Accept.'

Now that sounded bad.

Her face took on such an unhappy look that Erast Petrovich felt ashamed. He had played the little boy again after all. A genuine adult would have given the lady the satisfaction of feigning jealousy, while inwardly remaining unperturbed.

An actress and a millionaire – an ideal couple. Talent and money, beauty and energy, feeling and calculation, flower and stone, ice and flame. Shustrov will make her a 'star' right across Russia, even right round the world, and in her gratitude she will transform the entrepreneur's arithmetical life into a festival of fireworks.

Everything inside him was seething and bubbling.

'I b-beg your pardon, it is time for me to go.'

'You're leaving again? Will you not go into the hall?'

'A business matter. I completely forgot. I'll call in tomorrow,' he said abruptly.

'I have to do more work on myself. Self-control, restraint, discipline. And it's a very good thing that she is getting married. Every happiness to them. Now everything is completely finished,' Fandorin whispered as he walked down the steps. 'There was something I was going to do, wasn't there?'

But his thoughts were in a tangle.

All right, then. Everything later.

Four 1s

UNTIL THE BENEFIT PERFORMANCE

WHAT A FOOL!

'An excellent match. Accept.' How indifferently he had said it!

What a fool she was! How many days she had waited for this conversation, fantasising about all sorts of melodramatic scenes. She would announce her imminent marriage – and his face would be flooded with deadly pallor, he would start speaking fervent words of passion. She would say: 'My darling, my infinitely dear one, if you only knew . . .' and then a pause, that would be all. After that there would only be the trembling of her lips, the teardrop on her eyelashes, the pain in her eyes and the faint smile. Eliza had even glanced into the mirror to see how it would look. The effect was very powerful. The artistic half of her soul recorded the expression for future use. But the pain was genuine, and the tears even more so.

Oh God, oh God, how long he had been away! She had invented this love for herself, it didn't exist and it never had. If a man loves you, he cannot fail to sense that you need him desperately, madly. Never mind what you might have said or how you might have acted. Words were no more than words, and actions could be impulsive.

There could only be one explanation. He did not love her and he never had. It was all trivial. As Sima would have said: 'There's only one thing men want from our sister'. This Mr Fandorin had got what he wanted, he had gratified his male vanity, added a famous actress to his list of conquests, like a true Don Juan – and there was nothing more he needed. Naturally, he had been relieved to hear of her imminent marriage.

It had been stupid of her to wait for his return as if it could change something. It was enough to recall how Erast had behaved on that nightmarish evening when Limbach was killed. Not a word of sympathy, not a single affectionate touch, nothing. A few strange questions, asked in a cold, hostile tone of voice. And afterwards, before the rehearsal . . . She had been all tenderness, all eagerness to greet him, and he hadn't even come across to her.

There could be no doubt about it. He blamed her, as so many others did. He thought she had driven the poor youth insane with her flirting and he had laid hands on himself.

And the most horrific thing of all was that she couldn't tell the truth. Not to anyone. Especially to the man whose advice and sympathy she needed most of all . . .

Genghis Khan's fourth blow had been the cruellest.

Eliza had not seen the entrepreneur Furshtatsky and the tenor Astralov die with her own eyes. She had glanced into the dressing room where Emeraldov was lying, but had not yet guessed that he had been poisoned. But this time death – violent and crude – had presented itself to her in all its bloody hideousness and barbarous suddenness. What a spectacle! And the smell, the sickening, raw smell of a life that has just been eviscerated! She could never forget that.

How cruelly the khan had chosen his moment! As if Satan himself had prompted him, whispering when would be the best time to catch her unawares, so that she would be full of the joy of life, in festive mood, open to the entire world.

A premiere is a special day. If the performance has been a success, if you have acted well and the audience has been yours, totally and completely yours, then there is nothing that can compare with it, no other pleasure. To feel that *you* are the most loved, the most desired! On that evening Eliza, like her Japanese heroine, had felt herself shooting through the sky like a comet.

She had lived the role, but at the same time her eyes and ears had existed in their own right, able to follow the audience. Eliza had seen everything – even things that she could not possibly have seen: the rainbow waves of empathic feeling and rapture, shimmering above the rows of seats. She had even spotted Erast, sitting in the box for important guests. When Eliza was on the stage, he had hardly ever taken the opera glasses away from his eyes, and that had aroused her even more powerfully. She wanted to be beautiful for everybody, but for him more than for anyone else. At moments like that Eliza felt like an enchantress, showering her invisible spells on the audience – and that was what she truly was.

She also sought out her constant admirers. Several of them had come from St Petersburg especially for the premiere. But Limbach wasn't there. That had seemed strange to her. He had probably landed in the guardhouse again. What bad timing! She had been sure that the cornet would come to congratulate her, and then she could arrange a meeting with him. Not for any stupid nonsense, but for a serious conversation. If he was a paladin or a knight, let him free a lady's heart from the Dragon, from the vile Pagan Monster!

The monster, of course, was also in the hall. He deliberately came late to draw attention to himself. Khan Altairsky had walked in during her dance and demonstratively stood in the doorway, looking like Mephistopheles with his square, neatly outlined figure. In the reddish light of the little lamp glowing above the exit his bald cranium had gleamed like Satan's scarlet halo. According to the rules of Noah's Ark, no one was allowed in after the beginning of a performance, and the terrifying man did not flaunt himself in the doorway for long. An usher hurried over to the late arrival and asked him to go out. Eliza had seen this as a good omen that no one would cast a shadow over the premiere. Oh God, how appallingly mistaken she had been . . .

Following the performance, during the banquet, she had given herself a present: she had hugged Erast, kissed him, called him 'darling' and quietly asked him to forgive her for what had happened. He hadn't answered, but at that moment he loved her – Eliza had felt it! *Everybody loved her!* And the inspired speech about the mystery of the theatre that she had extemporised had been incredibly successful. To produce an impression like that on her fellow actors (and especially on her fellow actresses) – that was really a triumph!

When Shustrov asked her to go out to talk about 'something important', she had realised immediately that he was going to tell her he loved her. And she had gone, because she wanted to hear how he would say it – he was so very clever and level headed, and Stern himself wagged his tail for him. He had given her a rose, processed in some cunning technological fashion. How funny he was!

Andrei Gordeevich had surprised her. He had not said anything at all about feelings. The very moment they emerged into the corridor, he had immediately blurted out: 'Marry me. You won't regret it.' And he had looked at her with those eyes that never smiled, as if to say: Why waste words, the question has been asked, let's have an answer, if you please.

But of course, she hadn't let him off that easily.

'You have fallen in love with me?' She had raised the corners of her mouth slightly in a faint suggestion of a smile and lifted her eyebrows – just a tiny little bit. As if she were about to chuckle. '*You*? As Stanislavsky would have said: "I don't believe it"!'

Shustrov had started detailing the points, as if he were at a meeting of his management committee or board of directors.

'To be honest, I don't know what people mean when they talk about love. Probably everyone invests his or her own meaning in that idea. But it is good that you have asked. Honesty is the essential condition of that long and fruitful collaboration called "marriage".' He had dabbed at his forehead with a handkerchief. Evidently the millionaire found it hard to talk about feelings. 'What I love most of all is the work that I engage in. I would give my life for it. I need you both as a woman and as a great actress. Together we will move mountains. Would I give my life for you? Undoubtedly. Will I love you, if you cease to be of interest to my business? I do not know, I tell you that in all honesty, because without honesty . . .'

'You have already explained about honesty,' she had said, trying as hard as she could not to burst out laughing. 'When you gave me the formula of marriage.'

They were walking along the corridor of the artistes' floor, with only a few steps remaining to the door of her dressing room.

'I am not only offering you myself.' Shustrov took her hand and stopped her. 'I will lay the entire world at your feet. It will be ours – mine and yours. It will love you, and I shall milk it.'

'What do you mean, "milk" it?' She thought she had misheard.

'Like a cow, by the udder. And we shall drink the milk together.'

They had walked on. Eliza's mood had suddenly changed. She no longer found this funny. And she no longer wanted to tease Shustrov.

What if he has been sent to me by God? Eliza had thought. *In order to save me from a terrible sin. After all, I am intending, out of sheer egotism, to risk the life of a boy who is in love. Andrei Gordeevich is no green youth. He will be able to protect his intended.* She had turned the door handle and been surprised – the room was locked.

'The cleaner must have locked it. I have to get the key from the board.'

The millionaire had waited patiently for her answer, seeming perfectly calm.

'There is one complication,' Eliza had said when she came back, without raising her eyes. 'Formally speaking, I am married.'

'I know, I was informed. Your husband, a retired guards officer, will not give you a divorce.' Shustrov shrugged slightly with one shoulder. 'That is a problem, but every problem has a solution. A very difficult problem may have a very expensive solution, but it always has one.'

'Are you thinking of buying him off?'

But, really? Genghis Khan is accustomed to living on a grand scale, he loves luxury . . . No, he'll refuse. His malice is stronger than his cupidity . . .

Out loud she had said:

'You won't get anywhere with that.'

'That never happens,' he had replied confidently. 'I always get somewhere with everything. Usually precisely the place that I am trying to get to.'

Eliza had recalled the rumours circulating in the company: about the ruthless determination with which this merchant's son had accumulated his immense wealth. He must have seen all sorts of things and overcome a host of obstacles and dangers. A serious man! A man like that wouldn't waste time on idle talk. This was probably someone to whom she could tell the truth about Genghis Khan . . .

'I'll start dealing with the question of your legal freedom as soon as I have the right to do so – as your fiancé.'

He had taken hold of her hand again and looked at it, as if trying to decide whether to kiss it or not. But he hadn't kissed it – he had squeezed it.

'I need to consider all this. . . Carefully,' she had said in a weak voice.

'Naturally. Every important decision should be weighed thoroughly. Will three weeks be sufficient for your deliberations?'

He had released her hand – like a thing to which he had not yet acquired the rights of ownership.

'Why three weeks exactly?'

'Twenty-one days. That is my lucky number.'

Andrei Gordeevich had smiled for the first time since she had known him. And she had been as astounded as if the sun had suddenly peeped out from behind a cloud in the middle of the night.

Only at that moment had Eliza's heart faltered.

He's not an arithmometer! He's a live human being! He will have to be loved. And what if he should want children! After all, 'the fruitful collaboration called marriage' really does bring forth fruit. Millionaires always want to have heirs.

'Very well. I'll think about it . . .'

Eliza had turned the key and opened the door – and her nostrils had been assaulted by the smell of death. She had cried out and squeezed her eyes shut, but they had already read the bloody message sent to her by the monster. It said: 'You are mine. Anyone who dares to become close to you will die a terrible death.' No one apart from Eliza had understood, or could have understood, what had really happened. As usual, Genghis Khan had arranged everything with diabolical ingenuity. Everyone around had gasped, spoken about suicide and pitied the poor boy driven insane by love. They had offered Eliza words of sympathy that were mostly false and stared at her avidly, as if something about her had changed. Noah Noaevich, who was also horrified, had said: 'Well, Eliza, my congratulations. The suicide of an admirer is the supreme accolade for an actress. At the next performance they'll be storming the theatre to get seats.' There really was something frightening about a man who was so obsessed with theatrical effects.

She had sat in the green room, waiting to be summoned by the investigator; Sima had given her drops, Vasya had wrapped her in a shawl. Outwardly she had behaved as the situation and the nature of an actress required: she had sobbed with moderate ugliness, allowed her shoulders to tremble, wrung her hands, pressed them to her temples and so on. But it was the woman in her, not the actor, who was thinking. And in fact there had been only one thought running incessantly through her mind: *There's no choice, I'll have to marry a man I don't love*. If there was anyone in the world who could save her from this fiend of hell, it was only Shustrov, with his millions, with his confidence and his power.

How longingly Eliza had looked at Erast when he asked her his questions and tried to make sense of a mystery to which only she knew the answer. Fandorin had been magnificent. He was the only one who had not lost his head when everyone else was shouting and running around. Everyone had instinctively started to do as he said. How could it have been otherwise? He had so much innate, natural gravitas! It had always been palpable but it had manifested itself especially clearly at the moment of crisis. Ah, if only he had power and influence, like Shustrov! But Erast was only a 'traveller', a solitary. He couldn't cope with Genghis Khan. In any case, nothing in the world could have made her agree to put Fandorin's life in danger. Let him live, let him write plays. Marrying Andrei Gordeevich was a way to save not only herself, but also Erast! If the khan, with his satanic ubiquity, should get wind of the fact that she had *been intimate* with the dramatist, it would be the end of him. She had to stay as far away as possible from Fandorin, although the only thing she wanted to do was bury her face in his chest and cling to him as tightly as possible, with all her strength, and then let come what may.

This criminal desire had become almost unbearable after a long conversation with the Japanese. In the evening, after the rehearsal (it was the seventeenth of October, a Monday), Eliza had asked Masa to see her to the hotel. She hadn't wanted to ride in the automobile, because it was a glorious autumn evening, and she was afraid to walk on her own – she fancied that Genghis Khan was lurking behind every corner. She had also been frightened by the idea of an evening in an empty room and a sleepless night. And she had wanted to talk about *him*.

The conversation begun on the way to the hotel had been

continued at dinner in the Massandra restaurant and then in the hotel vestibule. Eliza had not invited her stage partner to her room – so that Genghis Khan, if he was following her, would not have any grounds for jealous suspicions. She had no right to endanger darling Mikhail Erastovich's life. She was very fond of him, and the longer she knew him, the fonder she became. That likeable, slightly lisping accent did not seem funny to her. After five minutes she stopped noticing that Masa pronounced some Russian sounds incorrectly. And the Japanese himself had proved to be more than just a capable actor, he was an extremely pleasant individual. Erast had been lucky to find such a friend.

Ah, how many new and important things Eliza had learned from him about her beloved! She had not even noticed how the night flew by. Following the restaurant, they had reached the 'Louvre' after midnight, settled into comfortable armchairs, ordered tea (Masa had asked for Danish pastries with his) and talked and talked. Then when they had looked, it was already getting light outside. She had gone up to her room, tidied herself up and changed her clothes, then they had taken breakfast together in the hotel buffet, and it had been time for the rehearsal. Eliza had never spoken so frankly and confidentially with anyone. And, moreover, about the one thing that concerned her most of all. What a pleasure it was to talk to a man who didn't look at her lustfully or strike poses, or try to produce an impression. Vasya Gullibin was also a member of the non-philandering tribe, but he was a poor conversation partner, no match for the Japanese in intellect or knowledge of life or aptness of observation.

The night had flown by so fast because they were talking about love.

Masa had told her about his 'master' (that was what he called his godfather). How noble, talented, fearless and intelligent he was. 'He roves you,' the Japanese had said, 'and it tortures him. The onry thing in the worrd he is afraid of is rove. Because those he has roved have died. He brames himserf for their death.'

Eliza had shuddered at that. How very similar it was to her own situation.

She had started asking questions.

Masa had told her that he had not seen the first woman whom his 'master' had loved and lost. It had been a very long time ago. But he had known the second. It was a very, very sad story that he did not want to remember, because he would start to cry.

But then he had told her after all – something exotic and amazing, in the spirit of the play about two comets. He really had started crying, and Eliza had cried too. Poor Erast Petrovich! How cruelly fate had dealt with him!

'Do not pray the usuar woman's games with him,' Masa had implored her. 'He is not suited for them. I understand, you are an actress. You cannot behave otherwise. But if you are not sincere with him, you wirr rose him. For ever. That would be very sad for him and, I think, for you too. Because you wirr never meet another man rike my master, even if you rive to be a hundred years old and keep your beauty for the whore hundred years.'

At that she had fallen apart completely. She had burst into floods of tears, quite unconcerned about how she looked as she did it.

'You do not rook rike an actress now,' the Japanese had said, handing her a handkerchief. 'Brow your nose, or erse it wirr be sworren.'

'What will it be?' Eliza had asked in a nasal voice, not understanding the word 'sworren'.

'Red. Like a prum. Brow your nose! That's it, very good . . . Wirr you rove my master? Will you terr him tomorrow that your heart berongs onry to him?'

She had shaken her head and burst into tears again.

'Not for anything in the world!'

'Why?'

'Because I love him. Because I don't want . . .'

To destroy him, she had been going to say.

Masa had pondered for a long time before he eventually spoke.

'I thought I understood a woman's heart werr. But you have surprised me. "I rove" but "I don't want"? You are very interesting, Eriza-san. Undoubtedry that is why my master ferr in love with you.'

And for a long time he had tried to persuade her not to be stubborn. However, the more vividly the Japanese described Erast Petrovich's virtues, the more unwavering her determination to protect him from disaster had become. But she had enjoyed listening to it anyway.

In the morning, when she saw Fandorin at the rehearsal, looking so hurt and so proud, she had been frightened that she might not be able to control herself. She had even appealed in prayer to the Almighty, pleading for His help to resist temptation.

And God had heard her. After that day Erast disappeared. He had gone away.

In her own mind she had held an endless conversation with him, all the time preparing to meet him. And now they had met . . .

She was a fine one too, of course. All the phrases she had prepared had simply flown out of her head. 'You know, I have received a proposal.' She had just blurted it out in passing – and taken fright herself at how frivolous it sounded.

He hadn't even raised an eyebrow. 'Aha, well now.'

Apparently the Japanese actor could also be mistaken. Masa didn't know his 'master' all that well after all. Or perhaps there had been love, but it had ended. That happened too. It happened all the time.

THE DAILY ROUND

It just happened that all the sincerity, all the passion of soul that, in her perplexity and torpor, had not been splashed out onto Fandorin fell to the lot of a man who was good, but unimportant – Vasya Gullibin. He was a faithful, reliable friend and sometimes Eliza had a secure, comforting cry on his shoulder, but she could just as well have buried her face in the fur of her dog, if she had had one.

Vasya glanced out of the auditorium a minute after Erast had turned round and walked away. Eliza's face wore an unhappy expression and she had tears in her eyes. Gullibin, of course, dashed over to her to ask what was wrong. Well, she told him everything, she unburdened her heart.

That is, not absolutely everything, naturally. She didn't tell him about Genghis Khan. But she did tell him the story of her drama of love.

She led Vasya into a box, so that no one would disturb them. Then she put her hands over her face and started talking incoherently through her tears – the dam burst. About how she loved one man and had to marry another; that she had no choice; or rather, she did, but it was an appalling one: either drag out a miserable life that was worse than death, or give herself to a man for whom she felt nothing.

On the stage Stern was rehearsing with Swardilin, going through his turn with the tightrope. Masa wasn't graceful enough. A romantic hero should observe a certain austerity in his gesticulations, but the Japanese spread his knees too wide and stuck his elbows out.

The other actors had taken advantage of this break to wander off in all directions.

Gullibin listened agitatedly and stroked her hair cautiously, but he simply couldn't grasp the most important thing.

'Who are you talking about, Lizonka?' he asked eventually. (Gullibin was the only one who called her that, they had known each other from their theatre school days.)

The expression on his face was puzzled and kind.

'Fandorin, who else?'

As if there was anyone else here she could love!

Vasya frowned.

'Has he proposed to you? But why are you obliged to marry him? He's old and completely grey!'

'You fool!' Eliza straightened up angrily. 'You're the one who's old and withered. At the age of thirty, you already look forty, but he . . . he . . .'

And she started talking about Erast Petrovich – she just couldn't stop. Vasya didn't take offence at that word 'withered', he wasn't the kind to take offence anyway, he forgave Eliza absolutely anything at all. He listened, sighed and suffered with her.

'So you love the playwright,' he said. 'But who has proposed to you?'

When she replied, he whistled.

'Oh boy! Has he now? That's a real turn-up for the books!'

They both turned round at the sound of the the door opening slightly. There were always draughts wandering about in the theatre.

'I haven't accepted yet! I have another four days to think about it, until Saturday.'

'Think it over, of course . . . It's for you to decide. But you know yourself that lots of women, especially actresses, have a way of arranging things. A husband is one thing, love is another. It's a perfectly normal business. So don't you go upsetting yourself. Shustrov's a millionaire, he'll go a long way. You'd be the owner of our theatre. More important than Stern!'

Yes, Vasya was a real friend. He wished her well. In recent days (there was no point in denying it), Eliza had contemplated this possibility too: giving her hand to Andrei Gordeevich and leaving her heart for Erast Petrovich. But something told her that neither man would agree to a ménage of that kind. They were too serious, both of them.

'Hey, who's that eavesdropping out here?' Vasya suddenly shouted out angrily. 'That's no draught, I saw someone's shadow!'

The door swayed and they heard steps – someone walking away quickly on tiptoe.

While Gullibin was squeezing through the narrow gap between the chairs, the curious listener had time enough to disappear.

'Who could it be?' Eliza asked.

'Anyone at all. This isn't a theatre company – it's a jar of spiders! The parish takes after the priest! Stern's theory of rupture and scandal in action. Well, congratulations, now everyone will find out that you're going to marry a man like that in four days' time!'

Wonderful Vasya was genuinely upset. But Eliza wasn't. So they would find out, and that was just fine. It would be one thing if she had boasted about it herself, but now the news had leaked out without her being party to it. Let them all eat their hearts out with envy. And she would see whether she really would marry 'a man like that'.

However, it had remained unclear whether the unknown spy had let the cat out of the bag or not. None of the others had started talking to Eliza about Shustrov directly. And as for their tangential, envious glances, she had always received plenty of those. The position of a leading lady was a bouquet of roses with extremely sharp thorns, and when it came to envy a theatre company could easily outdo the harem of a padishah.

But nonetheless, it *was* a bouquet of roses. Fragrant and beautiful. Every entrance, even during a rehearsal, brought that sweet oblivion in which she was cut off from the darkness and fear of real life. And a performance was sheer unadulterated happiness. The two shows that had been given since the premiere had turned out superbly. Everyone had acted with gusto – the play gave every actor an opportunity to hold the audience for a while, not sharing it with anyone else. And owing to the sudden disappearance of the ticket touts, the composition of the audience had changed noticeably. In the stalls there was less glittering of jewellery and gleaming of starched collars. Fresh, lively new faces had appeared, mostly young, and the emotional pitch had been heightened. The audience had started reacting more willingly and more gratefully, and that, in turn, had electrified the artistes. But most importantly of all, the faces had no longer radiated an avid anticipation of sensation and scandal, those constant companions of Stern's theatre – those people who once paid speculators twenty-five roubles, and sometimes even fifty, for a place in the front rows had wanted to see more for their money than simply a theatrical performance.

The charm of the role that had come Eliza's way lay in its difficulty of comprehension. The idea of a geisha – of a beauty that was incarnate and yet not of the flesh – thrilled her imagination. What an intoxicating craft – to serve as an object of desire while remaining inaccessible to embraces! How closely it resembled the existence of an actress, her own beautiful and sad destiny.

When Eliza, still simply Liza at the time, moved from the ballet department to the acting department of the college, a wise old teacher (a 'noble father' of the imperial theatres) had told her: 'Little girl, the theatre will reward you generously – and fleece you of everything. Know that you will have neither a genuine family, nor genuine love.' And she had replied blithely: 'Then so be it!' Afterwards there had been times when she regretted her choice, but for an actress there is no way back. And if there is, then she is not an actress – simply a woman.

Stern, for whom nothing existed in the world apart from the theatre, liked to repeat that every genuine actor was an emotional pauper and explained this, as he did many other things, with the help of a financial metaphor (Noah Noaevich's innate commercialism was both his strength and his weakness at the same time). 'Let us assume that an ordinary man has one rouble's worth of feelings,' he used to say, 'and he spends fifty kopecks on his family, twenty-five kopecks on his work and the rest on his friends and his interests. All hundred kopecks of his emotions are expended on the daily round. Not so with an actor! In every role that he plays he invests five kopecks or perhaps ten – it is impossible to play convincingly without this vitally essential mite. In his career an outstanding talent may play ten, at most twenty, first-class roles. What is left over for the daily round of family, friends and lovers? Three and a quarter kopecks.'

Noah Noaevich very much disliked it when people argued with him, and so Eliza listened to his 'kopecks' theory without saying anything. But if she had objected, she would have said: 'It's not true! Actors are special people, and they have a special emotional constitution. If you don't possess this special charge of energy, you shouldn't be on the stage. Let's assume that initially I only had a rouble's worth of feelings. But when I act, I don't spend my rouble, I invest it, and every successful role brings me dividends. It is ordinary people who spend their hundred kopecks' worth of emotions from birth to death, but I live on the interest and maintain my capital untouched! Other people's lives, of which I become a part on the stage, are not deducted from my life, but added to it!'

If a show went well, Eliza could physically feel the energy of the feelings that filled her. There was so much of this energy that it saturated the entire audience, a thousand people! But in their turn the people in the audience charged Eliza with their fire. This is a magical effect known to every genuine actor. The late Emeraldov, a lover of vulgar metaphors, used to say that regardless of his or her gender, an actor was always a man, whose responsibility it was to bring the audience to a state of ecstasy, otherwise he would merely break into a sweat and waste his energy, and the lover would leave unsatisfied and seek other embraces.

That was why Eliza was bored by the idea of the cinematograph that Andrei Gordeevich dreamed about. What good was it to her if spectators in hundreds or even thousands of electric theatres sobbed or lusted when they saw her face on a piece of cheap cloth? She wouldn't be able to touch this love and feel it, would she?

Let Shustrov think that she had accepted his proposal out of vanity, out of a yearning for worldwide fame. There was only one thing she wanted: for him to rid her of Genghis Khan. For that, she was prepared to be eternally in his debt. A marriage, even without love, could be harmonious. Did Shustrov value the actress in her more than the woman? Well then, she *was* an actress first and foremost.

But the other half of her nature, the womanly half, fluttered its wings like a bird caught in a trap. How much easier it would be to marry out of calculation, if only Fandorin didn't exist! In four days' time she would have to lock herself in a cage voluntarily. It was a cage of pure gold, offering reliable protection against any wild beasts on the prowl, but it meant abandoning for ever the flight of two comets in a starless sky!

If only she could know for certain, without any doubt, that Erast's feelings for her had cooled. But how could she find out? She didn't trust her stage partner Masa any longer. He was a very good person, but the soul of his 'master' remained as obscure to him as it was to her.

Provoke Fandorin into a frank conversation? But that was the same as flinging herself on his neck. Everybody knew how scenes of that kind ended. She wouldn't be able to run away from him a second time. Genghis Khan would find out about her infatuation, and she didn't need to guess what would happen after that . . . No, no, and a thousand times no!

After pondering over her doubts for a long time Eliza came up with the following solution. Of course, she must not permit any confessions of love. But in the course of some neutral conversation, she could attempt to sense – from his glance, from his voice, from some involuntary movement – whether he still loved her in the same way. After all, she was an actress, was she not, and her heart was particularly responsive to such things. If it didn't sense any magnetic attraction, then what reason was there to suffer? And if it did . . . Eliza hadn't decided what to do in that case.

The day after the encounter in the foyer, on Wednesday, when she arrived for the rehearsal, he was already there. Sitting at the director's desk, reading the entries in the Tablets, with such an unnaturally intense air that Eliza guessed he was doing it deliberately, in order to avoid looking at her. She smiled inwardly. This was an encouraging symptom.

She had prepared a topic for conversation in advance.

'Hello, Erast Petrovich.' He got up and bowed. 'I have a question for you as a dramatist. I'm reading a lot about Japan now, and about double suicides by lovers – in order to understand my character Izumi better . . .'

He listened intently, without speaking. The question of magnetism was not clear as yet.

'And I read something very interesting. Apparently, before the Japanese depart from this life it is customary for them to compose a poem. Only five lines long! I think that is so beautiful! What if my geisha were also to write a poem that would sum up her life in a few words?'

'It is strange that I did not think of that myself,' Erast said slowly. 'Very probably a geisha would have done p-precisely that.'

'Then write it! I shall read the poem before I press the electric switch.'

He thought about that for a moment.

'But the play is already written in verse metre. The poem will sound like an ordinary m-monologue . . .'

'I know what can be done here. You can retain the Japanese poetic metre: five syllables in the first line, seven in the second, five in the third and seven in each of the last two lines. To the Russian ear that will sound like prose and it will contrast with the iambic trimeter in which the monologues are written. For us, verse will fulfil the function of prose, and prose will fulfil the function of verse.'

'An excellent idea.'

His eyes flashed admiringly, only it wasn't clear if the admiration was meant for the idea or for Eliza herself. She had not determined whether Fandorin was radiating magnetism or not. Her own radiation must have interfered, it was too strong . . .

She had wanted to continue the investigation the next day, but Erast Petrovich had not shown up at the theatre either on Thursday or on Friday, and now the fateful day – Saturday – had arrived.

Eliza had not known what answer to give Andrei Gordeevich. *Let come what may*, she had thought in her hotel room in the morning, as she stood in front of the mirror, choosing her outfit. In fact, there was no doubt than she had to consent. But at the same time a lot would depend on Shustrov: the words that he said, the way that he looked at her.

The light purple with the black silk belt? Too funereal. Better with the dark green watered silk. A slightly risqué combination, but it suited both possible outcomes . . . The Viennese hat, of course, with the eye-veil . . .

At the same time, she had tried to picture what she would wear for the wedding. No corset, lace or frills, of course. And any mention of a bridal veil was absurd – for her third marriage! And all those orange blossoms were not for Eliza Lointaine in any case. The dress would have a close-fitting top and a sumptuous, full-bodied skirt. Quite definitely red, only not just red, but with black zigzags, as if she were being consumed by tongues of flame. She would have to make a sketch and show it to Bouchet, he was a magician, he would sew what she needed.

Eliza had imagined it: there she was, standing there like a blossom of flame, a single column of impulsive, upward aspiration; and there he was, erect and dignified, in black and white. They stood there in full sight of everyone, with flowers and crystal on the table, and her groom kissed her on the lips and she held out her arm in a long straw-yellow glove . . .

Brrrr! No, it was absolutely impossible for her, wearing a dress of flame, to kiss Shustrov on the lips to the sound of clinking glasses! Eliza only had to visualise this picture to realise immediately that it could not possibly happen. And what happened during the night that followed the wedding banquet was even more impossible.

Quickly, quickly, before the voice of reason intervened, she had dashed to turn the handle of the telephone and asked the operator to connect her with the Theatrical and Cinematographic Company. Eliza had been living in the Louvre again for almost three weeks now, Noah Noaevich had insisted on it – and Eliza had not tried to argue. She had grown accustomed to living without a bathroom, but poor Limbach would not be climbing in at her window again . . .

The secretary had answered, told her that Andrei Gordeevich was not expected in the office today and politely given her his home number. It must have been a compassionate fate's attempt to give Eliza a chance to change her mind. But she didn't take it.

When he heard her voice, Shustrov had said calmly:

'It's a good thing that you phoned. I'm just getting ready to come to your hotel. Perhaps you should cancel the rehearsal for an occasion like this? I ordered the table to be laid for breakfast and let the servants go. We can drink champagne together, just the two of us.'

'No champagne!' Eliza had blurted out. 'Nothing is going to happen. It's impossible. Impossible, and that's all! Goodbye!'

He had gulped and tried to object, but she had hung up.

For a moment she had felt an incredible sense of relief. And then horror. What had she done? She had spurned her lifeline, now she could only drown.

But the genuine horror was still to come.

LIFE IS OVER

For the first time in her career Eliza was almost late for a rehearsal. But then today she was in especially good form – for two reasons. Nervous agitation always intensified the fervour of her acting; and in addition, when she was performing the fan dance, Fandorin came in and sat down quietly at the back.

'Eliza's the only one working!' Stern shouted irritably (he was out of sorts today). 'All the others are counting crows! Lev Spiridonovich, once again from the words: "What a beauty! I could just watch and watch!"'

The shimmering Japanese music started up again from the gramophone record and the central doors swung open with a crash. A young man with tousled hair and no hat came running in through the opening. His furious-looking face was flushed, he was dressed foppishly and waving one hand about wildly, with something glinting in it – apparently a little metal box.

At this Noah Noaevich went absolutely berserk.

'Why is there an outsider here? Who let him in? What is this mayhem? Who is responsible for order in the theatre?' he yelled at his assistant, who shrugged, and Stern turned his fury on the stranger, who had run up to the stage. 'Who are you? And what do you think you are doing?'

Looking around, the young man handed him a business card. The director read it and broke into a toothy grin.

'Monsieur Simon! Dear colleagues, we have a visit from Andrei Gordeevich's partner! *Soyez*, so to speak, *le bienvenu, cher ami!*'

The Frenchman's wandering gaze settled on Eliza. She was

wearing that purple dress with the green belt, but in combination with Japanese lacquered sandals.

'Madam Lointaine?' the ill-mannered foreigner enquired.

'*Oui, monsieur.*'

She had already guessed that Shustrov had sent his partner Simon to persuade her to change her mind. A rather strange emissary of Cupid, and he was behaving rather strangely!

But Monsieur Simon howled in perfect Russian:

'You bitch! You murderer! What a man you've destroyed!'

He swung his hand and flung the little gold box. It struck Eliza directly on her breasts and fell to the floor, and a wedding ring with a diamond rolled out of it.

The troublemaker clambered up onto the stage, as if he intended to attack the leading lady with his fists. Vasya and Georges grabbed hold of his shoulders, but he shoved them away.

'What's happened? What's going on?' voices called from all sides.

The rowdy intruder shouted:

'Coquette, viper! You led him up the garden path for three weeks and then refused! I hate your kind. *Tueuse!* An absolutely genuine *tueuse!*'

Frightened and dumbfounded, Eliza backed away. What sort of wild Mexican passion was this?

Fandorin and Masa darted out onto the stage simultaneously from both sides. They grabbed hold of the madman's arms – and more securely than Gullibin and Nonarikin. Erast Petrovich turned Monsieur Simon to face him.

'Why do you call Madam Lointaine a murderer? Explain yourself immediately!'

From the side Eliza saw the Frenchman start to blink.

'Erast . . . Petrovich?' he babbled. 'Mr Masa?'

'*Senka-kun?*' Masa released his grip. '*Odoroita na!*'

Apparently he had recognised the stranger, And Fandorin also exclaimed:

'Senya, you? It's ten years since we last saw each other!'

'Eleven, Erast Petrovich! Almost eleven!'

Simon shook hands with Fandorin and exchanged bows with Masa, and the Frenchman (although what kind of Frenchman could he be, if he was 'Senya') bowed low, from the waist. All this was extremely bewildering.

'I was sure that you were in Paris . . . But wait, we'll come to that later. Tell me what has happened. Why did you attack M-madam Lointaine?'

The young man sobbed.

'Andriusha phoned me this morning. Disaster, he said. She turned me down. And his voice was so bleak. I got in my automobile. I have a Bugatti, Erast Petrovich, fifteen horse power – not like the old kerosene lamp we used to trudge around in, remember?' He livened up for a moment and then his face fell again. 'I got to Andriusha's house on Prechistenka. And there were policemen at the door, a crowd of people, flashguns flaring . . .'

'But what has happened? T-tell me in plain language!'

'In his desperation he slit his throat, with a razor. I saw it – it was horrible. Everything covered in blood. Slashed away at himself as if he was slicing sausage . . . And in the other hand he was holding the box with the ring . . .'

Eliza didn't hear how their conversation ended, or find out how Simon and Fandorin knew each other. The moment she heard about the razor and the slit throat, everything went dark and then something struck her hard on the back of the head. She had fainted and fallen, banging her head against the floor.

Eliza came round only a minute or two later, but Erast and Senya-Simon were no longer in the hall. Sima and Vasilisa Prokofievna were fussing over her, Sima waving a fan and Vasilisa Prokofievna thrusting sal volatile in her face – the theatre always had substantial reserves of that, because the actresses' nerves were easily agitated. Gloomy-faced Swardilin was sitting on the floor in the corner of the stage, with his legs crossed Japanese-style. The other members of the company were huddled round the director.

'. . . A tragic event, but there is no need to despair!' Noah Noaevich declared. 'The deceased was a great-hearted man, and he made provision for us! As you recall, he settled on the Ark a capital sum that will allow us to exist quite comfortably. And in addition, his partner has made a very pleasant impression on me – emotional and impetuous. I think we shall hit it off. My friends, one must seek the positive aspects of every misfortune, otherwise life on earth would have come to an end long ago! Imagine what the scene will be like at our next performance, as soon as the public learns of the reason for the latest suicide!'

At that point everyone looked round and saw that Eliza had recovered consciousness. How expressive all those glances turned towards her were! How much they said about each member of the company! It was clear from Vulpinova's face that she was bitterly envious of a woman for whose sake men killed themselves and who would be written about in the newspapers tomorrow. The 'philosopher' Lev Spiridonovich had a sad, sympathetic air. Vasya was sighing pitifully. Nonarikin was frowning disapprovingly. Mephistov ran one finger across his throat and applauded silently. Gullibin's face was contorted into a grimace that signified: 'Ah, gentlemen, what idiots you all are'. Shiftsky winked, as if to say: 'Well, you certainly played that faint well, bravo'.

And Noah Noaevich came across to Eliza and whispered:

'Hang on, little girl! Keep your head up! Nationwide fame, that's what this means!'

If anything, he was even more repulsive than Mephistov.

There won't be any performance for you, so you can stop rubbing your hands, Eliza told Stern in her own mind. The moment she came round she knew what to do. The idea had simply come to her. *But don't take it hard, Noah Noaevich. You'll soon recover your losses. A concert in memory of a great actress, immense box-office takings, newspaper headlines about the theatre – you'll have all that. Only without me.*

It was pointless to explain to them all that this was a murder. They wouldn't believe it. They liked the fairy tale of a Belle Dame Sans Merci, who drove admirers to their death with her cruelty. Well, so be it. If people wanted to remember Eliza Lointaine like that, so be it.

She felt a ghastly, infinite lassitude. She had no strength left to flutter her little wings. It was time to put an end to everything: the horror, the malevolence, the endless dance of death. No one else was going to die because of Eliza, no one. She had had enough. She was quitting.

Eliza didn't take the decision. It manifested itself as the only possible, natural one.

Noah Noaevich was in a state of high excitement. In anticipation of a siege by reporters and idle gawpers, he took measures: he moved Eliza to the Metropole hotel, where there was a special floor for important guests – with a special doorman who didn't allow strangers in. Of course, it wasn't a matter of protecting her from the press. The important thing for Stern was to demonstrate what a luxurious life was led by the leading actress of his theatre.

Eliza didn't argue. Aphrodisina and Gullibin took her to her new quarters in a luxurious three-room apartment with a piano and a gramophone, with a canopy above the bed, with voluptuous bunches of flowers in crystal vases.

She sat in the armchair without taking off her hat or cape, watching dully as Sima hung her clothes in the wardrobe. Killing herself also required an effort. And she didn't have any strength left at all. Absolutely none.

Tomorrow, she told herself. Or the day after tomorrow. But I won't live any longer than that, that's quite certain.

'I've set everything out,' said Sima. 'Shall I sit with you for a while?'

'Go. Thank you. I'm all right.'

They went.

She didn't notice it get dark. The street lamps came on outside in Theatre Square. There were lots of gleaming surfaces in the room – bronze, gilt, lacquer – and it all glittered and glimmered, casting little spots of light.

Eliza ran one hand over her thickly powdered face and frowned. She needed to have a wash.

As she wandered slowly to the bathroom, every step was a struggle.

She turned on the light and looked in the mirror at the white face with blue circles under the eyes, the face of a suicide.

There was something white lying on the toilet table, between the little bottles and boxes. A folded piece of paper. Where from?

She mechanically picked it up and unfolded it.

'*I warned you that you are mine for ever. Anyone you get mixed up with will die,*' Eliza read. Recognising the handwriting, she screamed.

Tomorrow won't do, let alone the day after tomorrow! This torment must be stopped immediately! Even in hell it can't be more terrible than this!

She didn't rack her brains over how Genghis Khan had found out about the move and how he had managed to slip the note into the bathroom. Satan, he was Satan himself. But the apathy and lassitude had been dissipated, as if scattered by a gust of wind. Eliza was shuddering in impatience.

No more! No more! Out of this world! Quickly!

Turning on the lights everywhere, she started dashing through the rooms in search of a suitable means of exit.

Death stood ready to take her into its embrace everywhere. The window was an open door into Non-existence – she only had to step across the threshold. The candelabra glittered with pendants, among which a place could easily be found for a dangling body. Lying in the medicine cabinet was a little phial of laudanum. But an actress could not leave this life like an ordinary woman. Even in death she had to be beautiful. The final scene, just before the curtain, had to be choreographed and played so that it would be remembered.

The preparations for this scene occupied Eliza's mind, distracting her, and the horror was replaced by a feverish animation.

She took the flowers out of the vases and scattered them across the floor in a bright, fragrant carpet. She positioned the armchair. With a crystal vase on each side of it.

She telephoned reception and told them to bring a dozen bottles of red wine, the very best, to her room.

'A dozen?' the velvety voice asked. 'Straight away, madam.'

While they were delivering it, Eliza got changed. The black silk dressing gown with Chinese dragons was like a kimono – a reminder of her final role.

Here was the wine. She told them to remove all the corks.

'All of them, madam?' the waiter asked, but he wasn't really surprised. You could expect absolutely anything from an actress.

'Yes, all of them.'

Eliza emptied six bottles into one vase and six into the other.

It was no accident that when women with a highly developed sense of beauty decided to do away with themselves, they usually slit their veins open. Some lay in a bath, after first filling it up it with lilies. Some lowered their slashed wrists into a basin of water. But crystal vases with red Bordeaux, so that the noble wine would consume the blood with its own colour – Eliza had never read about anything like that. It was exotic, it would be remembered.

Should she put on some music? She ran through the gramophone records and chose Saint-Saens. But then she put him back. When the record played through to the end, her own consciousness might not yet have faded away. She would have to die to the repulsive scratching of the needle instead of the beautiful music.

She imagined to herself what a furore would be stirred up by her death and – it was stupid, of course – regretted that she would not see it all. She could picture the kind of funeral that Noah Noaevich would arrange. The crowd behind the hearse would extend for miles and miles. And what they would write in the newspapers! What headlines there would be!

She wondered who Stern would take on for the role of Izumi. He would have to introduce the replacement urgently, before all the ballyhoo died down. He would probably lure Germanova from the Art Theatre. Or summon Yavorskaya by telegram. The poor things. It was hard to rival the ghost of someone whose blood had flowed out into wine.

Another idea also occurred to her. Should she not leave a letter, telling the whole truth about Genghis Khan? She could attach his note to it, that would be proof.

But no. That would be too flattering. The villain would milk the part, revelling in his role as the diabolical fiend who drove the great Eliza Lointaine into her grave. And he might even get clean away with it. One note would probably not be enough for the court. Better to leave everyone pondering and guessing at what kind of impulse had carried off the mysterious comet into the starless sky.

And so she sat down in the armchair, rolled up her wide sleeves and took out her sharp little manicure scissors. In an article about some decadent young woman who had committed suicide (there was, after all, an entire epidemic of suicides in Russia at the time) Eliza had read that before she slit open her veins the woman had held her hands in water for a long time – it assuaged the pain. Not that a mere trifle like pain was of any consequence now, but it was still best to avoid the intrusion of coarse physiology into an act of the pure spirit.

Ten minutes, she told herself, lowering her hands into the vases. The wine had been cooled, and Eliza realised that she wouldn't be able to sit like that for ten minutes – her fingers would go numb. Five minutes would probably do. Without thinking, almost indifferently, she started watching the clock. A minute proved to be a terribly long time, an eternity in fact.

Three times the minute hand shifted from one division to the next, and then the telephone rang.

At first Eliza frowned. Just at the wrong moment! But then she felt curious: who could it be! What signal was this that life was sending her at the final moment, and from whom?

She got up and shook off the red drops.

The hotel operator.

'A Mr Fandorin is asking for you. Shall I connect him?'

'Him! Surely he couldn't have sensed anything! Oh God, and she hadn't thought about him at all during these terrible hours. She hadn't allowed herself to. In order not to undermine her resolution.

'Yes, yes, connect us.'

Now he would say: 'My darling, my only one, come to your senses! I know what is on your mind, stop!'

'P-please forgive this late call,' said the dry voice in the earpiece. 'I have done as you asked. I wanted to give it to you at the theatre, but circumstances of which you are aware prevented me. I mean the verse. The pentastitch,' he explained when he heard no response. 'Do you remember, you asked me?'

'Yes,' she said in a quiet voice. 'It's very kind of you not to have forgotten.'

But what she wanted to say was: 'My beloved, I am doing this for you. I am dying, so that you can live . . .'

Eliza found this unspoken line very moving. She wiped away a tear.

'Will you write it down? I'll d-dictate it.'

'Just a moment.'

Oh God, this was just what was needed to render her departure ideally beautiful! Her beloved had telephoned to dictate her deathbed poem! It would be found on the table. But no one, no one apart from Erast Petrovich, would know all the beauty of what had happened. This truly was genuine '*yugen*'!

He dictated it in a monotonous voice and she wrote it down without thinking about the words, because she was looking into the mirror all the time. Ah, what a scene! Eliza's voice, repeating the lines, tranquil, even cheerful, a smile on her lips and tears in her eyes. It was a pity that no one would see or hear it. But it was absolutely the best thing she had ever played in her life.

She wanted to say something special to him at the end, so that the meaning would be revealed later, and he would remember those words to the end of his days. But nothing adequate to the moment occurred to her, and Eliza did not want to spoil it with banality.

'There, b-basically that's all. Goodnight.'

There was a note of anticipation in his voice.

'Are you not going to ask about Shustrov?' he asked after a pause. 'Are you not interested?'

'*That* does not interest me,' Eliza gasped in a rustling half-whisper: 'Goodbye . . .'

'Goodnight,' Erast said, even more coolly than at the beginning of the conversation.

The line went dead.

'Ah, Erast Petrovich, how cruelly you will repent,' Eliza told the mirror.

She looked at the piece of paper and decided to make a fair copy of the verse. Because her left hand had been occupied with holding the receiver, the lines had sprawled in higgledy-piggledy fashion, it looked untidy.

Only now did she really read it and grasp the meaning.

> *In another birth,*
> *Not a flower, but a bee*
> *Would I inhabit.*
> *Oh woe, this malicious lot –*
> *A geisha's timorous love . . .*

The part about 'another birth' was clear, the Japanese believed in the transmigration of the soul, but what was the sense of 'not a flower, but a bee'? What did that mean?

Suddenly she understood.

Not to be the eternal object of others' lust, but to be transformed oneself into desire, into resoluteness, oneself. To choose one's own flower, to buzz and to sting!

To wither and wilt without resistance or to be picked – that was the lot of a geisha and the lot of a flower. But a bee had a sting. And if an enemy attacked, a bee made use of its sting, with no concern for the consequences.

This was the signal that life had sent Eliza at the final moment.

She must not surrender without a struggle! She must not capitulate in the face of Evil. Eliza's mistake was that she had behaved too much like a woman: she had wanted other men to protect her against Genghis Khan, and when there were no defenders left, she had simply lost heart, dropped her hands and squeezed her eyes shut. What shameful weakness!

But she would become a bee right here and now, in her present incarnation! She would exterminate the enemy, save the one she loved and be happy as well! 'Only he is worthy of happiness and freedom who da-de-da-de-da follows them into battle!' In her agitation, part of Goethe's strophe had slipped her mind, but that was not important.

To strike down the Dragon herself! To appear before Erast strong and free!

The superb magnificence of this idea filled Eliza with ecstasy.

She called reception.

'Collect two crystal vases of Bordeaux from my room. Take them to the Madrid lodging rooms for the actors of the Noah's Ark theatre, from me,' she said. 'Let them drink to the victory of Light over Darkness!'

'How very high-tone that is, madam,' the receptionist exclaimed admiringly.

THE BATTLE WITH THE DRAGON

Kill him, in the same way that a mad dog is killed – with no moral compunctions, no Christian commandments. So that he can never bite anyone again.

And the most miraculous thing was that there would be no penalty for this deed. That is, of course, there would be a sensational trial, with a jury, with a crush in the courtroom, with journalists. The idea of a trial did not frighten Eliza at all. Quite the contrary. A deliberately casual hairstyle. Clothes that were simple, but eye-catching – all in mourning style, with a light glint of steel, as befits a female warrior. They would definitely acquit her. The case would definitely create a furore right across Europe. And quite definitely no Sarah Bernhardt or Eleanor Duzet had ever seen such glory, even in their sweetest dreams.

All *this* was wonderful and theatrical, with guaranteed applause. But first she had to kill a man. Not that Eliza felt sorry for Genghis Khan, she most certainly did not. She didn't even consider him to be a human being – he was an ugly anomaly, a cancerous tumour that had to be excised as soon as possible. But Eliza had no idea of how to kill a man. She had done it on stage many times – for instance, when she played the Comtesse de Teroir in *The Victim of Thermidor*. It had all been very simple there: she raised her hand holding the pistol, a worker behind the scenes struck a copper sheet, and the cruel Commissar of the Convention dropped to the ground with a howl. But in real life it must all be more difficult.

And it became clear to Eliza that she couldn't manage without a consultant or a second – in short, an assistant.

She started running through the potential candidates.

Erast was excluded immediately. In her play a completely different role was allotted to him: ashamed, admiring and forgiven.

Swardilin? Too conspicuous, with his oriental appearance. And then he was a celebrity too now. She didn't want to divide the glory between two actors.

Vasya? In the Japanese play he was a great swordsman, but in real life he was a ditherer. She was certain he had never held a gun in his hand in his life. What was needed here was some kind of military man . . .

What about Georges? Firstly, he was a former officer. Secondly, he was devotedly and quite patently in love with her. Thirdly, he was a genuine knight, a man of honour. Fourthly, he was a hero – it was enough to recall how he had grabbed hold of that snake, brrrr . . . He was discreet. And – very importantly – he was accustomed to remaining in the shade.

The following day she withdrew into an empty box with Nonarikin and, after making him take an oath of silence and obedience, she told him everything. He listened with his eyes blazing, sometimes even grinding his teeth at the villain who had caused her so much grief and had killed five entirely innocent people with impunity. Eliza's story did not arouse any doubts in Nonarikin, and she was especially grateful to him for that.

'So that's what it's all about . . .' the assistant director whispered, striking his fist against his forehead. 'Ah, it's all so . . . Fate, destiny! Now it's all clear. And we . . .'

'Who is this "we"?' Eliza asked cautiously. 'Who do you mean?'

'It is of no consequence. I am bound by my word of honour, obliged to maintain silence.' Georges set his hand over his lips. 'And I am eternally grateful to you for your trust. You don't have to tell me any more. Do you know the address at which I can find the ogre? Don't worry, I shall manage things without the police. I shall force him to shoot at two paces, by lots, with no chance. And if he refuses, I shall kill him on the spot!'

This was what Eliza had been afraid of.

'I have to kill him myself. With my own hands. The last thing I

291

want is for you to be exiled to hard labour because of me!'

'My lady, for your sake I would do more than serve hard labour – for your sake I . . . I . . . am prepared to save the entire accursed world from destruction!' And he reached his arm out above the hall of the theatre in such a funny, touching manner. 'Ah, if only your eyes could be opened, if only you could see what I am really like! If only you could love me – that would change everything!'

'Nowhere beyond the bounds of the stage has anyone ever declared their love for me so . . . majestically . . .' – it took Eliza a moment or so to find the right word. 'You are my knight, and I am your lady. That is a beautiful relationship. Let us not move beyond it. And there is no need for you to intercede for me. At the moment I am not in need of a protector, but an assistant. Remember, you swore an oath to obey. You are a man of your word, are you not?'

His fervour was extinguished. His shoulders fell and his head slumped.

'Have no fear. Nonarikin keeps his word. And the role of a deputy is nothing new to me. One in nine persons, as Noah Noaevich likes to joke . . .'

Feeling calmer now, she explained that his assistance would be clandestine. Otherwise it would not be a crime committed in a state of passion, motivated by the impulse of the moment, but a pre-meditated murder involving conspiracy – a horse of quite a different colour.

'Command me, my sovereign. I shall do everything you say,' Georges said in a voice that still sounded bitter, but calmer.

'Get me a pistol and teach me how to shoot with it.'

'I have a revolver, a Nagant. A little heavy for your hand, but you will be shooting point blank, will you not?'

'Oh, yes!'

This conversation took place on the sixth of November. For three days in succession, after the rehearsal they went down into the stone-vaulted basement, where the scenery from long-forgotten productions was stored, and Eliza learned to fire the gun without squeezing her eyes shut. The shots sounded deafening, the thunder rumbled and rolled about, unable to find any way out from under the heavy vaulting. But upstairs – they checked – the shooting could not be heard.

On the first day nothing went well. On the second, at least Eliza did not drop the revolver after a shot. She emptied the entire cylinder, but failed to hit the dummy even once. Eventually, on the third day, holding the heavy revolver in both hands and shooting at extremely close range, she shot holes in the dummy with five bullets out of seven. Nonarikin said that was quite a good result.

There was no more time left to practise. The next day, Thursday, after the performance, vengeance was due to be enacted.

Eliza had no doubt that Genghis Khan would show up at the theatre. He had never missed a single performance previously and now, over the freshly dug grave of the man who could have been her husband, he would certainly want to put in an appearance. Two days earlier, in the evening, she had seen him following her across the square from the theatre to the hotel, concealed in a gaggle of admirers. After the newspapers had reported – not openly, but in perfectly transparent hints – that the suicide of 'the young millionaire' had resulted from the intransigence of a certain 'only too well-known actress', curious theatregoers had lain in wait for Eliza at the stage door and dogged her footsteps but, thank God, they had not pestered her, only gaped reverentially from a distance.

That evening she played breathtakingly, as if there were some magical force bearing her round the stage, and at times it seemed that at any moment she would fly up into the air, flapping the sleeves of her kimono like wings. Never before had the public devoured her so avidly with its eyes. Eliza could feel that avid attention, she revelled in it and was intoxicated by it. In the wings Vulpinova, who had also been given a highly dramatic role, hissed: 'This is theft! Stop stealing my moves! Aren't your own enough for you?'

Genghis Khan was in the terraced stalls. Eliza didn't see him at first, but during the love scene in the third act a familiar silhouette suddenly rose up, towering over the seated viewers. The murderer, whose fate today was to be the victim, stood up and leaned against a column, crossing his arms. If he was counting on putting the actress off, then he miscalculated – Eliza only embraced Masa with even greater passion.

After the performance, as usual, they drank a glass of champagne. Stern was very pleased and said he would record his impressions of how they had each played their parts in the Tablets.

At the very end of the brief gathering Fandorin suddenly appeared. He congratulated the company on a successful performance – probably out of politeness, because Eliza had not seen him in the hall. She looked at him only once, briefly, and turned away. He didn't look at her at all. *Just you wait, Erast Petrovich, you'll be sorry*, she thought in sweet gloating. *And very soon.*

Then Nonarikin made an announcement: 'Ladies and gentlemen, tomorrow, as usual, we rehearse at eleven. But please bear in mind that from now on those who are tardy will be subject to the appropriate measures, without any exceptions. A fine of one rouble for every minute that you are late!' Everyone grumbled about that, clamoured briefly in outrage and started going home.

'The khan is here,' Eliza whispered to her second. She was trembling. 'Be prepared and wait. Today all will be resolved!'

'I simply can't settle my nerves,' Nonarikin said when they were left alone. 'What if you hesitate and he shoots first? Come to your senses! What sort of business is this for a woman?'

'Not for anything. The die has been cast.'

Eliza smiled bravely and flung up her chin. The sudden movement set her head spinning and she felt afraid that she might faint. But it was all right, it passed off. Only her knees were trembling.

Then Georges sighed and took something small, made of black metal, out of his pocket.

'You are a heroine. Who am I to stand in the way of your heroism? This is for you, take it.'

She took the light pistol that almost fitted her hand.

'What is this? What for?'

'A Bayard. A noble weapon with a noble name. I spent everything I had left over from my salary on it. And I'll keep the Nagant. If you are in danger, I shall be ready. This at least you cannot deny me!'

Tears welled up in his eyes.

'Thank you . . . Now I shall not be afraid. Almost . . . But how do I fire it?'

'Let's go down into the basement. I'll show you.'

They walked down the steps and she fired an entire clip. This was an entirely different matter! She could hold the weapon in one hand, she hardly felt any recoil at all, and the bullets made a neat, close pattern in the dummy.

Georges was pleased too. He put in new bullets, clicked something and handed the pistol back to Eliza.

'Now just take off the safety catch and fire away! Remember, I'm here. I'm watching out.'

On the way to the exit she repeated her instructions to her second.

'No matter what, do not look round. Do not interfere in anything. Only if I call out for you to help, all right?'

He nodded, becoming gloomier by the moment.

'Don't even think of taking out your Nagant. That will be the end of both of us!'

He nodded again.

'Only if the khan prepares to shoot. Is that all clear?'

'Yes, it's clear . . .' Nonarikin muttered.

At that moment they were walking through the auditorium.

'Wait a moment.'

She felt a sudden urge to look at the stage curtain. Perhaps she would never see it again. And if she did, it would not be soon. They would probably put her prison for the duration of the trial, wouldn't they?

The cleaners were already completing their work: they brought in Noah Noaevich's desk and stood it beside the stage – for the next day's rehearsal. Then they stood a lamp on it, precisely at the centre, as Stern preferred. Then they set out fresh sheets of paper and sharpened pencils and – with special respect – the Tablets.

Eliza suddenly felt a desire to read what Noah Noaevich had written about the way she had acted today.

It made pleasant reading: 'For E.L. – Miraculous nervous tension! The recipe for success: stretch the string to the limit. But do not snap it!'

That was on the stage. But in real life sometimes it had to be snapped.

Before she went outside, Eliza filled her lungs with air and looked at her watch. Precisely midnight. An ideal hour for bloodshed.

She stepped out onto the pavement like Mary Stuart stepping onto the scaffold.

Despite the late hour, there was a crowd standing at the entrance. There was clapping and exclamations, several men handed her bouquets, someone asked her to sign a photocard. A flashgun flared.

As she nodded and smiled, out of the corner of her eye Eliza followed the movements of a figure in a long black coat and a gleaming top hat.

He was here, here!

She handed the flowers to Nonarikin, who just barely managed to wrap his left arm round them, while keeping his right hand in his pocket.

Twenty steps farther on Eliza took her powder compact out of the pocket of her muff, in order to glance into the little mirror. About half a dozen admirers, both male and female, were following her at a respectable distance, and striding along at the head of them, with his heels clattering loudly, was Genghis Khan.

It would be easier to carry out her intentions in public view. She would just have to imagine that she was playing a part.

Eliza swung round. She shuddered, as if she had only just noticed the man in the long coat. He grinned under his black moustache.

She cried out and lengthened her stride a little.

The clatter of heels behind her also speeded up.

I mustn't hit the people walking behind him, Eliza thought. She counted to five in her mind.

'Torturer! Monster!' she exclaimed in a resounding voice. 'I can't take any more!'

Genghis Khan, startled, shied away to one side. Now she could fire at will, behind him there was nothing but the dark, empty square.

'As God is my judge!' Eliza improvised. 'I may perish, but you will also meet your end!'

She drew the pistol out of her muff with an elegant gesture and took a step forward. Her hand did not tremble, her supreme artistic elation rendered every movement irreproachable.

The khan shuddered and dropped his top hat.

'Die, Satan!'

She squeezed her forefinger as hard as she possibly could, but there was no shot. She pressed the trigger again and again – but it didn't yield.

'The safety catch! The safety catch!' Nonarikin hissed behind her.

Everything went dark in front of Eliza's eyes. This was a disaster!

The admirers started shouting and waving their arms about. Genghis Khan also came to his senses. He didn't reach into his coat to take out a gun, but simply turned up his collar, swung round and darted away at a trot, dissolving into the darkness.

A flashgun flared again. The camera recorded Eliza Altairsky-Lointaine in a most effective pose: with her arm extended and a pistol in her hand.

'Bravo! Is that from a future production?' the admirers babbled. 'How original! We adore you!' a woman exclaimed. 'I haven't missed a single one of your performances! I absolutely idolise you! I'm a reporter for the *Evening News*, will you allow me to ask a question?'

'What went wrong?' Eliza asked her second in an appalling whisper. 'Why didn't it fire?'

'But you didn't take off the safety catch . . .'

'What safety catch? What safety catch are you talking about?'

Georges took her by the arm and led her away.

'Oh, come on now! We fired in the basement, didn't we . . . You saw it! And I reminded you . . .'

'I don't recall. I was agitated. And then, when I fired the Nagant, there wasn't any safety catch.'

'Good Lord, every grammar school boy knows that, unlike a revolver, a pistol has a little lever like this, look, there it is!'

'I am not a grammar school boy!' Eliza sobbed hysterically. 'This is all your fault! Call yourself a second! You didn't explain anything properly! My God, get them away from me, will you? And you go away too! I don't want to see anyone!'

She ran on ahead, choking on her sobs. Nonarikin obediently hung back.

'Madam Altairsky is tired! Please show her some consideration!' she heard his voice say behind her. 'Please come to the performance, ladies and gentlemen. Please allow the artistes to have a private life of their own!'

The world of theatre is full of legends about the most shameful, monstrous fiascos. Not even the most famous of actresses does not have a nightmare in which she forgets her part or makes an appalling blunder that results in malevolent silence from the audience and then whistling and booing and the shuffling of chairs. Eliza had been certain that nothing of the sort would ever happen to her. But now she had flunked the most important entrance of her life quite disgracefully. As she stumbled blindly along the hotel corridor, she was not thinking of the consequences of her attack on Genghis Khan (there would definitely be some), but about her own absolutely hopeless incompetence.

Real life was not a theatre. There was no worker to strike a sheet of metal behind the scenes to make the shot ring out, and the villain would not tumble over of his own accord. The curtain would not descend to save her from the raging public. She could not simply take off her costume and her make-up.

I am talentless, my life is mediocre, and I have deserved my fate, thought Eliza. She sat there in the dark room, without taking off her hat, like some little bird huddling up in its feathers to warm itself, broken and exhausted. She fell asleep without realising it.

And she had a dream that was quite unbearable, absolutely terrifying. She was sitting in her dressing room, all the walls were covered with mirrors and she tried to look at herself – but there was no reflection. No matter which way she turned or which mirror she looked into – there was nothing. And although she had the feeling that there was something black right there beside her, she couldn't catch a glimpse of it. She sat there, turning her head faster and faster, right and left, right and left, but there was still no Eliza to be seen.

I've taken off my stage costume and make-up, and without the part I don't exist, she realised, and felt so afraid that she woke with a groan and with tears in her eyes.

If the sun had been shining outside the window, perhaps she would have felt some relief. But the dirty November dawn was even worse than the darkness, and her entire body was numbed from her uncomfortable pose during the night. Eliza felt dirty, unwell and *old*. She glanced fearfully round the room. The vague outlines of things, visible through the dim light, frightened her. A large mirror glimmered on the wall, but not for anything in the world would Eliza have glanced into it now. The real world pressed in on her from every side, it was menacing and unpredictable, she didn't understand the way its plot lines developed and she didn't dare to surmise what the denouement would be.

She jumped up and started dashing aimlessly round the room. She had to get away from here, away! But where to?

To where everything was familiar and predictable. To the theatre! Its walls were like an impregnable fortress. It denied access to strangers, and to real life with all of its dangers. There she would be in her own kingdom, where everything was familiar and comprehensible and nothing was frightening.

Following poor Limbach's death, Eliza had been given a new dressing room, at the opposite end of the corridor, a very bright and cheerful room – Noah Noaevich had given the instructions. And now she suddenly felt an irresistible urge, this very second, to run out of this appalling, absolutely alien hotel room and dash across the square, so that she would be there, among the posters and the photographs that reminded her of her former triumphs ... that reminded her that Eliza Lointaine really did exist.

It was only the habit of discipline in everything that concerned her appearance and her clothes that prevented her from dashing out immediately. With quite incredible haste – in about an hour – Eliza tidied herself up, changing her clothes, putting on her perfume and arranging her hair in a tight style. That lent her a certain amount of strength. She was at least reflected in the mirror. Well, she was pale and her eyes were sunken, but in combination with medium-blue velvet and a wide-brimmed hat, this morbid air actually looked rather interesting.

As Eliza walked along the street, men looked round at her. She was gradually starting to calm down. Once inside the echoing foyer of the theatre, she sighed in relief. There was more than an hour and a half remaining until the rehearsal. She would recover her spirits before eleven. And after that . . . But she didn't allow herself to think about what would happen after that.

Ah, how good it felt in the theatre when it was empty. The twilight wasn't frightening, and even the rustling of her footsteps was comforting.

She also loved the dark, deserted auditorium. Without actors, this wide space was lifeless; it was waiting obediently and patiently for Eliza to fill it with her light.

She opened the door slightly – and stopped.

In the distance the lamp was lit on the director's desk in front of the stage. Someone who was standing with his back to her swung round sharply at the creak. The figure was tall, with broad shoulders.

'Who's there?' Eliza called out in fright.

'Fandorin.'

So that is the force that drew me here! Eliza suddenly realised. *It is destiny. It is salvation. Or final annihilation – it is all the same now.*

She moved forward quickly.

'Did you also feel the call?' she asked tremulously. 'Was it instinct that drew you here?'

'It was chemistry that drew me here.'

Eliza was surprised for a moment, then she realised that he meant internal chemistry, the chemistry of hearts!

Only Fandorin's voice did not sound the way it ought to. Not agitated, but preoccupied. When she drew closer, Eliza saw that he was holding the Tablets in his hands.

'L-look. This was not here yesterday.'

She glanced absent-mindedly at the page with today's date on it. Written at the top in sprawling characters was: 'FOUR 1S UNTIL THE BENEFIT PERFORMANCE. PREPARE!'

'No, it wasn't. I was the last to leave, after midnight,' Eliza said with a shrug. 'But why are you concerned about this endless, stupid joke?'

What deep eyes he has, she thought. *If only he would look at me like that for ever.*

Fandorin replied in a quiet voice.

'Where there is murder, there are no jokes.'

Two 1s

UNTIL THE BENEFIT
PERFORMANCE

NEW AND OLD THEORIES

Erast Petrovich's words simply burst out of their own accord – he had still not recovered after she appeared here suddenly. But, thank God, Eliza didn't hear them.

'What?' she asked.

'Nothing. It d-doesn't mean anything . . .'

And he thought: *It's dangerous for me to look at her from close up. The symptoms of the illness are intensified.* He hid the extractor behind his back to avoid being drawn into explanations. Although he would have to justify his presence here in some way or other.

How she was looking at him. If any other woman were to look like that, he could be certain that she loved him with all her heart. But she was an actress . . .

The only time she had demonstrated unfeigned feeling was when she fainted at the news of her fiancé's death. At that moment a sharp pain had transfixed Erast Petrovich's heart. So she had not been planning to marry the millionaire out of calculation, but out of love?

This thought had tormented him afterwards for the whole day. Eventually he had committed an unworthy action. Late in the evening he had telephoned the Metropole hotel, after first enquiring from Stern which room Eliza was occupying, and then stuck in a hatpin: he read her the venomous tanka. The meaning of the pentastitch was obvious: your love is not worth a bent farthing, madam; perhaps in the next life you will prove more useful.

She had answered him in an absolutely lifeless voice. Pretended that she didn't care a fig for anything; she had even laughed, but she

305

had not fooled him. If even an artiste like her could not conceal her grief, then it was very great. But then why had she refused Shustrov? In truth, the soul of an actress was as dark as the twilight behind the stage.

Fandorin felt ashamed. He had promised himself he would leave Eliza in peace. And in the days that followed he had kept his distance. Only yesterday evening he had been obliged to appear where she could see him, but he had not gone close.

Yesterday it had been impossible not to come to the theatre. The interests of the investigation had required it.

Apart from anything else, Shustrov's death had struck a very powerful blow at Fandorin's vanity. The theory on which he had spent so much time and effort had burst like a soap bubble. Mr Whistle was dead and the Tsar was on the other side of the Atlantic. The gang of Moscow ticket touts no longer existed and could not have had anything to do with the millionaire's death.

Erast Petrovich had little doubt that it was not suicide. Shustrov was not the kind of man to do away with himself because of a rejected proposal of marriage. But he had had to visit the scene of the tragedy and check everything in person, and then castigate himself and set in order his raging feelings and tangled thoughts.

'Let's go to Prechistenka,' he said to 'Monsieur Simon' while the ladies were fussing over Eliza after she fainted. 'I have to see this.'

Masa cast an eloquent glance at his master, ran into a gaze that expressed nothing, sighed and turned away.

Erast Petrovich had not mended his relations with his comrade since returning from Europe. After learning of Eliza's impending marriage, Fandorin had returned home to Cricket Lane in a mood darker than a storm cloud. He didn't want to talk about anything. And he had nothing to boast about. After all, he hadn't managed to catch the Tsar. From the very beginning the operation had gone awry and it had concluded in failure, and Erast Petrovich had only himself to blame. If he had taken Masa to Sokolniki instead of the half-witted Georges, things would have turned out quite differently

'Leave me alone,' Fandorin had told his servant. 'No questions.'

And, naturally, the Japanese had taken offence. Not only had his master disappeared for almost two weeks without really explaining anything, but he didn't want to tell Masa anything either! Nothing of the kind had happened even once in thirty-three years.

'Then I won't tell you anything either!' Masa had declared, obviously meaning Eliza and his relationship with her.

'Certainly, by all means.'

In any case, Fandorin had not wished to hear anything about the rich love life of Madam Altairsky-Lointaine. Let her bill and coo with whomever she wished, and marry whomever she wished. That was her business.

All in all, Erast Petrovich's hope of recovery had been premature. Once again he was mired in depression. Exclusively in order to distract himself and occupy his thoughts with something, the next day he had gone to the theatre and done what he had been intending to do; he looked through the delinquent entries in the Tablets.

At that point there were three of them.

From 6 September: 'EIGHT 1S UNTIL THE BENEFIT PERFORMANCE. THINK BETTER OF IT'.

Then, on the second page for October, simply this: 'SEVEN 1S UNTIL THE BENEFIT PEFORMANCE'.

And the latest entry, dated 1 November: 'FIVE 1S UNTIL THE BENEFIT PERFORMANCE'.

The letters were large. The handwriting was the same. The messages were written in indelible pencil.

An obvious piece of nonsense. One of the actors was amusing himself – apparently in order to annoy the director and hear him roaring.

Erast Petrovich read through the 'sacred book' once again to see whether he had missed an entry about six units, but there wasn't one. Then he got angry and set the journal aside. The joke was not only stupid, but careless. These higgledy-piggledy characters did not deserve his attention.

The next time he appeared in the theatre was on the fifth of November, a Saturday – when Eliza was due to give her answer to Shustrov. He struggled with himself, but came anyway. What would she be like on this day? Would she be embarrassed by him showing up or not?

The bitter verse about a geisha's love was lying in his pocket. Erast Petrovich had composed the tanka the previous night, tormented by insomnia. But he didn't get a chance to give it to her. Events set off at a gallop when an old acquaintance of his, a character out of a previous life, came bursting into the auditorium.

Senya had changed greatly and Fandorin had not even recognised him immediately. He had been transformed into a lively young man of European appearance, who confused Russian words and French ones, but even so, every now and then his manners betrayed the semi-criminal youth from the Khitrovka, with whom Erast Petrovich had once lived through one of the very darkest adventures in his life as a detective.

On the way to Prechistenka, to the roaring of the Bugatti's engine, they had spoken – or, rather, shouted – a little.

'So how did it happen that you got involved in the cinematograph, dear sir? And why did you become Monsieur Simon?'

'Oh, Erast Petrovich, *s'il vous plaît*, don't take that formal tone, just talk to me the way you used to. I've been speaking to you and Mr Masa all these years. When I didn't know *que faire*, I always asked you. And you would *répondre*: "Do it this way, Senya". Or vice versa: "Don't do that, don't be a *crétin*".'

He chattered away without a break. He was clearly delighted by this unexpected meeting and for a while even forgot about the sad event. That was nothing new for Senya. He had never been able to remain despondent for long

'I became "Simon" because a Frenchman can't pronounce "Semyon", his tongue twists in a different fashion. And I fell in love with the *cinéma*, because there is nothing better in the world. The first time I saw *A Trip to the Moon*, I realised immediately that this was it, my *chemin dans la vie* – my path in life, as you say in Russian!'

'M-*merci*,' said Erast Petrovich, thanking his companion for the translation.

'*De rien*. I went straight to the great Monsieur Méliès. I still couldn't really speak their lingo then, my French would have made a cat laugh. *Vous êtes génie*, I told him. *Je veux vivre et mourir pour cinéma*! I wrote it on a piece of paper, in our letters. Learned it off by heart. But otherwise I didn't have a word.'

'And nothing else is needed. It says everything that matters. From an early age you had a qu-quite exceptional psychological talent.'

'Then I left Méliès. The old man started losing his *fleur*, not keeping up with life. What's the most important thing now for *cinéma*? Scale! Now Gaumont had got scale! Last year the two of us set up an electric theatre in Paris with three thousand, four hundred seats! But Gaumont wouldn't make me a partner, so I left. And then things are crowded in France, everyone's jostling for elbow space. You can only do real business here in your country, Russia. If you're *énergique*.'

Keeping one hand on the steering wheel and waving the other around, he glanced at Fandorin, who had raised one eyebrow at the phrase 'in your country'. But Senya misunderstood his surprise and started explaining.

'*Energique* – that's when you keep *révolver* all the time. It's the most important quality for success. You can get by without all the other qualities, but not without the *énergique*, no way. You have plenty of clever types here, plenty of hard workers, there are even some honest ones. But they're all dozy, feeble. A man thinks up something worthwhile, but he just sits there on his backside, like a bear. He turns a good deal – and he has to celebrate immediately. But you have to work quickly, quickly, *sans arrêt*. An *énergique* man, even if he's not so very *intelligent* – brainy that is – will stumble and fall ten times, get up eleven times and still outrun a man who's clever, but dozy. But here in your country, I see all the talk is about *révolution*, about *liberté* and *égalité*. But what Russia needs is not revolution, but a dose of turpentine, to make it run faster.'

Senya-Simon cleared his throat and took on a mournful air.

'Andriusha Shustrov – now he was a *génie*. I mean, how do you say that?'

'A genius.'

'Yes, a genius. What incredible business we would have done here. If not for that snake-woman. Men like Andriusha, they only seem to be made of stone, but they're really terribly *passionés* – intense. Heat a heart of stone up red hot and then pour icy water on it and – crack.'

'An elegant metaphor,' said Erast Petrovich, involuntarily rubbing the left side of his chest. 'But don't let me hear another word from you about the "snake-woman". I will not allow anyone to insult Madam Lointaine. That is one. And secondly . . .'

He was about to add that Eliza probably had nothing to do with this case, but he paused. Now, after this new death, Fandorin was no longer certain of anything.

Simon understood the pause in his own way. Forgetting the sad circumstances again, he winked.

'You should have said straight away. I see you're still the same as you used to be. Involved with the *femmes fatales*. Only you've changed your surname for some reason. Andriusha kept going on to me about you: Fandorin, Fandorin, he's going to write *fabules* for us, and I didn't have a clue that it was you. By the way, it has quite a ring to it. Sounds like Phantomas. That's someone a film should be made about! Have you read it? Real literature, none of your Emile Zola and Lev Tolstoy. Real power! We could try Mr Masa for the leading role. He's the "real Japanese Swardilin", isn't he? I only realised that today. Mr Masa can climb up walls, and kick someone in the face, and all sorts of things. And it doesn't matter that he has slant-eyes. Phantomas always wears a mask. Oh, a real *génie* of evildoing!'

And he started talking enthusiastically about some big wheel of the criminal world, a hero of modern novels. Erast Petrovich had known individuals of this type in real life, so he listened with a certain degree of interest, but the sports car was already flying into one of the side streets of Prechistenka. It pulled up with a squeal of brakes in front of a smart detached mansion house with policemen guarding the entrance.

The investigator was someone Fandorin didn't know, a certain Captain Drissen, from the chancellery of the Chief of Police. The death of a millionaire was a serious case, not like some little cornet of the Guards. It had not been entrusted to a modest old hand like Subbotin.

Fandorin took a dislike to the police officer. There had always been plenty of his type in the police, sweet with their superiors and rude with their subordinates, and in recent years they had spread everywhere. Naturally, the captain had heard about Fandorin, so he spoke in sugared tones. He showed Erast Petrovich everything, explained everything and even reported his own conclusions, which he had not been asked to do.

These conclusions amounted, in brief, to the following.

The questioning of witnesses had established that the deceased had been certain that this would be the happiest day of his life. Early in the morning he had been planning to visit the Louvre hotel to see his fiancée, the well-known artiste Altairsky-Lointaine, in order to set an engagement ring on her finger.

'By the way, where is it, Mr Simon?' Drissen asked, interrupting his report and giving Senya a look that was not sugar-sweet, but menacing. 'You grabbed it and ran off, and I'll be asked about it.'

'A mere trifle,' the Parisian said morosely with a wave of his hand. In his dead comrade's house he seemed to have shrunk and did nothing but sigh. 'If need be – I'll replace it. *Pas de problème.*'

The officer was delighted by the news that money wasn't a problem for the partner. He smiled sweetly and carried on with his report.

The picture that emerged was clear. At the last moment the fiancée had changed her mind and informed the deceased about this by telephone. Shustrov had gone insane from grief and grabbed his razor. His hand was trembling, so at first he had inflicted several small cuts on himself and then he had finally overcome his weakness and severed his artery, together with the trachea, and the end had followed without delay.

Erast Petrovich listened to the facts attentively and to the conclusions casually. He squatted down beside the body for a long time, examining the mutilated neck through a magnifying glass.

Eventually he got up with a very preoccupied air and spoke to the expectant captain.

'You know, there are policemen who for a certain f-fee let the gutter press have all sorts of piquant little details of events. So, if news that the investigation links Shustrov's death with the name of the actress whom you have mentioned should leak out to the press, I shall consider you personally responsible.'

'By your leave . . .' Drissen flushed, but Erast Petrovich flashed his highly expressive blue eyes at the officer, and he fell silent.

'And if such a mishap should occur, I shall employ all of my influence to ensure that you will serve the remainder of your career in Chukotka. I do not often burden the top level with requests, so they will not refuse me in such a trivial instance.'

The policeman cleared his throat.

'However, sir, I cannot take responsibility for others. Rumours might leak out of the theatre . . . the case will attract huge public interest. They have already had suicides there.'

'Rumours are one thing. An official theory is another. Do you understand me? Well, good.'

The suspicion that was so humiliating for Fandorin had been confirmed.

The Tsar and Mr Whistle probably had nothing to do with the deaths in the theatre. Because they could not have murdered the millionaire Shustrov, and he had been murdered. And to judge from the signature, by the same criminal who had murdered Emeraldov and Limbach.

The investigation would have to be started all over again from the beginning.

Usually, when there was a sequence of mysterious atrocities, the problem was that there was no reasonably plausible hypothesis. But here it was the opposite. Too many hypotheses arose. Even if one started from the basics of deduction – the two main motives that led one man to kill another: *'cui prodest'* and *'cherchez la femme'*.

Who could have benefited from the death of the millionaire?

Well, for instance, the whole of Noah's Ark and Mr Stern personally. Under the terms of the will, the company of actors received a substantial capital sum. That was one. The insistence with which the entrepreneur had tried to get the company to move into the cinematograph had irritated everyone and set their nerves on edge. The world of the theatre was pathological, filled with hypertrophied passions. If the character of the individual with the inclinations of a murderer had been formed in this environment (and this was almost an undoubted fact), the above reason could prove quite enough. Here one also had to take into account the psychology of the *artistic criminal*. This was a special personality type, for whom the 'beauty' of a concept could provide the impulse to commit a crime – in addition to the practical gain involved.

As for 'cherchez la femme', here there was no need to search for the woman. The candidate was obvious. However, if the murders had been committed because of Eliza, that threw up an entire bunch of theories.

Shustrov had proposed to a woman at whom many eyes gazed lustfully and to whom many hands reached out covetously. (It was disgusting that for a while Erast Petrovich himself had jostled in that crowd.) Madam Altairsky's admirers could well include someone whose jealousy could lead to them committing a crime.

In this case, unlike the version with *cui prodest*, it was easy to add in the previous two murders. The rumours about Limbach (it was not important whether they were true) claimed that he had won Eliza's affections. The same rumours had been spread about Emeraldov. Erast Petrovich himself had read in a revue of *Poor Liza* an extremely transparent hint about the 'intense sensuality of the acting of the leading players' not being the result of stage passion alone.

To the two basic motivations to which ordinary people were prone there should be added the exotic motivations possible only in the theatre.

In addition to amorous jealousy there was also actor's jealousy. The leading lady in a company was always fiercely envied. Cases were known of a prima ballerina's female comrades tipping ground glass into her shoes before a performance. Sometimes pepper was added to an opera singer's egg-nog in order to make her lose her voice. And anything could happen in a drama theatre. But it was one thing to stick a snake in a basket of flowers and quite another to cold-bloodedly dispatch Emeraldov, slit open Limbach's stomach and slash Shustrov's throat to ribbons.

The sugary Captain Drissen was, of course, mistaken concerning the sequence of the cuts. Examination of the wounds had demonstrated that the fatal wound had been inflicted first. The others had been added later, after the spasms had ceased. That was clear both from the traces of blood on the floor and from the minor cuts themselves: they were neat and even, as if they had been made along a ruler. What the murderer had needed this work of art for was an open question. But the signature of all the crimes was characterised by a certain fancifulness and theatricality. Emeraldov had been poisoned with wine from Gertrude's goblet; Limbach had been left to bleed to death in a locked dressing room; Shustrov's throat had been lacerated with a razor after he was dead.

And concerning the matter of theatricality. In the play that Erast Petrovich had written, one character, a merchant, had his head cut off in repayment for his perfidy. Shustrov was an entrepreneur, in a certain sense also a merchant. Was there some reference to the play here? Anything was possible. It would have to be clarified if any parallels could be traced between the actions of the Moscow millionaire and the Japanese moneybags.

There was also another theory that was absolutely insane. Erast Petrovich could not get out of his mind the 'benefit performance' and the accursed 1s mentioned in the Tablets. He even dreamed about them at night: pointed, glowing bright scarlet and then melting away, melting away. At first there were eight of them, then seven, then two had disappeared at once and five were left. And, by the way, the slashes on the dead man's throat had resembled scarlet 1s, one large, fat one and ten thinner ones. Eleven 1s in all and 11 was two 1s again. Raving lunacy, schizophrenia!

His head, already dulled by the humiliating torments of love, refused to perform its usual analytical work. Never before had Erast Petrovich been in such terrible intellectual form. Flowers with vipers, goblets with poison, bloody razors and fragile 1s were all jumbled up together in his brain, swirling round in absurd roundelay.

But the skills he had developed over years, his willpower and habit of self-discipline, eventually won out. The first law of investigation reads: when there are too many theories, their number has to be reduced, by first removing the most unlikely. Therefore Erast Petrovich decided first of all to get rid of the annoying 1s.

This would require identifying the joker who was making the idiotic entries in the 'sacred book'. Taking him by the scruff of the neck (or by the elbow, if it was a lady) and demanding an explanation.

It was a rather bothersome business, but basically simple – which was another reason why Fandorin decided to start with the 'benefit performance'.

On the evening of the tenth of November, after the performance, Erast Petrovich came to the wings to drink a glass of champagne with the company. Actors are a superstitious crowd and they take traditions seriously. So even the complete teetotallers, like Reginina or Noah Noaevich, clinked glasses with the others and took a sip of the wine. Fandorin remembered where each of them left his or her glass. When the green room was empty, he marked each one, put them all in his travelling bag and took them away with him. The buffet manager had already left, so no one would notice the disappearance until the next morning. And that night Erast Petrovich intended to come back here and put the glasses back in their places.

During the previous year, which had been devoted to studying chemistry, Fandorin had given over a lot of time to investigating blood groups, a new discovery that was of importance not only for medicine, but also for criminalistics. It promised even more interesting results in the future; however, even now the analysis of traces of blood could be of tremendous assistance to an investigator. The courts still refused to recognise this form of analysis as evidence for the prosecution, but there had already been a case in which blood analysis had helped to acquit an innocent party. A robbery and murder had been committed in a brothel. The police had discovered fresh spots of blood on the dress of one of the prostitutes who had come under suspicion, and on this basis they had decided that she was the murderer. The girl had no alibi and she had been in court before. The members of the jury were clearly inclined towards a guilty verdict. However, examination of the blood spots demonstrated that the blood belonged to a different group from that of the victim. The prostitute was released, and the hero of the day was not her barrister, but the medical expert.

Erast Petrovich had been greatly interested by this discovery and had taken it farther. In particular, he had established that the blood group could be determined from the saliva. This was the purpose for which the glasses from the theatre buffet had been temporarily purloined.

In the depths of the night in his home laboratory Fandorin took samples and performed his analysis. There were only ten glasses – he had excluded Masa and Eliza from the list of suspects. After some hesitation, he had kept Stern. Who could tell whether the director himself were not simply acting the fool – for the sake of his 'theory of rupture' or something else of the sort.

As followed from the science, the samples fell into four groups: three members of the company belonged to group one, two of them belonged to group two, three of them belonged to group three and two belonged to group four. Furthermore, in all cases the particles of liquid possessed additional individual characteristics. Microscopic admixtures of nicotine, lipstick and medicines that were present in the saliva made it possible to hope that identifying the hooligan might prove easier than Fandorin had been expecting.

Now he had to go back to the theatre and carry out another procedure.

It was already getting light outside. As he shaved and changed his clothes, Fandorin listened to check whether Masa was asleep. For the first time in a long time Erast Petrovich had a chance to boast of at least something to the Japanese. Of course, it was no astounding breakthrough, but at least there was something to tell.

However, Masa was snuffling away gently in his room – resentfully, or so it seemed to Fandorin. Well, that was only for the best. Today the author of the scribbles would be identified. Then he would be able to tell Masa the whole story, make peace with him and involve him in the investigation. There was a murderer on the loose, he was dangerous. This was no time for stupid nonsense.

The next stage would be to collect samples from the Tablets. All the entries about the benefit performance had been made with an indelible pencil that had to be wetted with saliva before use. Using a sample-extractor of his own design, Erast Petrovich intended to scrape away particles of the paper, together with the saliva that had soaked into them. Unfortunately he had not been able to do this the previous evening – the Tablets had been taken away to the hall by the cleaner, and Fandorin had not wished to wait until the service staff left. And in any case he would have to bring the glasses back.

*

He entered the theatre through the stage door, which he opened with a picklock. One of the rules established by Stern prohibited any of the service personnel from appearing in the building before the lunch break, so that they would not interrupt the sacred rites. Only the watchman was sitting in his booth, separated from the auditorium by an entire storey. So there was no reason to fear that this time Erast Petrovich would be seen by anyone.

Without encountering any complications, he first set the glasses back in their places and then entered the hall. The journal was lying where it was supposed to lie: on the director's little desk.

Fandorin switched on the lamp, prepared his extractor and opened the book. Then he froze.

On the empty page, immediately below today's date, there was a new entry in shimmering, blue indelible pencil: FOUR 1S UNTIL THE BENEFIT PERFORMANCE. BE READY.

The fourth time! And now there were four 1s too . . .

Astounded, he lifted the book right up to his eyes. He told himself: *Very good, fresh traces, now we'll find out who this joker is.* Although he no longer believed that this was a joke.

A door creaked beside him.

Fandorin looked round – and saw Eliza.

FANDORIN'S WORK OF DEDUCTION IS HINDERED

It was impossible to take the sample with her there. Erast Petrovich hid the extractor. There was still a lot of time to go before the rehearsal began, the actors would not start gathering for at least another hour. If Eliza left him alone for at least five minutes, that would be enough.

'Are you not going up to your dressing room?' he asked after an oppressive pause.

'Yes, I have to take off my hat and coat and change my shoes. Will you see me up? Let's go through the foyer. It's dusty backstage.'

It would be impolite to refuse, he thought, realising perfectly well that he was deceiving himself. To be beside her, to walk through the empty, dark corridors together, just the two of them – was this not happiness?

Feeling pitiful and weak-willed, Fandorin followed Eliza without speaking. Suddenly she took his arm in hers, which was strange – in enclosed premises ladies did not usually do that.

'Oh Lord, to walk like this . . .' she whispered about some thought of her own.

'What?'

'Never mind, never mind . . .'

She let go of him.

At the door of the dressing room, she apologised and asked him to wait while she put on her *tabi* – Japanese socks – for the sandals.

Five minutes later she called out.

'You can come in now.'

Eliza was sitting in front of the dressing table, but looking at

Fandorin, and he saw her immediately from every angle: the back of her head, her face, both profiles. In the light of the lamp her hair shimmered, like a golden helmet.

'Please stay with me for a while. Just stay. I'm in a really bad way . . .'

He lowered his eyes in order not to look into hers. He was afraid of giving himself away, afraid that he would dash over to her and start babbling pitiful nonsense about love.

Erast Petrovich gritted his teeth and made himself think about the case. The extraction of saliva from the Tablets would obviously have to wait until the evening, but even without the analysis there was plenty to think over.

So, a fourth entry had appeared in the journal. The chronology and the arithmetic were as follows: on 6 September there were eight 1s remaining until a certain benefit performance and someone was called upon to 'think again', on 2 October, there were seven 1s remaining, on 1 November, for some reason, there were only five; and finally, today, 11 November, there were only four 1s remaining and the unknown author admonished his reader to 'be ready'. Fandorin sensed a system in this arithmetical leap-frog, which at first glance appeared arbitrary. And if that was so . . .

'My sincere condolences on your l-loss,' he said out loud, because Eliza was clearly waiting for him to say something. 'It is terrible to lose a fiancé.'

'It is terrible to lose yourself! It is terrible to be in a state of despair and fear every minute!'

Is she crying? Why has she put her hand over her mouth?

Erast Petrovich moved towards her impulsively. And stopped. Then he took another step forward. Eliza turned towards him, put her arm round his waist, pressed her face against him and burst into sobs.

It's her nerves. It's very clear. The embrace only signifies that she needs support and consolation. Cautiously, very cautiously, he put one hand on her shoulder. He stroked her hair with the other.

Eliza wept for a long time, and for all that time Erast Petrovich's thoughts refused to return to the mystery of the 1s.

But when the actress raised her wet face to him and glanced at him, Fandorin longed unbearably to lean down and dry every teardrop with his lips. He stepped back and clutched at his deductions as if they were the straw that could save him.

The changing remainder of 1s signifies that originally there was a specific number of them. As a result of 1s being deducted in a manner that is in some way connected with the passage of time, this number is being reduced. The first question is: what was that number? How many 1s were there to begin with?

'I can't go on,' Eliza whispered. 'I must tell you . . . No, no!'

She turned away quickly, saw herself in the mirror and gasped.

'What do I look like? There are only fifty minutes left until the rehearsal! You mustn't see me like this! Please, wait outside. I'll tidy myself up and come out to you.'

However, the crying didn't stop. Standing in the corridor, Fandorin could hear her sobbing and muttering something.

Eventually Eliza came out, with her face powered and her hair freshly brushed.

'I'm having a nervous breakdown,' she said, trying to smile. 'I think I'll be magnificent in rehearsal today. As long as I don't go into hysterics. Please allow me to lean on your arm, it will give me strength.'

Their shoulders touched; he could feel her trembling and felt frightened that he might be infected with this trembling too.

X minus Y is equal to eight. X minus Y plus one is equal to seven. X minus Y plus three is equal to five. X minus Y plus four is equal to four . . . In the grammar school Fandorin had not been brilliant at algebra and remembered it only vaguely, and he had not included this seemingly useless discipline in the programme of fruitful ageing. He should have done. A mathematician might possibly have solved this crazy equation. Although an equation with two unknowns didn't have any solution, did it? Or did it? He couldn't remember. If not for the proximity of Eliza's hot shoulder, if not for the fragrance of her hair, his thinking wouldn't twitch about and skip like this, from one thing to another . . .

They tried to enter the hall via the side door, but for some reason it turned out to be locked. They had to walk to the central door.

'I can't put up with this nonsense about 1s in the journal any longer!' Noah Noaevich was shouting and waving his arms about. 'Whoever is doing this is trying to finish me off! He's jabbing his 1s into me like needles! Slashing me with them like razors!'

The assistant director's warning of the previous day about fines for lateness had had its effect. Even though it was only about twenty minutes to eleven, almost the entire company had already gathered. The actors were sitting in the front row, indolently listening to the director's howls.

'Let's slip in behind them,' Eliza said to Fandorin. 'I need to get a grip on myself . . . I just can't seem to manage it somehow . . . I'm about to shatter into fragments at any moment. Like a broken mirror.'

Slashing him with 1s like razors? Erast Petrovich thought with a start. *How many cuts were there on the millionaire's neck?*

'No more, I can't go on like this. So come what may!' Eliza said in a breaking voice, but Erast Petrovich was no longer looking at her, or listening to her. The figures were clicking away in his head.

'It's Genghis Khan who's killing everyone! My ex-husband. His jealousy has driven him insane! He killed two of my admirers in St Petersburg! He's not a man, he's a devil! He's going to kill me!' the actress babbled, choking on her tears.

'Genghis Khan lived in the twelfth century,' Fandorin said absent-mindedly. 'Twelve isn't right. The correct number is eleven. Eleven 1s. Right then. Eight is eleven minus three. Seven is eleven minus four. Five is eleven minus six. But why the sudden skip? Ah, damnation! Because it's 1 November! And on 11 November, today, there are only four 1s left. But what are those four 1s?'

She looked at him in alarm.

'Are you unwell?'

'What?'

'Were . . . weren't you listening to me?'

Erast Petrovich tore himself away from his arithmetic with an effort.

'Certainly I was. Of course I'm listening. Your former husband, Genghis Khan, is the one who is killing everybody . . . This is a psychosis. You've been through far too much. You need to calm down.'

The fear in her eyes intensified.

'Oh yes, a psychosis! You don't think it's of any importance! I'm not well. Promise me you won't do anything!' She clasped her hands as if in prayer. 'Forget all about it! I implore you!'

Vasilisa Prokofievna floated into the hall, looking red faced.

'Ooph, I was almost late!'

She glanced at Eliza's tear-stained face and enquired:

'What are you rehearsing, Elizochka? Ah, I've guessed. *King Lear*, Act Five. Cordelia: For thee, oppressed king, am I cast down, Myself could else out-frown false fortune's frown." Are we really going to play Shakespeare, then?'

We really are like father and daughter, Fandorin thought irritably. *She's a young woman and I have grey hair.* But Eliza flushed and moved away.

'Am I the last?' Reginina looked round. 'No, Georges Cerberus isn't here yet, the Lord be praised for that.'

It was true, everybody had already gathered except for the assistant director. At the very end of the front row Fandorin made out Masa's round head. The Japanese was whispering about something with Sima Aphrodisina, but squinting at his master at the same time.

Four 1s – it's time! Hours and minutes! But where do I put the 1s that fall out of line?

Eliza's breath tickled his ear.

'Do you promise to forget what I said?'

Stern appeared on the stage and looked round the hall.

'Geisha Izumi! Stop distracting the esteemed author! Join us, if you please! We're starting! Damn it all, where is Georges? A fine keeper of discipline. One minute to eleven, and he's not here yet! Has anyone seen Nonarikin? Where's Nonarikin?'

Fandorin swayed in his seat.

But of course! Nonarikin! The figure nine!

'Where's Nonarikin?' he exclaimed, echoing Stern, and got to his feet.

'Here I am, here!'

The assistant director appeared in the central aisle. Georges was looking different today: in a frock coat, with a starched shirtfront and a white chrysanthemum in his buttonhole. He swung round and locked the door for some reason. When he spotted Fandorin with Eliza, he seemed to be delighted.

'Erast Petrovich? I wasn't expecting you. But this is even better. Without the dramatist the picture of the world would be incomplete.'

'Nonarikin, I need to have a word with you.' Fandorin looked at the assistant director intently. 'Answer my questions.'

'I have no time for talking with you.' The miraculously transformed assistant director smiled confidently. 'And now the questions will all fall away of their own accord. I shall explain everything. Follow me, if you please, to the stage.'

'Why did you lock the door?' Eliza asked. 'Is that some new kind of rule?'

But Georges didn't answer, he moved between the seats towards the stage with a gliding gait. He darted lightly up the steps to the *hanamichi*. He took his watch out of his pocket with his left hand and displayed it to the assembled company.

'Ladies and gentlemen, my congratulations!' he declared triumphantly. 'The benefit performance will commence shortly. There are only two 1s remaining!'

The benefit performance

ELEVEN 1S AND THE FIGURE 9

Surprisingly enough, dandified Georges took it upon himself to address the assembled company without Noah Noaevich's permission and spouted drivel from the stage.

'It is now precisely eleven o'clock on the eleventh day of the eleventh month of 1911. That is nine 1s. In eleven minutes' time the number of 1s will reach eleven and the moment will be become perfect. Then I shall halt it! And my benefit performance will commence, ladies and gentlemen.'

Eliza wasn't exactly listening closely to this balderdash, she was preoccupied with her own sufferings. She cursed herself for falling to pieces and blurting out too much. Thank God, Erast had not taken her hysterical muttering seriously. He was acting rather strangely today. Was it just that kind of day, everyone as mad as march hares?

Choking on his assistant's impudence, Stern really blew his top when he heard about the benefit performance.

'Aha, so it was you!' he howled in a terrible voice, and flew up onto the stage. 'It was you who scribbled nonsense all over the sacred book. Why you, I'll . . .'

The assistant director struck his idol and teacher a deft, resounding smack across the face. Everybody froze and Noah Noaevich grabbed at his cheek and cringed, with his eyes goggling out of his head.

'Sit down in your place,' Georges ordered him. 'You are no longer the director! I am the director now.'

The poor man had lost his reason. It was obvious.

He strode over to the centre of the stage, where the scenery had been installed, and climbed up into the geisha's room. He stopped at the low table and lifted up the lid of the casket – the one connected to the wires that ignited the flight of the two comets in the finale.

The original stupefaction passed off.

'Hey, brother, you've lost it . . .' Shiftsky got to his feet, twirling one finger at his temple. 'You need calming down.'

Sensiblin got up.

'Georges, my dear man, what are you doing up there on the stage? Come here and we'll have a talk.'

'Nonarikin-san, you mustn't hit your sensei!' Swardilin said angrily. 'It's the worst thing you can do!'

But Stern, still clutching his cheek, whined:

'There's no point in talking to him, he should be tied up and sent off to a lunatic asylum.'

Suddenly everyone fell silent again. A pistol had appeared in Nonarikin's hand – the Bayard that Eliza knew so well, the witness to her shameful flop.

'Sit down! Everyone sit in the front row!' the assistant director commanded. 'Be quiet. Listen. Time is short!'

Sima started shrieking. Vasilisa Prokofievna gasped.

'Mother of God. He'll kill us, the raving lunatic! Sit down, don't provoke him!'

Kostya, Lev Spiridonovich and Stern backed away and sat down in chairs, while in his fright Sensiblin even sat on his former spouse's knees and she didn't utter a peep, although at any other time a liberty like that would have cost the philosopher dear.

The Japanese was the only one who wasn't frightened.

'Give me the pistor, you rittur foor,' he said affectionately, still walking forward. 'Ret's sort this thing out the friendry way.'

The acoustics in the hall were miraculously good. The shot thundered out so loudly that Eliza was deafened. In the basement, when they were practising shooting, the Bayard had fired more quietly. Masa was just stepping off the *hanamichi* onto the stage. He flung his arms up and went flying down into the seats of the front row. He was wounded in the head. There was blood pouring out of his torn ear and a red ribbon of it lay across his temple. Aphrodisina squealed despairingly, splattered with red drops.

Then it began! The actors went dashing in all directions, screaming as they ran. Only Swardilin lay there, stunned, on the floor, and Fandorin didn't stir from his seat.

Eliza grabbed him by the arm.

'He's gone insane! He'll shoot everybody! Let's run for it!'

'There's nowhere to run,' said Erast Petrovich, keeping his eyes fixed on the stage. 'And it's too late.'

All three doors of the hall turned out to be locked, and no one dared to run backstage – there was a madman sitting cross-legged on the stage and waving a pistol about. Then he threw up his hand, aimed upwards and there was another shot. Crystal crumbs sprinkled down from the chandelier.

'Everybody in you places!' Nonarikin shouted. 'Two minutes have been wasted for nothing. Or do you want to die like stupid animals without understanding a thing? I never miss when I shoot. If anyone is not in their place in five seconds, I'll kill them.'

Everyone came dashing back as promptly as they scattered. They sat down, breathing heavily. Eliza had stayed right beside Erast Petrovich, who lifted up Masa, seated him beside himself and wiped the bleeding wound with a handkerchief.

'*Nan jya?*' Swardilin hissed through his teeth.

'A concussion. I've forgotten the Japanese word.'

The Japanese nodded briefly.

'I didn't mean the scratch! What is that? That?' he asked, jabbing his finger in Nonarikin's direction.

Fandorin's answer was incomprehensible.

'Eleven 1s and one figure 9. I am very badly at fault. I realised t-too late. And I don't have a gun with me . . .'

Another shot thundered out. Splinters went flying from the back of the empty seat beside Erast Petrovich.

'Silence in the hall! I'm the director now! And this is my benefit performance! The fine for chattering is a bullet. There are eight minutes left!'

Nonarikin was holding his left hand on the casket with the buttons that switched on the electricity.

'If you make any sudden movements, I'll press it.' The assistant director was addressing Fandorin. 'I won't take my eyes off you. I know how nippy you are.'

'That's not just light switches, is it?' Erast Petrovich paused and gritted his teeth (Eliza heard the sound quite clearly). 'The hall is m-mined, isn't it? You're a sapper, after all . . . And I'm a damned stupid idiot . . .'

The final words were spoken very quietly.

'What do you m-mean by "m-mined"?' Noah Noaevich hissed. His voice was breaking. 'With b-bombs?'

'Now look, Erast Petrovich, you've ruined the entire effect!' Nonarikin complained, as if he were offended. 'I was going to tell them that right at the very end. Supremely fine electrical engineering work! The charges have been calculated so that the shock wave will destroy everything inside the hall without damaging the building. That's called "implosion". What lies beyond the boundaries of the world we share is of no interest to me. Let it remain. Quiet, gentlemen and artistes!' he shouted at his noisy audience. 'What are you all cackling about? Why, are you, my teacher, clutching at your heart? You said yourself that all the world's a stage and the stage is the whole world. Noah's Ark is the best theatre company in the world. All of us together, pure and impure, are an ideal model of humanity! How many times have you repeated that to us, my teacher?'

'That's true. But why blow us all up?'

'There are two supreme artistic acts: creation and destruction. So there must be two types of artists: the artist of Good and the artist of Evil, alias the artist of Life and the artist of Death. It is an open question whose art is the higher! I have served you faithfully, I have studied with you, I have waited for you to appreciate my boundless devotion, my zeal! I was willing to make do with the role of an artist of Life, a theatre director. But you mocked me. You gave my role to that mediocre Emeraldov. You said that I was just a mere jack of all trades, a make-weight, like a number nine in a deck of cards. But I have invented my own benefit productio. There are eleven of you here, all established artistes, all wanting to claim good roles and be number ones, aces. Now appreciate the beauty of my play. I have sought out the point at which eleven 1s will coincide with one figure 9. Precisely at eleven minutes past eleven o'clock on the eleventh day of the eleventh month of the year 1911 . . .' – Nonarikin laughed loudly – '. . . our theatre will go flying to kingdom come. When the time 11:11 appears on the electrical clock, there will be thunder and lightning. And if you get it into your heads to turn rebellious, I shall press the button myself – look, I'm holding my finger on it. The roof and walls of this ark will become our sarcophagus! You must admit, my teacher, that there has not been a performance as beautiful as this since the times of Herostratus! You must admit that – and admit that the pupil has outdone his teacher!'

'I'll admit anything you like, just don't press that button! Turn off the clock!' Noah Noaevich implored him, keeping his eyes fixed on the madman's left hand, which remained glued to the casket. 'Your concept with the figures is outstanding, phenomenal, brilliant, we all appreciate the beauty of it, we are all enraptured, but . . .'

'Shut up!' The assistant waved his pistol towards the director and Stern bit his tongue. 'There is nothing in the world apart from art. It is the only thing that is worth living and dying for. You have told me that a thousand times. We are all people of art. My benefit perform-ance is a supreme act of art. So rejoice together with me!'

Suddenly the little 'leading boy' jumped up off her seat.

'And love?' she cried out piercingly. 'What about love? All the world is not a stage, all the world is love! Lord, how much I love you, and you don't understand! You have brain fever, you're ill. Georges, I'll do anything for you. I don't need anyone but you! Don't destroy these people, what are they to you? They don't appreciate your great soul, then to hell with them! I'll adore you for all of them! We can get out of here and go away!'

She reached her arms out to him. Despite her panic and terror, Eliza was moved, although she thought the monologue was de-livered too fiercely. Eliza would have pronounced all those words differently – with no shouting, in half-tones.

'Ah yes, love!' Nonarikin squinted downwards at the electrical chronometer mounted in the little casket. 'I'd forgotten all about that. Have I not fought for my love? Have I not laid low the insolent who have come between me and my Fair Lady? But she spurned me. She did not wish to be united with me on the bed of Life, so we shall be united on the bed of Death! Today is not only my benefit performance, but also my wedding! Sit down, half-woman!' he shouted at Comedina. 'The sight of you is an insult to the final minutes of my existence. And you, cold goddess, come here! Quickly, quickly! There are only four minutes left!'

Staring into the barrel of the Bayard that was aimed at her, Eliza got to her feet. She looked round helplessly at Fandorin.

'Quickly,' he whispered, 'or else the psychopath will fire.'

She didn't know how she walked up onto the stage and sat down beside Nonarikin. Below her eyes, directly in front of her, the figures on the counter glowed brightly: 11.08 – and the rapidly changing seconds.

'At the final moment I shall take hold of your hand,' the assistant director said in a quiet voice. He smelled very strongly of floral eau de cologne. 'Don't be afraid, the genuine comets are you and I.'

At that Eliza started shuddering in earnest.

'L-listen, artist of Evil,' Fandorin said in a loud voice, after whispering something to the Japanese. 'Your arithmetic is faulty. The beauty of the benefit performance is marred. There are not eleven of us here before you, but twelve. One too many. Let me out of here.'

Nonarikin frowned.

'I hadn't thought of that. Yes, you are the twelfth. A playwright is entirely out of place here. I myself am the author of this play entitled *The Apocalypse*. Leave. Via the wings. And tell everyone about my benefit performance!' He menaced Fandorin with the pistol as the playwright ran up onto the stage. 'Only no tricks, now. If you hurry, you'll be in time.'

'Th-thank you.'

And the man whom Eliza loved so passionately, so awkwardly, ran away as fast his legs would carry him. Who could have imagined that he would behave in such a pitiful and unworthy manner! The world around her seemed to have gone completely mad. Her absurd and senseless life was ending in the same way: absurdly and senselessly.

TWICE ELEVEN

The tenth minute of the twelfth hour began.

The director of *The Apocalypse* sat there with a blissful smile on his face, keeping one hand on the button. The other was clutching the pistol.

'How fine this is, such great happiness,' the madman kept repeating. 'And you are with me. Just a little bit longer, only a minute and a half . . .'

They were sitting beside each other on mats, Japanese-style.

Noah Noaevich's mouth gaped open, but no sounds came out. In the final moments of his life his perennial loquaciousness had deserted him.

The 'villain' and the 'villainess' were weeping, with their arms round each other.

Poor Comedina was huddled up limply, like a rag doll that has been flung aside.

Sensiblin tried to take Vasilisa Prokofievna by the hand and seemed to beg her forgiveness, but Reginina shoved him away – she wouldn't forgive him.

Aphrodisina tried to smile flirtatiously.

'Georges, you're just joking, aren't you? There aren't any bombs, are there? You just want to give us a fright?'

The poor coquette! Women of that type are so full of life that they simply can't imagine their own death!

Shiftsky got up. His mobile features wrinkled up tearfully.

'Georges, let me go! I never aimed to be one of the leaders. If you're a number 9, then I'm no better than a number 6!'

'You're trying to be funny,' Nonarikin replied. 'Without artful dodgers the world is incomplete. Sit down!'

Eliza was astounded that with only a minute left, the only one to pray was Vasya Gullibin. He closed his eyes, folded his hands together and worked his lips.

'It's not good,' Masa said suddenly, pressing a red, blood-soaked handkerchief to his wound. 'If you want to die, it must be beautifur. But you have two zeros.'

'What two zeros?' Nonarikin asked with a frown.

'The seconds. They should orso be ereven.'

Georges looked at his electric clock.

'But then it won't be eleven digits,' he objected. 'Although, of course , two zeros . . . It's not really . . . I agree.'

'It wirr be thirteen digits. That's even better. The most beautifur number. And thirteen prus nine is twenty-two. Twice ereven – that's twice as good!'

'Why, that's right!' said Georges, brightening up. 'The Japanese know all about beauty! Eleven seconds won't change anything. I'll reset the chronometer this moment!'

And now I have time to pray too, thought Eliza. *Our Father, Who art in heaven . . .*

She raised her eyes. Of course, she was not expecting to see the sky. Up there the velvet top mask of the curtain was swaying slightly, there were dark girders and the black gangway with its dangling cables. What else should an actress look at as she prepared to take her leave of this life?

Oh God, what was that?

Right above Nonarikin's head, Fandorin was slipping down one of the cables used to secure the scenery to its fly-bars, moving rapidly hand over hand. In two minutes he had managed to run up onto the gangway, creep out to the very centre and start climbing down. But what for? He could have been somewhere safe now, and instead of that he would be killed together with everyone else! He wouldn't have time to climb down in the few remaining seconds in any case. And even if he did, Nonarikin would simply press the button – he was on his guard!

Her prayer was left unspoken.

The author of the benefit performance took his finger off the button and started turning a little wheel on the clock face, setting the number 11 in the second frame. He pushed a little lever, obviously changing the time of the detonation. At that very instant Fandorin jumped from more than twenty feet up in the air and landed directly on top of Nonarikin. Something crunched, Eliza was thrown aside, and when she got up, there were two motionless bodies lying beside her, one on top of the other. In the little middle window of the clock two single digits popped up, but the seconds were still blinking.

11:11:01, 11:11:02, 11:11:03, 11:11:04 . . .

Swardilin flew up onto the stage with a guttural croak. He swayed, unable to stay on his feet, and fell.

'The wires!' he shouted. 'Eriza-san, the wires!'

'What?' she asked in confusion, staring spellbound at the blinking figures.

11:11:05, 11:11:06, 11:11:07 . . .

Crawling sideways like a crab, the Japanese tumbled in over the threshold of the geisha's little house and jerked the casket towards him with all his might. The wires snapped, the display went blank and for some reason sparks showered down from the ceiling above the hall.

'That's orr,' said Swardilin, and he lay down on his back and squeezed his eyes shut. His head must have been spinning very badly. 'A beautifur death can wait. First a beautifur rife.'

There won't be any explosion. We're saved, Eliza thought. And she burst into tears. What good was that if *he, he* had been killed? It would have been better for them to die together. Enveloped in thunder and flame!

'Erast Petrovich . . . He saved us all and he's been killed, he's been killed,' she moaned.

Masa opened his eyes and sat up. He looked at his master, lying there face down, and protested resentfully.

'I saved orr of us. My master herped me. He onry tord me: "*Masa, jyuichibyo!*" – "Masa, ereven seconds!" and ran off. And I had to puzzur out what he meant. My head was broken anyway, it hurt. It was hard to think. But I understood!'

'What difference does it make, who saved everybody . . . He has been killed! He fell from such a great height!'

She crept across to her beloved on her knees, fell against his back and started crying.

Swardilin touched her on the shoulder.

'Ret me see, prease, Eriza-san.'

He gently moved Eliza aside, then felt his motionless master for a short while and nodded in satisfaction. He turned Fandorin over onto his back. Erast Petrovich's face was pale and motionless, quite unbearably handsome. Eliza bit herself on the wrist to stop herself howling with grief.

The Japanese, however, treated the fallen hero disrespectfully. He pressed on his neck with one finger, leaned down and started blowing into his nose.

Fandorin's eyelashes fluttered and his eyes opened. The blue eyes gazed at Masa – first indifferently and then in astonishment. Erast Petrovich pushed the Japanese away from him.

'What on earth do you think you're doing?' he exclaimed, and started staring around.

It's a miracle!

He's alive, alive!

Swardilin shook his head and said something reproachfully. Fandorin's face took on an embarrassed expression.

'Masa says that I have completely forgotten how to jump from a height. I haven't p-practised it for a long time. He's right. There are no bones broken, but the impact knocked me unconscious. I'm ashamed. Well now, how is our artist of Evil doing?'

He and Masa started massaging and probing at Nonarikin. The assistant director cried out. He was alive too.

'A quite exceptionally hardy constitution. He got off with a broken collarbone,' Erast Petrovich summed up, and turned towards the hall. 'It's all over, calm down! Those who can get up may do so. Those who are too agitated had better remain in their seats. Gentlemen of the company, bring the ladies some water! And sal volatile.'

Cautiously, still not fully believing that they had been saved, several of the actors got up. The first to jump to her feet was Comedina.

'Don't touch him! You're hurting him!' she shouted at Masa, who was tying the assistant director's wrists together with a leather belt.

'He should be sent off to serve hard labour! He almost did for the lot of us!' Mephistov brandished his bony fist at Nonarikin. 'I'll testify at the trial. Oh, I'll testify, won't I just!'

Noah Noaevich mopped the top of his head with a handkerchief.

'Forget it, Anton Ivanovich, what trial are you talking about? He's a violent lunatic.'

The leader of the Ark was recovering before their very eyes. His expression grew firm again, and his eyes started glittering. Clambering up onto the stage, the director assumed a majestic pose, standing over the groaning Nonarikin.

'Congratulations on a phenomenal flop, my talentless pupil. An artist with this specific gift belongs in the aforementioned lunatic asylum. They employ progressive means of treatment there, and I think there is even a drama circle. When you have recovered a bit, you can lead it.'

Suddenly Stern was almost sent flying as Comedina jumped up and crashed into him from behind.

'Don't you dare make fun of him! That's mean and base! Georgy Ivanovich is unwell!' She went down on her knees and started rubbing the dust and dirt off Nonarikin's face. 'Georges, I still love you anyway! I'll always love you! I'll come to visit you in the hospital every day! And when you get well, I'll take you away. The only problem is that you imagined you were a titan. But there's no need to be a titan. Titans are always huffing and puffing, so they're unhappy. It's better to be a little person, believe me. See how little I am? And you'll be the same. We were made for each other. You'll come to understand that. Not now, but later.'

Stunned and in pain, Nonarikin couldn't speak. He merely tried to move away from the stage fool. If his grimace was anything to go by, he didn't wish to be a little person.

'Well now, colleagues,' Noah Noaevich exclaimed. 'The benefit performance turned out rather impressive, as a matter of fact. It was only a shame that there was no audience. And if we tell anyone, no one will believe us. They'll think that we acted out the whole thing ourselves and stuck dynamite all over the place for the sake of the publicity . . . By the way,' he added anxiously, switching to a whisper, 'dynamite can't simply go and detonate for some reason or other, can it? Quiet, I implore you! Konstantina Petrovna, don't shout like that, please!'

After the benefit performance

RECONSTRUCTION

A woman in love spoke beautiful words to the man who had almost blown up the theatre. Then an ambulance carriage arrived and orderlies led away the madman, carefully supporting him from both sides. Soft-hearted Vasilisa Prokofievna, forgetting the terror she had suffered, threw a coat over the shoulders of the wilted assistant director and also made the sign of the cross over the sick man.

People are compassionate with the insane, thought Fandorin, and that is probably right. But at the same time, the type of psychological disorder known as manic obsession gives rise to the most dangerous criminals in the world. They typically possess steely determination, absolute fearlessness and brilliant inventiveness. The greatest threat is represented by manic obsession on a grand scale. Those who are not possessed by the petty demon of lust, but by the demon of global transformation. And if they cannot manage to transform the world in accordance with their ideal, they are willing to kill everything that lives. Fortunately, as yet it is not possible for any Herostratus to incinerate the temple of life, that is beyond their reach. But progress is creating ever more powerful means of destruction. The imminent war – which is clearly, unfortunately, inevitable – will be unprecedentedly bloody. It will break out not only on the land and the surface of the sea, but also in the air and in the depths of the waters, everywhere. And the century has only just begun, technical progress is unstoppable. The tragicomic Georges Nonarikin is not simply a theatre director driven insane by his artistic vanity. He is the prototype of a new kind of villain. They will not be satisfied with just a theatre as a model of existence: they will want to transform the entire world into a gigantic stage and present on it the plays that they themselves have penned, to allocate to mankind the role of obedient extras, and if the production is a flop – to die together with the Universal Theatre. That is exactly how everything will end. Madmen obsessed by the grandeur and beauty of their conceptions will blow up the Earth. The only hope is that people will be found to stop them in time. Such people are essential. Without them the world is doomed.

But these people are not all-powerful, they are vulnerable and prone to weaknesses. For instance, a certain Erast Petrovich Fandorin, faced with a catastrophe not on the scale of the universe, but on the scale of a doll's house, almost allowed the model of existence to be destroyed. It must be admitted that in this absurd story his behaviour has been pitiful.

Of course, there are extenuating circumstances.

Firstly, he was not himself. Blinded and deafened, he forfeited his clarity of thought and lost his self-control. In this case both parties – the criminal and the investigator – were in a state of insanity, each in his own way.

Secondly, it is hard not to lose one's way in the labyrinths of an unnatural world where play is more genuine than reality, the reflection is more interesting that the essence, the articulation replaces the underlying feelings and the face under the make-up cannot be discerned. Only in the theatre, and among people of the theatre, could a crime take place with such motives and in such a setting.

The little officer from the distant edge of the empire would have dragged out a dreary army career, like Chekhov's Solyony, acting out demonic poses for the garrison ladies. But the swirling tornado of the theatre flew down to the Asiatic backwoods, swooped down on the lieutenant, tore his feet off the ground, swirled him round and bore him off.

The little man wished to become a big artist, and in order to satisfy this unassuageable hunger, he was prepared to sacrifice absolutely anything and absolutely anyone, including himself.

His love for Eliza was a desperate attempt to take a grip on life, to move away from the self-destruction to which his obsession with art was leading. And in his love Nonarikin behaved exactly like

Lieutenant Solyony: he conducted an absurd siege of the object of his passion, suffered fierce jealousy and exerted cruel revenge on his unfortunate Tuzenbach rivals.

What could possibly be more absurd than the trick with the viper? Georges was there beside Eliza and was the only one out of all of them who did not lose his head, because he was the one who put the snake in the basket. In the steppes of Central Asia Nonarikin had probably learned to handle reptiles – a hobby of that kind would suit the demon lieutenant. (Let us not forget that Nonarikin kept a phial of cobra venom, with which he smeared the tip of a rapier.) He knew that the bite of a viper in September is not particularly dangerous and deliberately offered it his hand. He was counting on arousing in his Fair Lady a passionate gratitude that would subsequently grow into love. Georges certainly did arouse her gratitude, but was unaware that in women gratitude and love are administered by different departments.

Simultaneous with this disappointment there was another, an artistic one. Nonarikin was not given the role of Lopakhin for which he had been hoping so badly. It went to Hippolyte Emeraldov. Devastated by the ingratitude of Stern, his adored teacher, the assistant director rebelled – as another assistant, the angel Satan, once rebelled against the Eternal Teacher. Any personality with a maniacal bent, teetering on the edge of insanity, can undergo a sudden qualitative shift. Something clicks in the brain, a certain *idée fixe* arises and takes shape, and its false irrefutability is absolutely blinding, it takes over the mind and that's it, there is no way back.

For Georges it was the crazy idea of eleven 1s and one figure 9 that became such an epiphany. Apparently it arose suddenly, in a moment of total despair, and Nonarikin was spellbound by its brilliance. And yet at the beginning he was still prepared to spare the world and not destroy it. The first entry in the Tablets says: 'Take thought!'

The future benefit performance artist gave the theatre world a chance to do that. He killed Emeraldov, who had not only 'stolen' his role, but was also pressing his attentions on Eliza in a way that was provocative and insolent. Nonarikin's calculation was obvious and at first seemed to have proved correct. The director instructed his assistant to play the part of Lopakhin at rehearsals, until a worthy replacement could be found for Emeraldov. There can be no doubt that if Stern had done as he intended and invited in a celebrity from outside – Leonidov or someone else – then Russian theatre would have suffered another loss. On the eve of the premiere, some accident would have happened to Lopakhin, and Nonarikin would have had to be allowed out onto the stage. But Fandorin had appeared with his Japanese drama and the plan, composed with the thoroughness of an engineer, collapsed.

And when it became clear to the assistant director that it was pointless to hope that his feelings for Eliza might be requited, he gave himself over completely to his apocalyptic idea. In the subsequent entries, which were made as a new 1 appeared in the calendar, there was no 'Take thought!' The sentence had been pronounced and confirmed. The theatre world would be sent flying to kingdom come and Eliza, having failed to become his bride on earth, would become his Heavenly Bride.

A bride must maintain her chastity until the wedding. Therefore the 'bridegroom' killed those whom he suspected of endangering her virtue.

And so the young fool Limbach died. Of course, the cornet received his pass to the actors' floor from the assistant director. The boy must have been tremendously pleased by the idea of waiting for Eliza in her own changing room – in order to congratulate her on the premiere tête-à-tête.

The scene was set skilfully. It is well known that maniacal personalities in the grip of their overarching idea can manifest incredible ingenuity. The blow with the knife across the stomach was intended as a reminder of the hussar's threat to commit hara-kiri. In case that trick didn't work (and by this time Nonarikin already knew that Fandorin was conducting an investigation and that he was a man of experience) the criminal took precautionary measures. Firstly, he acquired a clasp knife – the preferred weapon of Moscow's bandits. Secondly, he wrote the letters 'Li' in blood on the door. This was a cunning trick, and it achieved its purpose. If the investigation or Fandorin did not believe in the 'hara-kiri', a different interpretation of the incomplete name could be hinted at – which Nonarikin did very deftly. Apparently by chance he turned the conversation to the subject of Mr Whistle's past, and before the former policeman's real name – Lipkov – could be pronounced, the maniac immediately withdrew into the shadows – he knew that the bait would be swallowed.

It was painful for Erast Petrovich to realise how many mistakes he had made. How long he had allowed the murderer to lead him around by the nose!

The most annoying thing of all was that his very first theory, the most obvious of all, had led him directly to Nonarikin, but the assistant director had managed to wriggle his way out of things and even gain Fandorin's trust . . . How shameful, how very shameful!

The initial miscalculation had been that Erast Petrovich thought the poisoning of the leading man to be a cold-blooded, carefully planned murder, but in actual fact it was the action of an artist who unhesitatingly laid his own life on the line. Unfortunately, Fandorin failed to guess that the poisoner had played a game of equals with Emeraldov, tempting his own fate. Strictly speaking, it had not been a murder, but a dual. Only poor Hippolyte had not been aware of that, he had not known that in selecting a goblet he was deciding his own fate. It is quite possible that the drinking companions clinked goblets and both drank – the 'demonic personality' also wanted to test Fate, to confirm his own chosen status.

Nonarikin decided to proceed in exactly the same way with Fandorin after he picked up the trail – only using a poisoned sword instead of wine. What a great directorial innovation these striking interludes with a fatal outcome must have seemed to Georges! But Erast Petrovich's perennial good luck did not let him down. The hunter almost fell into his own trap, but he managed to scramble out of it – thanks to the remarkable ingenuity and false testimony of Comedina, the woman who was in love with him and was certain (he had no doubt) to shield him.

This risky episode did not bring the 'artist of Evil' to his senses. The morbid idea of a benefit performance had taken too strong a hold of his inflamed brain. It was easier to abandon his faith in Fate. 'Fate is blind,' said Nonarikin, as we recall. 'Only the artist is sighted.'

He was undoubtedly a very gifted artist. Stern underestimated this 'player of third-level roles'. Georges played the part of a stupid but noble blockhead with great talent.

The Sokolniki operation was quite dangerous for him. His entire, painstakingly constructed story could have collapsed if Fandorin had backed the Tsar up against the wall and forced him to talk frankly. Probably, as he walked through the park with Erast Petrovich that night, the maniac had hesitated – would it not be safer to shoot the overzealous investigator in the back? However, intuition whispered to the schemer that it would be best not to do that. Fandorin's very gait (the tiger's stride of a *sinobi* keyed up for action) indicated that it was impossible to take a man like this by surprise.

Nonarikin acted more cunningly than that. He led the pinschers away from the house and came back himself in order to eavesdrop. As soon as the conversation with the Tsar took an undesirable turn, Georges put in an appearance – once again displaying a total lack of fear in the face of danger. Like a total blockhead, Erast Petrovich raced halfway across Europe, following a false trail. It was a good thing that he didn't go sailing off to America. On the day after his arrival, the twelfth of November, he would have read in the *New York Times* about a mysterious explosion in the theatre.

In killing Shustrov, yet another pretender to the hand of the Bride, Nonarikin did not try very hard to disguise his work. He permitted himself the incautious artistic gesture of decorating the throat of his rival with eleven 1s. But even with this hint, Fandorin failed to guess the criminal's concept in time and avert the psychopathological 'benefit performance'. Because of the conflict between his reason and feelings, Erast Petrovich very nearly allowed the theatre company, this molecular model of humankind, to be annihilated.

When he reread *The Apocalypse*, Fandorin often paused over the line that speaks of how 'those watching over the house will tremble', and he thought that those who watch over a house have no right to tremble. They must be firm, keep their eyes wide open to avert danger in good time. All his life he had numbered himself as a member of this army. And now look – he had trembled, manifested weakness. In the house that he had undertaken to protect, the apocalypse had very nearly come about. *No more trembling*, Erast Petrovich told himself, when the sick man was led away by the orderlies and the hysterical tension in the hall dissipated somewhat. *I am a mature individual. I am a man. No more playing the child.*

He lowered himself into a chair beside Eliza, who was the only one not screaming or waving her arms about in terror, but was simply sitting there, looking dully straight ahead.

'That's it, the nightmare is over, the chimera has been dissipated. I have a suggestion.' He took hold of her cold, feeble fingers. 'Let us not play at life, but live.'

She did not seem to have heard his concluding words.

'Over?' Eliza repeated, and shook her head. 'Only not for me. My personal nightmare has not gone away.'

'You mean your ex-husband? Khan Altairsky? It is him that you call Genghis Khan, is it not?'

She shuddered and looked at him in horror.

'My God, Erast Petrovich, you promised to forget . . . It is my psychosis, you said so yourself . . . I didn't mean at all . . .'

'Now then. You got it into your head that Emeraldov, Limbach and Shustrov were murdered by your ex-husband, out of jealousy. And they certainly were murdered. Only it was not Altairsky who did it, but Nonarikin. He is no longer dangerous. So don't worry any further.'

Erast Petrovich wanted to move on as quickly as possible to the most important thing – to the reason why he had sat down beside Eliza. To talk to her at long last without leaving anything unspoken, without any stupidities, in a manner that befitted adults.

But Eliza did not believe him. He could still read only fear in her eyes.

'Very well,' Fandorin said with a gentle smile. 'I shall meet with your husband and have a talk with him. I shall get him to leave you alone.'

'No! Don't even think of doing that!'

The others turned round at her shout.

'It's all over and done with,' Stern said nervously. 'Get a grip on yourself, Eliza. The other ladies have already calmed down, don't start up all over again.'

'I implore you, I implore you,' she whispered, holding Fandorin's hand. 'Don't get involved with him. He's not like poor, crazy Georges. The khan is a fiend from hell! You are mistaken if you think that Nonarikin killed everyone. Of course, after the "benefit performance", it is possible to believe absolutely anything, but it is coincidence! Georges is not capable of cold-blooded murder. Since I have let it slip, you may as well know everything! Genghis Khan is the most dangerous man in the world!'

Erast Petrovich could see that she was on the verge of breaking down, so he tried to talk to her as judiciously as possible.

'Believe me, the most dangerous people in the world are madmen with the ambitions of an artist.'

'The khan is absolutely insane! He lost his mind from jealousy!'

'And does he have any artistic ambitions?'

Eliza was flustered slightly by that.

'No . . .'

'So he and I will c-come to some sort of arrangement,' Fandorin concluded, getting to his feet.

The conversation about the most important thing would in any case have to be postponed until a later time, when Eliza had stopped worrying about her Caucasian Othello.

'My God, aren't you even listening to me? Emeraldov was killed in exactly the same way as Furshtatsky! Shustrov's throat was slit with a razor – just like Astralov's. All of it was done by Genghis Khan. He told me: "The wife of the Khan Altairsky cannot have lovers and cannot marry anyone else!" What has Nonarikin got to do with anything? When Furshtatsky was killed (he was an entrepreneur, he got engaged to me in St Petersburg), I wasn't acting with the Ark yet and I didn't even know Georges!'

'Astralov, the tenor?' Erast Petrovich asked with a frown, recalling that the famous St Petersburg singer really had slit his throat with a razor several months earlier.

'Yes, yes! When Furshtatsky died, the khan telephoned me and confessed that he had done it. And at Astralov's funeral, he did this!'

She ran one finger across her throat and started shuddering.

'There's nowhere I can hide from him! He knows every step I take! I have found notes from him everywhere. Even in my dressing room! Even in the room in the Metropole! As soon as I moved in, I found a note in the bathroom: *"Anyone who dares to become close to you will die"*. At that time no one but Stern even knew which room I was going to be in! And Nonarikin didn't know!'

'Really?' Fandorin sank back down into the chair. 'In the entire company only Noah Noaevich knew exactly where you were staying?'

'Yes, he was the only one! Vasya and Sima took me there. Vasya opened the suitcases and Sima hung up my dresses and set out my toiletries . . .'

'Where, in the bathroom? Please excuse me,' Erast Petrovich interrupted her. 'I have to leave you. We will definitely talk again. Later.'

'Where are you going?' Eliza sobbed. 'I implore you, do not try to do anything!'

He gestured reassuringly as he looked around for Masa.

He was sitting sulking in a chair.

'Don't be offended with me,' Erast Petrovich said to him. 'I have treated you quite terribly. Forgive me. Tell me, what do you think about your lady friend Aphrodisina?'

The Japanese replied sadly.

'I'm not offended with you, master. What point is there in being offended with someone who is unwell? I am offended with Sima-san. How did you know that I was thinking about her now?'

The subject of discussion was close by, only about ten steps away. Flushed after all the turmoil and agitation, Sima was telling Shiftsky something heatedly, holding one hand on her breast.

'. . . My poor heart almost burst with the terror of it! It's still fluttering now!'

Kostya looked at the spot where Aphrodisina's heart was fluttering and couldn't tear his eyes away.

'It needs someone to blow on it, then it will settle down. Just give the word,' the 'scamp' suggested mischievously.

Masa complained.

'That empty-headed girl only loved me for my beauty. Now that a bullet has mutilated my features, she does not even want to look at me. I walked over to her and she said to me: "Masik, you're a rear hero, of course, but you smerr singed." And she wrinkled up her nose. And she turned away from my wound in disgust! Kind Reginina-san bandaged me up. She's still quite good looking, by the way. And in a good body . . .'

'I'm interested in whether Aphrodisina is fond of money?'

'That's all she ever talks about. How much everything costs and what things she would buy herself if she had a bigger salary. The only time she doesn't talk about money is when she makes love, but immediately after the love she starts asking for presents. I was wounded and bleeding to death, and she turned away from me!'

Sensing that she was being watched, Aphrodisina looked round, folded her lips into a rose bud and blew Masa a kiss.

'Master, tell her that I do not want to know her any more!'

'Straight away.'

Fandorin walked across to Sima and gave Shiftsky an eloquent glance – he immediately disappeared.

'Mademoiselle,' Erast Petrovich asked in a quiet voice, 'how much does Khan Altairsky pay you?'

'What?' Aphrodisina squealed, fluttering her long eyelashes.

'You spy on Eliza, you report everything about her to her husband, you plant notes, and so on. Do not dare to lie to me, or else I shall announce this to everyone, out loud. You will be thrown out of the c-company in disgrace . . . Very well, I shall amend the question. I am not interested in the amount of your remuneration. I need to know where I can find this g-gentleman.'

'I beg your pardon! How could you!' Sima's eyes filled up with pure tears of the highest quality. 'Eliza is my very best friend! The two of us are like sisters!'

Fandorin twitched the corner of his mouth.

'I shall count t-to three. One, two . . .'

'He rents an apartment in Abrikosov's tenement building on Kuznetsky Most Street,' Aphrodisina said rapidly. She blinked and the tears dried up. 'You won't give me away now, will you? Remember now, you promised!'

'How long have you been in the khan's pay?'

'Since St Petersburg . . . Oh, dear, darling man! Don't destroy me. Noah Noaevich will blacken my name in the world of theatre! I'll never get work with any decent company! Believe me, I know how to be grateful!'

She started breathing rapidly and moved closer to Erast Petrovich. He squinted into her décolleté, winced and moved back.

Once again, with fantastic ease, the tears started flowing down Sima's face.

'Don't look at me with such contempt! It's unbearable! I'll lay hands on myself!'

'Don't venture beyond the bounds of the "coquette", mademoiselle.'

He bowed slightly and set off quickly towards the exit, simply gesturing for Masa to follow.

ON LOVE AND MARRIAGE

Before all the other business, he had to take the Japanese to a specialist in cerebral traumas. Erast Petrovich was concerned by the way that Masa was swaying from side to side and the greenish tinge of his complexion. His unusual loquacity was also suspicious. Fandorin knew from experience that when his servant chattered continuously, he was concealing the fact that he felt terrible.

On the way to Virgin's Field the concussed man no longer spoke about Sima and inconstant women, but about himself and heroic men.

It began with Fandorin apologising for his unsuccessful leap and praising his assistant for the alacrity he had displayed.

'Yes,' Masa replied solemnly. 'I'm a hero.'

Erast Petrovich remarked guardedly: 'Quite possibly. But let others decide whether you are a hero or not.'

'You are mistaken, master. Every man decides whether he is a hero or not. You have to make the choice and then not betray it afterwards. A man who has first decided to be a hero, but then changed his mind, is a pitiful sight. And a man who, in the middle of his life, has suddenly changed from being a non-hero to being a hero risks damaging his karma.'

Raising his automobile goggles onto his forehead, Erast Petrovich squinted at his passenger in alarm to see whether he was delirious.

'Can you clarify that?'

'A man who is a hero devotes his life to the service of some idea. It is not important what or whom he serves. A hero can have a wife and children, but it is better to do without that. The lot of a woman who has bound her destiny to a hero is a sad one. The children are even more to be pitied. It is terrible to grow up, feeling that your father is always ready to sacrifice you for the sake of his service.' Masa sighed bitterly. 'It is a different matter if you are a non-hero. A man like that chooses his family and serves that. He must not play the hero. That is the same as if a samurai betrays his lord in order to show off to the crowd.'

Fandorin listened carefully. Masa's philosophising could sometimes be intriguing.

'And what do you serve?'

The Japanese looked at him in resentful amazement.

'Can you still ask? Thirty-two years ago, I chose you, master. One choice for the rest of my life. Women sometimes – quite often – bring solace to my life, but I do not promise them much and I never become involved with those who expect me to be faithful. I already have someone to serve, I tell them.'

And Erast Fandorin suddenly felt ashamed. He coughed in embarrassment, trying to clear away the lump that had risen in his throat. Masa saw that his master was embarrassed, but he misunderstood the reason for it.

'Are you reproaching yourself for your love for Eliza-san? There is no need. My rule does not apply to you. If you wish to love a woman with all your heart and do not feel that it hinders your service, then go ahead.'

'And ... what, in your opinion, does my service consist of?' Fandorin asked cautiously, recalling that only a quarter of an hour ago he had been thinking about those who 'watch over the house'.

The Japanese shrugged nonchalantly.

'I have no idea. That is all the same to me. It is enough that you have some idea and you serve it. But my idea is you, and I serve you. It is all very simple and harmonious. Of course, to love with all your heart is a very great risk. But if you wish to know the opinion of a man who knows women well, one like Eliza-san would suit us best of all.'

'Us?'

Erast Petrovich gave his servant a severe look, but Masa's expression was clear and open. And it was immediately obvious that

353

there had never been anything between Eliza and the Japanese, that there never could have been. Only with his reason clouded could Fandorin have imagined that Masa was capable of regarding his master's chosen one as an ordinary woman.

'Surely you don't want a jealous woman to come between us, who will hate me because you and I are bound together by so many things? That is the way any normal wife would act. But an actress is a different matter. In addition to her husband, she has the theatre. She doesn't need a hundred per cent of your shares, she's happy with forty-nine.'

The automobile crossed the Garden Ring Road, skipping over the tramlines.

'Have you seriously decided to marry me off?' Fandorin asked. 'But what f-for?'

'So there will be chirdren and I will teach them,' Masa replied. After a moment's thought he added: 'I probably can't teach a little girl anything useful.'

'And what would you teach my son?'

'The most important thing. What you cannot teach him, master.'

'Interesting. What is that I can't teach my own son?'

'How to be happy.'

Fandorin was so terribly surprised, he couldn't think of anything to say at first; he had never thought that from the outside his life could seem unhappy. Surely happiness was the absence of unhappiness?

'There is no happiness, but there is peace and freedom,' he said, recalling Pushkin's famous formula, which he had always liked so much.

Masa thought for a few moments and disagreed.

'That is the mistaken reasoning of a man who is afraid to be happy,' he said, switching back to his own language. 'It is probably the only thing that you are afraid of, master.'

His condescending tone of voice infuriated Fandorin. 'Go to hell, you home-grown philosopher! That's a line from Pushkin, and the poet is always right!'

'Pushkin? Oooo!'

Masa put on a reverential face and even bowed. He respected the opinions of authorities.

In the reception room of the university clinic, as the Japanese was being led away for examination, he suddenly looked at Erast Petrovich with his piercing little eyes.

'Master, I can see from your face that you are going out on business again without me. Please do not punish me like this. My ears are ringing and my thoughts are a little confused, but that does not make any difference. You will do the thinking, and I will only act. For a genuine samurai, a concussion is a mere trifle.'

Fandorin prodded him in the back.

'Go on, go on, let the professor-sensei cure you. A genuine samurai should be yellow, and not green. And anyway, my business is quite trivial, there's nothing to talk about.'

However, Erast Petrovich did not set out on his business immediately. First he called into the telegraph office, and the long-distance telephone station. It was twilight before the Isotta drove up to Abrikosov's tenement building on Kuznetsky Most Street.

Khan Altairsky lived in the *bel étage*, occupying the entire left half of it.

'How shall I announce you?' Fandorin was asked by the doorman, a sturdy black-haired young fellow with a black moustache wearing a long-waisted Circassian coat with a massive dagger in the belt. He looked Fandorin up and down suspiciously and announced: 'His High Dignity is busy. He is dining.'

'I'll announce m-myself,' Erast Petrovich replied good-naturedly.

He took the young fellow by the neck, pressed simultaneously on the *sui* point with his thumb and the *min* point with his index finger and supported the limp body so that it wouldn't make too much noise. This manipulation guaranteed an unhealthy but deep sleep lasting from fifteen to thirty minutes, depending on the strength of the organism.

Fandorin left his top hat and coat in the entrance hall, and checked in the mirror to make sure that his parting was straight. Then he set off along the corridor towards the melodic jingling of silver.

His High Dignity was indeed dining.

A balding man with dark hair and bushy eyebrows, with puffy facial features that seemed vaguely familiar to Fandorin, was chewing food and sipping on red wine. To judge from the beverage, and also from the carved piglet and Dutch ham, the khan did not adhere to the sharia law in his diet.

At the sight of the stranger the khan forgot to close his mouth and froze with a piece of the bread that he had just bitten off between his teeth. A manservant, who looked like the twin brother of the sleeping doorman, also froze, holding a jug in his hands.

'Who are you? Why did they let you in?' the khan rumbled menacingly, spitting the bread out onto the tablecloth. 'Musa, fling him out!'

Fandorin shook his head. How was it possible to marry a crude oaf like his, even if only for a short while? This woman quite definitely had to be saved – not from her enemies, but from herself.

The servant put down the wine and dashed at Fandorin, hissing like a goose. The visitor gave Musa the same treatment as his presumptive brother: he put him to sleep and gently laid him out on the floor.

The blood drained away from the abandoned husband's bald patch. Expecting the uninvited guest to be bundled out immediately, the khan had taken a gulp of wine, but had not yet swallowed it, and now it flowed down over his chin onto his starched napkin. It was an appalling sight – as if the man had suffered a stroke with haemhorraging from the throat.

'Who are you?' he repeated, but in a quite different tone of voice. Not with outrage, but in fear.

'My name is Fandorin. But perhaps for you I shall be Azrail,' said Erast Petrovich, naming the Muslim archangel of death. 'Everything will depend on the outcome of our c-conversation.'

'Fandorin? Then I know who you are. You're the author of that idiotic play and also an amateur detective with big contacts. I have made enquiries about you.'

The khan tore off his stained napkin and grandly folded his hands, glittering with rings, together on his chest.

'I see you have calmed down a little.' Fandorin sat down beside him and toyed absent-mindedly with a dessert fork. 'That's a mistake. I'll be b-brief . . . You stop persecuting Madam Lointaine. That is one. You immediately grant her a divorce. That is two. Otherwise something nasty will happen to you.' Erast Petrovich considered it unnecessary to specify the meaning of the threat. His opponent was clearly not worthy of having pearls scattered before him, and the tone of the voice and glance of the eye are always more eloquent than words.

The khan was mortally afraid, that was clear. A little more of this and he would keel over in a faint.

'I have already decided that I shall never go near that madwoman again,' His Most High Dignity exclaimed. 'She tried to shoot me with a pistol!'

This was the first time Fandorin had heard about the pistol, but the news did not surprise him. It is dangerous to drive a woman of artistic temperament to extremes.

'You have only yourself to blame. You should not have pretended to be a murderer. So on the first point we are agreed. That leaves the second.'

Altairsky thrust out his chest.

'I shall never give her a divorce. It is out of the question.'

'I know,' said Fandorin, screwing up his eyes thoughtfully, 'that you told Eliza that the wife of a khan cannot have lovers and cannot marry anyone else. But the widow of a khan is a different matter.'

The other man was perhaps not really frightened enough. Erast Petrovich took him firmly by the scruff of the neck and set the silver fork against his throat.

'I could kill you in a d-duel, but I won't fight a scoundrel who frightens helpless women. I'll simply kill you. Like this p-piglet here.'

The khan's bloodshot eye squinted at the dish.

'You won't kill me,' the stubborn man hissed in a choking voice. 'That's not your line of business, rather exactly the opposite. I told you. I've made enquiries about you. I make enquiries about everyone who hangs around Eliza . . . But then, kill me if you like. I still won't give her a divorce.'

Such firmness aroused distinct respect. Evidently Erast Petrovich's first impression of His High Dignity had not been entirely accurate. He took the fork away and moved back.

'Do you love you wife so very much?' he asked in surprise.

'What the hell has love got to do with it!' Altairsky slammed his fists down on the table and started choking on his hate. 'Eliza, that bi . . .'

Fandorin's face twitched furiously and the khan bit off the swear word.

'. . . That lady destroyed my life! My father deprived me of the rights of the firstborn! And if I get divorced, he'll leave me without any support! A hundred and twenty thousand a year! And what would I do then – go and get a job? Khan Altairsky will never blacken his hands with labour. It would be better if you killed me.'

This was a weighty argument. Erast Petrovich pondered it. Perhaps he really should kill this weak potentate and cunning, balding fop.

'As far as I understand it, you wish to marry Eliza. And does a civil marriage not suit you?' the husband asked ingratiatingly. He evidently also wanted very much to find a compromise. 'It's fashionable now. She would like it. And you would never hear anything about me again. I swear it! Do you want me to go away to Nice, for ever? Only don't demand the impossible from me.'

Fandorin went back from Kuznetsky Most Street on foot. He had to gather his thoughts and prepare for the conversation with Eliza. The November evening attempted to tear the hat off his head and he had to hold it on.

Something trivial has happened to me, Erast Petrovich told himself. *Probably every second man goes through it. Where did I get the idea that this cup would pass me by? Of course, in other men this sickness that is commonly referred to as 'no fool like an old fool' seems to occur for other reasons. I've read about it. Some suddenly get the feeling that they do not have much time left to be a man, and so they start panicking. Some suddenly realise that they didn't sow enough wild oats in their young days. Neither the former nor the latter would appear to have anything to do with my case. What has happened to me is not a sickness, it is more like a trauma. It is well known that a bone breaks more easily at the site of a previous break. In the same way, owing to a chance confluence of circumstances, the old break in my heart snapped again.*

But does it really matter what whim of fate is responsible when love overwhelms you? It comes and it swings the door wide open. Your usual dwelling place is suddenly illuminated with unbearably bright light. You see yourself and your life differently, and you don't like what you see. You can pretend to be an experienced gallant and turn the whole thing into a courtly adventure; but at any moment the glow might fade. You can shove the uninvited guest back out of the door and turn the key; in a little while the dwelling will once again be immersed in its customary gloom. You can turn frantic, jump out of the window, go running off to the ends of the earth. I have actually tried to do both of those things. But now I have to try another method – simply take a step forward and not turn my eyes away. This requires courage.

Such was the rational monologue that Erast Petrovich rehearsed to himself, but the closer he approached to the hotel, the more agonisingly nervous he felt. In the foyer a cowardly thought even occurred to him: 'Perhaps Eliza is not in her room?'

But the porter sad that Madam Lointaine was in and politely telephoned upstairs and enquired:

'How shall I introduce you?'

'Fandorin . . .'

His throat turned dry. Was this the puerility starting all over again?

'She says to go up.'

In any case I am obliged to tell her that her husband offers her complete freedom! Erast Petrovich shouted at himself. *And as for everything else . . . That is her business.*

In this same angry mood he began the conversation.

He said that there was nothing more to be afraid of.

That Khan Altairsky was a villain and a petty wretch, but not a murderer. That in any case from henceforth he would disappear from her life. He would not give her a divorce, but he offered her complete freedom.

He told her that the matter of the two deaths in St Petersburg had been clarified. Following the death of the Kiev entrepreneur Boleslav Ignatievich Furshtatsky, as always in such cases, an autopsy had been carried out on the body. From the telegrams sent by the coroner's office, it followed that the cause of death had been heart failure, and no traces of poison had been discovered. Khan Altairsky had only exploited the sad event for his own purposes.

The case of the tenor Astralov was different. In a telephone conversation with the investigator who had conducted the case, it had transpired that the marks of the razor were almost identical to the wounds that had broken off the life of Mr Shustrov. A sliding blow with a light inclination from left to right. A blow like that could be struck either by someone sitting in a chair, or by someone who was standing behind the victim. On 11 February, the day Astralov died, Eliza was already a member of the Noah's Ark theatre company; she was acquainted with Nonarikin and, as was not in the least surprising (Fandorin felt it possible to put that in), he had immediately conceived a passionate love for her. Exactly how the murderer had managed to approach first Astralov and then Shustrov with a razor was not yet entirely clear, but the maniac himself could be asked about that. After everything that had happened, he had no reason to conceal anything; and in addition people of a certain kind adored boasting of their great feats. Nonarikin would be glad to tell them everything.

Eliza listened to his report without interrupting, with her hands folded on the table in front of her, like a diligent grammar school girl. She kept her eyes fixed on Erast Petrovich, but he preferred to look away. He was afraid of losing the thread.

'I believe you,' Eliza said in a quiet voice. 'I believe *you*. But the fact remains that all these men were killed because of me! It's appalling!'

'Read Dostoyevsky, my lady. "Beauty is a terrible and appalling thing".' Fandorin deliberately started talking more drily. 'It makes some strive for the heights and drives others down into the depths of hell. Megalomania led Nonarikin implacably along the path to self-destruction. However, if the madman had found his feelings for you to be requited, he would have stopped wishing to r-rule the world. He would have been willing to settle for your love. As I am . . .'

The final phrase slipped out involuntarily. Fandorin finally looked into Eliza's eyes – and what he had been intending to come round to only after a thorough introduction simply spoke itself. It was too late to retreat. And in any case, it was actually better without any diplomacy and tactical preludes.

Erast Petrovich gave a deep sigh and started speaking, not like a boy, but like a potential husband (even if only a civil law one).

'You remember I said that I was in love, enamoured with you? Well, I was mistaken, I *love* you,' he began in a gloomy, almost accusatory voice, and then paused in order to give her a chance to react.

'I know, I know!' she exclaimed.

Having once assumed a morose tone, Fandorin could no longer abandon it.

'It is splendid that you know everything. But I had hoped to hear something else. For instance: "I love you too".'

'I have loved you all this time,' Eliza exclaimed immediately with tears in her eyes. 'I love you madly and desperately.'

She reached her arms out to him, but Erast Petrovich did not yield to temptation. He had to tell her everything that he had been intending to.

'You are an actress, you cannot manage without exaggerations, I accept you as you are, I hope that you will take the same attitude to me. Please listen to everything I have to say and then decide.'

Until this moment Erast Petrovich had been standing, Now he sat down at the opposite side of the table, as if establishing a barrier between them, and now the conditions for crossing would have to be negotiated.

'I have lived in this world for a long time. I behaved with you like an absolute idiot . . . Don't object, just listen,' he said when she shook her head and threw her hands up in the air. 'I knew from the very beginning what I could expect and what I could not. You see, it is always written on a woman's face whether she is capable of a great love or she is not. The way she will behave if life forces her to choose between her beloved and herself, between her beloved and children, between her beloved and an idea.'

'What choice do you think I will make?' Eliza asked timidly.

'You will choose a role. That part of you suits me. We are cut from the same cloth, you and I. I will also choose a role. My role is not a theatrical one, certainly, but that does not matter. Therefore I suggest an honest alliance, without any lies or self-deception. You and I shall have a marriage of convenience.'

'That is the same thing that Shustrov offered me,' she said with a shudder.

'Possibly. But our convenience will not be one of commerce, but of love. To put it in entrepreneurial terms, I propose a love with limited liability. Don't frown. We love each other, we want to be together. But at the same time, we are both invalids of love. I am not willing to abandon my manner of life for your sake. You will not sacrifice the stage for me. Or if you do, you will soon regret it and become unhappy.'

He thought he had managed to break through her habit of affectation. Eliza listened to him seriously and attentively – without wringing her hands, without assuming an air of glowing love.

'You know, I think we are ideally suited for each other,' said Fandorin, moving on to the second point, which was no less delicate. 'I am a mature man and you are a mature woman. There is an ancient formula that can be used to calculate the correct combination of a man's and a woman's ages at the moment of their alliance. The number of years that the bride has lived should be equal to half of the bridegroom's years, plus seven. So according to the Chinese rule you are slightly younger than the ideal age for my chosen one. You are thirty, and according to the formula you should be thirty-four and a half. This is not a great difference.'

As he had expected, Eliza was interested by this dubious Chinese wisdom. She wrinkled up her forehead and worked her lips.

'Wait . . . I can't count it up. How old are you, then? Thirty-four and a half minus seven, multiply by two . . .'

'Fifty-five.'

She was upset.

'As old as that. I didn't think you were more than forty-five!'

This was a painful subject for Erast Petrovich, but he had prepared well for it.

'A man has three ages, and their link to the number of years he has lived is only relative. The first is the age of the mind. There are old men with the intellectual development of a ten-year-old child, but some youths have a mature intellect. The older a man's mind is, the better. The second age is spiritual. The supreme achievement on this path of life is to reach wisdom. It can only descend on a man in old age, when the vain commotion has receded and the passions are exhausted. As I see now, I still have a long way to go to get there. In the spiritual sense, I am younger than I would like to be. And finally, there is physical age. Everything here depends on the correct use of the body. The human organism is an apparatus that is amenable to endless improvement. The wear and tear is more than made up for by acquired skills. I assure you that now I have much better control of my body than I did in my youth.'

'Oh, I saw how in just two minutes you ran up onto the gallery gangway and climbed down the cable!' Eliza lowered her eyes demurely. 'And I have had other opportunities to appreciate how well you control your body . . .'

Erast Petrovich, however, did not allow the conversation to be diverted from its serious vein.

'What do you say, Eliza?' He felt his voice breaking and coughed. 'What do you think of my p-proposal?'

Now everything depended, not so much on her words, as on the way she pronounced them.

If his sincerity had not broken though the actress's defensive guise, nothing worthwhile would come of their union.

Eliza turned pale and then blushed. Then she turned pale again. And a terrible thing – her eyes seemed to have rid themselves of their perpetual squint, and they were both looking straight at Fandorin.

'One condition.' She also seemed to have suddenly turned hoarse. 'No children. May God allow me not to be torn apart between you and the stage. If we cannot get along with each other, it will be painful for us, but we will manage somehow. But I would feel sad for the children.'

This is not a mask speaking, Erast Petrovich thought with immense relief. This is a real, live woman. The way she speaks to me is already an answer. And he also thought that there was a disappointment in store for Masa. It was not the Japanese servant's destiny to teach a little Fandorin how to be happy.

'That's reasonable,' Erast Petrovich said out loud. 'I wanted to ask you about that myself.'

Here, however, Eliza's reserves of reason and restraint ran out. She jumped up, knocking over her chair, dashed to Fandorin, huddled up against him and murmured devotedly.

'Hold me tight, never let me go! Otherwise I shall be torn off the earth, blown away, up into the sky. I shall be lost without you!

God sent you to me to be my salvation! You are my only hope, you are my anchor, my guardian angel. Love me, love me, as much as you can! And I shall love you as well as I know how and with all the strength I have.'

And now he couldn't tell whether she was being genuine just at that moment or whether, without even noticing, she had slipped into some role. If she had, then how magnificently it had been played, how magnificently.

But Eliza's face was wet with tears, her lips were trembling and her shoulders were shaking, and Fandorin felt ashamed of his scepticism.

Essentially, whether she was acting or not was not really important. Erast Petrovich was happy, unconditionally happy. And now come what may.

APPENDIX

E.F.

TWO COMETS IN A STARLESS SKY

***

**A PLAY
FOR THE PUPPET THEATRE
IN THREE ACTS**

***

**WITH SONGS, DANCES, TUMBLING TRICKS,
FENCING SCENES
AND MITIYUKI**

***

DRAMATIS PERSONAE

OKASAN
Owner of the Yanagi tea house

KUBOTA
Counsellor to the Prince of Satsuma

O-BARA
The owner's adopted daughter, a geisha of the first rank

YUBA
Her pupil

IZUMI
The owner's adopted daughter, a geisha of the first rank

SEN-CHAN
Her pupil

KINJO
A thief

FIRST ASSASSIN

SOGA
Nicknamed 'First Sword', a Ronin
who lives in the tea house

SECOND ASSASSIN

FUTOYA
A rich merchant

THE INVISIBLE ONE
The Jyonin of the Sinobi clan

THE INAUDIBLE ONE
A warrior of the Sinobi clan

The stage is divided into two parts, alternated by rotating it. In one half the scenery is permanent – this is the garden of the tea house and Izumi's room: in the other half the scenery changes. On the left a little platform or hanamichi is attached to the stage, running out into the hall to approximately the fifth row. Between the hanamichi and the hall there is an empty space. On the right, the Storyteller sits at the edge of the stage throughout the performance, wearing a severe black kimono with crests. He is gently lit by a paper lantern.

ACT ONE

Scene one

At the gates of the Yanagi tea house, which are flung open wide in welcome. Lying on a stand at the very centre is a shamisen, or lute, and at one edge there are two pillows: one larger and rather more luxurious, the other smaller and more modest. Quiet music is playing.

STORYTELLER *(he strikes a drum lying in front of him with a wooden stick – the sound is a low, quiet rumbling)*

This is the Yanagi tea house, throughout the capital
It is famed for the art of its exquisite feasts.
The respected owner, to secure her own success,
Adopted two peerless geishas as her foster-daughters,
Since when the house's fame has multiplied most greatly,
And now the Yanagi is celebrated far and wide.
Today from distant Satsuma a noted visitor
Is honouring this refuge of refinement with his presence.
For an occasion such as this the main gates
Have been flung wide open, so that all might see
How celebrated is this house of tea today.
Since morning old and young have gathered at the stage,

For when else could they see the dancers and the singers
Who charm the ears and eyes of only noblemen and merchants?

Before uttering his final phrase, the Storyteller strikes the drum, and the public streams up onto the hanamichi. *Trying to occupy places closer to the stage, the viewers sit down with their backs to the hall. At the front are the trainee geishas – the young woman Yuba and the teenage girl Sen-chan – behind them are the merchant Futoya and the First Assassin (he is dressed like a monk, with a large straw hat on his head) and then the thief Kinjo and the Ronin Soga (in a patched kimono, but with two swords in his belt).*

STORYTELLER *(he strikes the drum)*
And here we see the owner – Okasan her name,
Which simply means 'mama' – for she is like a mother to all here –
Trembling in her joy, leading her dear guest along
To take the place of honour at the very finest spot.
Mr Kubota's duties are exalted ones,
As counsellor and minister to the Prince of Satsuma.

Bowing repeatedly, Okasan seats the samurai in the place of honour, and sits down modestly beside him. At the appearance of the guest all the spectators on the hanamichi *lean towards him. While a conversation takes place between Kubota and the owner, everyone remains respectfully motionless, with only Sen-chan fidgeting and squirming in her place.*

OKASAN Oh, what happiness it is that you, Kubota-san, have not forgotten me, even after so very many years! Ah, of course, I have become ugly and old, but seeing you, I tremble once again in joy.

She covers her face elegantly with her hand, performing the gesture 'Pleasant Embarrassment'.

KUBOTA Ah, but how could I forget you? Ah, those golden days! But weeping tears for spring is foolish on an autumn day. Yes, we are not as we once were. What once was is now past, and yet it would be strange to be offended at our fate. What a high grandee I have now become, and you are now the owner of the finest of all tea houses. But I have come to you today not in remembrance of the past. I have been sent here on an errand from my prince. His

Lordship wishes to choose from among the geishas of the capital one who will be a concubine for his sweet delectation.

Okasan flutters her sleeves elegantly, performing the gesture 'Great and Joyful Amazement'.

My prince is well accustomed to trusting my judgement. My instructions were to hasten to the capital. Before the prince arrives I must go round all the tea houses and select ten of the very finest geishas. During a presentation he will make his choice of one. For a geisha truly an enviable fate! Think how much money you would receive. And how greatly your establishment's prestige would be enhanced!

OKASAN I do not dare to dream of such a matchless honour. My best reward is simply to behold your face.

She performs the gesture 'Most Profound Gratefulness'.

I shall show you forthwith what brings my house its fame. I shall reveal my treasure, holding nothing back. It was no accident that I ordered the gates to be flung open. My house and my heart are both alike open to you.

She performs the gesture 'Boundless Sincerity'.

First my daughter O-Bara will demonstrate all her art for you. Do not be strict with her.

She claps her hands.

The owner's adopted daughter O-Bara appears and walks up onto the stage. She is wearing a magnificent brocade kimono with a scarlet lining. Her tall hairstyle is decorated with slides in the form of butterflies. Her face, as befits a geisha, is thickly whitened. Her movements are precise and bold and every gesture is replete with sensuality.

Yuba gets up and minces to the stage. She bows, hands her mistress a little drum and goes back. The performance begins. O-Bara first dances to fast music, beating out the rhythm with blows on a drum. The geisha keeps her eyes fixed on the guest all the time, demonstrating in every way possible that she is performing only for him.

371

STORYTELLER (*during the dance*)
　　For good reason is she called O-Bara – 'a rose'.
　　Her thorns instantly pierce any male heart.
　　O-Bara has no equals when she wishes to kindle
　　The flames of passion and awaken generosity.
　　It is no secret to O-Bara why this guest has come
　　(the rumour of it filled the tea house long ago).
　　She has in mind to captivate Kubota,
　　So he will help her to become the prince's concubine.

The dance is over. The pupil takes the drum, the geisha sits down with the shamisen *and sings in a beautiful, low, slightly hoarse voice, looking at the samurai.*

O-BARA (*sings*)
　　Even as the convolvulus winds
　　Around the mighty cedar,
　　Thus too would I, my master,
　　Around your body twine myself.
　　My tender leaves and petals,
　　My aroma and my flowers
　　Would I devote to you alone,
　　My precious sovereign lord!

Kubota listens, swaying his head to the rhythm. Okasan glances sideways at him to see whether he is pleased.

　　During O-Bara's performance, the following takes place on the hanamichi.

　　Kinjo, taking advantage of the fact that the spectators are absorbed in the performance, sets about his thievish business. First he deftly frisks the Ronin beside him: he searches under his belt and in his broad sleeve, and raises the hem of his kimono from behind. But he finds nothing of any value and shakes his head in disgust. He creeps a little farther forward, walking on tiptoe, and sets to work on the merchant. Here he has much better luck. He takes a purse out of the man's sleeve and a silk pouch and gilded pipe from behind his belt; in the lining of the merchant's kimono he discovers a secret pocket, from which he fishes out several gold coins.

　　The geisha's performance comes to an end. She bows deeply, exclusively to Kubota, and heaves a deep sigh, which is accompanied by the gesture

'Sensual Agitation', then walks away to the far side of the stage and sits down there.

KUBOTA (*to the owner*) What a seductress! I could have watched and watched. I am no longer young, and yet my blood still boiled. The prince will like her even more. Of course, it is embarrassing even to compare her with the princess. For after all, my lord's wife was chosen by his father, who was thinking, not of beauty, but of profit for the treasury . . .

OKASAN Will you permit me now to call Izumi? She is in a different style, but also very fine.

Kubota nods and the owner claps her hands.

Izumi appears. She is wearing a muted but elegant kimono of bluish-white with silver embroidery. She moves smoothly, almost weightlessly. Her eyes are lowered. She bows first to the guest, then to the owner, then to the public. Her pupil Sen-chan abruptly gets up, runs to the stage and hands Izumi a fan, after which she takes her time returning to her place.

Izumi begins a slow, elegant dance.

KUBOTA (*moved*) Oh, such nobility! The patterning of the dance is pure! She is exactly like a willow tree above a quiet river!

SEN-CHAN (*very clearly*) Did you hear, my sister? He has approved the dance. He likened you to a willow tree above a quiet river!

OKASAN Such naughtiness! Intolerable child! She has not been with us for long. Forgive her, my lord!

Kubota is so entranced by the geisha that he has not heard either the shout or the apologies. Sen-chan comes running back and takes the fan from Izumi, who sits down with the shamisen, *plays and sings.*

IZUMI
All genuine beauty is hidden,
It dazzles not, it does not catch the eye
Beauty's voice is soft and delicate,
Not everyone is capable of hearing it.
The lovely captivates with its perfection.
Filled with a mystery ineffable,

It reveals but a tiny morsel of itself,
And for the devotee, that is enough . . .

SEN-CHAN (*turning towards the auditorium*) Did you all hear? Did you hear? Oh, how she sings! In all the world there is no one more beautiful than my Izumi-san!

Yuba nudges the girl in the side with her elbow, and she falls silent. During Izumi's performance the thief carries on working. After cleaning out the merchant, he moves on to the 'monk'. Here there is a surprise in store for him. Not having discovered anything in the sleeve, Kinjo lifts the hem of the robe – and sees the gleaming blade of a naked sword. The thief backs away fearfully and takes up a position behind Yuba. He tries to thrust his hand in behind her belt, but, unable to resist, lovingly strokes the firm, cloth-wrapped thigh.

Without turning round, Yuba slaps the unknown rascal on the hand. Kinjo calms down.

Izumi finishes singing. She bows again in three directions, lowers her eyes and walks away to take a seat beside O-Bara.

KUBOTA (*loudly*) If it were up to me, I would already halt the search! A concubine such as this is the very one we need! Modest, with excellent manners, and so comely! No stain would she inflict on my lord's honour. And above all, in her one sees that genuine *yugen*, without which any beauty is but vulgar.

He bows to Okasan and says something to her fervently.

STORYTELLER
The samurai extols Izumi's virtues at great length
He is a connoisseur of *yugen*, 'the hidden beauty'.
Izumi's gentle song enchanted the old man,
Naming all seven of the hidden beauty's qualities.

And in conclusion, speaking from his heart,
Kubota gave his one-time lady friend a piece of good advice.

KUBOTA Although the prince is learned in the arts, he is still young. It would be good to embellish the performance, to enliven it. I shall let the Yanagi house perform last . . .

374

Okasan performs the gesture 'Undeserved Offence', but Kubota smiles at her cunningly.

The prince will have had time to grow weary of geishas and their songs and dances.

And then you will present your goods to him. First you bring out the rose (*he nods towards O-Bara*) in order to arouse him. And then do this: hire a jester or a juggler who is full of fancy twists and tricks. The prince loves acrobats. Let him laugh at some simple spectacle. But then Izumi will come out and he will be transfixed. The vulgar entertainment will provide a superb contrast for appreciating the exquisite pattern of *yugen*.

STORYTELLER

>The exalted guest departs. As he is leaving
>Okasan bows to him and she is moved to tears.
>His goodwill and his cordial advice
>Promise the owner of the house unprecedented profit.

Okasan, bowing repeatedly, sees the samurai on his way. Everyone there bows low, with their foreheads to the ground; only Soga, as befitting a man of noble rank, does not bow down as low as that.

This is why he is the first to see that as soon as Mr Kubota and the owner of the house are hidden in the wings, the 'monk' abruptly straightens up, jumps to his feet, pulling out his concealed weapon, and dashes forward.

All of this happens in an instant.

Sen-chan squeals and grabs the killer by his robe. He stumbles and pulls himself free, but in that second Soga also has had time to get up and bare his sword.

The killer rushes at Izumi with a furious scream, raising his sharp blade. She freezes in horror and puts her hands over her face.

O-Bara nimbly darts out of the way.

The viewers shout and mill around.

But the Ronin moves even faster than the 'monk', jumping up onto the hanamichi *and shielding Izumi with his body.*

A sword-duel ensues, the killer making guttural sounds, Soga remaining silent.

STORYTELLER (*beating very rapidly on his drum and declaiming briskly*)
   Sharp is the killer's blade, his movements swift!
   Both from the front and from the side he makes his thrusts!
   But Soga well deserves his title of 'First Sword',
   And in the swordsman's art he truly is the best of all.

Eventually, following a precisely aimed blow from Soga, the 'monk' falls dead. The Ronin freezes in the pose of his thrust. Everyone else also freezes motionless: some with their hands over their faces, some with their arms raised in the air.

The light dims. The curtain closes.
The stage revolves.

Scene two

The front section of the stage represents the garden of the Yanagi tea house. This is the basic stage set, which remains unchanged. There is a small, decorative bridge, a young apple tree and a large stone lantern. A little farther back there is a narrow, raised veranda, or engawa, *running round a pavilion. At each end of the* engawa *there are oil lamps, which are lit or not, depending on the time of day. The* shoji *(the paper walls of the pavilion) can also either be parted or moved together. At the moment they are closed. A light is burning inside and we can see Izumi's silhouette as she sits there, slowly strumming on the strings of the* shamisen. *A sad, faltering melody is heard.*
   Night. The garden is dark.
   The Storyteller strikes his drum – Soga walks soundlessly along the engawa *and disappears, holding the hilt of his sword in his hand.*

STORYTELLER   When mayhem broke out at Yanagi's gates
   Our thief was quick to seize this easy chance.
   He gave his stolen booty to his partner
   And in the noisy clamour crept into the tea house.
   He hid until night came, but once the darkness fell,
   The sly rogue went in search of further loot . . .

He beats on the drum.
   Kinjo appears. He gazes all around and sees the geisha's silhouette. He

freezes, enchanted by the music.

STORYTELLER
Since the attack this afternoon a mere six hours have passed.
Izumi is not sleeping, she cannot overcome her trepidation.

Yuba enters the garden, walking backwards. Bent over double, she is sweeping the path with a broom.
She bumps into Kinjo with her backside. Both of them cry out in fright and turn to face each other.

YUBA Who are you? And how could you have got in here?

KINJO (*keeping his presence of mind*) Ah, what rare good fortune! Oh, what a lucky man I am!

YUBA (*suspiciously*) What is it, my good sir, that makes you so delighted! Upon my word, I'll call the guard this very moment!

KINJO (*taking hold of her sleeve*) There is no need call the guard. I made my way in here with only one intention – to meet you once again! Today I saw you there beside the stage, close to the gates, and my poor reason was stunned by an insane love. I crept into the garden here by stealth and I am wandering about, bewildered and bemused. I did not think or dare to hope to meet you at this hour!

YUBA (*relenting, but still on her guard*) My mistress is out of sorts today, she keeps shouting. She has sent me out to sweep the paths in the middle of the night . . .

KINJO (*trying to keep her talking*) Did you see that sword fight here today? What a performance! I was absolutely fascinated. I thought at first that it was all in earnest, that at any moment blood would spurt out in a fountain. Hey, hey, a classy trick. It was only a pity that the noble guest left without seeing it, the actors played the deadly fight so deftly.

YUBA What actors? I'm still shaking even now. It was our enemies who tried to kill Izumi yet again!

KINJO Your enemies have tried again? What do you mean, I do not understand . . .

YUBA Probably you're not from hereabouts. Why, it's the talk of all the town that our Izumi has a secret enemy. This is the third time he has sent a man to kill her. But every time she is saved by Soga-san. He is a homeless samurai, with no wealth but his sword, and he is boundlessly devoted to her, like a faithful guard dog. Being a famous geisha is no easy fate. The love of men can sometimes be quite dangerous. Some admirer, spurned by Izumi, must be seeking his revenge for the insult that he has suffered.

KINJO You geishas are so cruel! A beauty such as you can pierce a man's heart like an arrow, but you care nothing. It's wrong to dance and sing your songs to us and then pretend to be a touch-me-not.

YUBA Well, I am not a geisha yet. I'm only learning to be one, although my mistress thinks I do not have an ounce of promise.

My lady O-Bara knows all about men, and no one could call her a touch-me-not. She tells me that lady Izumi arranges everything herself. That in this way she wishes to acquire scandalous fame, to be on everybody's lips. That her faithful Ronin, the fearsome Soga-san, deliberately hires tramps and vagabonds, and then he kills them, the unfortunate fools. For after all, he knows them all by sight. And with his skill, why it's nothing at all to slice some blockhead hireling into shreds. And all this means a double profit for the mistress: the geisha's fame increases, and the bold warrior's fame spreads far and wide.

KINJO Oh, but that monk did not look like a simpleton. His swordplay was quite glorious, he was clearly a master.

YUBA All that's none of our business. But why don't you tell me where you are from and what your name is?

KINJO Call me Kinjo. I dare not reveal my family name to you until I know that our feelings are mutual, that your response to my passion is love and we have become one. I am the young heir to a trading house and it would be indecorous for me to blacken the honour of my father's firm.

378

When she heard that, the lovely girl thought this:
'Perhaps I will "become one" with him then.
He has good looks and his manners are bold.
And in addition he is rich, so what else could I want?'

Kinjo starts embracing Yuba. She does not resist very strongly. They put their arms around each other passionately.

Once a thief, always a thief. In that ardent moment
Kinjo looks to see what he can filch.

Kinjo feels inside Yuba's belt, glancing over her shoulder. He hides a tor-toiseshell comb and little mirror in his sleeve and then cautiously removes a beautiful slide from her hair.

But Yuba also is no fool. She wishes to discover
Whether her gallant wooer is truly rich.

At the same time Yuba feels behind the belt of her passionate admirer. She discovers a thin purse and rummages in it.

But what bad luck is this! The purse is almost empty!
His embraces have lost all their sweetness for her now.

The young woman stamps her foot angrily and tries to free herself.
Suddenly Soga appears at the end of the engawa. *He jumps down with-out making a sound, runs over to Kinjo and grabs him by the collar.*

SOGA Who is this here with you, girl, answer me! Do you dare to bring your lovers here to the Yanagi?

YUBA (*embarrassed*) Why, no indeed, my lord! This is my own dear brother, who has come to visit me. We have not seen each other for so long . . .

The Ronin brusquely searches the frightened Kinjo, taking the stolen items out of his sleeve: the little mirror, the slide, the comb. Yuba throws up her hands in outrage but says nothing. Failing to find a weapon, Soga loses interest in Kinjo.

SOGA Well, so he is your brother. I couldn't give a damn. But just mind now, you fidget: keep quiet here, do not disturb the peace!

He disappears as silently as he appeared.

YUBA You villain! You rogue! You're a thief and a scoundrel. Some fine merchant you are, when all your wealth is a mere two farthings!

She pounds him on the chest with her fists. Kinjo chuckles.

KINJO Well look at that! The she-devil has rummaged in my purse! And I didn't even notice! What skilful hands!

YUBA Well, I may be a she-devil, but I am not a thief! I did not take your things, but you have stolen mine.

KINJO A fine reason that is for pride! If you would like to know the truth, the thief's lot has no equal in this world. I am freer than the wind. No one can order me around. The whole world is my booty. I am a true king among men!

But there is still one thing that vexes me: I live all alone in the world.

I am a king, but with no queen my rule is wearisome. Come and be my companion. The two of us will go away together!

There is no guile in what I'm saying to you now. You are astute and nimble, and you have a pretty face. Together as a couple we would do great things . . .

He leans down to her and whispers in her ear. She turns away again, but then starts listening. His arms embrace her once again.

STORYTELLER
Sweet-tongued Kinjo calls her to follow him.
He promises a life of freedom with all the sweetness of love.
But they must set off laden with booty, not travel light.
The girl must give him some serious help now –
In this rich house they could make a fine haul.
Let Yuba sniff out where the valuables lie.
She is inclined to yield to his persuasion,
She feels the lure of wanderlust, karma's imperious call . . .

The lovers merge into a kiss. And then Kinjo takes Yuba by the hand and leads her into the depths of the garden. The moment they disappear from the stage, a black figure emerges from behind a stone lantern. This is the Second Assassin, who was hiding there. He takes a small crossbow out from behind his back, sets a bolt on the string and aims at the silhouette of Izumi playing on the shamisen.

But as suddenly as the previous afternoon, Soga appears on the engawa. *He leaps down and runs the Second Assassin through with a single thrust. The assassin screams and falls.*

The sound of music breaks off. We see Izumi get to her feet.

Soga puts his sword back in its scabbard and drags the body under the veranda.

STORYTELLER
The loyal bodyguard has turned a blow aside once more.
Ever-vigilant is bold Soga, the staunch First Sword.
Now he is agitated and alarmed. Yet another attack!
He hurries to conceal the body out of sight,
Wishing to spare Izumi's peace of mind.
The poor soul need not know that death was hovering here.

Izumi opens the partitions: seeing Soga, she relaxes and moves the shoji *wide apart. We can see the inside of her room. It is carpeted with straw mats and decorated with flowers. At the centre there are two low tables. The* shamisen *is lying on one and a large lacquered casket with drawers is standing on the other.*

IZUMI Ah, it is you, my glorious, my priceless guard. I thought I heard a shout.

SOGA It was a night bird. Everything here is calm. Lie down and take some rest. I shall be here on watch.

IZUMI (*shivering*) I cannot think of sleep tonight! Who is this savage enemy whose sole wish is to see Izumi killed?

SOGA I have asked you, I have questioned you: try to recall the men whom you have spurned.

IZUMI But how can one recall them all? They are just like a swarm of

381

flies. They buzz and pester: 'Be mine, be mine!' They do not understand that true *yugen* entices but then slips away, that it cannot be clutched. I have no need of men's embraces or of oaths. There is no man in all the world whom I shall love.

Soga listens, hanging his head. Izumi's voice softens.

Only you, dear friend, have proved able to understand me. And yet at the beginning you too begged for love. But you are noble-hearted and for you it is enough that I value your true nobility and devotion.

She gestures to invite the Ronin up into the house. As he enters, he parts the shoji even wider and leaves them open. They sit down: Izumi in front of the casket, in profile to the hall, Soga facing her.

SOGA I behaved absurdly, as if I wished to crumple and pick the flower, not to admire it. I look at you and I am happy. When you are here, my life is full. I would serve such perfection for an entire lifetime.

Izumi raises the lid of the casket – there is a mirror in it. The geisha looks sadly at her whitened face.

IZUMI 'An entire lifetime' is short for a geisha. When beauty fades, there is no more perfection, merely a dried-up leaf ... When a net of wrinkles creeps across this skin, I shall not wait for long – I have sworn to myself. What good is life when all the Beauty in it fades away? For that, here in my casket, I keep this (*she takes out a sharp stiletto and looks at it*). A quick blow, a little pain, and my flower will be cut. I will not let it wither, I will not betray *yugen*!

SOGA What kind of talk is this! You are only twenty years old. Believe me, there is another beauty in this world. It comes in place of corporeal beauty, if you have walked your path through life beautifully ...

IZUMI (*in a frivolous tone, putting the stiletto back*) Yes, you are right, it will not soon be thus. Youth will continue for another five or seven years.

The Storyteller strikes his drum.
   The geisha's expression changes, her voice trembles.

Ah, how could I forget? It slipped my mind completely: some other person's hand wishes to cut my flower . . .

She turns in fright towards the garden, as if it conceals some invisible danger. Soga also turns, setting his hand on his sword. They both freeze motionless.

The light slowly fades, the curtain closes.
The stage revolves.

Scene three

A deserted temple. Night. In the background there is the vague form of a large statue of the Buddha.
   The Storyteller strikes his drum. Futoya enters, looking round nervously. He is holding a small but heavy sack in which something is jingling.
   He waits, glancing around and shuddering at every rustle. Every now and then there is a peal of thunder and a flash of lightning.

STORYTELLER
   On a dark, inclement night the merchant Futoya-san
   Has secretly sneaked into a deserted temple.
   Why would a haughty merchant, richest of the rich,
   Suddenly come alone to such a fearsome place?
   Ah, a dark business, this! A meeting has been set here
   By the mysterious one known to all as 'Invisible'.
   We all have heard of *Ninjas* and *Sinobi*,
   Those well-known killers, but few have seen them in the flesh.
   They take commissions to perform dark deeds
   And no power on earth is there more cunning and more terrible.
   The *Jyonin* is the title of their fearsome leader,
   Whom Futoya has asked to meet with him in secret . . .

The Storyteller strikes on his drum and lightning flashes.

VOICE OF THE INVISIBLE ONE (*a rumbling sound, it is hard to tell where it comes from*) I am here, now we can get straight down to business.

It must be important, if you have asked to meet with the Sinobi.

Futoya almost jumps up in the air in surprise. He does not know which way to look. In the end he speaks to the statue.

FUTOYA Yes, yes, a most great need has brought me here to you. I simply cannot kill a certain person. Four times have I sent assassins to her. Wandering samurais and intrepid bandits . . . But alas, the woman is well guarded. I cannot manage this without the help of the Sinobi.

THE INVISIBLE ONE What is her name? When? And how much? This is all that I need to know.

FUTOYA Her name? Izumi, a geisha. When? There is one difficulty here. It would be best not to carry out this commission straight away, but only at the moment when I give the signal. In the garden of the Yanagi tea house there is a little apple tree. I will break off one of its branches to show when the time has come . . .

THE INVISIBLE ONE Aha, a delayed commission, requiring readiness to act at any moment. That is a contract of the highest class of difficulty.

FUTOYA *(hastily)* Your go-between informed me of your charges. And I have brought the sum – this is exactly one thousand *ryo*.

He holds up the sack, but does not know how to hand it over.

THE INVISIBLE ONE And did the go-between tell you that, once having placed a commission, you can never cancel it? Such is our ancient law: those who have been condemned must die.

FUTOYA *(bowing)* Why would I cancel the request, if I have paid the money?

THE INVISIBLE ONE Put the sack at the statue's feet. Our contract is concluded.

The Storyteller strikes his drum.
Futoya places the sack at the feet of the statue and backs away.

THE INVISIBLE ONE My finest warrior will fulfil your request.

384

'Inaudible One' is the name that I myself have given him.

FUTOYA (*timidly*) I have been told that it is usual for you to give a certain item in place of a receipt . . .

THE INVISIBLE ONE Yes, my jade dragon. I have a dagger with a dragon on the hilt – the symbol of my rank. You must return the sacred talisman to me when our contract with you has been fulfilled.

FUTOYA How shall I know to whom to give it?

THE INVISIBLE ONE My messenger will show you a dagger with a blade like a snake.

A single drumbeat. The beam of a spotlight illuminates the statue of the Buddha. We see a hand thrust out from behind it, holding a long dagger with a sinuous blade like a snake. The other hand unscrews the pommel from the handle and tosses it to the merchant, who picks up the jade dragon, presses it respectfully to his forehead and bows. The beam of light goes out.

THE INVISIBLE ONE But know this, merchant Futoya, you are responsible for this token. If it is lost, you will pay for it with your life.

The merchant freezes in a pose of horror. A simultaneous drumbeat and flash of lightning. Darkness.

The curtain closes.
The stage revolves.

Scene four

The garden in front of Izumi's pavilion. The shoji are closed. Okasan is sitting on the engawa, with her adopted daughters beside her. At the sides are the pupils Yuba and Sen-chan, holding large fans in their hands. The sun is shining brightly. It is hot.

Soga is peeping out from round the corner. As always, he is on the lookout.

STORYTELLER
Following the advice of wise Kubota,
Okasan spread the rumour through the city:

'The venerable Yanagi tea house wishes to invite
Jugglers, acrobats, comedians and jesters'.
This call spread though the fairs and circuses
And next day all the show folk came along.
The choosy owner, though, was difficult to please,
Being concerned for the honour of the tea house.
No one suited her taste, but then, at close of day,
A most strange man arrived at the Yanagi . . .

*The Storyteller strikes his drum. Everybody starts moving: the ladies and
the pupils with the fans; Soga, who appears and disappears by turns.*

*The Inaudible One walks out onto the stage. He is not dressed in a
kimono, but in a close-fitting black leotard painted with jester-like vari-
coloured stripes. His face is completely covered by a silk mask with a foolish
face drawn on it, the mouth stretching from ear to ear. He is carrying a
bag with his props. The Inaudible One walks over to Okasan with a
waddling, clown-like gait. Sen-chan giggles and puts her hand over her
mouth.*

*With the gesture of a conjuror, the Inaudible One produces a paper rolled
into a tube, seeming to extract it from the very air, and holds it out to the
owner.*

STORYTELLER
He handed her the sheet of paper with a bow.
She took it and read what was written there:
'I have been dumb from birth. My name is *Nobo-ji*.
My face is disfigured and I always wear a mask,
And I shall show you now what I can do.'

*Okasan shrugs and shows the letter to one of her adopted daughters, then
to the other. She gestures for the show to begin.*

*The beam of a spotlight rises and illuminates a tightrope stretched above
the stage. The Inaudible One takes a rope with a hook out of his bag, deftly
casts it onto the tightrope and clambers up in a jiffy. He walks along the
tightrope, acting the fool, pretending that he is about to fall off at any
moment. He starts juggling with knives that he takes out of his belt. The
spectators watch admiringly. Sen-chan forgets to wave her fan and squeals
in delight.*

386

It is not hard to guess that this indeed is he,
Whom the Sinobi leader dubbed 'Inaudible'.
His face is hid beneath a mask for a good reason:
A Ninja may not show his face to strangers.
He can only appear unmasked in token of
Absolute trust – and then only among his own.
And he has not been dumb from birth. The tale
Of how he lost his speech is worth the telling here.
One day he was instructed to assassinate the leader
Of another Ninja clan – an extremely dangerous order.
The killer might be taken alive by the bodyguards
And tortured to set his tongue wagging.
Not hoping to remain alive, before the mission
He cut his own tongue out with an untrembling hand.
And from that time his friends called him 'Inaudible' –
For them he was a paragon of honour and of skill . . .

The acrobat jumps down and hands the owner another sheet of paper.

OKASAN (*reading aloud*) 'And now permit me to show you the Hoo
bird. The wings of the phoenix burn but they are not consumed.
I know a magical gesture, with which the fierce element of fire
can be subdued.'

*The Inaudible One shows them an impressive trick. He takes a pair of
jester's bird's wings out of his bag and attaches them to his sleeves. Then he
takes an oil lamp that is lit from the engawa and pours oil onto his 'wings'.
He makes the 'magical gesture', squats down comically and spreads out his
arms. Then he strikes one finger against his knee, and the finger bursts into
flame. He runs the flaming finger along one 'wing', and then the other, and
they flare up. The conjuror spins round on the spot, fluttering his burning
'wings'. Everyone gasps in horror.*

At this point the Storyteller explains how the trick is managed.

STORYTELLER

This trick, impressive though it is, is easy to perform.
In pouring burning oil onto his wings of rag,
The conjuror in no way risks being burned himself.

That cloth has been soaked in a special fluid.
The fire will not touch his skin, nor even scorch it.
And the magical gesture has nothing to do with the case.

Sen-chan repeats the magical gesture.

OKASAN (*in a pleased voice*) Well now, this will do for us. You are hired, Nobo-ji. Until the performance you will stay here in the Yanagi. Please, Soga-san, show the actor the way to the servants' wing, he can settle in there.

Soga walks up to the conjuror and looks him over suspiciously. He pulls the knives which the Inaudible One used for juggling out of his belt and keeps them.

SOGA No carrying of weapons is allowed here. Especially since you are far too skilful with your knives. My heart mistrusts your jeering grin, my lad, and I shall keep a sharp eye on you. Why are you standing there? Come on now, follow me.

The Ronin leads the Inaudible One off the stage.

The owner gives a sign to the pupils and they open the shoji. The owner and her adopted daughters walk into Izumi's room and sit down. Okasan gestures for the pupils to go. They leave with a bow, and then Sen-chan runs off, hopping and skipping.

OKASAN Well, now I feel assured for the performance. This wibble-wobble monster will provide the perfect foil for your ardent appeal, O-Bara, and for your style too, Izumi. Kubota is our ally. He thinks that you, Izumi, will catch the prince's fancy. But the prince's taste may differ from the servant's. The call of the flesh, as we know, is stronger in the young, and I think it is quite possible he might choose you, O-Bara. If anyone knows men, I do! And let me tell you frankly, it is all the same to me which of you triumphs and is chosen for the prince's concubine. I love you both, my daughters. May this great prize not go to someone else's house . . . But then, you have no rivals in the entire capital. I know that one of you is destined to win this victory.

O-BARA In a rich princedom I would shine bright as a star! No, not a star, the sun! And I would soften the prince with my rays, softer than wax. I would take charge of all Satsuma in a trice. What a great dream! If only fate would grant me this good fortune! I would be forever grateful to you, my mother!

OKASAN And what say you, Izumi?

IZUMI I am resigned to karma. If I had my way, truly, I would live here for ever. But a geisha is not entitled to choose her own fate. Since you have decided that there is more money to be made by handing me over to a man, then so be it.

OKASAN Could that be resentment I hear in your voice? As if I were selling you to some ugly old man or a filthy merchant! The prince of Satsuma is young and handsome, so they say. Perhaps with him you will know the joy of love. And then you will be grateful to Okasan and fate.

IZUMI I have heard many times about the joys of love. And I have sung songs of them for my audience. But what they are, I have no wish to know. All men bore me and I do not believe in love.

OKASAN You are wrong not to believe. Love does exist in this world. To be precise, there are only three loves. One love is earthly. And all, whose spirit is bowed down low to the surface of the earth, are in its power. Such people are at least nine out of ten. Sinful and sordid, but sweet is this kind of love.

Then there are those who are seduced by hell. I call their poisoned love 'infernal'. It is an igneous potion that burns away the soul, leaving nothing, and vanishes in black smoke.

And sometimes, although rarely, one may find another kind of love. It captures those souls that aspire aloft, therefore the poets call it heavenly. But its time is not long, like the flight of a butterfly. Or the flight of a comet, tracing its luminous path across the sky once in two hundred years . . .

IZUMI A comet is alone, it has no need of anyone. Ah, if I could fly through life like a comet! The flight may not be long, but what great beauty!

O-BARA Love? A comet? Oh really, this is comical to hear, I say, soar across the sky or go down into hell, but squeeze out everything this life can give. A miraculous, luscious fruit has fallen straight into our hands. We must squeeze out the juice, every last drop!

OKASAN (*with a sad sigh*) Both of you, my daughters, are renouncing love. But here it is for karma, not for us, to choose. Heavenly, earthly or infernal love: the path is set out and we cannot turn aside.

All three women freeze in various poses. Okasan folds her hand together in Buddhist style and closes her eyes; O-Bara raises one hand to adjust her hairstyle; Izumi sits there with her head elegantly lowered.

The light goes out, the curtain closes.
The stage revolves.

ACT TWO

Scene one

O-Bara's room, brightly lit and richly decorated, with predominant tones of gold and scarlet. When the stage is revealed, we see two motionless figures. They are O-Bara and a man wearing a straw cloak and a hat pulled forward over his eyes. They are sitting facing each other and leaning forward – as if they are whispering. The room is dimly lit.

STORYTELLER
    After nightfall a visitor slipped in to see O-Bara.
    (Sometimes men did come to visit her.)
    And this one, who conceals his face behind a hat,
    Probably comes more often than the others.
    Not for amorous games has he come here today.
    They sit there, making quiet conversation . . .

He strikes his drum. The light in the room becomes brighter and the figures start moving.

O-BARA (*impatiently*) Take off that hat and look me in the eyes. And speak more clearly, I can hardly hear you! Have you settled this business, as you swore to recently? I relied on you and hope my trust was not in vain.

The man removes his hat and cloak. It is Futoya.

FUTOYA (*in a low voice, after glancing round*) You know, I feel uncomfortable shouting about this. I have arranged it all just as you wished. Now all you have to do is give the sign. When you decide the time has come, break a branch off the apple tree. I have done all the dirty work alone. The horror I went through, God only knows. They could have finished me, those savage brutes. I contacted that rabble only out of love for you.

O-BARA And this one also fancies he should talk to me of love! I thought you more intelligent than that, Mr Futoya. You and I love money. We love strength and power. And we shall leave the nonsense and the sighing for the others. And if on this occasion you have taken a great risk, you have your own reasons for that. You know that if I tame the prince, then all trade with Satsuma will fall into our hands. And spilled blood – surely I do not need to explain this to you – will bind us together for ever, more firmly than any glue.

FUTOYA (*sighing*) All this is true, in our souls you and I are twins. I have not simply thrown away a thousand golden coins. I count on earning my costs back many times over. But still, it is a bitter thought that we shall part. God willing, you will become the prince's concubine. You will transform him into a tame monkey. (Oh, you know very well how to do that, you have no equals there.) But I shall never lie in your embrace again . . .

O-BARA You are intelligent, strong and mature. Exactly as I am. You and I both know how much an embrace is worth.

FUTOYA Tell me then, O-Bara, how much is it worth?

O-BARA Enough of this, we know the true value of embraces. They are bought and sold easily. He who does not know this is more stupid than Izumi.

FUTOYA Then tell me this. I have condemned Izumi to death for the sake of profit, I feel no enmity for her. But it seems that as soon as Izumi's name is mentioned, you turn black in the face from hatred.

O-BARA (*furiously*) I hate that haughty air she has! That rotten *yugen* of hers is like a bone stuck in my throat! Tell me, who needs a beauty that cannot be touched and seen? But there are fools walking this earth who prefer languid Izumi to me! No, I do not understand! I cannot understand this! And what I cannot understand . . .

FUTOYA (*joining in*) . . . You must destroy. Ah, poor Izumi. And the prince is no more than an excuse for all of this. If not for him, you would have found some other reason.

O-BARA Are you going back on your word? Do you pity her now?

FUTOYA Whether I pity her or not is idle talk. Under the Ninja laws the commission cannot now be rescinded. Consider her already dead.

O-BARA (*with a pensive smile*) Then I shall wait a while before I break the branch. It will be my great pleasure now to watch the fool. Breathing in the gorgeous aroma of Izumi's hair, I shall smell the stench of carrion.

FUTOYA Since you have mentioned carrion, there is one little hitch that bothers me. To warrant the completion of our deal, their Jyonin gave me a secret token, which I have to keep safe. And if it should be lost, consider me a dead man. Here it is, a dragon made of jade, it has been burning a hole in my bosom . . . (*he takes out the little figure*). Let me tell you what I am afraid of. The accursed Sinobi are guileful and cunning. What if they should decide to steal this token from me?

O-BARA What for? I do not understand.

FUTOYA I have sworn to answer for the safety of the token. They will come and ask me: 'Where is the jade dragon? Pay us either with your life or with all your fortune.' Where can I run from them? They will beggar me completely. A cunning trick like that is well within the customs of the Ninja. But you are not known to them. Our liaison is a secret. So take the dragon now and hide it well.

Futoya hands the jade dragon to the geisha. O-Bara takes the token that the deal will be completed. They both freeze in this pose.

The light goes out.
The stage revolves.

Scene two

The garden in front of Izumi's pavilion. The lanterns on the engawa are not lit. The Inaudible One is standing on the apron of the stage in a strange pose: his hands are held out in front of him, clutching several wooden knives. Soga is standing equally motionless on the edge of the engawa. Sen-chan is sitting beside him.

Too look at, in Yanagi all is peace and quiet.
But the great day is near when all will be decided.
The owner is agitated, and the entire house along with her,
As if the world's fate has been staked upon the outcome.
But omnipresent karma observes this bustle
With impassive features. She already knows
The ending of the drama known as 'Fate'.
Nobody can escape what has been decreed on high . . .

He strikes his drum.

The Inaudible One starts moving – juggling the wooden knives. Sen-chan claps her hands. Soga steps down off the veranda and walks resolutely towards the juggler, who shows him that the knives are made of wood. But it is not the knives that interest the Ronin.

SOGA Listen, my friend, I do not like you. You may fool the women, but you don't fool me. Take off your mask. I want to see what kind of face you have, perhaps this is some trick.

The juggler makes clownish gestures to explain: This is impossible, my face is disfigured!

Nonsense! I have seen many terrifying faces. With no nose and no eyes, hacked by a sword . . .

He tries to take the Inaudible One by the shoulder, but the juggler deftly dodges away. This is repeated several times. Soga begins to lose his temper.

Hey, brother, I'm not going to play jokes with you. How would you like to feel some solid punches?

Izumi comes out of the pavilion onto the engawa and watches. At this moment, taking advantage of the fact that no one is watching her, Sen-chan goes over to a lantern and starts pouring oil on her sleeves.

IZUMI I beg you, Soga-san, do not torment him. To live in this world with no face is a hard fate.
A brave man who has not been broken by the worst of all misfortunes is deserving of respect.

She touches her own face and shudders.

Sen-chan repeats the 'magical gesture' that the Inaudible One performed before his trick with fire.

SOGA I do not teach you how you should dance and sing, my lady. Do not teach me how to keep guard . . .

SEN-CHAN (*she strikes a spark with a flint, sets tinder alight and shouts*) Look, everybody, look! Having performed the magical gesture, I too shall demonstrate the phoenix bird to you!

She sets fire to her kimono and it flares up. Izumi screams in despair. Soga freezes in uncertainty. Only the Inaudible One does not lose his head. He dashes to the little girl, tears the kimono off her with his bare hands and flings it to the ground. The little girl cries in fright, but she is unhurt. The Inaudible One has fallen to his knees, doubled up in pain, and pressed his burned hands to his chest, but has not uttered a single moan.

Soga and Izumi dash to Sen-chan.

IZUMI Ah, what have you done! You silly thing, are you all right?

SOGA (*examining the little girl*) A miraculous rescue! There are no burns at all. But if the Inaudible One had reached you a moment later, you foolish child, you would have burned up like dry grass.

Izumi hugs her pupil close and the Ronin walks over to the Inaudible One and looks at his hands.

But this one is in a bad way . . . Terrible burns. With these injuries he cannot perform. Okasan will be upset now. And I feel sorry for the lad. He acted so bravely. What a fine thing to do!

Everybody freezes: Izumi and Sen-chan hugging each other; Soga with his hand on the Inaudible One's shoulder; the Inaudible One with his head lowered.

The light goes out. The curtain closes.
The stage revolves.

Scene three

A room in the tea house that has been set aside for the juggler. Paper partitions. A floor covered with straw mats. No decorations and no furniture, apart from a low table on which the items required for his tricks are laid out. Standing on a bench in the corner is a tub with water for washing.

The Inaudible One is sitting on the floor, hanging his head, with his hands, bound up in rags, crossed on his forehead. He is motionless.

STORYTELLER

The killer sits alone in his small, wretched room,
A violent conflagration raging in his soul.
He curses himself for his stupid impulse.
In saving the girl he has ruined the whole business.
For now his hands are blistered all over,
His fingers now are burnt and helpless.
How can he kill someone with useless hands like this?
Only death can atone for such disgrace.

He strikes his drum.

The Inaudible One jumps up and mimes a pantomime of despair: he dashes randomly around the room, trying to find a way to take his life. He tries to take something out of a sack, but his hands will not obey him. He picks up the rope on the table, but he cannot form a noose. Finally he falls face down on the floor and rolls about in silence, beating his head against the mats.

STORYTELLER (*continuing*)

But how can he take his own life, if he is crippled?
He cannot draw a dagger and he cannot tie a noose.
No fate exists more terrible, no despair is darker
Than when you cannot even let death in.

The Inaudible One lifts himself up and crawls on his knees to the tub. An idea has occurred to him: he can drown himself! He lowers his head into the water and remains in that pose.

STORYTELLER (*continuing*)

The Ninja has found his solution. His honour will be saved!
The water in the tub is a mere three *suns* deep,

But the Sinobi has a will of iron.
If not blood, then water will wash away his shame!
Fate herself, as if taking pity on Izumi,
Seems to have set aside the sword already raised.
But karma's mystic pattern is so tangled!
And often we destroy ourselves unknowingly . . .

He strikes his drum.

IZUMI'S VOICE (*coming from behind a partition*) Will you permit me
to enter your room? Can you hear me? I have come to visit you!
May I come in?

*The Inaudible One's body starts shuddering convulsively, but he does not
change his pose. The* shoji *slide apart. Izumi is there, seated on her knees.*

STORYTELLER
Seeing this picture, she thinks to herself:
'Poor fellow! He cannot even wash without his hands.
He cannot take his mask off and is obliged to soak
His damaged face like this, straight through the cloth.'

*Izumi gets up, hurries across to the Inaudible One and touches him on the
shoulder. In his surprise he straightens up abruptly. His mask is soaked
right through and clinging to his face.*

IZUMI Permit me to remove your mask and wash your face. I swear
I will not look if that is painful for you.

He shakes his head furiously and backs away.

Very well then, I won't. That is not what I came here for . . . I am
so grateful to you for saving Sen-chan! (*She bows deeply to him.*)
In the garden I was completely numb with fear, I could not say a
single word.

He looks at her without moving. A furious fire glitters in his eyes.

I expect you feel distressed because your hands will not allow you
to take part in the performance. But there is a certain cure for all
burns. My father was a healer, I inherited a chest of potions and
ointments from him, and one of them is a miraculous soothing

balm. In a single hour it can make burns close over and help heal up the skin. In just a day or two your hands will be as dexterous as they ever were. I only ask you, please, to follow me.

She walks to the way out, looking round at the Inaudible One. He watches her but does not move from the spot.

STORYTELLER

He does not know what to believe. Oh, wonder of wonders!
A whimsical joke by a droll, mischievous Fate.
The innocent moth has flown to the flame herself.
The victim is rescuing her own murderer.

Izumi freezes on the threshold, holding out her hand to the Inaudible One. He starts getting up and also freezes.

Darkness. Curtain.
The stage revolves.

Scene four

Izumi's room. The shoji are opened wide. The Inaudible One is sitting on a mat, with his hands bound up in snow-white bandages. Sen-chan is there beside him. There are refreshments on the table.
Sen-chan tries to thrust chopsticks holding a rice ball in through the opening in the mask for the Inaudible One's mouth.

SEN-CHAN How disobedient you are. My lady told me to take care of you and serve you everything. While the soothing balm is healing your burns, I must be your hands. Come on, open your mouth!

The Inaudible One turns away.

SEN-CHAN Don't you want to eat? Then I'll eat it myself.

She eats the ball of rice and carries on talking with her mouth full.

Why don't I loosen up your shoulders and your neck? Sometimes I give lady Izumi a massage like that.

She jumps up, sits behind him and starts giving him a massage. He tries to move away, but she won't leave him alone.

For you I will do anything you want! Just let me know! Since you saved my life, I am yours for ever. And if the balm doesn't help to heal your hands, then I'll be your hands and I'll never leave you. You'll stay with us and live here as our guest. I'll do as I am told by my lady and by you. Where could you go, with no hands and no tongue? But here I'll put your clothes on, and take them off, and feed you.

The Inaudible One shudders at this prospect.

No one in all the world is kinder than my Izumi-san, and no one is nobler than you. What more could I want? What happiness it will be to serve you both! . . . But have I worn you out? Do you want to lie down?

Izumi comes out onto the engawa. *She is wearing an elegant kimono and holding a fan in her hand.*

IZUMI I won't be in your way here, will I? Let the soothing balm take effect and I'll carry on practising my dance.

Sen-chan sits down with the shamisen. *Slowly and painstakingly, sometimes making mistakes, she accompanies Izumi in her dance. The Inaudible One watches Izumi without taking his eyes off her.*

STORYTELLER
The helpless villain follows the marvellous dance,
Admiring all the beauty of the movements despite himself.
What does Izumi's dance have in common with the craft
To which this Ninja has devoted his whole life?
At first sight, one would think, not much. And yet there is a likeness,
A unifying law: to raise mystery to the level of an art.
Yugen conceals the radiance of beauty from the eyes.
The way of the Sinobi conceals the blackness of murder.
Like Yin and Yang, these two forces strive towards each other.
Without darkness there is no light, without light there is no darkness.
Shaken by a strange trembling, the Inaudible One
Sits there, not understanding what is happening to him.

Izumi stops dancing and goes over to the Inaudible One.

IZUMI I think an hour must have gone by now. So let us take a look
and see if my secret balm has helped you as it should. Please, let
me have your hand . . . That's right, thank you. And if it hurts, let
me know straight away.

She cautiously unbandages one hand and examines it, nodding in satisfaction. She unbandages the other one.

There now, that's a quite different matter. But there is still some
redness and the swelling has not yet gone down completely. Now
I'll give you a sleeping draught to drink. A healthy sleep will complete the course of healing.

She prepares the potion. The Inaudible One looks at his hands in amazement and wriggles his fingers.

STORYTELLER
He looks and he cannot believe his eyes. The burns are gone!
He can control his hands, strength has returned to them.
It hurts to move them, but that is a trivial thing.
The assassin can perform his duty with no difficulty.

IZUMI (*handing him a cup with a bow*) Here, drink this please, and
soon you will fall asleep. And I shall stay with you awhile and
watch over your sleep.
(*To her pupil.*) And you go and run around for a while. With your
character you won't be able to sit still in any case. You will start
squealing and fidgeting, and we don't want that. Nobo-ji-san must
sleep soundly now.

*The little girl bows and goes out. The Inaudible One hesitates and does not
take the cup.*

Ah, it must still be painful for you to hold it. Let me give you the
medicine to drink myself.

*She gently takes the Inaudible One by the neck and raises the cup to his lips.
He shudders and squeezes his eyes shut. He pauses again, then drains it all.*

400

In his heart the assassin feels a sudden strange desire,
An absurd, nonsensical dream. He tells himself:
'Oh, if there had been deadly poison in this draught,
How gladly would I have drunk the fatal dose!
And in the next life – who can tell, all things are possible –
I could be born to a quite different destiny.
Perhaps Providence would bring us together once again.
And then I would behave quite differently with her.

Izumi lowers his head onto the pillow, which is a wooden support. The Inaudible One instantly falls asleep, his chest rising and falling smoothly. The geisha sits there, looking at the sleeping man.

STORYTELLER

Two feelings arise now in Izumi's heart
For this man, who saved her pupil from an awful death:
Firstly, admiration: He is a genuine hero!
When everybody lost their heads, he still kept his.
Secondly, there is pity. He is dumb and he has no face!
Oh, how hard it must be for him, living in this world!
She looks at him and sighs. By turns she feels
Her admiration flare up and pity get the upper hand.
A woman's heart filled with rapture can bring disaster,
But pity is more dangerous to the compassionate soul.
When these two feelings are suddenly combined in one,
Nothing good can come from this combination.
To this we can add mystery. The man without a face
Frightens and fascinates her with his strange allure.
No matter how handsome might be an ordinary man,
Izumi's pride would not have let her love him.
But this one she beholds with a hundred thousand faces –
As if all men lie there in supplication at her feet.
There is only one way to banish this strange vision –
To glance under the mask while he is sleeping.
The sight of gross deformity will bring her down to earth.
She reaches out to raise one corner of the mask –
Then suddenly, driven by a strange impulse,

She moves away and seats herself before her mirror . . .

Izumi sits down in front of the dressing table, raises the lid of the casket and looks into the mirror. The sleeping man is left behind her back.

IZUMI (*in a low, agitated voice*) *Yugen* is always invisible! Beauty remains concealed! To tear away its veil means only to destroy the mystery. A beloved with no face! That is true *yugen*! Here my imagination can create the world's loveliest face, a magical face! I shall love him! Yes, it is decided: we shall be such a couple as the world has never seen. I the best of women and he the best of men. I fine, he finer still, as dream is finer than reality. Anybody can easily see me. But his beauty shall be revealed to me alone!

Suddenly the Inaudible One gets up and walks out of the room. Izumi does not notice.

We women are corporeal creatures, weak and timid. Thus nature's female Yin created us. My chosen one shall be fearless and disincarnate. A true man is a disembodied Spirit! My face will wither, but an ethereal Spirit is eternal. He is the very one I need!

She looks round abruptly and sees that the sleeping man has disappeared.

Truly he is incorporeal . . . And, truly, like a Spirit . . . Could he have heard my words and run off in embarrassment?

She grabs her head in her hands.
The shoji slide open and Sen-chan glances in.

SEN-CHAN A man has come to see you. He wants to talk to you. His face is hidden, and he did not give his name . . .

IZUMI His face is hidden? He has come back to me! Nobo-ji, come in! Why did you go away?

SEN-CHAN No, my lady Izumi, this is a different man. And from his dress, he looks like an important samurai.

The samurai enters, wearing a straw hat pulled low in front of his face. He gestures impatiently for the pupil to leave. She bows respectfully and disappears. The samurai walks into the room and closes the shoji behind him. He responds to the geisha's bow with a curt nod, then sits in front of her and removes his hat.

KUBOTA I hope the girl did not recognise my voice. I would not want any loose talk about my visit.

IZUMI You, Mr Kubota? What an unexpected visitor! Ah, to what do I owe this most singular honour?

She bows again, even lower.

KUBOTA Having arrived in Edo, the prince has ordered the presentation of the geishas to be held forthwith. Tomorrow he must attend at court, but on the day thereafter he summons all of you to visit him.

Izumi bows and performs the gesture 'Joyful Anticipation'.

I advised him to take special notice of a geisha from the Yanagi tea house.

Izumi bows and performs the gesture 'Boundless Gratitude'.

I said that she is elegant and she, alone of all of them, embodies true *yugen*.

Izumi bows and performs the gesture 'Oh, Undeserved Praise'.

I told him that you combine nobility with delicacy of soul and heavenly beauty.

Izumi bows and performs the gesture 'Pleasant Embarrassment'.

Now I am almost certain of his choice, but even so a vague disquiet troubles me. I know His Lordship. He is overly susceptible to the influence of others, credulous and passionate. The concubine who moves into our castle will win instant control of his heart and thoughts. The princess is no hindrance, she is dull of mind and year after year gives birth only to daughters. And if the concubine should bear the prince a son, nothing will shake her domination. It is appalling to consider what might happen if the prince should bring some shrewish vixen back from Edo.

Izumi performs the gesture 'Delicate Commiseration'.

I have gathered all the finest geishas of the capital, but you alone are worthy to become the prince's concubine.

Izumi bows and performs the gesture 'Respectful Doubt'.

Are you afraid of life in foreign parts? I shall help you, and you will quickly settle in with us in Satsuma. As reliable allies, we shall be able to protect the prince from errors.

Izumi bows and performs the gesture 'Oh, Your Wisdom is Boundless!'

But first we must make quite sure that no chance is left to your rivals. I have made a most thorough study of my good lord's tastes. Remember what I tell now: the prince's favourite dance is 'The Babbling Brook'.

Izumi nods.

Wear something very simple, a kimono with no glamour. Lower the neckline and reveal your elbows. His Lordship has always been a great admirer of an elegant female neck and elbows that are white.

Izumi raises her arms and her sleeves slip down, revealing her elbows. Kubota nods his head in admiration.

I see you grasp advice at the first telling. I have no need to fear the outcome of this presentation.

He gets up and they exchange bows. Kubota puts on his hat and leaves. Izumi is left alone. She presses her hands to her temples and sways slightly, like a willow tree in the wind.

In the garden the Inaudible One appears, concealing himself from Izumi. He watches her.

STORYTELLER
The old man's advice is truly priceless.
Of course, in following it, Izumi will win the prize.
But why is her lovely face so unhappy?
What thoughts have cast this shadow on her brow?

O-Bara walks into the garden, strolling under a parasol. She stops in front of the blossoming apple tree, as if in admiration of its beauty. The Inaudible One hides deeper in the shadow.

Izumi notices O-Bara and throws up her hands.

IZUMI Ah, my sweet sister. Please, come over here! I need to tell you something urgently!

O-Bara walks up into the pavilion and sits down facing Izumi. They start to talk. The words cannot be heard, but the gesturing is eloquent: Izumi speaks passionately. O-Bara listens agitatedly, every now and then bowing as a sign of gratitude.

STORYTELLER (*commenting on their conversation*)
Izumi does not wish to be a concubine.
She has betrayed Kubota's trust in her.
But the honour of the house must not be sacrificed,
So let another geisha from Yanagi take the prize.
She has informed O-Bara of the cunning tricks:
About the dance, about the song and the modest kimono.
And about the open neck and whiteness of the elbows.

O-Bara tugs the neck of her kimono down excessively and pulls her sleeves almost right up to the shoulders. Izumi nods: Yes, yes, that is exactly right.

Izumi promises that she herself will perform poorly
And in her joy O-Bara is completely lost for words.
The two embrace each other firmly, overcome by emotion.

The geishas embrace elegantly, without allowing their cheeks to touch, in order not to spoil the layer of ceruse.

O-BARA Izumi, my dearest one! Oh, this is such a happy day! It is a bitter thing for me, competing with my sworn sister! Withdrawing before the battle, you have conquered me. Never could I have expected such nobility!

IZUMI No, this is not nobility. But I have realised that the lot of a concubine leaves my heart cold. You would be better suited to this destiny, and I prefer to keep my freedom.

The geishas embrace once again, and O-Bara cautiously removes a teardrop from her eye with a napkin. She bows and leaves, closing the shoji behind her. Stepping down into the garden, she stops in front of the apple tree and looks round at the pavilion.

O-BARA Thank you for passing on those hints. Now I know everything I need to be quite sure that I shall hook this golden fish. But I shall be even more certain of success if I compete alone from the Yanagi house of tea. The other rivals do not worry me at all, but you, my sweet Izumi, must now be on your way to the next world.

With a furious gesture, she breaks off the most beautiful branch of the apple tree and walks away, waving it in the air.

The Inaudible One emerges from the shadows at the other side of the stage and watches her as she leaves.

Darkness. Curtain.
The stage revolves.

ACT THREE

Scene one

O-Bara's room. At one side a paper lantern is lit. At the centre the branch of the apple tree is displayed in a gilded porcelain vase. O-Bara is touching up her make-up. Yuba is sitting beside her, handing her mistress little jars, brushes and creams. They both start moving after a single drumbeat is heard. O-Bara is in a wonderful mood. She sings, every now and then glancing at the branch.

O-BARA *(after a pause)* And who is this rascal?

YUBA What do you mean, my lady?

O-BARA Who is your lover? Come on now, tell me.

YUBA Ah, what are you saying. I swear to you, no one . . .

O-BARA Oh, come on. I do not believe in oaths. But I can always tell from the eyes and a hundred different signs if someone has a lover, and if she does – whether he is good. I see that yours knows how to bring you joy. But I am curious about where he appeared from. Ah, you're blushing, you fool. But what cause is there here to feel embarrassment?

YUBA There is no hiding anything from you. He . . . is just a man.

O-BARA Well, is he rich at least?

YUBA Not very.

O-BARA Oh, I just knew it. So it is amorous embraces that make you glow like this, not gold coins and rich gifts? You were always a fool, Yuba, and you will die a fool. But mind now, don't you dare to bring me home a belly! Don't get intoxicated with the follies of the flesh. Love is a heady potion, but it is not good for much.

YUBA But without it there is no joy in life, or so they say . . .

O-BARA The price of that joy can be very high.

YUBA I do not mind a high price, if the wares are good.

407

O-BARA (*turning round in surprise*) My, my, what news is this? Are you going to argue with me now? Earthly love is foulness. It will smear you with mud, abandoning you in a pool of filth. You will be left with nothing. You worthless girl! Ah, how stupid you are! I think that I shall go to Satsuma without you. As the court favourite, I need a she-fox for my confidante! A lynx! A she-wolf! A serpent! But not someone like you.

YUBA (*bowing down to the floor*) Forgive me, I shall mend my ways! Ah, do not throw me out! I swear to be your diligent pupil!

O-BARA Very well, we shall see . . . I think I'll go into the garden. I wish to pick some flowers for an *ikebana*.

YUBA What kind would you like? If you tell me, I can pick them.

O-BARA (*stroking the apple tree branch lovingly*) Oh no, I shall choose worthy companions for this branch myself. But you can tidy up in here.

She goes out.
Yuba sticks her tongue out after her. She turns rounds and gives a sign.
To the sound of a drumbeat, Kinjo steals in from the other side of the room, with a sack over his shoulder.

KINJO I have cleaned out the owner, taken all her money and her pearls and silk. And now let's pluck your dear lady O-Bara. Have you found out where she hides her precious things?

YUBA I took a sly peek yesterday. She has a hiding place in here.

She points to one leg of the table.
Kinjo lifts up the table, removes the leg to expose the secret compartment and takes out the jade dragon.

KINJO And is that all? I was told she keeps a nest egg and has a rich lover.

YUBA She must have a hiding place for her money too. But, forgive me, I could not find it.

KINJO (*sticking the dragon in the sack*) To hell with it! The dragon's made of jade, it must be worth a lot. Or what would be the point of hiding it like that? But my main booty from the house of Yanagi is you! Now let us leave this cursed place behind, we have a long journey ahead of us!

They walk out onto the hanamichi.

The curtain closes behind them.
The light goes out.

The first mitiyuki

In the mitiyuki *all the action takes place on the* hanamichi *platform. Kinjo and Yuba walk in 'koaruki' style, that is, imitating walking, but barely moving from the spot. He strides along with the sack over his shoulder, leading her by the hand. Yuba has lifted up the hem of her kimono and she walks, not with a woman's gait, but a man's, taking long strides. This symbolises her break with 'the world of flowers and willow trees', where all is artificiality and affected femininity. At first she glances back occasionally at the closed curtain, but then stops doing it. The wind has tousled her hairstyle.*

YUBA But what if they come after us?

KINJO I couldn't give a damn!

YUBA But what if they put us in jail? Then what?

KINJO I couldn't give a damn!

YUBA But what if we don't find any shelter?

KINJO I couldn't give a damn.

YUBA You won't abandon me, will you? Tell me!

KINJO I couldn't . . . (*he stops himself and gestures broadly with his arm*) . . . Not for anything!

STORYTELLER

They hasten on, leaving these parts as far behind as possible.
The wind mischievously tosses their hair about.
Their earthly love leads them on an uncertain route,
Along the springy pathways of the Earth –
The cruel, kind, abundant, meagre Earth.
The travellers will wander it until at last
Their earthly love is consigned to the earth
And scattered by the careless wind, a mere handful of dust.

The light goes out.
In the darkness Kinjo and Yuba disappear.

Scene two

O-Bara's room again. The geisha comes in, carrying flowers. Futoya follows her, shrouded in a cloak. O-Bara turns towards him and they both freeze on the spot.

STORYTELLER

O-Bara has summoned her accomplice once again,
To tell him all is ready, she has given the secret sign.
But the villainess is unaware that now a silent spy
Is tracking her, watching her every step.

He strikes his drum. The Inaudible One appears on the other side of the paper partition and parts the shoji *slightly. O-Bara and Futoya start moving again.*

O-BARA Today or tomorrow we shall see the end of her. There will be no obstacle to my success.

She sits down at the little table and starts arranging an ikebana thoughtfully.

Now everything that we desire, dear friend, will come about. There is no doubt of it.

FUTOYA Most welcome news. And now I ask you to return the token that I entrusted to your safe keeping. The sign has been given and Izumi's final hour has come. The Sinobi execute a sentence promptly. Their messenger may appear at any moment now, and I must return the dragon instantly.

O-Bara takes her time to finish arranging the bouquet. Then she lifts the table up slightly, opens the secret compartment and rummages in it. She thinks she has tried the wrong leg and looks in each of them by turn.

STORYTELLER (*in the meantime*)
The Ninja hears this conversation and the background
To the situation is revealed to him.
The instigators of the murder are both here before him.
It is their fault that he must take Izumi's life!
What satisfaction he would feel in putting to a cruel death
O-Bara and the merchant, and accept no payment for it!
But the Sinobi laws prohibit any punishment of clients
Without some weighty and compelling argument . . .

O-BARA Where has it got to? I remember very clearly that I put the dragon in my secret hiding place.

FUTOYA This is no time for foolish joking! Give me back the talisman!

O-BARA Oh, damnation! It has been stolen! I simply can't believe my eyes. Look, the table leg is hollowed out. No hiding place could possibly be safer!

Futoya overturns the table.

FUTOYA I understand! I realise everything! Oh, you vile serpent! You wish to get rid of me now! You no longer have any need of me! My usefulness has been exhausted! You wish to hand me over, so that they can torture me to death! (*He grabs her roughly by the shoulder.*) The Jyonin will kill me for losing his dragon! And that is what you want. Give it back!

O-BARA (*resisting*) What is this, have you lost your mind? Let go of me, you idiot! You and I are allies! Why should I wish to have you killed? Yuba must have robbed me. I had noticed a strange new wilfulness in her behaviour . . .

FUTOYA (*not listening to her*) Give me back the dragon, you bitch! Out of my love for you I have sinned and marred my karma for ever.

She breaks free and he chases her around the room. He knocks her down, but O-Bara is strong and agile, and she breaks free again. Eventually they both fall and start rolling about on the mats, punching and scratching each other. All this takes place with no words spoken and no shouting, in pantomime.

STORYTELLER (*during the pantomime*)
Fate, the joker, lays out her traps for us,
Righteous and sinners both. None are protected.
It brings her great delight when a cunning fisherman
Blunders into the nets she has flung out.
The Sinobi rejoices. What's this? The dragon has been lost?
Now he can rightfully call to account
These petty people who arranged Izumi's death!
The Inaudible One takes paper and a brush . . .

The Inaudible One takes a scroll out of his belt and tears a piece off it. He takes out a portable inkwell and a little brush and writes something quickly.

And writes: 'The sentence has been carried out.
Now please return the dragon, as the Jyonin ordered.'

A single drumbeat.
The Sinobi tears open the shoji and walks into the room.

O-BARA Enough of this! Stop it! You and I are not alone! (*to the Inaudible One*) How can you dare to enter uninvited, you buffoon?

O-Bara and Futoya disentangle themselves. They both sit up, trying to put their clothes and hair in order. The Inaudible One, taking no notice of the geisha, holds out the piece of paper to the merchant.

FUTOYA A piece of paper! What's this now? And are you giving it to me? (*He reads it and cries out in a loud voice.*) All-merciful Buddha! She is already dead!

The Invisible One takes a dragon with a snake-like blade out from behind his back and reaches out his hand for the dragon.

FUTOYA (*creeping away in a squatting pose*) We are joint clients in

412

this contract. I gave the dragon to this honourable lady for safe keeping.

O-BARA He lies! This is the first that I have heard of this. I do not understand what you are saying. What contract do you mean?

The Inaudible One picks the branch of the apple tree up off the floor and shows it to the geisha.

O-BARA (*realising that her denials are pointless*) Yes, yes, please, I'm sorry. I was simply being cautious to begin with, in order to make sure. So she is dead? So quickly? Our commission has been carried out? Can this be possible? I want to see her body.

FUTOYA (*in a loud whisper*) You'll be the death of us, you fool! Do not insult him! In cases like this the Sinobi never tell lies to their clients! Give him back the dragon! Your trick has failed! Or he will kill us both this very moment!

O-BARA (*also whispering and creeping towards the paper lantern standing on the floor*) It's you who are the fool, dear sir. The dragon's not here, it has disappeared. If you want to live, keep your mouth shut. And don't get in my way!

Bowing to the formidable messenger, Futoya creeps towards her, still squatting. The Inaudible One watches them, holding out his hand demandingly. He has hidden the dagger away again.

O-Bara overturns the lantern and it goes out. Darkness.

O-BARA'S VOICE Now save me, legs!

FUTOYA'S VOICE Wait! What about me?

The sound of scurrying feet.

The curtain closes.
During the *mitiyuki* scene
the scenery is changed.

413

The second *mitiyuki*

Caught in a patch of light, O-Bara and Futoya run along the hanamichi, *without moving from the spot. Their feet seem to be sticking in sand: they run agonisingly, as people do in nightmares; their breathing is fitful and laboured. The geisha has outrun the merchant. She has thrown off her lacquered sandals and tucked the hem of her kimono in her belt so that she can run more freely.*

FUTOYA It is pointless to flee! There is no way to escape them! They will find us anywhere, even on the bottom of the sea!

O-BARA (*not looking round*) I am not running from the Ninja, but from you, you blockhead. I did not take the dragon, and I should not have to answer for it!

Futoya runs faster and catches up with her.

FUTOYA Did you really not love me, even just a little bit?

O-BARA Yes, I loved you, of course I did. But what good is love now?

FUTOYA You are right, as you always are. And your advice is good. Let him finish you off, and I shall get away.

He grabs hold of her sleeve and flings her to the ground. Then he races ahead.

I only need to run from death today. Afterwards I shall buy the Jyonin off with money.

O-Bara grabs the hem of his kimono and he falls. They both get up and carry on running in panic, jostling each other.

STORYTELLER
Now you can see in all its fetid charm the rank love
Termed 'infernal' by Okasan in the first act of our play.
The lovers blaze with a bright, glowing flame,
Yet this fire does not warm, but chills their souls.
Where all scurry along in haste, pursuing profit,
Hell's mouth gapes wide open at the end of the road . . .

He strikes his drum.

    A beam of light picks out the Inaudible One, standing in front of the curtain. He raises a bamboo blowpipe to his mouth, and spits out a poisoned dart – and Futoya falls. Another dart – and O-Bara falls.

    They squirm on the ground and then grow still.

    The Inaudible One walks up to the bodies. He takes the snake-blade dagger out from behind his back, bends down and does something.

    The beam of light goes out.

    Darkness. We hear the Inaudible One walk back onto the stage.

        The curtain rustles.
        A single drumbeat.

Scene three

The deserted temple again. It is dark inside, and the Inaudible One is picked out by a solitary beam of light. He is sitting there without his mask, but his face cannot be seen, since the actor has his back to the auditorium. His arms are extended to the sides: in his left hand he holds a woman's head, and in his right, a man's.

STORYTELLER
    An unheard-of business. Without completing his assignment,
    The Sinobi has arranged a meeting with the Jyonin,
    Presenting a request to be released from his commission,
    Since the client has violated the conditions.

A single drumbeat.

    The statue of Buddha is lit up dimly from behind. We hear a voice.

    The Inaudible One places the heads on the ground, clasps his hands respectfully on his knees and lowers his head.

THE INVISIBLE ONE Inaudible One, on reading your request, I was so indignant, I could scarcely contain my wrath. If not for the great service you have rendered, I would have ordered you to put an end to your own life . . .

The Inaudible One takes out the snake-blade dagger and sets it to his throat, demonstrating his readiness to carry out such an order immediately.

THE INVISIBLE ONE (*continuing*) . . . And transferred the commission to another valiant warrior. The sentence must be carried out, no matter what. The client is of no importance here. And the victim likewise. We Sinobi bear a sacred duty of honour. We transgress every law of man, and rumour names us denizens of hell. Our path lies through the darkness, but a single star still guides our stealthy stride.

Man does not know why he lives in this world. He thinks up toys with which he can amuse himself. He has invented Good and Evil, Ugliness and Beauty, using them as chains to bind himself. But the Buddha alone knows what is Good and what is Evil; the Beautiful is easily transformed into the Ugly. And there is only one thing of true value: having once chosen a Way, never to stray or turn aside from it.

The Way of the Sinobi is killing. That is our craft, elevated to the high standing of an art. Always keep faith with honour. Follow the light of the star. Who are you without honour? Merely a wretched, murderous thug.

The Inaudible One lowers his head even further. Eventually he stretches out face down as a sign of unquestioning obedience.

Well then. Carry out the assignment to the letter, and I shall forgive your weakness, so be it. And one more task. Find the dragon. For that talisman you are answerable with your life . . .

The backlighting of the statue fades out. The Inaudible One straightens up abruptly. He sits there, motionless, precisely reproducing the silhouette of the Buddha.

STORYTELLER
Shamed by the Jyonin's severe words,
The Inaudible One acknowledges their truth.
Why has he lived in the world? And why has he sown death?
What has it all been for, if he turns off the Way?
Such a life is bereft of honour and of meaning.
The shark and lion must shed blood to live.
And the Sinobi cannot live without allegiance to the Way.
All this he tells himself, to buttress his drooping spirits.

In the battle of love and duty, duty wins the day.

A single drumbeat.

The Inaudible One jumps up and freezes, with the snake-blade dagger glittering in his hand.

Darkness. Curtain.
The stage revolves.

Scene four

The garden in front of Izumi's pavilion. Night. The shoji are closed, but a light is burning inside. We see the geisha's silhouette. Izumi is melancholically plucking the strings of the shamisen.

The Invisible One creeps out stealthily. He stops in front of the engawa and takes out his dagger, then freezes motionless.

STORYTELLER
And that very same night, submissive to his fate
The Sinobi sets out to pay his debt of honour.
Today will come to pass what karma has decreed.
For man is powerless to correct the course of destiny.
And yet, setting his eyes on that familiar silhouette,
The Inaudible One has slowed his silent stride . . .

A single drumbeat.

Soga appears on the edge of the engawa. He sees the Inaudible One with a dagger in his hand, draws his sword and, without saying a word, attacks the assassin furiously.

An unusual duel follows: it takes place in absolute silence; both opponents move without making a single sound. The distinctive feature of a Sinobi's swordmanship is that he defends himself from blows, not with his blade, but by rapid movements and jumps, sometimes even by turning somersaults. Soga's long sword repeatedly slices through empty air. The Inaudible One hides his dagger away in the secret scabbard behind his back.

The duel is reminiscent of an acrobatic ballet or pantomime; musical accompaniment is provided by Izumi playing the shamisen.

The fight concludes in the following fashion: the Inaudible One, finding himself beside the blossoming apple tree, dodges yet another blow and

417

Soga's sword slices right through the trunk. The Ronin involuntarily glances round at the falling tree and that instant is enough for the Inaudible One to whip out his dagger and thrust it into Soga's chest. At the same moment the music breaks off and the light in the pavilion goes out.

The Sinobi catches the body, as if embracing it, and slowly lowers it to the ground. After glancing round at the pavilion in almost exactly the same way as Soga in the first act, he hides the body under the engawa. The dagger is already back in its sheath.

Then the Inaudible One walks up onto the veranda. He opens the shoji *slightly, slips inside and closes them together behind him.*

A pause.

The Storyteller strikes his drum rapidly but quietly, imitating the sound of a pounding heart.

IZUMI'S VOICE Who is breathing here? Who is watching me in the darkness?

The lantern is lit again. We can see two silhouettes. Izumi is sitting up on her bed, with the Inaudible One standing over her. What follows is in the style of a shadow theatre.

IZUMI Ah, so it is you? I knew that you would come to me!

The Inaudible One backs away.

Now why are you embarrassed? Was your heart bold, but then turned cold? Do you think I will push you away in disgust? Then let me tell you, I was waiting here for you impatiently.

She holds her arms out to him.

I have heard so many vows of love from others, I am not ashamed to make my own confession first. I love you with all my heart, you were sent to me by destiny. And it does not matter to me whether you are ugly or not. Ah, what stupid nonsense is that? Now your face will become the ideal of heavenly beauty for me. From henceforth pretty faces will seem ugly to me, disgusting even to behold. Quickly, take off your mask! I shall accept your trust with great delight, as a most precious gift!

A single drumbeat. The Inaudible One tears off his mask.

IZUMI (*in confusion*) But you have not a single flaw! Your face is handsome! I do not understand, why did you hide it? My dearest chosen one is silent and handsome, like the moon in a black sky, like a bright star! Without my make-up, also without my mask, do I appear before you now. You see me, too, just as I am ... let us swear that never again shall we hide our faces from each other. I do not wish to be a geisha! I shall go away with you. We shall simply be together, two of us – the same as everybody else. Or almost the same ... It is no misfortune that you are dumb. You will see. I shall be talkative enough for two.

Ah, but does it really matter what will happen afterwards? Here and now we are together, my love, you and I!

He reaches out his arms to her and she pulls him onto the bed.
The light goes out in the pavilion again, and then on all the stage.
Quiet music.

Curtain

The third *mitiyuki*

The Inaudible One walks out onto the hanamichi, *holding a lantern in his raised hand. The audience sees his face for the first time – it is impassive. Izumi walks behind the Inaudible One, carrying a bundle. Her face, with no ceruse or make-up, is lit up by a beam of light. She is dressed in a simple, dark kimono. They both freeze motionless.*

STORYTELLER
In the dark hour before the dawn the two of them set out,
Leaving the house of Yanagi, casting off their former world.
Or so Izumi thinks ... Which way their path lies,
She has not even asked. It leads wherever it goes.
She babbles constantly in a happy, piping voice.
The bleak night seems quite lovely to her now ...

He strikes his drum.
They are both walking in 'koaruki' style. But the Inaudible One is

419

taking broad strides and Izumi, in keeping with the canonical rules of femininity, is taking small steps.

IZUMI There are no stars to be seen in the sky, there is no moon. We shall disappear now, you and I, dissolve into the night. I used to think my life would streak past like a comet, trace a path across the sky and vanish without trace. But fate has prepared another destiny for me: I shall live with my beloved, just as thousands live. One leaf among the other leaves, one blade of grass among the others. With you I am happy to be like this, like everyone. But why did you tell me to bring with me the kimono in which I used to perform for an audience? (*She points to the bundle.*) It is too luxurious for a modest life, I cannot go out in it, or wear it for receiving guests . . .

Suddenly the Inaudible One stops and turns towards her.

IZUMI (*putting down the bundle*) Have you chosen this spot to make a halt? You're right, it is so lovely here, with this cliff and the river down below . . . (*She walks to the edge of the* hanamichi *and looks down.*) That is the genuine *karyukai*, the world of flowers and willow trees, where Beauty lies concealed, faithful to *yugen* . . .

Meanwhile the Inaudible One takes the kimono out of the bundle and spreads it out on the ground. Then he takes a scroll of paper out of the sleeve and hands it to his companion.

IZUMI (*laughing quietly*) Yes, you wrote something before we left, I remember. Only you wouldn't let me read what you had written. But I have realised now: is it love poems? Have you chosen this place to show them to me?

Taking the piece of paper in one hand and the lantern in the other, she reads. After a little while the lantern starts to tremble.

STORYTELLER
Oh, poor Izumi! This is not poetry at all.
The Sinobi confesses his accursed trade.
He writes that she is doomed to die,
And her only salvation is to disappear without a trace.

She must leave the capital, nevermore to return,
And start a new life in some distant place.
He is releasing her, rather than destroy his own honour.
Without honour a man's life in this world is pointless,
He is bound to atone for his offence with death.
But first he wishes to throw the assassins off the trail.
Here on the clifftop they will find Izumi's kimono,
Splattered with blood, but no body inside it.
They will think that he threw the body in the river
And the current carried the dead woman off.
It matters not if the Sinobi's own body is found,
Everything will be clear to the Jyonin in any case.
He will think his emissary carried out the sentence,
But clearly was unable to locate the dragon
And, faithful to his vow, took his own life.
This is the action of a Ninja who values his honour.
And in the final lines of this appalling missive,
The Inaudible One gives her his final behest:
'Run! Live! Save your own life and forget me.
Let me remain for you a shadow with no face.'

The Inaudible One puts on his mask.

Numbed to her soul, Izumi knows not what to say.
She cannot stir, she thinks this is a dream,
An absurd, senseless dream. She must awaken from it!
Her parting from the dumb man takes place without words . . .

He strikes the drum.
    The Inaudible One pulls the snake-blade dagger out from behind his back.
pierces his own throat with it, leans down so that the blood pours out onto
the outspread kimono, turns round and falls over the cliff (into the dark
corner between the hanamichi *and the hall). We hear water splashing.*
    Izumi gives a piercing scream. She drops the lantern and everything is
plunged into darkness.
    We hear the singing of the funeral sutra to the steady beating of the
drum. At this point the actress must creep behind the curtain, taking the
lantern and kimono with her.

Scene five

Izumi's room.

She is standing motionless on the threshold of the room, to which she has only just returned.

STORYTELLER

Knowing not her path and seeing nothing,
Izumi wandered blindly through the night,
But, coming to herself, she saw that her haphazard steps
Had led her back to this very same house.
Just so a theatre puppet, when the show is ended,
Is set away again, lying lifeless in its customary chest . . .

He strikes the drum.

Izumi slowly gazes round the room, as if seeing it for the first time, and sits down in front of the casket, in profile to the audience. She looks at the casket and raises the lid with the mirror.

STORYTELLER

Half her life she has spent before the mirror,
Admiring the reflection of a lovely face.
And now she looks into that gleaming surface
As if seeking a vision of the truth there.
'He was an assassin, a Ninja. But who are you?
Who are you, in real truth? Why were you born?'
She interrogates the mirror avidly,
As if the reflection in it can answer her . . .

IZUMI (*ecstatically*) 'Without honour a man's life in this world is pointless,' he said, and abandoned me there in the desolate night. Frozen in horror, I had no chance to ask: 'And can a woman live in this world without honour?' Who, then, am I? I am a geisha, my Way is to bring forth feminine beauty, in its imperishable image. And to become imperishable there is one excellent recipe: to make the story of Izumi legend. Let them write poems, let them compose plays about the geisha and the Ninja who gave up their all for love. Both of them were faithful to their art. But when suddenly love blocked off the Way and the barrier was impassable, then they soared into the sky, high above the earth, to where honour and love abide in harmony . . .

She takes the stiletto out of the casket and looks at it. Then she continues quietly, with no affectation.

All this is foolishness, my beloved. I wish to be with you. And all the rest is no more than a geisha's empty chatter. Throughout the blackness of eternity you and I are destined to fly, like two comets in a starless sky . . .

She plunges the stiletto into her throat. The lights go out and immediately two bright beams blaze up above the auditorium, like two comets.

Curtain

The Erast Fandorin Mysteries

'Think Tolstoy writing James Bond with the logical rigour of Sherlock Holmes'
Guardian

'Erast Fandorin is a delightful character like no other in crime fiction'
The Times

Available from W&N in paperback and ebook

'Full of incident and excitement, swift-moving and told with a
sparkling light-heartedness which is impossible to resist'
Evening Standard

Available from W&N in paperback and ebook